ANGEL

BY THE SAME AUTHOR
Copy to follow

ANITA MASON

ANGEL

HAMISH HAMILTON

LONDON

HAMISH HAMILTON LTD
Published by the Penguin Group
Penguin Books Ltd, 27 Wrights Lane, London w8 5tz, England
Penguin Books USA Inc., 375 Hudson Street, New York, New York 10014, USA
Penguin Books Australia Ltd, Ringwood, Victoria, Australia
Penguin Books Canada Ltd, 10 Alcorn Avenue, Toronto, Ontario, Canada m4v 3b2
Penguin Books (NZ) Ltd, 182–190 Wairau Road, Auckland 10, New Zealand

Penguin Books Ltd, Registered Offices: Harmondsworth, Middlesex, England

First published 1994
1 3 5 7 9 10 8 6 4 2

Photoset by Datix International Limited, Bungay, Suffolk
This book proof printed by Antony Rowe Ltd, Chippenham, Wiltshire
Set in 10.5/12.5 pt Lasercomp Ehrhardt
A CIP catalogue record for this book is available from the British Library

ISBN 0–241–00202–8

For Mary

AUTHOR'S NOTE

This novel began as an attempt to write a fictional treatment of the career of the German pilot Hanna Reitsch (1912–79). I abandoned the attempt because of a complete lack of sympathy with the personality of Flügkapitän Reitsch as it emerges from the records. However, since I was still drawn to the material, I set about inventing a German woman pilot of that period. I then found I was getting close to my original conception of the book by a different route. In effect, I have used the broad outline of Hanna Reitsch's flying career until 1945, but given it to a fictional character (who has a fictional personal life: of Freddy's friends, only Ernst has a real counterpart). I have taken a few liberties with time but not, I hope, with history. The aeroplanes are not invented, or not intentionally so.

Of the books I have consulted, I should like to acknowledge Judy Lomax's *Hanna Reitsch: Flying for the Fatherland*, Marie Ziegler's *Rocket Fighter* for its information on the Me 163, and Trevor-Roper's brilliant *The Last Days of Hitler* for making me want to write about this subject and illuminating it for me. Hanna Reitsch wrote her own, remarkably uninformative, autobiography, published in English as *The Sky My Kingdom*.

I would like to thank Hanna Kusch, who made me think about Germany and was there for some of the thinking.

The Arts Council generously awarded me a Writer's Bursary during the writing of this book.

Lomax   Biog. Reitsch
T. Roper   Biog. Hitler

CHAPTER ONE

In the stained dark we flit along the hedgetops like a moth and that
ridiculous trick of Ernst's comes to my mind in which he used to
pick up a handkerchief with his wingtip.

I fancy I can hear the roar of the crowd as he picks up the small
white square and climbs away and the band strikes up a jolly march;
but it is another roar, more distant but more dangerous, and as for
marching . . .

The general shifts heavily behind me. His foot is bad. It has not
been dressed since yesterday morning, or do I mean the day before?
I suppose I should look at it when we stop; but then, what is the
point? Unwrap the stiff bandages, hard with a substance like varnish,
lower my eyes to the blue-red smashed yolk, and then cover it all up
again. We have no dressings and no drugs. The first-aid kit in this
aeroplane is a revolver.

It worries me when he moves around. This little Bücker, which
flies so slowly that it can be guided into every hollow of the ground,
can clothe itself in shadows, can slip between trees, this little acrobat
can also be thrown out of balance by a very tall general doing
something anguished and impulsive in the back seat.

He is a pilot, I mustn't forget that. Perhaps he doesn't trust my
flying.

That would be too much. That really would.

There was to be a helicopter at Rechlin, that's why I'm on this
lunatic flight. I was to fly the general to headquarters in it. He had
been summoned, against all reason. The general can't fly a helicopter: not many pilots can, and there are not in any case many pilots
about these days. I learnt to fly a helicopter seven years ago. It was
one of the very earliest. It had an aeroplane's fuselage and tailplane,
and two rotor blades where the wingtips ought to be. It looked as if

it wasn't sure what it was. I had to demonstrate it inside a covered stadium containing several thousand people, at a motor show. It was not a sensible idea, and it frightened the wits out of everybody except Ernst, whose idea it was, and it even frightened him on the night.

It nearly crashed. The audience, all busily breathing away, was depriving the engine of oxygen. If I'd known at the time who was in the audience, I think it might have crashed. After that I had to fly with the stadium doors open. It was very windy. I don't know how much the spectators saw, as they clutched their hats, of my carefully executed dance beneath the roof; but the ministry was pleased, and my picture was in the papers again.

When we got to Rechlin there wasn't a helicopter. It had received a direct hit, and been reduced to the pilot's seat, the radio and a rotor blade.

'General,' I said, heel-clicking, while he gave me one of his gentleman-officer smiles (that was before he got the armour-piercing bullet in his foot), 'General, even I cannot fly a seat, a radio and a rotor blade.'

There then appeared from nowhere a pilot and a Focke-Wulf 190. A nice plane, that. I don't know how it happened, the Focke-Wulf, how it got through, when everybody knew that the priority in the ministry at the time was to produce planes which if possible could not fly at all. It is a single-seater but this one had had a second seat fitted in the bit of space behind the pilot's seat. You can't ask for more. However, the pilot could not be separated from his Focke-Wulf. I don't blame him. This wasn't a problem from anyone else's point of view. The pilot could fly the general to Gatow – the only airfield in or near Berlin which was still usable – and return to Rechlin, and another pilot could later fly in and bring him out again, if there were any more pilots, if there were any more aeroplanes. But it was a problem from my point of view because, now that I was denied my flight into Berlin, I was overcome by an imperious desire to go there.

My reasons for this mainly concerned a sense of unfinished business with the general. And these days I like to be on the move. Nevertheless, it was undeniably rash, since my chances of surviving the trip – I calculated quickly as I inserted myself into the tail section of the Focke-Wulf's fuselage, which fitted me like the sides of a coffin, and might indeed be the sides of a coffin– were approximately one in sixteen. I don't know how I arrived at this figure and have no wish to go over the calculation again. But in a trice there I was, in the pitch dark behind the general's seat, hands before my face, looking at the luminous dial of my watch as if it were a sacred writing (and it was: in that darkness, any writing is sacred writing); there I was, and there, for a time which did not seem to be at all the time measured by the creeping green hand of my watch, I stayed.

I exaggerate when I say it was pitch dark. Most of the time there was a thin line of red, a fuzzy glowing line, on either side of the general's seat. It was the glow of the burning towns over which we flew. Periodically the red was obliterated in a dazzling bluish-white of such intensity that it illuminated the whole interior space in which I lay, and a moment later the aircraft would rock and plunge in the explosion. My body, intimately tucked into the metal ribs, was driven onto them by every shock wave. It was curious to be in the midst of this violence and not hear it. All I could hear was the roar of the Focke-Wulf's engine. I heard, as it were, with my bones.

Afterwards it would be about a minute before my eyes could distinguish the green figures on my watch dial again.

Twenty minutes into the flight the aircraft dropped like a stone. I swore. I was so angry, to have to die like this, stowed like a parcel in the back of someone else's aeroplane. I bellowed with anger in the tiny space as we plunged downwards, as I held out my hands before me like a diver, like a supplicant. Let it be quick. Let her remember me. Let me be forgiven.

Abruptly we levelled out. I caught my breath as the blood left my temples and surged to my hollow legs. How wonderful the reek of sulphur and petrol.

The pilot had dived, the general told me, to avoid fighters.

I remembered another dive.

Blue sky over golden fields. Far below, the brick buildings and runway of the Glider Research Institute.

I was at ten thousand feet. Ahead of me the tow plane banked and turned.

I was up there to test the glider's dive brakes. A new development in aviation. Flaps were attached to the wings, extending automatically when the aircraft dived so as to obstruct the airflow. On the first tests the vibration had threatened to shake the glider apart. The brakes had been re-designed. This was the final test of the new design, and the severest. It involved putting the glider into a vertical dive for nine thousand feet.

No one knew what would happen in those nine thousand feet.

I ran my eyes, yet again, over the instruments, and my fingers over the safety harness. The sky was full of golden light. It was a beautiful morning and I was going to die.

I checked the sky for other aircraft. My tongue felt like cloth.

I told myself that I didn't have to carry out the test that day. Any one of a dozen reasons would serve. Conditions admittedly were perfect, but the weather forecast was as good for the following day. I could say that the seat had moved. (Hadn't it?) In an hour's time I could have made my report and be sitting over a cup of coffee in the canteen, talking to Dieter. In an hour's time . . .

I rolled the glider on to its back and put the nose down.

Ah, that drop into the abyss.

The glider plunged, and I hung above the nose in my transparent bubble as before my face the fields grew larger, rising towards me like . . . like what? Milk in a saucepan.

I fixed my gaze on the dials. If the needle moved beyond 125 mph, it meant the brakes weren't working properly. The vibration would start. After a short time it would become uncontrollable.

Seven thousand feet.

I crouched, or hung, like a sharp-eyed animal. And sharp-eared. My ears missed nothing. They relayed to my brain, and it analysed, every sound made by the plunging aircraft. Every whine, every tap, every rattle. I was listening for one particular sound. It was a high-pitched, papery rustling in the wings. After a few seconds the rustling would become a creak like that of fabric stretched to the limit before it tears. This sound I prayed not to hear.

At five thousand feet, with the needle steady at 125, I felt a wildness begin to grow in me. I had never felt it before on a test flight and I could not permit myself to feel it: I was a professional. But I did feel it. My blood surged with a forbidden excitement. On and on we plunged to the spreading fields, and it seemed to me that everything that had preceded this dive had been a preparation for it, for the intoxication of hurtling like an arrow at the heart of the earth. And when the altimeter showed a thousand feet and I must bring the stick towards me there was a moment, before I was buffeted back in my seat and the world rocked level beneath my wings, there was a moment when I did not want to pull out of that dive.

Which was why I understood Ernst.

At Gatow I pulled and wriggled myself out of the Focke-Wulf's metal tail. The clouds were sulphur-yellow, and the air held a burning edge. As soon as I dropped down from the aircraft the pilot began his take-off run. I saw the general's long legs weaving a path among the craters, and followed him under a sky, which flashed and thundered like a gong, into a low concrete building.

Inside it was dark. We kept to the wall, instinctively still sheltering from the lethal rain. Then we heard footsteps. A man came down a passageway carrying a torch. He flashed it over us, and led us through unlit corridors to the control room.

It was heavily blacked out and was lit by paraffin lamps. The polished wooden tables were covered in plaster dust, and a half-eaten hunk of bread stood on top of the radio. Still on the far wall, as it had been on all my previous visits, hung the coloured map of Berlin. It was the only thing that looked normal.

It struck me that it should not look normal. I studied it. Streets, canals, railways, with their familiar configurations and comforting names. To the east, the curving course of the River Spree; on the west, the graceful lakes and fine green expanse of the Grünewald, just across the Havel from where we stood.

Of the shattered city whose fringes we had just reached there was no sign. There were not even any markers to show which areas were in Russian hands. It was a map of a previous life.

I turned to the airman who had brought us here. He had recognized me, with a faint smile, when I took off my helmet. I didn't know him.

'There's nothing plotted on this map,' I remarked.

'What is there to plot?'

'Where are the Russians?'

He laughed. 'Everywhere.'

His face was gaunt and, in the uncertain light, he looked a little mad.

'So which roads are open into the city?'

'None.'

'None at all?'

'Berlin is encircled.'

He sat heavily on a stool and motioned me with his hand to another. I preferred to walk around the room, massaging my still-cramped muscles.

The general paused with his hand on the telephone and said, 'There must be some way of getting in. It's only ten miles.'

He then spoke curtly into the receiver. It was extraordinary that the telephone link was still open. It might be cut at any moment. The general took off his cap and laid it on the table among the dust and breadcrumbs. Then he picked it up again with a look of irritation and put it on his knee.

'I don't care if he is asleep, get him to the phone,' he said into the receiver. His patience cracked. 'That is an *order*!'

The airman on the stool watched him with a strange expression. He had not saluted when he found us. He was a lieutenant. It was all over, I realized. The saluting and the orders, it was over. Now there would be something else.

He said to me, 'I don't suppose you have any cigarettes?'

I shook my head. 'Sorry.'

The general took an unopened pack out of his pocket and tossed it over. The airman fell on it, mumbling thanks. He held the pack to his nostrils and sniffed the aroma. He took out a cigarette and rubbed it between his fingers, listening to the sound it made. Eventually he placed it between his lips and lit it with a loose match picked up from the table.

The general, still holding the telephone to his ear, said to him, 'Are you here alone?'

That hadn't occurred to me. It would have seemed fantastic.

'Alone, yes sir.'

I could see in the general's eyes that the general, too, knew that the saluting and many other things were over.

'What happened to the rest? Deserted? Or dead?'

The lieutenant did not reply. The general's gaze moved round the room, taking in the disorder, the pointless map, the plaster dust.

The telephone crackled and he returned his attention to it.

'Von Below? Thank God. I'm at Gatow. Yes, it's still open, but apparently all land routes are closed. Does he still require me?'

A precise, metallic voice enunciated. The general listened intently. An expression of hopelessness grew on his face.

'Yes, as soon as possible,' he said after a while, and put the receiver down.

He sat looking at his hands. He has long, rather elegant hands, always well manicured. Not that he is a vain man, so far as I've noticed.

He said, 'I am still wanted at headquarters. I have to find a way to get there, if it's humanly possible.'

Obviously he was prepared to die in the attempt. He had no idea why he was required to go there, and had not asked. I made these silent observations as I kneaded my calf muscle.

He stood up and put on his cap.

'I must find a truck, or some such thing. There must be something on an airfield.'

'There's a Stork under a tarpaulin at the end of the runway,' said the lieutenant.

The general's mouth dropped open. 'Good God, why didn't you tell me before?' He looked at his watch.

The lieutenant looked at his. 'It's almost light by now,' he said. 'And she needs fuelling up. You'd do better to wait for nightfall.'

We listened deliberately, for the first time since we had arrived, to the scream and thump of artillery outside, trying to estimate how far away it was, how long we had.

'He's right,' said the general. 'Let's try and get some sleep.'

We slept on blankets on the bare floor of an adjoining room. It was too cold to sleep much. The lieutenant brought us some oily-tasting acorn coffee as we sat rubbing our wrists and ankles to make the blood flow.

The general said to me, 'You must stay here. Give yourself up. You'll be all right as long as you make sure it's an officer.'

'You're joking.'

7

'I am ordering you to stay here.'

I reminded him that I was not subject to his orders.

'Then I am asking you to stay here.'

'Then I refuse. I'm coming with you. You need a co-pilot.'

We drank our acorn coffee.

I said, 'I know the compass bearing from this airfield of the only landmark I can guarantee to be still standing in the centre of Berlin. I can navigate us to the Chancellery even if the whole city is rubble. Which it almost certainly is.'

I had made it my business to know how to get in and out of the capital when the roads could no longer be used and when the city was no longer recognizable. I had memorized compass bearings, distances, and the course of rivers and canals. It had been one of the things I did at a time when it was difficult to know what to do.

We uncovered the Stork as the light faded. The lieutenant swung the propeller and stepped back into the shadows. The last I saw of him, he was cupping his hands to light one of the general's cigarettes.

We roared down the pocked runway, the general at the controls, and lifted quickly to climb above the dark water towards the treetops of the Grünewald.

I wonder what the general remembers of that flight into Hell. He hasn't said much to me, and thanks might be in order, but one must be reasonable in one's expectations. I can't talk to him in this aeroplane: we have no radio. I can shout, but unless he is leaning right forward the noise of the engine drowns my voice.

He has settled down now. Perhaps he's asleep. Everything around is peaceful. No helmet glints below. The pale lanes, the dark copses, are empty.

Where are the Americans? Where are the Russians?

A definition of war: a state in which anything might be anywhere.

As the general took the pilot's seat of the Stork and buckled his harness I had leant over his shoulder.

'What are you doing?'

'I want to see if I can reach the controls from behind you.'

He gave a bark of a laugh.

'Sit down and strap yourself in. I'm flying this kite.'

He opened the throttle and we moved, gathering speed, into the night.

From the cabin of the Stork you can see a great deal. It is like sitting in a greenhouse. The transparent canopy extends all round and above you, and is wider than the fuselage, so that with the slightest turn of the head you can see the ground. You see, too, right below you, the stalky undercarriage, so fragile-looking, so easily shot away; and to either side of you rise the long struts that brace the plank-shaped wings.

So frail a thing, an aeroplane.

Against the mass of the earth so tiny. Against the sky so huge: how can the gunner fail?

We climbed steeply and for perhaps the first half-minute flew without incident. Then, looking up through the transparent roof of the cabin, I saw the fighters. They dived and swarmed, showing black against the strange colours of the sky. On each one, I fancied I could see the red star burn.

'Fighters above!' I shouted.

He didn't hear me. I unfastened my seat harness and stood up and shouted in his ear.

He dropped at once to treetop level, then jerked the nose up again. We were right over the Grünewald, and the forest was crawling with Russians.

Tanks stood in smashed clearings, surrounded by groups of upward-staring men. The long barrels of guns nosed towards us. In the tops of trees sat infantrymen, with the light glinting off their weapons. I saw their faces clearly: the blackened cheeks, the beards, and staring from each face the whites of the eyes, implacable.

The general rammed the stick sideways as the forest erupted into fire, and I saw part of a wing slat fall away. I was thrown about by the plane's twisting and turning and the explosions around us. We banked steeply again in machine-gun fire, and seconds later there was a brilliant upward streak of colour beside the engine, followed by a loud bang.

The general screamed.

I jumped for the controls. I could only just reach them: his head, fallen sideways, was in my armpit. I heard his breath rasp. I was fighting the aeroplane, which, with his feet jammed on the rudder pedals, would not answer properly but I had to keep twisting to avoid the ground fire. Punches of air threw the plane in all directions. My stomach felt liquid and nauseous. It was hard to breathe, in the smoke and sulphur and stench of fuel.

Fuel.

I glanced up, to right and left where the tanks were. And there I saw it, the ghastly snail-trail of leaking fuel across the fabric of each wing.

The ground fire slackened as we passed over the black edge of the Grünewald, but moments later visibility dropped to a few yards. The air was yellow and red, hideous with burning, lit by occasional lurid lights. In the obscene glare of those lights I saw hallucinatory shapes. A jagged, moving landscape, the dead walking.

The general's hand moved convulsively for the stick. I knocked it away and it fell back on to his thigh.

I saw, then, the shape, the real shape, for which my eyes had been straining. A squat, fortress-like flak tower, the landmark to which I had plotted our course. There it was, directly ahead; and five degrees to the east of it gleamed the scar of the East-West Axis. Cratered and rubble-strewn, in places all but extinguished. But its line of Morse could still be read.

I turned the Stork's nose until it pointed along the scar.

Seconds later a shell landed directly ahead of me and fragments of rock spun at the plane as we shot upwards. I felt them strike the underside of the fuselage and the leaking, battered wings. A stone bounced off a wheel strut: the metallic clang cut sharply through the engine's roar and the thunder of gunfire.

Unbelievably, the area below us was still being defended. Answering fire spat from the rubble, and a *panzerfaust* bazooka flared.

Something was coming towards us out of the swirling dust: something massive, columned. I thought at first I must have culled this image from memory and projected it on to the red mist that pressed against the canopy, because of all possible silhouettes it was the one I most wished to see. Columns defiantly surmounted by a team of capering bronze horses. But it was real and solid. The Brandenburg Gate, against all probability, was still standing.

In front of it was a little bit of uncratered road. A Stork can land on almost nothing. This one would have to.

I pulled back the throttle. I tried to reach the flap lever but couldn't. As the speed dropped, we were blown about even more violently by the constant explosions and rushes of air from collapsing walls. The plane veered crazily, denied the balance of the rudder; with the stick, which was all I had, I struggled to keep control. Above me I fancied I saw petrol now actually spurting from the starboard wing. I lifted the nose fractionally, felt the speed drop further, felt her go down, and prayed that the undercarriage was intact.

There was a long, long moment when the dangerous ground streamed towards us. Then we were down, a rough bouncing crabwise landing that drenched me cold with sweat. I switched off the engine and for a second could not move. Then I unbuckled the general's harness, flung open the cabin door and hauled and dragged him out, and he was so tall and his legs were so long and at the end of one of them was a pulped mass of bone and blood.

I got him out. I half-carried and half-dragged him a little way into the shelter of a wall. I was shaking. He came round again. I took off my tie and made a tourniquet for his leg. I asked him if he thought he could crawl, and he said yes, so we crawled on to within a few yards of the Gate. Then we sat at the side of the road, or what used to be the road, so that we could be seen if anyone came to investigate the Stork.

A lorry came after a few minutes. Five or six SS troops with the faces of exhausted children piled out of it. I told them where we had to go. They pulled a stretcher from the back of the lorry, lifted the general on to it and then into the back of the truck. I climbed in beside him.

We lumbered past ruined ministries, and entered a heavily guarded area. The truck halted. The SS boys scrambled out, I jumped down with them and we lifted down the stretcher with its burden.

Shells screamed overhead and landed close by. Half-stifled by the burning dust, we moved slowly towards a colonnaded building. At some point we passed from the lurid light and jagged shadows of a courtyard into the vast remains of rooms where the sky showed biliously through the ceiling and the stiff figures of tapestries moved on the walls.

11

We reached a narrow passageway, at the end of which was a stair rail.

I set my foot on the top step. The stairs went on down into darkness.

CHAPTER TWO

Ernst.

I think of him often these days.

What a dazzler. Dazzling smile, dazzling style. A dazzling pilot. Make no mistake, Ernst was the best. I waggle my wings in salute, and hope the general won't notice.

He started off in style. A fighter ace in the Great War, sixty-two victories. A tally second only to that of von Richthofen, with whom he flew. You can't do better. The Fat Man did rather worse, with a total (whisper it) no one was ever quite able to verify. And the Fat Man, who in the last days of the war was sent to command the Richthofen Squadron, never flew with the Baron.

Ernst and the Fat Man met in a shed in Flanders. Ernst described it to me. The wind blew through the gaps in the walls. On one of the walls a drawing was tacked: a man with a serious face, his tunic half–unbuttoned, relaxing in a wicker chair. Against the wall was a small table, and on the table, under the drawing, a vase of wild flowers.

Balancing this arrangement at the other end of the hut, a large table covered in maps and pencils and, standing behind it, the Fat Man, not yet fat, and smiling his wide, thin smile.

Ernst saluted.

The Fat Man returned his salute.

The Fat Man was wearing the *Pour le Mérite*. Ernst averted his eyes. It was the highest decoration for gallantry. He had one, too. You didn't wear them on the airfield, not this airfield.

'I expect you've heard that I've been sent to take over,' said the Fat Man amiably.

The eyes of the man in the drawing watched the back of Ernst's head.

'Yes, sir,' said Ernst.

Such was the banality of their first exchange. Such was the disposition of power between them. Thus it would remain.

'I'd like to meet all the members of the squadron as soon as possible.'

'Certainly, sir. There are five of us.'

'How many?'

'Five, sir.'

'I see.' The Fat Man had a ring on his finger. A broad gold ring. He played with it.

'Well, I hope we're sent some replacements soon. Five isn't much of a squadron.'

It was raining on the tin roof and on the mud outside. Ernst listened to the rain.

The Fat Man walked round the side of the table.

'That sketch on the wall. Who did it?'

'I did, sir. I sometimes draw in my spare time.'

'Really? It's good. Strong lines. I have an eye for that sort of thing. Who is it, by the way?'

A fractional pause before Ernst said, 'Baron Manfred von Richthofen, sir.'

'Ah.'

After a few moments the Fat Man walked over to the drawing, unpinned it and handed it to Ernst.

'All the same I don't think we can have it here,' he said. 'It's morbid, don't you think? This is my squadron now.'

Ernst put the drawing in his map case, and saluted.

Away from the glare of Berlin, the night has dropped over the landscape like a cloth. We fly in its folds. We hug the contours of fields and hide in the lee of hedges. Often my wheels are kissing distance from verdure. Praise God for this dainty aeroplane which nothing can induce to stall.

I startled some rabbits just now. They shot through the waving grass like fish when a stone is dropped into water.

Enough moon to see all this. In the moonlight the grass is green-black, the rabbits dun. Woodland is densely black along a ridge. Canal a blade of silver.

Craggy moon. Childhood's face-in-the-moon. Serene, unearthly, unbearably beautiful moon.

Lovers' moon.

Leave it. Think of something else.

Bombers' moon.

Ernst bobbed about like everybody else in the flotsam and jetsam of after-the-war. He survived. A *Pour le Mérite* became a curious thing, twin-faced and unreliable: a talisman and a thing spat upon. Ernst kept away from the spitters. At the same time he didn't much like the talisman-worshippers, but they would give him his dinner.

He flew for the crowds. Wherever he could find a crowd and borrow an aeroplane. There weren't many aeroplanes. Then suddenly there weren't *any* aeroplanes. Aeroplanes were forbidden by the victors.

Every pilot in the country became a fanatic. Aeroplanes were made in bedrooms and garden sheds. Parts of aeroplanes were taken along the roads disguised as shelving or farm equipment, and were put together by torchlight in forests. Naturally, as soon as they took to the skies they were seen and impounded.

Ernst stopped flying because there was nothing to fly, and became a salesman. The problem here was finding customers. Money had gone mad and people were paid twice a day because the morning's wage would be worthless by evening.

Ernst was twenty-five now, and I was ten. I had no idea that the fabric of the world was disintegrating. My world was safe. My father was a doctor in a country district.

Ernst scraped by, and when money got back on its feet so did he. Aeroplanes had come back, too, modest ones, ones that couldn't fly very fast or very far or very high, but aeroplanes non the less. Ernst became an aeroplane salesman.

Soon, with a partner, he was making and selling his own sporting aircraft. It was a good business. Ernst had a flair for aircraft design and the kind of smile that made you want to buy things. But his heart wasn't in it. He didn't really care whether people bought his aeroplanes or not, as long as he could go on flying them.

In the end he went back to flying for a living. He worked up a series of aerobatic routines, ending with the handkerchief stunt. To publicize his shows, he did the flying-under-the-bridge stunt and the can-I-really-squeeze-between-these-two-towers stunt. Both illegal. He put skis on his undercarriage and landed in the Alps.

15

The Alpine Club complained. The air police were frantic. The public laughed and went through the turnstiles.

It was some years before Ernst met the Fat Man again.

I followed Ernst's career in the newspapers. He seemed to me godlike. I did not utter his name for fear of profaning it. I became upset if a newspaper containing a photograph of him was disrespectfully treated.

The idea of flight possessed me, as a small child. One of my earliest memories is of a dream in which I flew for hours, soaring and swooping in my nightclothes, over the woods and valleys around our house. I woke with a longing so intense that I wept. The dream returned throughout my childhood, and each time devastated me. They came like irruptions from another life, these dreams, they were like messages from somewhere I had lived. I could tell no one about them. I mourned in secret my loss, my fall.

The dreams became less frequent and less vivid as I grew older. Life was a practical affair, and I got on with it. Sometimes I looked up and watched an aeroplane crossing the sky. It interested me, in a distant sort of way. Flight, yes, but mechanical. The mere existence of such a machine was an acknowledgement that human beings could *not* fly.

All the same it must be beautiful up there, I thought. The sky was a country: peopled by birds, haunted by storms. It was a sea, with cliffs of cloud. It was a place of secrets.

An echo of the old yearning came back. I shrugged it off roughly. I knew what was possible.

Then one day I saw a glider. I was twelve, and out with my family. We were picnicking near a brook on the grassy lower slopes of a hill. The day was warm, and clouds of yellow butterflies danced above the water where it ran white over stones. Peter was sunk in unhappy contemplation of his shoes. Father had just reprimanded him for something. My mother was cutting cake.

The cruciform shadow moved across the tablecloth on which our meal lay spread, and I gasped as if something had struck into my heart. I looked up.

Grace. Effortless riding of the air. Moving in majestic silence.

I had risen to my feet. Dimly I was aware that they were telling me to sit down. There were tears in my eyes. Through them I watched the glider's path above the treetops. It was lower now, and turning, and as it turned I saw the pilot's face.

With terror I realized it was going to land.

But I must see. I raced on shaking legs to the top of the hill, and arrived panting at the field gate as it swooped down.

The suddenness, and its materiality, shocked me. There it was, in common wood and fabric. I had dreamed a thing; and there was this, which was real. What connection could there be between the two? Did I want reality?

For a moment longer I clung to my dream, and then I let it go. This would do. Oh, this would do.

In the seconds before it touched down I had heard it singing.

It was not, as I had thought, quite soundless. The air sang in its wings. A sweet, wild note, like that of a shepherd's pipe.

Heart, mind, soul, I gave myself to it.

My brother Peter, two years older than myself, was the eternal target of my father's wrath. Why, what had he done? A kind boy, who liked stamp collecting.

It was because my father was proud of him but wanted to be prouder. It was out of a profound sense of duty that he harried and laid snares for Peter, engaged tutors renowned for their strictness, refused to accept anything he did as good enough, and finally sent him to a boarding school which was a place of horrors, and from which he returned like a starched ghost for the holidays.

Never can a father have been more scrupulous in his harshness.

Peter was untidy. His collar was askew, his hair too long. Peter had been impolite to his aunt. Peter was not good at Maths. Peter was lazy. Peter had neglected his violin practice. Peter slouched.

Peter stood at attention, a tic working in his cheek, as pale as milk.

When the offence was grievous the cane would come out from its lair. Grievous offences were lying and outright disobedience. Peter's rare lies were told in confusion and panic, and his acts of disobedience committed in frenzy, but there was no mitigation. Honour and authority are not matters for compromise.

Naturally I never saw him punished. It was utterly private, this struggle for Peter's manhood. But I heard it. I have a cat's hearing.

In the woods behind the house one day Peter stood among fallen leaves, picking without seeing it at a beech nut.

I went to stand beside him.

'Father hates me,' he said.

'No, he doesn't.'

'He does.'

The shape of what I wanted to say was clear in my mind but I lacked the words for it: that Father didn't hate Peter, he simply didn't know how to express love. That an idea had bitten through the vital connection and severed it.

The idea was to do with discipline. Yes, that idea. It is of course a national obsession. But what is unusual about my father is that any idea, strongly held, would have done the same thing. That is the measure of his seriousness.

A village below us has been bombed. Perhaps the pilot was off course and dumped his bombs where he could. Or perhaps he thought the village was really an underground weapons factory. Anything might be anything, these days.

The rafters of the bombed houses stick into the sky like the masts of sinking ships.

My father used to bring home eyes for us to dissect.

He was an eye specialist. He wanted us to share his love of anatomy.

They were usually pigs' eyes. I suppose these were the easiest to obtain, from the abattoirs and vets' surgeries he found time to visit while out on his rounds. He would withdraw them with care from the rubber-lined pouch in which he carried them, and place them in a white porcelain dish in his study. The first time I saw him do it I thought, so carefully did his fingers reach inside the pouch, he was bringing out some delicate treat for us, like a chocolate.

A suffused jelly laced in gore.

Peter was sick. He bolted into the bathroom: it was at the other end of the house, but I heard him. I stood my ground, although the blood had left my face.

My father waited for Peter to come back. When Peter didn't, but after an interval my mother came instead, saying that Peter had gone to bed with a headache, my father looked surprised and disappointed.

'But I was going to show them how to dissect,' he said.

He seemed to think that if he explained his purpose, Peter would return.

My mother's eyes darted to the thing in the dish, dwelt on it for a frozen moment, and dragged themselves away.

'You will have to do it some other time, Otto,' she said, in a level voice which didn't sound like my mother's at all.

With sadness my father put the eye away. He would not give a dissection lesson to me alone. That would have violated his ideas of rightness.

He persevered. There were more eyes in the pouch a few evenings later. Peter flinched, but he was made to look at them, trembling like a horse, while my father stood behind him holding his arms.

('What is the matter with the boy?' I heard him say to my mother afterwards. 'How can he be frightened of a pig's eye?'

'He's frightened of you,' my mother replied.

Silence.)

It must have been hard for my father, this shame of a son who flinched like a girl, but he bore it with cold fortitude. The pouch continued to yield up its contents. I would know before dinner when my father had visited an abattoir, because there would be a fleck of blood, or something more intimate, on his normally spotless cuff. And the time came when both Peter and I, wearing white coats, stood with a scalpel in front of a porcelain dish, looking at an eye which looked back at us.

My father, also white-coated and standing before a porcelain dish containing an eye, would bend and with a deft, cruel movement begin the separation of the tissues.

He would look up and, with a nod, indicate that we should begin on our own specimens.

I learnt something about my father on those agonizingly long evenings. (How Peter and I glanced every few minutes at the big clock on the wall, with its picture of Nuremberg, willing the hand onwards.) I saw his passion, the thing to which he had given himself, and for the first time he interested me because I had thought he was a passionless man. And for the first time I saw his skill, and I was humbled by it. Watching his fingers draw apart the delicate, unbelievable layers, I was proud that he was my father.

But I did not want his skill. Even my fumbling attempts to practise it laid a cold hand on me. I could hardly wait to get out of the stifling study with its reek of preserving fluid and blood, out of the silence that was broken only by the steady ticking of the clock, the crisp slicing of the scalpel and the faint sounds, audible only to me, of Peter's unhappiness. As I walked to the door at nine o'clock with the lightness of one released from prison, I dreaded that my father would see my eagerness. For, clearly, in the midst of my revulsion, boredom and anxiety, I knew that he was doing this for us. He wasn't enjoying it: it pained him.

We didn't learn. We were slow, clumsy, and the intensity of his expectation frightened us. The harder we tried, the more idiotic we became. Peter knocked his dish to the floor once and it broke. My father said nothing, with an effort which made the air vibrate, but picked it up and gave him another dish and another eye.

He could not understand why we were so bad at it, what he had done wrong.

We progressed from dissecting to preparing samples of tissue for the microscope and describing what we saw. The nightmare deepened. Now we had an instrument to contend with as well. I hated my microscope. I couldn't focus it properly. Once my father, in exasperation, moved me aside and corrected the focus himself; but then, when I looked down the eyepiece, I saw that the specimen was still slightly blurred and I realized that this imperfect image was the best the contraption could do for me.

I was very disappointed. I had thought that the microscope, once I succeeded in focusing it, would let me into a new world, a place of fantastic landscapes and seas more extraordinary than the landscapes of my imagination because they really existed. The image I saw, resembling a white plain bisected by a red river, was flat, dead-looking, and rigidly defined by the sides of the tube down which I looked at it.

I straightened up.

'What did you see?' asked my father.

I looked blankly at him. The poverty of what I'd seen, compared with what I'd hoped to see, was all I could think of. I knew I must not say this. Not because he would be angry, but because it would hurt him.

'I don't know,' I said.

'Don't be silly. You must have seen something. Describe it.'

I faltered out a lacklustre description of what I had seen. He listened bitterly.

'You've no imagination,' he said.

He turned to Peter.

'What can you see, Peter?'

But Peter was still trying to get his specimen into the right position on the slide for viewing.

All that autumn and winter, as the days grew short like small pictures in a big frame, my father went on bringing home blood-encrusted jellies in his pouch. Wednesday evening became an evening we must haul ourselves through, minute by minute, and after a while not an evening at all, but something quite different, a pit dug in the middle of the week.

Then one Wednesday my father said at breakfast, 'I've decided not to hold any more dissection lessons, since you don't enjoy them.'

Peter and I looked at each other and gasped. It was impossible to conceal our joy. A moment afterwards we stared at our plates, faces burning. My father sat on at the table a little longer, then folded his newspaper and left the room.

The Wednesday evening sessions were never referred to again.

Another scene from my childhood.

I walked into the drawing room and saw something I had witnessed many times before, but this time it was different.

Peter was being taken to task for writing in the pages of a school book. Normally I would have left the room at once: this was between Father and Peter. But I knew that Peter had not written in the book: it had been done by a friend to whom he had lent it. Peter never wrote in books. Moreover, you could see that it wasn't his writing.

As I entered the room, Peter was saying that it was someone else who had written in the book. My father interrupted him.

'I detest lying in a boy, and even more than lying I detest the cowardly habit of blaming other people.'

Something happened, I do not know what. Something took control of me. I was standing before my father with my fists clenched, and shouting, 'He didn't do it, it isn't even his writing! Why don't you believe him? Why can't you leave him alone?'

A long, shocked interval. Then my father said coldly, 'Go to your room.'

I didn't. I resolved to leave home and live in the wild. I would eat berries and mushrooms. It would be quite easy. Home was insupportable. In a day or two Peter would come and join me.

I stayed in the woods all day. Several hours after nightfall, unexpected cold and ravenous hunger (I had found no berries, and did not trust the mushrooms) drove me back to the house. By this time the situation had become very confused and had to be resolved by my mother.

My father couldn't deal with me. I saw it then for the first time. He didn't know how to behave towards me. And he knew I was stronger than Peter.

My childhood is like a kaleidoscope; perhaps everyone's is. Turn it one way, and the brightly coloured pieces arrange themselves in a particular pattern; turn it another, and they assume a quite different pattern. Which is the real pattern? A kaleidoscope has no real pattern, only a multiplicity. Yet a childhood ought to make sense.

From the beginning there were two of me. There was what I was supposed to be, and what I was. Yet, in a way, I was both. And for a very long time no one noticed. I hardly noticed.

I remember vividly the summer a cousin from Dortmund came to stay with us. There was some family trouble which meant that his parents were unable to look after him. His name was Hans, and we had never met him before.

My father brought from the station a thin, knobby-kneed boy of Peter's age with a funny accent and angry brown eyes under a thatch of hair. He and Peter sized each other up as they submitted to introduction, and hostility vibrated between them. It consolidated itself during dinner, while my parents did their best to draw Hans out in conversation and Peter and I communed in glances and ankle-kicks.

At the end of dinner my father, with visible relief, said, 'Why don't you show Hans the woods, you two?'

We didn't want to show Hans the woods; the woods were our special place. However, Hans was going to be with us for three months and we could hardly keep him out of the woods all that time.

Peter and I walked in silence along the track that led from the house past the barley field and the paddock which never had anything in it but stones, and Hans whistled and threw sticks at the birds. When we arrived at the edge of the woods Peter stopped, as if he was going to refuse to go in, but I said, 'Oh, come on,' and led the way, because I knew that it had to be done and it was better to get it over with. Behind me I heard a derisive chuckle.

'These are the woods,' I threw over my shoulder as we walked.

I went on down the slope, creeper-covered and still dense with the late foliage of bluebells, which led to the stream in its deep bed. A bridge of planks crossed this stream, but Peter and I always preferred to jump across from one projecting rock to the other. As I jumped I heard Peter say, 'This is the stream,' and an answering snigger.

We went up to the clearing. Peter and I stood side by side at the edge of that light-filled, always mysterious space.

'This is the clearing,' Peter said disastrously, and turned away.

Hans cackled. 'This is the wood, this is the stream, this is the clearing,' he mimicked. He walked round to face me, placed his hands on his hips and said with contempt, 'And what's *that* supposed to be?'

I was wearing lederhosen and a shirt of Peter's which no longer fitted him. I always dressed like that when I wasn't at school. Everyone was used to it.

Peter leapt on him. There was a short and furious exchange of blows. I waited until they broke apart and then I flung myself at Hans, yelling at Peter to keep off. It was my fight. Also in my mind was the idea that if Peter fought a guest, Father would do something terrible to him.

I fought to kill. That I didn't still surprises me. I came to myself, eventually, sitting on my enemy's chest and punching his ear.

'Pax,' he said, hardly moving his lips. It would have been difficult to move them, I could see.

I got off with reluctance. Hans sat up. His face was covered in blood, and underneath the blood it looked in rather poor shape. His once-white shirt bore in numerous places the imprint of my blood-stained fist.

Peter made us shake hands. We went to clean ourselves up at the stream, and realized that the real damage could not be cleaned up. Discussing the problem and what tales we might plausibly tell, and illustrating my father's behaviour with gruesome anecdotes for Hans's benefit, Peter and I made our peace with our guest. He was not so bad. He had a reason for being objectionable. He told us about it, the trouble at home which he had been sent away from. His father was leaving his mother; his father, Hans told us, had another wife.

Peter and I were thrilled. Nothing like that ever happened in our village.

I was elected the one to approach Mother. I hid in the shrubbery until I knew my father had gone into his study, and then intercepted her on the way from the dining room.

She steered me into the bathroom and shut the door.

'What on earth has happened to you?'

'I fell down,' I said.

I had fallen down, among other things.

My mother went to the washbasin, ran cold water, tipped my head back with one hand and with the other produced from a cupboard lint and iodine. Her hands were quick and sure.

'Where did you fall down?'

'In the woods.'

'Let me see your hands.'

She inspected the palms, which were virtually undamaged, and the bruised and torn knuckles.

'All right, what were you doing?'

'We had a fight. Please don't tell Father.'

'A *fight*!'

I started to hang my head, and then raised it again, impelled by a kind of honesty.

'With whom did you have a fight?'

'With Hans.'

She was shocked. '*Liebchen*, how could you? Don't you understand that he's a guest?'

Of course I did. Why were grown-ups so stupid?

'And what was Peter doing?' she asked as an afterthought.

I said, striving for lucidity and succeeding beyond my expectations, 'Peter started to fight Hans because Hans was rude to me, and then after a bit I fought him because I knew if Peter was in a fight Father would kill him.'

She looked at me sharply, but said only, 'so Peter and Hans are in the same state as you?'

'Peter doesn't look too bad.' I grinned: I couldn't stop myself, 'Hans looks awful.'

'It's nothing to laugh about.'

'Sorry.'

From a tin she took a strong-smelling ointment and spread it on my knuckles.

'You'd better tell them to come here to me separately.'

'You won't tell Father?'

'How can I possibly keep it from him? Look at you.'

'Please, mother. Please. Think of something.'

'Are you asking me to lie?'

'No,' I said.

'You know you are.'

'He's so beastly to Peter,' I said.

I hadn't meant to say this. A shadow crossed her face.

'That is not your business,' she said.

She took a pair of scissors and cut a square of lint. Then she drew me to her and kissed the top of my head.

'Go and send Hans to me,' she said, and I did.

Father left the house early the following morning and we didn't see him at breakfast. He did not come home for lunch, and during the afternoon he sent a message to say that he would be dining out with a colleague, as he occasionally did. By the time he was able to take a good look at Peter, Hans and me we were almost presentable.

He said he'd heard that we'd taken a tumble when climbing a tree, and would Peter and I try to behave more responsibly now that we had a guest. It was all my mother's doing, of course, and I never really thanked her.

All my childhood seems concentrated in that summer. Almost every day the three of us went swimming in the river. We dived for treasure, after Hans had found a rusted pair of binoculars in the mud, but we never found anything else. We fished. The fish would nose up to our trembling bait, give it a disdainful nudge and slip away again.

We camped in the woods and nearly started a forest fire.

We built a dam across the stream.

As we were building it, Hans said with confidence, 'I'm going into the army when I'm older.'

'Is your father in the army?' Peter asked him.

'No. He's a civil servant.'

'What d'you want to go into the army for, then?'

'Adventure.'

'Adventure!' scoffed Peter. 'It's boring, the army. It's all manoeuvres. I want to go into the navy. You go all over the world, in the navy.'

'But your father's a doctor!'

'Doesn't matter. Well, actually, it does, because he wants me to be a doctor. I daren't tell him.'

Peter inserted a stone with care into the hollow he had made for it in the stream bed.

'But I am going to go into the Navy, whatever he says.'

Hans nodded approvingly.

The chill of exclusion fell over me like a cloak.

Hans's visit must have been the year before Peter went away to boarding school.

It had been an unthinkable thing, his going away, a reef in the distant future. All of a sudden it was upon us.

Peter, trying to seal off his feelings, became withdrawn and snappish with me. I didn't understand, and felt wounded. I was too proud to go to my mother for comfort. In any case, I could see that she was unhappy, too.

The morning came when I was summoned to my father's study to say goodbye to my brother. Why he was not allowed to come and find me, why this farewell had to take place under my father's eye, I don't know, unless it was that my father feared a last-minute breakdown in the front Peter was so desperately maintaining. He stood like a terrified marionette in his new suit and shining boots.

I grasped the hand of this apparition. It was cold. In horror, I tried to croak out something appropriate.

'I look forward to seeing you at Christmas,' said Peter stiffly. 'Please would you remember to feed Hengist.'

Hengist was his goldfish.

I got out of the room as soon as I could. I lay on my bed and listened to the sound of the cab drawing away: I could not watch.

A part of my childhood came to an end as cleanly as if a guillotine had been brought down on it.

CHAPTER THREE

I was in disguise.

My arms were not the arms I ought to have. My face was not the face I ought to have.

It came and went throughout my childhood, this perception of wrongness. There were long periods when it was dormant. Then, if anyone had suggested to me that I felt dispossessed, I would have denied it. There were other times when the anger would rise in me like molten stone.

I stared at my face in the bathroom mirror. Whose face? It must be someone's. It was quite a nice face, but I could not love it. Where was mine?

Perhaps Peter had mine.

Perhaps Peter . . .

It was true, we were back-to-front, I should have been him and he me, everybody said so and laughed, but because everybody said so and then laughed, that made it silly and stopped it meaning what it really did mean. And what it really did mean . . .

The trouble was I couldn't work out what it really meant. Which was the bit of a person which made them who they were? It was difficult, and as I tried to think about it the ideas dissolved and made me dizzy.

'I want you to call me Peter,' I announced one evening at dinner, to a family circle turned suddenly to stone.

After a long time my father pointed to where his firstborn sat, goggle-eyed, on his left, and said clearly, 'That is Peter.'

We were eating liver. Liver has tasted of humiliation to me ever since.

The year was turning into autumn when Peter went away. Alone, I waded through the deep drifts of leaves, collected conkers, looked for beech nuts and stared at the fairy rings in the clearing. The conkers lost their shine and I threw them away. I fed Hengist, and wandered round Peter's room looking for Peter. I wished my mother would let the dust gather on his possessions, but every time I went in there the room shone with emptiness. In the end I moved Hengist into my room.

I found that I hated my father. I had grown up with his tyrannizing of Peter, and recognized that in some way he could not help it. But the sending away of Peter was something new; it passed all previous boundaries. He had acted as if he were God, I thought: with the same confidence of rightness.

I studied him covertly across the dinner table, as he separated his lamb cutlet from the bone with a surgeon's economy of movement. Father. What did it mean? I had no doubt what 'mother' meant. It meant necessary to life. But 'father' did not mean anything that corresponded to this. Reduced to its essentials, it seemed only to mean the word 'No'.

People had a great reverence for this word, I thought. And fathers were its priests. Like priests, they were regarded with awe and a certain pity, because what they did seemed difficult and to go against the grain of human nature.

I decided that I did not accept these ideas: the importance of 'No' and the specialness of fathers on account of it. I resolved that when I grew up I would not take any notice of them.

Peter's departure left me in the centre of a suddenly empty stage. I had sometimes been the focus of my mother's attention, but almost never of my father's. Now his gaze rested on me daily. Much of the time it was faintly puzzled.

I wanted to hide from this gaze. I knew that he wanted to know my thoughts. I was determined he should not. Wasn't he powerful enough as it was? I would not give him the smallest bit more power over me than the world gave him already. So I rebuffed his overtures, and dug traps for his attempts to get to know me. Once or twice, sensing I had made him unhappy, I felt sorry about it. But there was nothing I could do. We were at war, and he should know that. If I capitulated once, I would have capitulated for ever.

I realized that, with Peter gone, I had to start again; I had, as it were, to re-invent myself as a child who had no brother.

I began to spend more time with my mother, although from the beginning something made me wary of this. It was too easy. Being with her was almost like being with myself. But I loved to hear her laugh. She would toss her head back and laugh with the naturalness of a girl. Then, if it was I who had made her laugh – and often I did, I did it on purpose – she would give me a quick, adult's glance of gratitude, as if she had needed to laugh but I was not to know that.

Of course I knew it. I had always known more than my mother knew I knew. As far as I could, I tried to look after her. I did not want anything hurtful to come near her. If I saw it coming – an unpleasant piece of news, a painful thought – I fought it off. But I was powerless to guard her against the pain of my father's hounding of Peter. I would retreat when I saw it in her eyes, because I knew that anything I said would only make things worse. When Peter went to boarding school she seemed to shrink. I did say something, then. I said, 'He'll soon be home, *Mutti*,' and from the pressure of her fingers on mine knew how near to tears she was.

I saw my father a few minutes after this, on the way to his study, and backed into the doorway because I was afraid he would see the murder in my eyes.

I had a friend called Mina. She was three months older than me and I thought her grown-up. This was because she wore a gold watch, had an air of responsibility and sang in the school choir. Her parents were wealthy and kept horses. Sometimes Mina and I went riding together.

When Mina rode, she seemed to blend with the horse. My own performance was more ragged. However, what I lacked in skill I made up for in enthusiasm and daring. At least, I thought I did. Mina took a different view.

'You're reckless,' she said to me, after I had galloped my pony along the edge of a beet field and over a patch of heath strewn with boulders. 'You only just managed to hold him. And Prinz might have hurt himself.'

It was true. I said I was sorry, because after all it was her pony I had endangered. But I caught a gleam of satisfaction in her eye, and wondered whether I really liked Wilhelmina Huber, and whether she really liked me.

In Peter's absence, I started spending more time with Mina. She lived in a big gabled house on the other side of the village. The house was an object of contempt to the children of the farm workers who lived along the lane. Mina in her turn was scornful of them and of a great deal else, often including me.

When Mina showed disdain for something I had done, I thought it was because I hadn't done it well enough. And it was true that I rode like a scarecrow, that my singing voice was more robust than pure, and that I could not do the pretty drawings of animals with which she decorated her notes and invitations. However, it seemed to me that I could do other things. I could swim and climb trees, I played the piano well enough to satisfy my father, I was good at learning poetry and remembering dates, I had a reasonable grasp of geography and was so much better than Mina was at Maths that more than once I had helped her with it.

Stung, one day, by a scornful comment, I referred to these accomplishments. She was silent for a few moments. Then she said, 'Yes, but who cares? Those are all boys' things, except for the piano.'

'Boys' things?'

'Climbing trees especially.' She inked in a bit of forest glade.

'I think your drawings are stupid,' I said. 'And at least I haven't got freckles.'

I went home and refused to tell anyone why I was in such a temper.

I turn the kaleidoscope of my childhood, and the pieces fall into a bright tableau: a summer day, a holiday perhaps, the colours of lawn and shrubs vivid outside our house, the hills lavender above the tiled rooftops.

I rushed down the road shouting to someone, all the vigour of youth in my voice and my running feet.

My mother called to me from the garden.

I went, singing. Probably she wanted me to fetch something from the baker.

She told me not to run, and not to make so much noise in the road. It was unladylike, she said.

I opened my mouth to protest, but I never said what I intended to because in that moment my world rearranged itself. With a feeling of suffocation, I saw them all there, the rules for what you were. 'Unladylike' was a snake of a word that had lain for years in the undergrowth of my childhood: now it had struck. It was a statement that certain things were over. It was a statement that certain things were to come.

I felt as if someone had told me the date of my death.

'Why is it unladylike?' I demanded. It was not the question I meant.

'Don't be silly, darling, it just is.'

'I don't want to be ladylike.'

'But I want you to.'

My mother's eyes were serene. She pushed a lock of hair back from her forehead with a finger. I loved her hands, I loved her face. I was filled with rage.

'Why? Why do you want me to?'

'Because you're growing up. Soon you won't be a child any longer. You must learn not to behave like one.'

'Is running down the road behaving like a child?'

'Yes.'

'Helmut and Klaus and Fritz all run and shout in the road, and they're older than I am.' They were Peter's friends, or had been, until Peter went away to school.

'*Liebchen*, they are boys. You are a girl.'

I gazed bitterly at her. I had heard this said before, in other houses, but it had never been said to me. I had always assumed it wasn't said because everyone realized that it wasn't applicable. I didn't *feel* like a girl, so what was the point of asking me to behave like one? Inside me, something had whispered that it was only a matter of time. But that it should be my *mother*, who was supposed to love me, who was holding the manacles to snap on my wrists . . .

I would refuse.

'I'm not going to do the things girls are supposed to do,' I shouted. 'I don't want – '

And then the enormousness of what I didn't want, and the impossibility of my defiance, showed themselves to me for an instant, and I turned and blundered away.

*

32

Two weeks before Peter came home for Christmas, I took from the drawer the presents I had bought for him and carefully wrapped them.

I had bought him a number of small presents rather than one big one, in order to prolong the pleasure. Nevertheless, one of them was quite big. It had cost a lot of my pocket money. It was a stamp album. It had a red cover and a picture of the globe printed on it in gold.

Peter needed a new stamp album. He had run out of pages for Switzerland and Italy, and his British colonies were in a muddle. The new stamp album had twice as many pages as his old one, and coloured maps at the back. I thought he would be very pleased with it.

We heard the cab drawing up and were in the hallway to welcome him as my father opened the door. He was taller, but there was something else. For a moment, as they stood framed in the open doorway with the snowflakes falling behind their shoulders, I did not know who the boy was. My heart went cold as he came forward and, rather awkwardly, raised my mother's hand to his lips.

She stood rigid for a second or more. Then she said, 'Peter!' and hugged him to her. He submitted like a trapped animal.

I wondered if he would kiss my hand. It would not have surprised me. But he gave me an awkward pat and a kiss on the cheek so swift he must have practised it, and turned to Trudi, who had been our housekeeper for years, standing by the kitchen door. He knew what to do with Trudi. He gave her a warm smile, grasped her hand, said how nice it was to see her again, and flung away up the stairs with a suitcase, scattering snow.

My mother and I stared at each other. Trudi went quickly back into the kitchen, and my father, meeting no one's eyes, took off his scarf and hung it on the hatstand as if it were a sacred vestment.

Dinner was horrifying. We had a stranger in our midst, a stranger who made stilted conversation, seemed unfamiliar with a hundred trivial household details, had acquired an abrupt, hollow laugh, looked either at his plate, or at the tablecloth or at the wall behind your head, and ate his food as if afraid of the physical process of swallowing.

At the end of this painful meal, my father, rising from the table, said, 'I'll talk to Peter in my study.'

And that was as much of my brother as I saw that evening.

The following day Father announced at breakfast that he was taking Peter into town. I sought Peter out before they left. He was flicking a finger against the front of Hengist's tank, as if trying to drive the fish back from the glass. He turned his frown towards me.

The smile died on my face.

'Peter – ' I faltered.

His eyebrows went up slightly, as if I had said something illogical.

I tried again. 'Peter, what is the matter?'

'What are you talking about? Nothing's the matter.'

'Aren't you glad to be home?'

'Of course I am,' he said angrily.

'But you don't . . . you don't seem very pleased to see us.'

'I am pleased to see you. Now will you please leave me alone,' he said.

The next day was Christmas Eve. We had already put the tree up, and fixed the candles. I got my presents out of the drawer, took them downstairs when no one was about, and arranged them under the tree. It would be all right. Christmas was always all right.

In the course of the day we visited neighbours, were visited in turn, and made last-minute preparations. Peter stayed in his room most of the time. In the evening my father lit the candles on the tree and we gathered round the piano, with my mother at the keyboard, to sing carols, as we always did. This for me was the best part of Christmas: the singing, the little flames dancing, and outside the snow falling in the immense night.

After the carols we began to open our presents.

I don't remember any of my presents. Nor do I remember those I gave. I remember only Peter's controlled face as he unwrapped the stamp album, and the momentary loss of composure as he took the last sheet of wrapping away. I saw that he had not wanted it, was ashamed of it, and could not bear this Christmas evening with its presents, or anything else. Then he called to mind what was expected of him, and tried to thank me.

All the next week, Peter was inaccessible. He was out, or he was with Father, or he was just, mysteriously, absent. At mealtimes he was uneasy with me. He alternated between the jocular and the insulting. Or he tried to patronize me. 'Little sister' passed his lips twice. On the second occasion I banged down my fork and shouted at him, earning a simultaneous rebuke from both parents in which I nevertheless detected a trace of sympathy. Peter crumbled a bread roll with violence, and said nothing.

On New Year's Eve I put on my warmest jumper and went out to the woods.

The snow lay thick, but a rough path had been cut along the track. Inside the wood, where the trees had caught the main weight of the snow, it was only ankle-deep over the crisply snapping bed of twigs. Here and there was a high drift, like a collapsed battlement, where the branches had given way beneath their load. Standing in the frozen air, in the white twilight under the tents of snow, I heard the near thunder of another snowfall, and saw the mist plume.

A snowball struck me on the shoulder.

I turned, already scooping and forming my own. Peter. It must be: and there he was, the trail of his blue knitted scarf betraying the tree he had dodged behind.

I made two snowballs and threw them in quick succession. He would dodge the first and the second would catch him as he poked his head out to see where I'd gone.

It did, and I heard his grunt of surprise.

I made two more snowballs. I decided to move from tree to tree and try to creep up on him.

But he was doing the same. For a while we circled, hitting the trees more often than each other, and then, catching him in the open, I came into the open myself and threw from where I stood. He stayed where he was, too, and in moments we were scooping and throwing, scooping and throwing, in a fast unbroken sequence of movements that had no pleasure in it, only purpose.

One of Peter's snowballs smashed into my ear as I bent down, sending me reeling with unexpected pain. I straightened up, dimly aware that he had stopped making his next missile. I raised my hand to my ear, saw the blood on the fingers, and saw the ugly small grey stone beside my foot.

I looked at him in disbelief.

'I'm sorry,' he said. He said it with defiance.

There was no point in words. I kicked the stone towards him. I turned and began to walk home.

He caught up with me at the edge of the wood, and fell into step beside me. I walked on with my hands in my pockets, eyes on the path ahead.

'I'm sorry, Freddy,' he said again. This time he did sound contrite.

'So you said.'

'Aren't you going to forgive me?'

'Why should I? You've been behaving like a pig ever since you came home.'

'You've been fairly piggish yourself.'

'*I* have?'

'Yelling at me at dinner.'

'You deserved it. *And* I came to talk to you and you told me to leave you alone.'

He muttered, once again, 'I'm sorry,' and said it with an emptiness of spirit which seemed to make the sky dark.

I stopped walking. It was now or never. I said, 'What's the matter, Peter? What is it?'

'There's nothing – ' he started to say, but I threw myself at him and thrashed him with my fists, shouting 'There is! There is!' until he caught my wrists and held them firmly – he was stronger than I remembered – and said, 'All right. I'll tell you. But you must never tell anyone. Promise.'

'Promise.'

We sat on a snow-covered log at the side of the track.

He said, 'It's that –' and he was trying to say, 'it's that school,' but he couldn't finish it. I watched in horror as something unbearable exploded out of him and he lowered his head and wept.

It seemed to go on a long time. I put an arm round him and gave him a handkerchief which was not very clean but was all I had. He blew his nose and we sat and looked at a robin which was hopping over the snow.

'You get bullied,' he said. 'There's a sort of system to it. It happens to everyone. But some people get it worse than others.'

'Do you get it worse than others?'

'Yes.'

I didn't ask why.

'There's something called the Lock,' he said. 'It's a sort of torture. It happens in the dormitory, after lights out. They take someone and some of them sit on his arms and some of them sit on his legs. So he can't move.'

'And then what do they do?'

'That's all. They just go on sitting there.' He took a deep breath. 'You can't imagine it. Your arms and legs start to go numb, and then you get cramp, you want to double up with it, but you still can't move, and your heart starts pounding, you can't breathe properly, and you still can't make a sound.'

'What?'

'You mustn't cry out. If you do, they – '

'They what?'

'Well, it gets worse.'

I waited for my own breathing to subside.

'They burn you, if you make a sound,' he said.

'How do they burn you?'

'With a match.'

I said, 'But it shows, a burn. Why don't the masters stop it?'

'They burn you where it doesn't show.'

'Where?' Perhaps the armpits, I thought.

He shook his head. His eyes were so dark they looked like bottomless pools.

'Where do they burn you, Peter?'

'It doesn't matter.'

My mind hovered over a wickedness I could barely formulate.

'There are things I can't tell you,' he said. 'There are other things they do. You're a girl, I can't tell you.'

At another time I would have protested vehemently. I thought, perhaps I am imagining all this.

'It doesn't happen every night,' he said.

We sat for a while. It was cold.

I said, 'Have you told Father?'

'Of course not.'

'Then I'm going to.'

He turned to me in a frenzy.

'You mustn't! *Please*, Freddy! You promised!'

'But Peter, it's horrible! He can't make you go back!'

'He will! No, that's not what I mean. Don't you see – ?' He clutched his head in his fists, trying to make me understand something he did not understand himself, and I gazed at him, not understanding, but also understanding.

'I have to go back,' he said at last. And I saw that he did.

He made me, again, promise not to tell. To tell no one, ever, 'not even if they kill me,' he said.

I promised. It was hard, but I told no one. When he said goodbye at the end of the holidays and turned his face again towards his doom, I gave him my piece of lucky meteorite. I told no one of the insane bravery of my brother.

I realized one day that something had been happening.

Mina had gathered round her a coterie of girls, who were to be seen whispering in huddles at the school gate or in Mina's bedroom. In so far as I understood it, they were whispering rather for the sake of whispering than because they had anything to whisper. I was not excluded from this group by any conscious decision on their part. Sometimes they would try to include me. 'Freddy,' they would say, 'come and sit with us,' or 'Freddy, come and look at this!' extending, with giggles, a photograph of someone's elder sister dancing in the arms of a tailcoated beau.

On these occasions I would often see Mina watching me with a little smile. It was a smile of secret knowledge, and I hated it. I did not consider that Mina had any knowledge, secret or otherwise, which warranted an assumption of superiority. In fact I had decided that Mina was rather stupid.

And yet there was a difference between us, and it was everything. She had one foot already in that other world of things that were not spoken of but lay beyond the horizon like a feared and longed-for dawn. I had no footing there and did not think I wanted one. But I did not know what else I wanted, or what else there was.

After I had seen the glider I did not talk about it to anyone. I wanted to think about it. It had been almost like a supernatural visitation. I felt it had been meant for me.

The question was what to do with it. I thought about it by day, and hoped to dream of it at night. (I didn't.) I kept the memory of it bright by constantly re-creating the details of the scene in my mind: the wooded slope, the bare hilltop, the astonishing descent to earth. But how long could I go on doing this? The vision would fade.

It was several weeks before it occurred to me that the place where I had seen the glider was a real place, accessible by road, and that I could get to it if I tried.

Nervously I asked my father where we had picnicked that day. He told me. I consulted a map that hung on a wall at school. It wasn't very far: I could get there on my bicycle.

I went, alone, the following Saturday. I would have asked Peter, but he had gone back to school.

They were flying when I arrived. I saw the first glider as I freewheeled out of the tunnel of beeches on the next hill. I parked my bicycle in the hedge and went to lie among the gorse, my face turned to the sky. All afternoon I lay there, watching the gliders wheel and soar. They came in to land, I saw, always in the same direction. And they took off always in the same direction. And, coming in to land, they always performed the same low circuit beforehand. There was a reason for this. It was the way it had to be done. With a thrill I realized that flying was *learnable*.

I cycled home and, instinctively defensive, parried the first questions from my mother. Then I thought better of it, and started to talk to her.

Peter only spoke again once about being bullied at school. I had asked him a direct question, the second time he came home. I saw that he didn't want to be asked.

'Yes,' he said, 'of course it's still going on.'

I said, 'Can't you fight them?'

'It isn't like that,' he said. 'I can't explain. If you fought, you'd be . . . well, it would be like saying you didn't want to be there.'

'But you don't want to be there!'

He shook his head. 'I can't explain,' he said again.

I said, 'Do *you* sit on anyone's arms?'

'The older boys do that.' He raised his eyes to me. 'I don't want to talk about it any more,' he said.

I think he wished he hadn't told me. Yet he needed me. His

39

friends at home compounded the problems he faced at school by forcing him to deny that there were problems. There was no one but me in whose presence he could drop his mask.

He was trying to become a man. I pondered this process. It was mysterious, and appeared very difficult. Part of me envied Peter what he must go through, because in spite of its extreme unpleasantness there was a great deal of glamour attached to it – and attached, it seemed, to the unpleasantness. The obligation of silence under suffering was part of the whole scheme and was absolute. That was why Peter regretted his confession to me and why I should never again remind him of it. This I could comprehend: it was our childhood code elevated to a fierce discipline. But there was nothing childish in the bleak resolution with which Peter returned, term after term, to take his punishment; and when I saw that something in him had begun to welcome it, would fight against any diminution of it, I assumed that that, too, was part of the necessary process.

You get what you want.

Peter, one spring day in his eighteenth year, carefully suited and a little pale, caught the early train into town and wasn't back until evening. When he came home, there was a flush over his paleness but he still seemed pale. He kissed Mother, winked at me, and said he would like to see Father in the study after dinner.

He was there for two hours. I heard an initial angry exclamation from my father, and Peter's voice, raised, too, in protest. Then their voices dropped to an almost normal level, not quite conversational, but as if they were addressing each other in alternating monologues.

I went to my room and tried to read one of my books on gliding. I couldn't concentrate.

The stars were out, and I was at my window looking at them, when Peter knocked on the door. He looked exhausted, and as if he had slain a dragon.

'Come for a walk,' he said.

I slipped on a jacket and went with him. As we stepped out of the garden, he put an arm round my waist and waltzed me along the road. He was laughing.

'I've joined the navy,' he said.

*

It was not long after this that I asked my father if I could have gliding lessons.

He gave me a searching look, and said, 'I wish you could find an interest more suitable.'

He took out his pocket watch and started swinging it, a trick he had when he was, or wished to appear, deep in consideration.

'I suppose you're drawn to it because it's become fashionable,' he said. 'There seem to be gliding clubs all over the place these days.'

I did not reply to this.

'Every Saturday when it isn't raining,' said my father, 'you get on your bicycle and you disappear. We don't see you until the evening.'

'You know where I am, Father.'

'Oh yes, we know where you are. We know that you prefer the company of glider pilots to that of your own family.'

I had never spoken to the pilots. I did not dare. I had spoken only to the helpful groundsman, who had told me there were beginners' courses every summer.

I followed the pattern in the carpet so my father wouldn't see the hope in my eye. If he was going to say no, would there be this preamble?

'I will pay for you to have a course of gliding lessons,' said my father, transfixing me with delight, 'on two conditions. The first is that we don't hear another word from you about flying, because your mother and I are heartily sick of it, and the second is that you do well in your school-leaving examination.'

I could not believe for a moment that he had said this. I was a reasonably good pupil, except when it came to cookery and sewing, but that was not the point. The *Abitur* was not for another two years. Then I realized that I must have misunderstood.

'You mean that I can have the lessons, and you'll trust me to work hard?'

My heart warmed towards him. It is lovely to be trusted.

'Certainly not. You must take the examination first.'

Two years. I stood silent, looking at the rock face I would have to scale.

My father cleared his throat, and left the room.

I climbed my rock face. Enduring those two years of waiting, while keeping silent about the goal which obsessed me, is the most difficult thing I have ever done. The most difficult because I had no training for it: it was the training. The most difficult because implicit in it was that I could say to no one, Look what I am doing, look how hard it is.

I passed my school-leaving examination with credit.

My parents gave me a gold watch.

I held the watch in my hand, feeling the weight of it, the value. It had been chosen with care. I was angrier than I have ever been in my life.

'I don't want it,' I said. 'You promised me gliding lessons.'

There was a terrible silence. Then my mother turned and left the room.

My father took the watch back from me with a movement of surgical precision in which his fingers did not touch my hand.

'If you still wanted gliding lessons you should have reminded me,' he said. 'We thought you'd forgotten all about it.'

'You forbade me to talk about it.'

His glance jumped through me, surprised again.

He replaced the watch in its presentation case and said, 'I suppose I must honour my promise.'

I said nothing. Did he expect me to release him from it?

'You're a strange one,' he said softly.

I learnt to glide that summer.

It seems to take place very slowly. It seems slow because of the height, because of the majesty of the movement, but you are travelling a mile with every minute, the needle says so. Air, strangely solid beneath, buoys you. Your long wings bear you.

The stick is in your right hand, lightly grasped. Your left adjusts the trimmer. Correctly trimmed, she will fly herself. In the cockpit you have little room to move, can hardly move in any case, so firmly are you strapped. You are not separate, you are the glider. From your shoulders the wings extend.

Below you lie fields and houses, woods, a railway line. The sun bathes them, and across them drifting clouds play shadow games.

It is quite silent, except for the creak of your leather harness.

You are doing what you always knew you could do. You have come home.

You scan the sky and then move the stick a little to the left, and push the left rudder pedal with your foot. A lovely thing happens.

The left wing dips down and the glider turns as if speaking to the earth. It uncovers the earth, which rises towards it like a lover. The wing cleaves and the horizon tilts.

The moving air holds you.

CHAPTER FOUR

One fifty-four by the green hands of my watch.

The transparent windshield above the Bücker's instrument panel is flushed with pink. I admire this effect, reminiscent of clouds at sunset: so cheerful in the surrounding dark. It is Berlin, behind us, burning.

My gaze is never still. It flickers constantly over the ground, the sky and the instrument panel. My brain calculates speed, fuel, distance and compass bearing. In spite of all this activity, my mind is a blank.

It is partly lack of sleep. Did I sleep at all in that rabbit-hole under the Chancellery? Nobody was sleeping there. They had their minds on something else entirely.

We are flying back to Rechlin. Where else? We are flying the return half of the journey which cost the general his foot. At Rechlin we have urgent business to perform. Urgent, that is, if you believe the order the general has to transmit stands any chance of being carried out.

Then we must fly on to see Doenitz in the north. To which roughly the same applies.

I hope the general lasts the trip. I really hope he does. I'll fly the aeroplane, but he will have to do the other part of it. I don't think they'll take orders from me. Let alone these orders.

I flew my first aeroplane on a cool morning in June.

Dismounting from my bicycle and propping it against the hedge, I walked for the first time through the open gate into the gliding field. As I joined the group of pupils chatting on the concrete pad in front of the hangar, a silence fell. It was broken by the biggest of the group, a ruddy-faced youth with button eyes like a rodent's.

'Well, what's this then?'

'Hello,' I said. 'I'm Freddy.'

'Come to fly, have you, sweetheart?'

Guffaws.

'Yes,' I said.

The laughter went higher, and I could hear the uncertainty in it alongside the derision. My nails bit into my palms.

'Oh dear, oh dear,' said the ruddy-faced youth. 'Well, now I've seen everything.'

The instructor arrived.

As he strode towards us his eyes swept round our circle and fixed at once on me. They fixed without astonishment, but with a kind of unbelieving, furious distaste.

He pulled a list from his pocket and read out our names. He read mine last. When I answered, he folded the list and put it away again.

'I don't approve of having a girl on the course,' he said, and as always the word was like cold water, like an undeserved slap, and silenced me. 'Unfortunately, there's nothing in the rules that prevents you from flying. But I can't make any special allowances. You must expect to be treated just like everyone else.'

I said that I wanted to be treated just like everyone else.

He gave me a hard stare, then turned on his heel and walked to the hangar.

Why is it like this? But it is.

We pass from broad fields through a narrow gate in which all that we are is squeezed into the answer to a single question. The question is binary and primitive: one word suffices to answer it, and only two words are available. On, off, the current flickers. This is the way the universe is.

The question cannot be avoided.

The gate must be gone through.

Once you have gone through it, you have accepted definition. This is what you are, for life. For eternity. All characteristics, all qualities, all possibilities of fulfilment, your relation with your peers, your society and your God, will find their base in this, the answer your cells have given to the idiot's question of your gender.

*

I found ways, in time, of not acknowledging the idiot's question, and in the end they left me alone.

But then I was too young to know a way of refusing. I could not imagine how I could deny what I appeared to be, however little I felt myself to be it. I was convinced I was unlike anyone else on earth. But I was also proud. I would not betray myself.

And yet you have to live in the world. And the world must be lied to, if it cannot hear the truth. Lying by omission and implication, accommodating the intolerable, making shift . . . do you know when you have betrayed yourself?

You know when you haven't. But sometimes you have to go close to the edge.

We brought the training glider out of the hangar. I had never been so close to a glider before. With intense curiosity I laid my hand on the thing's blunt, blind nose. It was warm where the summer sun was playing on it.

I was fascinated by how visible were its working parts: the wires, hinges and rods controlling ailerons, elevator and rudder. I noted the curved piece of wood, called the skid, under the belly, which took the shock when landing: it looked flimsy, but wasn't. The cockpit contained more wires, extending backwards into the fuselage, a rudimentary seat, and a wooden dashboard in which were set three dials.

It was not a sophisticated machine. But it flew.

A smell came from it, oily, dusty, rubbery. A workshop smell. The smell of flying.

It was the following morning before we flew. And then we flew along the ground.

This was not a dual-control glider. Such sophistication had not yet arrived in gliding circles; or, if it had, it had not got as far as my local club. With no instructor sitting behind you, you had to learn to fly before you took off. You started by doing a belly-slide down the slope, and worked up to a bunny-hop. Your task was, using the stick, to keep the wings level, and to counteract any sideways swing with the rudder.

On the third day we were allowed to bring back the stick just a little as we moved forward. This raised the nose. And then I felt it at last: the long-dreamed-of lifting, the exchange of earth for air.

By the second week we were hopping the length of the field, and by the third we were really flying. The weather stayed fine and we went up every day. At home each evening I rushed through my meal, raced upstairs and, with my grandfather's alpenstock doing duty for the control stick, practised flying my bed. I already knew everything the instructor put on his blackboard, and more. It was all in the gliding books.

I was a good pupil. The instructor didn't much like this, but there was nothing he could do about it. I was at least as good as anyone else on the course: I had a natural balance, learnt quickly, was willing and never complained about having to pull the glider back up the hill. If these things had earned me the instructor's favour, the hostility of the other pupils would have increased; but it was clear to all that they didn't. After a few days my presence was accepted. Rodent-face retreated to sarcasm, but had no allies. Even so, there remained something, a trip wire, which I knew I must not cross.

The day came for us to take our Class 1 test. It was rare for pupils to pass at the first attempt. The chief officer of a neighbouring club had come to judge.

I went fifth. So far, no one had passed. I stepped into the cockpit, and the control stick slipped into my hand as if picking up the thread of an old conversation.

I flew a faultless circuit and landed lightly on the spot at which I had aimed. It is like that sometimes.

I did not have to look at the judge's face, or see the blue and white badge in his hand. I got out of that cockpit into a silence as clear and brittle as glass.

By then, Ernst had met the Fat Man again.

When Ernst met the Fat Man again, the Fat Man shook him by the hand, clapped him on the shoulder and gave him a glass of champagne.

And this was surprising because, on the last occasion when Ernst and the Fat Man had met, Ernst, as chairman of the Richthofen Veterans' Association, had been presiding over the Fat Man's expulsion from the membership for declaring as his own the unclaimed enemy aircraft credited to the squadron.

The Fat Man bore no grudge. It is not in his character to bear a grudge. He is a sportsman. This fact makes no sense, it is like a goldfish in a pigeon loft, but it is a fact.

'Delighted to see you again, old chap,' said the Fat Man, or something of the sort. He was very amiable. He was stouter, although not yet fat, and his pussycat face with its wide, wide mouth had become the face of a bigger man. It was both more accommodating and more ambitious.

Each inquired with courtesy what the other was doing these days. Each knew perfectly well what the other was doing. Much of what they were doing was reported in the papers, and what wasn't was circulated by word of mouth. They moved in the same circle, these men, and it was a small circle. One of them would be trapped by this circumstance.

Ernst was doing 'the Flying Professor'. He dressed in a frock coat, top hat and long white beard and taxied around in his Flamingo for ten minutes trying to take off. When he was at last airborne he seemed unable to fly in a straight line. First he flew in circles and spirals, then he could not stop looping. He pulled out of the last loop but now he was flying upside down. He made a supreme effort to right himself and a cloud of coloured smoke burst from the exhaust. Eventually, having flown like a madman with great skill for twenty minutes, Ernst put the plane down in a landing disdainfully precise. Smoke at once poured from every part of the machine. The crowd was delirious.

Naïve, yes, but they loved him, and he needed to be loved. The money was useful, too.

The Fat Man, who was also a showman but had barely entered yet on this stage of his career, had returned from a spell abroad. He had become a parachute salesman, but he had done rather better than most parachute salesmen and had married a Swedish countess. She hadn't brought him much money but the title was useful. The Fat Man did a lot of entertaining.

He didn't sell parachutes any longer. He had gone into politics. He had espoused a sect of fanatics who ranted race-mysticism and revolution on street corners, and was one of a handful of their representatives in the Reichstag. Everyone made mistakes, thought Ernst.

The Fat Man appeared to nourish hopes that Ernst might join him in his indiscretion. He said something about it.

This was embarrassing. Ernst listened to the bubbles fizzing and crackling in his glass. He lifted it to his mouth and the coldness flared deliciously into his nostrils.

'Politics isn't my sort of thing,' he said.

The Fat Man laughed. 'I never thought it was mine. Terrible bore. I don't understand half of it.'

'Then why are you a deputy?'

'Strategy, Ernst! Staying legal these days. Undermine from within.' He tapped his upper thigh in a curiously frank gesture. 'We don't want any more of that if we can help it.'

The Fat Man's involvement with politics dated back some ten years. His spell abroad followed immediately on a botched attempt to seize power which had been quelled by the bullets of the police. One of the bullets lodged in the Fat Man's groin. There were rumours of impotence. There were rumours of morphine.

Despite all this, the Fat Man looked pleased with himself.

'We particularly need people like you,' he was saying. 'And let me give you a tip.' He lowered his voice. 'Get in on the ground floor.'

'Thank you.'

'This isn't politics,' said the Fat Man. 'Politics you can wipe your arse on, as far as I'm concerned. This is the future.'

Ernst looked into the pussycat face and saw only the wide, infinitely self-indulgent mouth. He did not see the infinite coldness of the eyes above it.

He found it hard to keep the contempt out of his smile, but he was a gentleman and managed it.

Ernst was called a playboy. It was true that he enjoyed playing. He threw a lot of parties and was seen with a lot of women. He had not found a woman he could stay with for long. They left, or he left. It wasn't surprising. The fast lifestyle, the deliberate risks, the adulation of the crowds. The constant travelling. The money: he was making, and spending, a lot of it. There were rich friends, expensive hotels.

He was outrageous sometimes. He dressed in tails and rode his motorbike around a ballroom. He danced on tables routinely. He baited policemen. Perhaps it was not very grown up. (But the grown-ups were so *serious*.)

It was certainly not conducive to stability.

Ernst was easily bored, and didn't want stability. As for the women who pursued him (and they did), they wanted excitement.

He was sometimes lonely. There was no one – of course – to whom he could say this.

He threw a party when the baroness, his mistress of eleven months who wasn't a baroness at all, departed. He would remember for some time the dramatic catharsis of their quarrels. Once she had drawn a pistol on him. The bullet struck a stuffed tiger's head on the wall and knocked out a tooth.

Ernst was living in a small flat in a fashionably bohemian quarter of Berlin when the baroness packed her many suitcases and left. From the window he watched her settle herself in the front seat of a cream and black Bugatti. The driver was a wiry little man wearing a leather cap: Ernst despised him, he was a racing driver. At the same time Ernst had room for a feeling of relief. The racing driver could face the bullets and the IOUs.

The baroness had expensive tastes and a perpetual shortage of cash. She had left Ernst a great many IOUs.

Ernst leafed through these pieces of paper as he sat by the telephone ringing his friends to invite them to a party. Most of the friends accepted. Ernst's parties were fun and he was lavish with the food and drink. By the time the guests arrived Ernst had pinned the IOUs to a wall and was using them for target practice. Well, they were no use for anything else.

The guests joined in. Ernst had a collection of pistols: he was a keen shot. He levelled his Walther and shot dead the baroness's IOU for twelve hundred marks.

Ernst and his friends divided themselves into teams. Rules were agreed on and a score sheet was kept. As the evening wore on and crates of drink were consumed the noise became deafening, and a window was found to have been broken without anyone noticing it. Several bullets which should not be there were found in the stuffed tiger's head. Ernst stopped the shooting at this point and put a jazz record on the gramophone. In the acrid smoke that filled the rooms of Ernst's ravaged flat, they danced.

Ernst danced well. He seemed to do everything well. There were men here who envied him, who, calling themselves his friends, would not have been sorry to see him in trouble. Ernst knew this but chose to ignore it. He thought he could cope with whatever came to him. And if most of your friends are fair-weather friends, you still only need a few of the other kind.

In the pause as a record was changed, a new sound came to the fuddled ears of the guests. They went to the windows to look. Colour was falsified by the streetlamps, but there was no mistaking that shit-brown uniform. The guests watched, some uneasily, some with derision, as the troop passed by with its banner. Then they went back to their dancing.

Ernst drew the velvet curtains. The marchers belonged to the Fat Man's party. It was a party that liked marching. And it was doing well, all of a sudden: a hundred and seven seats in the Reichstag at the recent election. A fluke of the troubled times, thought Ernst.

At eighteen, I was expected to indicate what I was going to do with my life.

The path I was expected to follow was plain. One by one, with wonder and a touch of pity, I watched the girls I had known at school disappear behind the high walls of marriage.

I had never considered marriage as a possibility. It seemed utterly alien to me. I did not consider it now.

That was all right. My family appeared perfectly content that I should not marry. But I had to do something. Presumably I envisaged a career?

There were a number of professions open to women who were clever and prepared to work hard. They included education, the various branches of medicine, the arts and the law.

I cast an unenthusiastic eye over the field.

I knew what I wanted to do. I wanted to fly. I said this to a few people. They looked at me as if I were either mad or mentally retarded.

I had a series of unsatisfactory and rather unpleasant conversations with my father on the subject of my future. I was in a state approaching desperation (and was not alone in this) when, one evening, I drifted into the local church hall and found myself listening to a talk on the work of flying missionary doctors.

St Paul's revelation on the road to Damascus was as nothing to the light which illuminated me. Why had I not thought of it before? No one could object to my becoming a missionary: ours was a Christian household. (Thoroughly Christian: my mother was a Catholic and my father a Lutheran. A result of this was that religion was never mentioned.) Certainly no one could object to my becoming a doctor: my father would be delighted. Therefore no one could object to my flying.

I would have to learn to be a missionary and a doctor. I thought briefly about what this might entail.

The missionary part, I decided, would not be a problem. I'd been to church all my childhood; and presumably they trained you. It would take years, on the other hand, to become a doctor. Moreover I had a suspicion, sown years previously in the dissection lessons in my father's study, that I was not going to like anatomy.

But it would be worth it. It was a way, apparently the only possible way, of incorporating flying into a career.

I went home, took a deep breath and informed my parents that I wanted to study medicine. The news was greeted with amazement, then cautious pleasure. Over the next few months, inquiries were made, procedures followed and financial matters attended to.

In due course, I packed my suitcase and went to Berlin to be a medical student.

The worst of the Depression was over, but only just. Berlin shocked me.

On the Ku'damm, smartly dressed people ate cream pastries with silver forks at pavement tables. Behind them, in the mirrored recesses of the café, waiters flitted. Store windows displayed jewellery, watches, furs, soft leather; in showrooms stood gleaming automobiles. Turning away from this brilliant scene I would all but stumble over a maimed war veteran in rags selling matches, or simply holding out his hand.

There were hundreds of beggars. They stood in doorways or huddled at underground stations, or sat like sacks against walls with their legs extended, as if the most they could hope for from the world was to make it walk round them. They had given their sight, their limbs, their sanity, for Germany, and Germany could not feed them. I gave them what money I could: it was little enough, I was living on an allowance from my father. I tried to talk to them. Some were philosophical about their state, but many were bitter. They had been betrayed, they said.

I had grown up with that word. The country had been betrayed, stabbed in the back by politicians who had made a coward's peace while the army was undefeated. It was the work of Communists, it was the work of Jews. Such talk was not accepted at home: my father said that the army *had* been defeated and the business about Jews was pernicious and unscientific. But among most of the people I knew, the story went unchallenged.

And even my father, scrupulous and pedantic though he was, shared the popular indignation over the Treaty of Versailles. 'That infamous document,' he called it. It decreed, among other things, that we must have an army of not more than one hundred thousand men ('the nation of Bismarck!' snorted my father), that we should have no air force, that East Prussia should be cut off from the rest of Germany by a slice of Poland, and that we must pay huge, unpayable sums in reparation for a war for which it was alleged we had been solely responsible.

By the age of twelve I had heard enough about the Treaty of Versailles to last me the rest of my life, and had laid the foundations of an enduring distaste for politics. But in Berlin you couldn't get away from politics. And in Berlin, its streets haunted by the limbless and sightless, I first understood that politics referred to something real.

The war veterans were not the only beggars. There were the men who were simply unemployed because there weren't jobs for them. Some held placards saying how many children they had to support. I didn't give them money, because I gave all my spare coins to the war veterans. Once, feeling sorry that I had to refuse, I explained this to one of them.

He looked at me at first as if he didn't understand what I was saying. Then he smiled, rather weakly, and said, 'That's all right, *Fräulein*. You give your money to who you want.'

I was touched by this, and was about to give him what money I did have in my pocket, which roughly amounted to my tram fare, when the man standing next to him spat on the ground and said, 'Give it to the SA, then.'

I walked away. I didn't know how to deal with it.

I didn't know how to deal with the SA.

They were the street troops, the bullyboys, of the National Socialist Party. You saw them everywhere in their brown shirts, lounging and swaggering. Collecting tin in hand, blackjack in pocket.

They frightened me. I shrank from them in public places: their noise, their aggression, their bulking maleness, their smell of sweat and beer. They frightened me because I knew they would do anything. They had no morals and no religion, no compassion and no justice.

Yet it struck me that, in their own way, they were disciplined. They were even selfless. It was visible when they marched. They cared for nothing except the movement and their leader, but for those they would sacrifice everything. The movement was an idea: you could see it in their eyes. They had fallen in love with it. The idea was the idea of the regeneration of Germany. For that, everything. If it took lives, if it took revolution . . . still, everything.

I found I could not despise that.

And what if they were rough? They had been roughly treated. They were unemployed, many of them, through no fault of their own but the mismanagement of politicians. They were war veterans, many of them, come home to a land for which they'd fought bravely, to find those living well in it were the friends of politicians. And if the country was going to be turned around, dragged out of the mire, who was going to do it? These men, or the white-gloved politicians?

The SA marched and paraded with military precision. Four hundred thousand of them.

The army looked on in thoughtful silence. But in the streets people cheered.

For someone who hated politics, I could not have gone to Berlin at a worse time. The chancellor was ruling by emergency decree. Coalitions were formed and fell apart again. There was warfare in the Reichstag and warfare on the streets. On the streets, the SA fought the Red Front.

Hindenburg's term as president had expired: in spite of his age, he was standing again. The presidential campaign opened in the spring, and election then succeeded election until the year drew to an exhausted close. A second election for the presidency, because the first had failed to produce a majority; elections for the Prussian state parliament; then two elections for the Reichstag. The screaming posters were plastered to the walls in February, and there they stayed – torn down and replaced almost daily, but always there – until November. Meetings broke up in violence. Bombs were thrown. And at the end of it, still nothing had been decided, still nobody knew who was to govern the country.

There seemed to be a deliberate cruelty in it, this incessant electioneering. It was like being bludgeoned. We hadn't asked for it. Why, then, was it happening? Well, it was democracy. If this was democracy, did we want it? Hang democracy, ran a savage current of feeling.

'Hang democracy,' the National Socialists bellowed joyfully. 'Vote for us and you'll never have to vote again.'

In the July elections they emerged as the largest single party in the Reichstag.

The Bücker sings to me. A light, sweet note, which develops, as I push the throttle forward, what might almost be called a rattle, but never develops it fully.

I have a certain knowledge of aircraft engines. You come to, when your life depends on it. There's much I have been required to know. Some of the engines I know about are still on the secret list, if at this stage there can be said to be such a thing as a list, secret or otherwise. One or two should never have got out of the factory. I have built my knowledge up in layers, geologically, over the years, flying whatever's flyable; but the bottom layer, the bedrock, is what I learnt when I was a medical student in Berlin.

It was horribly predictable.

I did intend to study. I intended to study hard. The sooner I qualified, the sooner I could become a flying missionary doctor. I found myself a room in an attic and bought some books. I went to an introductory lecture. Then, in the course of conversation, another student mentioned to me that there was a flying club on the southern outskirts of Berlin. They flew sports planes, he said.

I took the bus out there. It was a long journey, but at least, I told myself, if I made this journey regularly I could use the time for reading. Perhaps they didn't give lessons. And perhaps I wouldn't like the place. But when I got there, I saw the little single-engined Klemms on the grass, lifting their noses into the breeze, and I knew what I was going to do. The rate for lessons took my breath away, but I found myself enrolling.

That was virtually the end of my studies. I paid the rent in advance, lived on bread and apples, and flew.

When I wasn't flying I was hanging around the clubhouse, making one cup of coffee last all morning and picking up information like a dog picking up scraps. Or I was in the workshops. On the bus I read the flying manual. I told myself that one day soon I would settle down to serious work.

Learning to fly the Klemms I didn't find difficult. Flying is mostly a matter of concentration, and that had never been hard for me. But engines . . . I knew nothing about them.

I turned up in the workshop with my lunch apple in my hand, wearing a pair of baggy overalls obtained under an oath of secrecy from Peter. I looked, I suppose, as I usually look: small, fierce and of indeterminate sex.

'Hello,' I said. 'I'm Freddy. I'm learning to fly and I need to know about aircraft engines. D'you mind if I watch you?'

It makes no difference what you say. The look they give you is always the same. It is not a response to anything you've said or ever will say. However, it doesn't last long, this look, because they are embarrassed by it.

They let me in. I worked hard to be useful. I ran errands and held spanners, and made coffee on the petrol stove for them. I did odd jobs. In time the odd jobs became real jobs. They had not come across anything like me before, but because I wouldn't go away, and was always the same, they made a special category for me, like a box in the corner for the cat.

I lied to them. I had to. I lied about being a student. How could I tell them that I should, at the very moment when I was dismantling a carburettor, have been at a lecture in the university medical school? They would not have understood. It would have made them angry. I told them I was waiting for a place and had a year to spare.

During that time I met a girl called Lise.

I was still making occasional fevered attempts to study, in the hope that a few days' concentrated work could make up for missed weeks. I went one morning to a lecture on the spine. Within ten minutes I was lost. I gave up trying to take notes, since I did not understand what was being said, and began instead to draw from memory the circuit I was learning to fly at the airfield. I put in all the landmarks I could remember, and the places where I had to gain or lose height. I hate wasting time.

'What on earth is that?' whispered the girl sitting next to me, a tall girl with a long, high-browed face made more intimidating by glasses.

'A circuit,' I whispered back.

'A what?'

Clearly she thought it was a wiring diagram. I giggled. So did she.

'Shh!' reproved somebody behind us. My neighbour went pink. She was a serious girl, whom I had several times seen deep in a textbook. I was sure no one had ever said 'Shh!' to her in a lecture before.

As we picked up our books at the end, she said, 'Come and have lunch. There's a good place by the art gallery.'

I couldn't afford it, but it was the first time I had received such an invitation. She took me to a basement café which had red candles, sunk into snakes of melted wax, on the tables, and French and Spanish posters on the walls. We ate bean soup and rye bread, washed down with beer. I wasn't used to beer and it gave me the exhilarating sense that anything might happen.

We went to the park at Charlottenburg, where we bought bags of bread and fed them to the squirrels.

She said, 'Why do you come to so few lectures?'

'I go flying.'

'Flying?'

'Yes.'

'Isn't that expensive?'

'Terribly.'

'Can you afford it?'

'No.'

She laughed. 'But your father can.'

'He doesn't know.'

She gave me a curious look.

'Aren't you going to get into a lot of trouble?'

'Yes,' I said, and grinned, because the sun was slanting through the treetops and I was walking through a wood with someone I liked.

'You take risks, don't you?' she said.

This pleased me. 'Yes,' I said.

'Mmm.' She did not appear to find it impressive. 'Probably compensating for something.'

'What?' The afternoon collapsed around my feet.

'Oh lord, I've done it again,' she said. 'I'm sorry. My father's a psychoanalyst.'

I was feeling injured and did not care who her father was.

'It means that nothing is ever simple,' she said. 'You analyse everything. At home we all sit round doing it. If the Nazis get into power, Father's going to be in trouble. We might have to leave the country.'

I had not the remotest idea what she was talking about. But a sense of large and dangerous issues tugged at my imagination. I wanted her to go on talking about herself, her family and the obscure danger in which they stood; but she turned the conversation back to me.

'Flying must be very important to you.'

'It is.'

'Tell me about it.'

'Promise you won't analyse it.'

'I promise only to analyse it inside my own head.'

I didn't go to the flying club that day. I didn't feel like it. I walked through the woods with my new friend, and talked, and marvelled at the way the sun brought out the paleness of her hair, so that it gleamed almost silver. The squirrels played around us as if we weren't there. How beautiful Berlin was, I thought, in the spring-time.

At the few other lectures I attended, I saw her but she was with other people. Some time later I wrote to the address she'd given me, but her family had moved.

After some months had passed, the workshop foreman gave me an engine to strip down and reassemble by myself, over a weekend.

By this time I had begun to enjoy engines. I had realized they had a dual personality. There is the logic, the unyielding set of rules; and there is the quirkiness, the daemon hidden among the valves and washers. Thus every engine has a character, and demands from you a personal relationship.

Laying the parts out carefully on newspaper in the echoing workshop, I worked late into the Saturday night and all through the day following. At some time after midnight on the second night, something strange happened. The engine began putting itself to-gether. Of themselves, the parts moved from my hands into sockets and on to spindles, and fitted with an oily click.

I finished the job at six-thirty, and was sitting on a packing case eating a sandwich when the foreman came in. Without comment he inspected the engine. Then he nodded. 'You've made a good job of it,' he said, and went off to start his work.

I was triumphant. Dazed with sleeplessness and hubris, I took the bus back to my lodgings and went to bed.

I woke in the early evening and took stock of the situation. Over me flooded everything I had repressed for months: the guilt, the doubt, the fear. My parents were spending hard-earned money on my education. There was I, grubbing about in a workshop among oily bits of metal.

I looked at my broken, blackened fingernails and in my mind's eye saw, with shame, the well kept hands of my fellow-students. They were all going to be doctors. What was I going to be?

As I sat on the side of my bed in the dowdily furnished attic, I heard a troop of Brownshirts march singing down the street. A full-blooded, roaring, cheerful noise. It struck at me like a knife.

I went to the window and looked out. The lights were coming on in the houses. The last file of S A men swung round the corner, bellowing out their song. Passionately I envied the certainty of their lives. They were what they were and they did what they did, as unselfconscious and free of doubt as animals. I wanted to be like that. I wanted to be like that more than anything else in the world.

What was wrong with me?

I wasn't interested in anything I was supposed to be interested in. I didn't want anything I was supposed to want. I cared about only one thing: and that thing, I was constantly told, I could not have.

The trouble was that, in that inner place where one confronts the truth about oneself, I did not feel there was anything wrong with me. Oh, I was guilty of deceiving my parents, I was consumed with worry over the work I hadn't done, and I was lonely because, in the nature of the situation, I had no one to confide in. But these things were superficial. As I watched the lights spring on in the houses opposite, illuminating other lives, lived – presumably – as they should be, I knew that I was living mine as I should. I really could not do anything else.

As for the world's blessing, I would have to manage without it.

I laughed. I don't know where that laugh came from, but it freed me, and for ever. I scrubbed the oil from my skin and went out to explore the city.

CHAPTER FIVE

You get what you want, don't tell me otherwise. Be careful what you want.

I must have wanted this.

This flight in the dark through the tatters of a war, the man with his putrid foot sitting behind me. Where else could I be?

I have to fly.

Ernst had gone into films.

There was an inevitability about it. Flying was the rage, motion pictures were the rage: put them together and you have a steady demand for stunt pilots.

And who better than Ernst? He loved it. The glamorous company, the exotic locations. If the flying turned out tamer than he liked, there was always a way of livening it up. He flew over the Sahara, crash-landed with an engine fault and had to wait by his aeroplane to be rescued. In the Serengeti, a lioness leapt at his plane and tore a strip of fabric off the wing.

He tried to take Africa with him when he left. Skins, masks, assegais, a tribal shield, drums. They lent his flat an air of danger: you never knew what you might come face to face with in the bathroom.

He coasted through the Depression, sometimes close to disaster but never quite caught by it, as he was never caught by anything. As things picked up he applied for an instructor's post at Rechlin, the secret air-testing station and research establishment, but they turned him down. The reply was couched in terms which did not trouble to conceal officialdom's contempt. They had not forgotten the Flying Professor. They thought he was a clown.

He was a clown.

The Fat Man was Speaker of the Reichstag.

*

I went into films, too. I suddenly needed rather a lot of money.

I had known I could fly, and I could. After the initial, uncomfortable gliding course I had come to the notice of the head of the gliding school. He found me interesting, encouraged me and, as I improved, gave me special lessons. Within a fairly short time, I was on the gliding field nearly every day I was at home. I began to do long-distance flights and altitude flights, and set a few modest records (in those days it wasn't difficult to do).

My adventurousness outran my knowledge. I learnt my lesson the day I flew into a thundercloud, allowed myself to be sucked up to nine thousand feet and found myself on the wrong side of the Czech border in a zone where aircraft were not permitted. There was intense diplomatic activity, my photograph was in the papers, I had a very heavy cold (it is literally freezing inside a thundercloud at nine thousand feet), and I had nearly destroyed a new training glider. My relations with the head of the gliding school recovered sooner than my relations with my father, who was furious and said I had made a shameful exhibition of myself. It was the photograph in the newspaper he couldn't forgive. The fact that I had set an altitude record didn't impress him at all.

I wasn't sorry that he was angry with me, because it meant that he didn't want to speak to me. I had come to dread being alone with him. I expected him to ask me questions about medical school, what I was studying, and how I liked it. I went to the gliding field partly to get away from him. I was profoundly grateful for the demands of his work, which kept him so busy and occupied so much of his mind.

When I thought I had enough gliding experience, I went to the Rhön championships. They were held every summer; I was the only woman competing. That made it all the harder to cope with what happened. My glider wouldn't fly. I don't know why. Sometimes you just get a run of bad luck. Every day it took off and flew down into the valley, where it ran out of height and landed. The spectators were in no doubt as to the reason. Ribald cheers greeted my arrival on the third day, and there was some shouted advice to go home. I felt like going home. But I refused to. I gritted my teeth until my jaw hurt. I was going to see these contests through.

And I did.

A week later a letter arrived for me. I read it twice, then asked my mother to read it because I could not believe what it said.

It was from the director of the Glider Research Institute in Darmstadt. The Institute had great prestige: it carried out studies into aerodynamics and meteorology, and was the most important centre of its kind in the world.

The director said he had been present at the Rhön championships and had admired my 'perseverance in adversity'. He said there was nothing a pilot needed more than determination, and invited me to join an expedition the Institute was making to study thermal conditions in South America. I would have to find my own expenses.

'What about your studies?' said my father. He seemed at a loss to understand why I wanted to go.

'It's only a postponement, Father. People do take six months or a year out. Even more.'

This was true. The system accommodated it.

'Yes,' he said, 'but to do it for such a trivial reason.'

'It's not trivial to me, Father.'

'Clearly.'

He took a few turns up and down behind his desk. His face was heavy with disapproval. Watching him, I felt suffocated.

'South America is a dangerous place,' he said. 'How do we know you will be safe?'

'The Institute will have made proper arrangements, Father. It's not some amateur organization.'

'Doubtless it has experience of this sort of thing. But you're a young woman. How can we be sure they will take proper care of you?'

'I'm not a child.'

'You're still in my care, and as long as you are, you will not go gallivanting around the world on some harebrained scheme to do with gliders.'

'Father, *please*! *Please!*' I would have flung myself at his feet if it would have done any good, like the woman in the etching of Coriolanus in the dining room, but I knew it wouldn't. It would just disgust him.

He glanced at me sideways. He had not expected this passion.

'And what of the expense?' he said. 'Have you any idea what a transatlantic crossing is likely to cost?'

'I can earn it,' I said. 'There's a film company advertising in the paper for a female stunt pilot.'

'Then that settles it,' he said. 'You will do no such thing. I never heard of such an idea. My daughter in a film!'

'You wouldn't be able to see it was me,' I said. 'That's the point of stunt work. The audience think it's the film star.'

'I am aware of that!'

He had almost lost his composure. He cleared his throat a few times.

Sensing an opening, I said, 'It's just like any other work, but it's well paid. They probably wouldn't even put my name on the credits.'

'Where is the film being made?'

'Near Hamburg.'

'That's a long way away.'

'They would put me in a good hotel. But if you didn't like that, I could stay with Aunt Ettie.'

'You've thought all this out, haven't you?'

'Yes.'

He stroked his small, neat moustache. I really expected him to say no. If he had, I don't know what I would have done.

He said, 'I shall need to know a lot more about this. I shall write to the director of the Glider Research Institute . . .'

I drew in my breath. It would embarrass me intensely if he did that.

'Oh yes,' he said. 'I must. That is the least I must do. And if I receive a satisfactory answer – *if* – and *if* I decide this expedition is a suitable place for you, and if you assure me that you will continue to study while you are away and will resume your place at the university as soon as you return . . . well, then, *perhaps* . . .'

I met Dieter that year.

Poor Dieter. I have almost stopped being angry with him. Now that I've won. That is a brutal thought, but it comes to me. For here I sit, at the controls of the Bücker, flying still, after everything. And there he lies, in his hospital bed. Well, I suppose he is sitting up by now. Awaiting the arrival of the Americans, to whom he will certainly be very rude.

I don't forgive easily. I have a confession to make. When I heard that he'd crashed, dropped his aircraft onto concrete with nothing to take the shock, I smiled.

That was after I knew he was alive, be it added.

I went to see him, and we had a terrible argument and the nurses asked me to leave. It bucked him up considerably, I think. We hadn't had an argument for nearly a year.

He is lucky to be alive. Pale phrase, limply signposting the chasm between what happened and what by a hairsbreadth didn't happen. In Dieter's case, by a complete absence of fuel in the tanks. But for that, there wouldn't have been enough left of him to put in a bed. Not if you wanted to be sure of finding it again.

When I think of South America, I think of the light, and the space, and the vultures.

I went to a Brazilian beach one day and there they were. *Urubú*, an Indian word. Black-feathered, the size of a turkey, bald, red-eyed and vile. There were four of them, heads together, thrusting themselves into the carcass of something or other. Under the beat of the surf, I could hear the soft tearing.

There was nothing on the beach except me and the four vultures.

I stood and watched. I had never been so close to one before. When I followed them up through the thermals, they wheeled out of their trance as the glider came near. They could hang quite motionless. Seeing them above me I almost stopped breathing, it was such perfect artistry.

I gazed around. Behind the beach ran a dusty, unpaved road, and on the other side of the road was the village. Half a dozen houses, looking somehow unfinished, their doors open on to a dark interior. Smoke came from chimneys in spite of the heat of the day: they are cooking, I thought, on open fires.

In front of me, stretching to an indistinct horizon, was a sheet of glistening water, milky blue in the shallows, deepening to a dark, glassy green. On either side of me unrolled a carpet of pale sand the hue of peach.

My gaze returned to the vultures. One of them was now perched on the ribcage, and was gorging itself on the mess within.

I turned and walked away, the movement occasioning no more than a reptilian lifting of heads.

On the way to the place where the bus stopped I was joined by a little girl in a pink dress and a small black pig.

Back at the hotel, Dieter was hanging about in the lobby.

'Where have you been?' he asked as I came in, my shoes trailing sand.

'To a beach.'

His face fell. 'We were going to go to the beach tomorrow,' he said.

'It wasn't that beach I went to. I don't know where it was. I just got on a bus.'

'You just *got on a bus*?' He looked aghast.

'Why not?'

'This is *South America*!'

'Don't be silly, Dieter,' I said. 'I'd be in more danger in the middle of Frankfurt.'

I said I'd see him later, and crossed the lobby to the creaking lift with its imitation bronze doors and was whooshed upward to my room.

Dieter worried about me. He was concerned that I would get overexposed to the sun, or get bitten by mosquitoes, or get lost. In fact my skin was faring wonderfully in this fierce sun, and the mosquitoes bothered me not at all: it was his arms which turned red and peeled, his sandalled feet that acquired itching bumps. Poor Dieter. His attempts to protect me against nameless hazards were entirely inappropriate but I supposed that he had to do it. He sought my company a lot; rather more than I wished for his, but it was not easy to tell him so. He was sensitive to rejection. And one of the many differences between us was that while I liked company but could do without it (I had had to learn to do without it when Peter went to boarding school), Dieter appeared to find it a necessity. He seemed to feel incomplete on his own.

I had become aware of this on the boat from Bremen. Many times he had joined me at the breakfast table when I had been enjoying my coffee and my thoughts, assuming that I no more wanted to breakfast alone than he did. Or I would be standing at the rail as the sun went down, watching the water darken and the sun fling its path of fire across the swell; and there would be Dieter at my elbow, saying something about it. Again.

But he was pleasant enough. And there was something about him I found interesting. It was the intensity of his seriousness. He was a passionately committed National Socialist. That party was now in power, but Dieter had joined it years previously when it was struggling for a foothold in Berlin. When he talked about it, I sensed under the words a reservoir of feeling barely held in check.

I found myself envying this. What he said often bored me, or I couldn't follow it because it took flight into something rapturous and mystical. Occasionally it repelled me, because there was a deliberate brutality in it, although I saw no brutality in Dieter. But I envied his certainty over many questions about which I had never been able to make up my mind, and I envied, too, his unselfconscious belonging. I did not feel myself to be a member of anything in the way in which he seemed to feel it, and there were times when I longed to trade my freedom for its opposite. In such moods, it seemed to me that comradeship was a far more comforting thing than independence, and that to accept the Party line or the group teaching must simplify one's life wonderfully. In such moods, I could have joined the National Socialists myself. But the moods did not last long.

And I was a hater of politics.

Dieter, to whom I had not expressed my ambivalence but who sensed it none the less, said that National Socialism wasn't politics. I mocked him for saying this, but it seemed in some way to be true. The movement overflowed its political bounds. And there was something consuming about it.

Dieter, I thought, wanted to be consumed. I didn't. Nor did I at all like the views of the Party on women. These were, briefly, that the role of a woman was to serve her man and rear his children. That was her 'fulfilment'.

So what was I doing here, in Brazil, flying gliders, on a government sponsored expedition? They could easily have stopped me. That they hadn't gave me hope that the new regime would be more comfortable to live under than it had threatened; that they did not, in fact, mean what they said.

67

That would not be surprising. Politicians, surely, never meant what they said.

I lay on the wide, hard bed in my room, watching the curtains move in the draught from the electric fan. A mysterious thing, air, which we had come all this way to investigate. It really was a long way, I thought, to come to study thermals. And to promote international understanding.

Wolfgang was cynical about the stated aims of the expedition. Wolfgang, the third member of our four-person team, was cynical about everything. He was in the Foreign Office. He was roughly Dieter's age and liked to tease him. Dieter reacted like a porcupine. I watched them, and kept out of it.

I was having a wonderful time. I flew every day, and I had enough free time to look around. The country excited me: it could not have been more unlike the country I had left behind.

After an hour I got up, ran water in the blue-crazed hand basin, changed and went downstairs. We were invited that evening to a concert arranged by the German-Brazilian Cultural Fellowship. Public relations: we did a lot of it.

We are ten minutes' flying time from Rechlin. Five days ago I came here to fly a helicopter; it feels like half a lifetime.

I am supposing, we all are, that Rechlin is still operational. That there is a radio on which the message the general has to send can be sent, that there is electricity, a negotiable airstrip. There is no reason why there should be any of those things.

There was no way of finding out before we left. Telephone communication with headquarters is now cut off. The last call that went out was made at 3 pm yesterday; that was the last chance they had, down there, to ask a question of the world and get an answer. Now they have only the tap–tap–tap of the transmitter key, like a blind man's stick.

I hear in my mind the tapping of the blind man's key in the deserted control tower of Rechlin.

Then all at once I am uncertain whether it was 3pm yesterday or the day before. How long were we down in the rabbit-hole? Was it five days? What does 'day' mean? In the dark that was always there, even when the lights were on. The rhythmic thudding, like being trapped in someone else's body. The voices.

It is months since it was the headquarters of anything, but the habit of thought is powerful still. Witness the general behind me. He was a sensible man before he went down the rabbit-hole. Now look at him. This mission which is out of some saga, some comic book.

And look at me, flying him on it.

I found Dieter staring at an American newspaper in the bar of the hotel one day.

He was looking at a photograph of a large bonfire. In the background was a building I vaguely recognized. People with avid faces stood around the fire. A man in uniform was throwing something into the flames. The uniform was an SA uniform.

Dieter said, in a hushed, thrilled voice, 'They've burnt the books!'

'Who?' I said stupidly. 'What books?'

Dieter said, 'All the rubbish that should have been burnt long ago.'

I looked at him. Then I studied the picture. I didn't like it. I particularly didn't like the expression on the faces of the people around the fire.

I wondered what was burning on that fire. It was symbolic, of course; you couldn't destroy a book by burning copies of it. I wondered why anyone should want to. I was not a bookish person, but there were books that had been important to me. As a child I had worked my way steadily through the set of Alexandre Dumas in my father's study. I liked historical books and books about exotic places. At fourteen, I had read about Schliemann excavating Troy, and I would never forget the shudder of wonder that ran through me as I realized that Troy had been a real city. And there were certain poems I loved, and which I could not imagine not having in my memory.

Were some of the books I had cared about burning on that pyre? It was quite possible.

But that wasn't the point. Perhaps for everyone there was a book, I thought, and you would never know what it was. And for that reason no books should ever be burnt.

The expression on Dieter's face was boyish and shining.

'Now we can really make a new start in Germany,' he said.

The idea evolved that we should catch some vultures and take them back with us. We would present them to the Glider Research Institute.

They were wonderful as thermal detectors. Many times I had been indebted to a soaring *urubú* for pointing out a rising air current of which there was absolutely no other sign. What a boon they would be at home, we agreed. They would cut the cost of meteorological research by half, and be of invaluable help to many a long-distance glider pilot.

Somehow the joke turned into a serious project. Hans-Eric, the leader of the expedition, remarked one evening that if we simply notified the director of the Institute that the birds were being shipped back for research purposes, he would probably obtain the necessary authorization. 'There's a lot of money going into glider research,' he said. 'What's a vulture or two?'

A slow smile spread across Wolfgang's face. He had an odd face: long and cadaverous, with a hint of the dissolute which I think he cultivated.

'Right,' said Wolfgang.

Wolfgang and I went to talk to the manager of the hotel. The manager was unable to understand why we wanted to keep vultures in a cage in his back yard, but agreed that we could do so if we did not tell any other hotel keepers about it.

The boy who worked the lift said he had a brother with a truck who could make us a cage and transport it, and us, wherever we wanted to go.

A fortnight later Dieter, Wolfgang and I, with the lift-boy's brother, returned to the beach where I had seen the four*urubú*. We had with us as bait on the back of the truck a portion of a bullock's carcass in a fairly advanced state of decay.

The beach had occupants. A group of little boys in ragged shorts ran in and out of the shallows, playing with a homemade raft. Further away, where the haze began to confuse the outlines of things, was *urubú*. Solitary, intent, it picked at a mound of something.

The children watched us as we unloaded the wooden cage from

the truck and started to drag it in the direction of the vulture. Above the back of the truck a swarm of flies hung like a black inverted pear.

We reached the vulture. It lifted its head and looked at us, then went on pecking.

'We should have brought a net,' murmured Wolfgang.

The lift boy's brother shook his head vigorously. 'No net. He fly away. *Urubú* quick. See.'

He made a sudden grab for the bird, which flapped its wings and rose in a single sure movement.

'He come back soon.'

And indeed the vulture was circling, waiting for us to finish whatever silly game we were playing and let it get back to its meal.

With a piece of driftwood the lift-boy's brother picked up the thing the vulture had been eating – it looked like a dog, I glimpsed a dark-furred paw – and tossed it into the bottom of the cage. Then he propped the lid of the cage wide open with a stick he had brought for the purpose, and tied a length of rope around the stick so that from a distance it could be jerked away. It was not a sophisticated trap, but it would work on a sufficiently stupid vulture.

Our vulture was not stupid. It wheeled away and began to take an interest in what might be on the back of the truck.

'Damn,' laughed Wolfgang. His black hair was plastered to his forehead with sweat. 'We should have left the cage *and* the carcass on the truck.'

'I get the truck,' said the lift-boy's brother, and took off over the sand, which flew from his heels like little white wings.

We heard the engine start, and saw the truck roll for a short distance along the unmade road and then turn lurching on to the foreshore. It proceeded towards us for about twenty yards, at decreasing speed and with increasing noise, and stopped, its wheels churning in the sand.

This was the signal the little boys on the water's edge had been waiting for. It was the first thing we had done they understood. They ran to the truck and broke over it like a wave. Pushing, heaving, and scrabbling in the sand around the wheels, they laboured to free it. Wolfgang, Dieter and I went to help. We struggled for a

71

while, before Wolfgang said, 'How stupid!' and sprang on to the back of the truck and jumped up and down on it, at which the engine roared and the truck leapt away over the sand like a horse at the starting gate, careered towards a concrete ramp, rushed up it and on to the road and came to a halt with squealing brakes.

The little boys danced and capered.

Wolfgang was somehow still aboard. We caught up with him. 'I don't know about you,' he said, 'but I could do with a drink.'

Wolfgang could always do with a drink. Fortunately he was also good at finding places of refreshment. He consulted the lift-boy's brother, who consulted the children. Yes, they said, there was a café, they would take us to it.

From its height the vulture watched us. It had been circling continually since we disturbed it. I peered up at it: unwholesome, voracious, logical, with its angel's gift of flight.

The café consisted of a circular iron table in the corner of the village shop, which sold soap, matches, paraffin, tinned beans, sugar and not much else. The shopkeeper produced chairs for us and we sat in the paraffin-smelling gloom drinking weak beer and trying to converse in Portuguese with the lift-boy's brother. I began to feel bored.

Someone touched my hand. It was one of the children: he had stolen into the shop so quietly, in the shadows, that I hadn't seen him. He beckoned. I got up and followed him.

He led me through the sun-parched lanes back to the beach. He pointed to the cage. I followed the direction of his finger and saw between the bars something move with a jerky, thrusting movement.

My head swimming a little from the beer and the sun, I stared around for the rope, which had been flung down casually and was almost invisible against the sand. I found it. The boy was jigging up and down, urging me to hurry because the vulture might fly off. I knew it would not fly off. I knew it was mine.

I picked up the end of the rope. I nearly put it down again. But some things you have to do, because that's the way the world is.

I pulled the rope, the stick jumped from its place and the lid of the cage fell with a crash. From inside came an anguished beating of wings, and a series of horrible thumps as the bird hurled itself against the wooden lid and sides. After a while this frantic protest subsided and I went closer to look at my prisoner.

He stared at me through the bars, unwinking. I have always thought of it as a look of outrage, but it occurs to me now that perhaps he didn't even see me, just the bars and the sky.

A few evenings before we left, Dieter came to my room. I knew his knock, a quick triple-rap with the knuckles of the middle and third finger. But in any case I knew it was him.

I opened the door. There he stood, with his short blond hair and his sharp Adam's apple and his challenging look which masked shyness.

'Come in,' I said.

He sat on the edge of the bed, which was covered in a white bedspread embroidered with yellow flowers. There wasn't really anywhere else to sit. It was that sort of hotel.

'Would you like some pineapple?' I offered.

'No thanks.'

There was an awkward pause. Finally he got going.

'I wanted to talk to you.'

'Yes?'

'We've spent quite a lot of time together, haven't we?'

'Yes,' I said. We had.

'We've got . . . I mean, we've got a lot in common'

I looked at his clear eyes which only saw things they understood, and the little hooked cross on his jacket.

'Have we?' I said.

'Freddy . . . we're good friends, aren't we?'

'We're friends, yes, Dieter.'

'Do you – like me?'

'Yes.' I did not put too much enthusiasm into the word. It was fairly clear where this was leading. I had hoped not to have this conversation with him. I hoped he would get it over with quickly.

'I admire you,' he said. 'I've never said that before, but I really do. As a woman, and as a flyer. The first time I saw you get out of a glider . . .' His fingers began making nervous pleats in the bedspread. 'You climbed out of the cockpit and smiled at Wolfgang and me, and I thought . . .' He took a deep breath. 'I thought, that's the only girl for me.'

I was propped against the edge of the dressing table as I listened to this, and taking an interest in the yellow flowers on the bedspread. His eyes sought mine.

'How can you say that?' I said. 'The world is full of girls.'

'Not like you, Freddy.'

'I'm sorry, Dieter,' I said, 'but I don't feel the same way about you.'

His face contracted a little, but I thought he had expected it.

He said, 'Do you think in time you might?'

I laughed, and realized I shouldn't have when I saw the hurt on his face, but I wasn't laughing at him, I was laughing at the sheer unreasonableness of the question. How could one possibly foresee such things?

I explained this. I saw his expression clear, then cloud, then clear again. Ominously.

'You mean it's possible?' he said.

'I don't think so.'

'But you've just said you don't know.'

'Dieter . . .' It was late, I was tired, it was too much. 'I must ask you to go now.'

He stood up at once. He was very correct.

'Of course. I'm sorry if I've kept you up.' He moved towards the door, then stopped. 'May I ask you something?'

'Yes.'

'Is it Wolfgang?'

'I beg your pardon?'

'I wondered if . . . I know you like him. If it's that, well . . . I understand.'

I was angry.

'No, it isn't Wolfgang,' I said. 'Now good night, Dieter.'

He went out, and I closed the door behind him.

I didn't want to go back to Germany.

I had been in South America for nearly five months, and had flown almost every day. I had given aerobatic displays, I had flown north along the coast and ventured into the vast interior. I had come to think of flying as my occupation. Now I had to go back to scrounging it.

Worse, I had to go back to being a student, and being a student had become a nightmare. When I was honest with myself I acknowledged that I was never going to qualify as a doctor, and I did not know how to tell my parents this. Throughout the voyage home I hoped that a miracle would happen which might divert the ship. As we steamed slowly up the Elbe towards Hamburg, and smiles of recognition lit the faces of other passengers, I stood at the rail looking at the mist-shrouded, flat, utterly German landscape and felt despair.

We were welcomed off the boat, to our astonishment, with a grand reception. A deputation of saluting Party officials met us as we emerged from Customs and took us in a very big car to a marquee set up on the side of the Alster. There for three hours, although we had just had lunch, we ate, drank and listened to speeches about the spirit of the new Germany. Almost everyone in sight was in uniform. Wolfgang, sitting beside me, wore a sardonic smile.

After the speeches there was music from two military bands. Then some SA men gave a gymnastics display. Inside the tent, a group of Party functionaries got steadily drunker.

At some point Hans-Eric touched my shoulder.

'You must meet Ernst Udet,' he said.

I was startled. *He* was here?

In fact it was an obvious place for him to be. He was a founder member of the gliding fraternity and on the committee of the national association. Only my childhood belief that he existed on a different planet had prevented me from picking him out earlier. He was exactly like his photographs, except a little shorter than I had expected. He was wearing a dark suit with a carnation in the buttonhole, and holding a large cigar the smoke of which wreathed his smiling face.

He rested the cigar in an ashtray before taking my hand.

'We should have met long ago,' he said.

For a moment I could find nothing to say. I was intimidated by his fame, his glamour and his charm. Then I gathered the courage to look properly into his face. I saw two things. I saw that he was a kind man, and that he was interested in me. And I knew what sort of interest it was. It wasn't the thing I would not have welcomed, the thing which was such a nuisance because you had to negotiate your path around it and it got in the way of friendship. He was simply curious about me.

I said, 'I feel I've known you half my life.'

'Then you have the advantage of me,' he said, releasing my hand.

'I doubt that very much.'

'Well, we shall see. I've heard a great deal about you. Were I a man to worry, I should be feeling threatened.'

'Start worrying when I start picking up handkerchiefs.'

'Oh, I shall. At the first sign. Tell me, do you have it in mind to start picking up handkerchiefs?'

'Not really. The position is taken. In any case, I'm not sure there's a career in it.'

'Between ourselves, neither am I.'

The people around us gave up trying to insert themselves into this conversation, and moved away.

Ernst said, 'Seriously, what are you going to do? Next, I mean.'

I said, 'I'm a medical student.'

'Oh, I see. And that's what you want to do, is it? Become a doctor?'

'No.'

'What do you want to do?'

'Fly.'

He looked at me. I looked at the white linen tablecloth with its winestains and grape stalks and crumbs of cheese.

He said, 'There's nothing to stop you flying as a hobby, if you can afford it.'

'A hobby,' I repeated. I was too weary of the business even to put any contempt into the word. I said, 'I want to fly for my living.'

'Of course you do,' he said. 'But there are no jobs in aviation for women.'

I struggled with a spasm of intense anger. I could have torn the marquee from its moorings and thrown all their cosy little world into the Alster.

Ernst, watching my face, said gently, 'I wish you luck. I really do.'

His cigar had gone out. He relit it. Blowing out the match and replacing the box in his pocket, he said, 'Who knows? Things may not look promising at the moment.' His gaze was on the Party functionaries, one of whom had wandered off to be sick on the grass. 'But there is always the unpredictable. We live in unpredictable times.'

'I believe that you get what you want,' I said.

He was surprised, and showed it. His features were very mobile.

Then he laughed and said, 'You're right. It's the most sensible remark I've heard all afternoon. Let's drink to it.'

I lifted my glass of *Sekt*, and we drank to it.

Back in my homeland, I gazed around me with the clear sight of the stranger.

It was as if the whole nation had decided to stop being grown-up and to play a game. The men dressed as soldiers, whether they were or not. Half the population was in one uniform or another. Little boys drilled and saluted. The young men of the Labour Service marched and presented arms with shovels, and you smiled at your peril. Bands and parades filled the streets, which were decked with banners.

The parades were colourful and well staged, but it was obligatory to enjoy them. There was something deeply unpleasant in this game, something frightening. You had to have a flag to hang out of your window when a parade had been organized. If, when an SA troop passed, you did not salute the standard with the outstretched-arm salute now known as 'the German greeting', you were in danger of physical assault.

It was not all right to be an outsider. In fact it was impossible. I felt a chill as I saw this. The community was sacred. You had to belong.

Various clearly identified groups did not belong. The most important were the Jews.

There was uniformity, there was unanimity. The newspapers all said much the same thing and used the same words. These words always included 'honour', 'community', 'blood' and 'soil'. There was an obsession, which I could not comprehend, with farming.

It was not a good thing to be clever. What mattered were feeling and instinct. It seemed that if you were German, your instinct was necessarily sound. Science and the arts were being re-examined in the light of a new criterion: 'Is it German?'

I thought: 'They can't be serious!'

But they were. That was the thing about this game. Once it began to be played, it stopped being a game because you had to go on playing it. Not just because there were so many eyes watching to see that you did, but also because a great deal of the game was fun. The music and the banners, and the organized entertainments, they were fun. There was always something to do, something to look at. Belonging to a community was reassuring, and it told you who you were.

Above all, there were jobs now. Factory wheels turned, new roads and public buildings were being constructed, everywhere there was activity. And there was excitement. The game was a great adventure.

I was no more immune to the exhilaration than anyone else. At the same time I knew there was something terribly wrong with this game. How long could one go on not being grown-up?

I was confused about what I saw. And after a week or so I ceased to see it clearly. There were moments when I was aware that my vision was narrowing, that a filter had started to screen out certain things.

Realizing this, I was both disturbed and relieved.

The letter arrived a fortnight after my return from South America. I had been gloomily sorting out the clothes I needed to take back to Berlin. I had already confessed to my father that I had not studied while I was away, and relations between us were frosty.

A long grey envelope lay on the dining-room table, bearing my name. The postmark was Darmstadt. I picked it up with a wild surge of hope, at once checked. It would be a letter of thanks, or something.

It was from the director of the Institute. He was offering me a job carrying out research flights.

It was almost too much to bear. I seemed to have been willing it for so long.

Then I composed myself, and burst into the kitchen, where my mother was making an inventory of the bottled fruit. She looked in bewilderment at the letter end at my radiant face and, finally understanding what I was telling her, said, 'But, *liebchen*, do you mean that you do not *want* to be a doctor?'

It wasn't until later that she expressed what was on both our minds.

'I don't know what your father will say.'

'I don't think I understand what you're telling me,' he said. 'Do you mean that you wish to give up medicine?'

The light was behind him and I had to squint.

'Yes. Father. I've been offered a job.'

I heard how it sounded. How cheap.

He said with contempt. 'And is that all it takes, to make you give up a medical career?'

'It is not just a job, Father.'

'I suppose you found the work harder than you expected,' he said. 'Too much to learn. Is that it?'

I let it pass.

'There is of course a great deal to learn,' he said. 'And it has to be learnt. Anatomy. The bones. Muscles. The nervous system. I remember the armfuls of textbooks I had to carry. Hours spent in the dissecting theatre. But I wouldn't have thought you'd admit defeat.'

He looked me over. He grunted. 'Well, it seems I was wrong.'

I kept my eyes on a small engraving on the wall which I had always liked. A man on a horse, picking his way through a towering forest. As a child I had worried that he would never get out of this forest.

'You've disappointed me,' he said. 'I know that you're capable of applying yourself. And you've a good brain. You've got a better head than Peter. And although there are some people who would say that the professions aren't a suitable place for a woman, I don't agree. I've always believed women have as much ability as men, taking into account the natural differences. And medicine is expanding. You'd find plenty to interest you. Psychological medicine is an area which seems to appeal to women. It's out of favour at the moment, but that will pass. Some people find general practice the most rewarding of all. Certainly no doubt as to its usefulness.'

He brought his hands emphatically together. Then his eyes fell again on me and he recalled the facts of the situation.

'Well, I shan't allow you to throw away your future,' he said abruptly. 'And that's that. I insist on your continuing your studies.'

'Father – '

'Not another word, please. You must write to the Institute and tell them you aren't free to take up this post. Whatever it is.'

'I have already written accepting it.'

He stared at me.

'You have accepted it?'

'Yes.'

Words entirely escaped him. His face was wiped clean of expression in its amazement. Then it assumed a look of such cold anger that I was, for the first time in that interview, really afraid.

'You wrote a letter which accepted the job, and committed you to giving up your studies, without any consultation with me? Before you had even *informed* me that you had been offered the thing?'

'Yes.'

'May I ask what possessed you to behave in such a way?'

Controlling my voice was difficult. It felt as if it wanted to jump out of my mouth and fly out through the window.

'I knew you'd try to stop me.'

'You think you can defy me,' he said.

And when he said that, something happened. Inside me. Something laughed.

I lowered my gaze so that he shouldn't see it.

He said, 'You will write another letter, cancelling the first one. Politely, of course.'

'No.'

'I beg your pardon?' he said after a moment.

'No.'

'Frederika, the games are over. You will write that letter.'

I raised my eyes to his. I met his furious gaze.

'No,' I said.

I felt the huge shock of his will against me. I thought it would crush me. With every ounce of strength I had, I held it back.

Then it was done.

'I see,' he said, in a remote, chill voice which denied that I was his child.

There remained only the details.

'I cannot pretend to understand why you are doing this,' he said, 'and I presume you will not seek my blessing on it. As for the money I have thrown away on your education – '

'I'll pay it back,' I said. 'As soon as I'm earning enough.'

I had always hated my financial dependence on him.

'I suppose I should have listened to my patients,' he said. 'They all believe education is wasted on girls.'

I heard myself shouting. Something about my life being my own, about how he made everything impossible.

Then there was silence, and the room ringing with my voice.

My father walked to the door and, without a word, opened it and motioned me to leave.

It was sad, I thought the following day, hiking with a knapsack through the hills, that it had to be like this. I would have liked him to rejoice with me. But I had known that if I got what I wanted, it could not be what he wanted.

I was already pushing it to the side of my mind.

My life was about to begin. I would extract from this chance everything it possessed. There was nothing I couldn't fly. There was nothing I wouldn't fly. And nothing would stop me. I swore it.

CHAPTER SIX

Ernst had been to the USA. He went there as often as he could – on business, or any other excuse. He liked the place. At an air show he saw something that changed his life.

High up in a clear sky, a gleaming dot grew larger. It grew with surprising speed. Then Ernst heard the engine's roar. The aircraft was right above him and hurtling almost vertically at the ground. Ernst fought the impulse to throw himself flat. At what seemed the last possible moment for the pilot to pull out of the dive, there was a swoop of air, the engine note changed and the aircraft rushed away in a shallow climb. Ernst saw it circle, and come in to land on the far side of the airfield.

He started to run. He knew what he had just seen, but had thought it could not be done. It was a power dive. It involved putting the aeroplane into a steep dive without reducing engine throttle. The stresses when levelling out might break a wing or tear off the tail section. As Ernst ran, the idea seized him that he had to reach the aircraft before anyone else did: that all over the showground were men running towards it, who would steal its secret from him. He arrived breathless at the enclosure, pushed through the crowd and flashed his pass at the guard. He caught up with the pilot as he was walking to the hangar, unlacing the strap of his helmet.

'I'm Ernst Udet,' said Ernst, heart hammering against his ribs. 'I've just seen –'

The pilot stopped. Ernst never knew whether his name would be recognized or not. There was a new generation of pilots, and the exploits of the Great War were a thousand years ago to them.

'You *are*? Oh, *great!*' said the pilot.

They shook hands, and a look was exchanged above the handclasp. The pilot turned and led Ernst back to the aeroplane. It was a tough-looking little biplane. The mechanics were checking it over.

'What is it?' asked Ernst.

'A Curtiss Hawk. Want to sit in it?'

He did more than sit in it. The following day he flew it. The pilot was proud of his plane and eager to show it off. He was a tall, gum-chewing boy with the open face they all seemed to have. He ran with Ernst through the procedure for power diving, banged his hand on the fuselage by way of a 'Good luck', and walked away over the cropped grass.

Ernst flew a few circuits to accustom himself to the aircraft's handling, took it up to twelve thousand feet and dived it.

He knew in the first few seconds that something new had come into his life, and that he had been waiting for it. The blood surged in his head as the Hawk plummeted, his skull throbbed with the engine's beat, and in his ears began a dull, long-forgotten pain, an ache of war-damaged tissue. But his blood sang, too, as the air stormed at him; it sang as he plunged earthwards. He shouted with exultation. He felt like a matador, like a king; he felt like a fighter pilot again.

Choked by engine fumes, his veins rioting, the pain in his ears now intense, Ernst had become, by the end of that dive, a man of purpose. His country must have an aircraft that could do this. He would create it.

We needed aeroplanes.

German aviation at the start of the 1930s inhabited a shadowy borderland between what was permitted and what wasn't. In that region, things often were not what they seemed. It wasn't just aeroplanes that were affected, and the game of pretending to have what you didn't, and pretending not to have what you did, had been going on since I could remember.

I recall the day in my sixteenth year when we were sitting in the garden having tea, when something which wasn't a lorry but wasn't anything else either clanked down the country road which ran past our gate.

We stopped talking to stare. Beneath overhanging skirts of metal, shaped like boat hulls and painted camouflage green, revolved four conventional spoked lorry wheels. A radiator and headlamps peered from below the boxlike front. The top was crowned with something resembling a saucepan, and from the front of the saucepan projected a tube.

This thing moved down the road slowly and with a loud banging of its metal sides. Behind it, at exactly spaced intervals, came five other heaps of hardware just the same.

They were on their way to army manoeuvres, and had taken a wrong turning. The NCO in charge was worried it would be reported. We weren't allowed to have tanks. Therefore we weren't supposed to have anything that pretended to be a tank, either.

The Treaty of Versailles again.

The aircraft clause gave rise to systematic sleight-of-hand. First we had not been allowed aircraft at all, not even models; then we had been allowed civilian planes but with crippling restrictions on engine power, range and particularly numbers. So aircraft were built abroad. As for numbers, you can do a lot with a paint pot. For years, there wasn't an aeroplane in the Lufthansa fleet which didn't have a considerably greater thickness of paint where the identification markings were than anywhere else on its surface.

And there was Lipetsk. A really dangerous conjuring trick.

Imagine. On a field in the middle of Russia, buildings one day spring up like mushrooms. Hangars, workshops, living quarters. Every scrap of material used in the construction, down to the hammers and nails, has come from Germany. Smuggled, with false papers. The really serious contraband is brought in by cargo planes flown at high altitude, or slipped on to fast boats in the Baltic. Bombs and ammunition. The little, vital aircraft are sent in sections, crated.

The pilots travel in small groups, posing as tourists. On arrival in the Soviet Union they vanish. Many months later they come back, as if from the dead. Some of them are dead. 'Machine parts', say the crates in which the bodies are returned.

It's the forbidden fighter school for a forbidden air force. It is absolutely top secret. But Ernst knows about it.

On his return from America Ernst went to see Milch.

Erhard Milch, at the time in question, was the managing director of the civil airline, Lufthansa. But since Lufthansa was also the air force which the Treaty of Versailles did not permit us to have,

Milch was, among other things, managing director of the air force. He had built it up, disguising it as this and that, with care and patience over the years.

That was, and is, Milch's method in all things. Nothing deflects Milch. Nothing confuses him. He is probably the most competent man on the face of the earth.

I have disliked Milch from the moment I met him. He cannot abide me. Not so Milch and Ernst, in those days. They were good friends.

'We have to have an aeroplane that can power dive,' announced Ernst.

Milch permitted himself a smile. 'So that you can fly it?'

'Think of the military applications. Bombing, ground attack.'

Ernst had no interest in the military applications. He just wanted the plane.

'We have experimented in the past,' remarked Milch. 'The trials were unpromising. You stress the airframe for diving, you're bound to pay a price in terms of general performance.'

'I flew an aircraft in the States which performed beautifully.'

'What was the engine?'

Ernst produced a slim notebook from his pocket. Milch took and studied it.

'They let you write all this down?'

'I wrote it down in the lavatory.'

'Do you like America?'

'Yes, very much.'

'It might not be wise to say that too loudly.'

'It's funny how people think they should give me advice.'

'We care about you, Ernst. And you can do with advice. You go away a lot, don't you? Things happen quickly here.'

He shut the notebook and handed it back. 'I'm open to argument. But I'll have to see the aeroplane.'

'Can you get me the money to buy one?'

'Of course I can't,' said Milch. 'You know who to go to for money.'

'These are historic times,' said the Fat Man.

'Indeed,' agreed Ernst.

'Victory,' said the Fat Man, 'will be ours very soon.' He cupped his fleshy hand, then closed it. 'Have you thought any further about joining the Party?'

Ernst was silent.

'Don't wait too long,' said the Fat Man amiably. 'As soon as we get into power there'll be a stampede.'

Ernst lit a cigar to cover his distaste.

'I've been in America,' he said.

'So I hear. How was it?'

'Interesting. They have a very fine aeroplane which can power dive. A Curtiss.'

'Oh yes?'

'We ought to build one like it.'

The Fat Man chuckled. 'So you can fly it?'

'Military applications. It could bomb with great accuracy. A psychological weapon, too.'

'Mmm. Have you talked to Milch?'

'Yes. He'd like to see the Curtiss. I could import one for testing, there's no restriction on them, except that I don't have the money.'

'How much would you need?'

Ernst told him and the Fat Man did not turn a hair.

The conversation moved on to other matters.

A month after that, the Fat Man's party was in power.

Ernst stood at a hotel window and watched as, hour after hour, the brown-clad street fighters paraded past their leader. They didn't look like street fighters any more. They looked like an army. Above their heads the flames of smoking torches leapt into the night. Above their heads the banners marched. Black, white and red. How it throbbed, that passionate arterial red.

The Fat Man was made minister for Air, with Milch as his secretary of state.

After an interval, a letter embossed with the Air-Ministry seal landed on Ernst's doormat in Pommerschenstrasse. It said that the ministry intended to purchase two Curtiss Hawk aircraft from America and, after testing them, was prepared to grant Ernst the use of them for demonstration purposes.

In the course of that week, Ernst joined the Party.

We slip like phantoms into the graveyard of Rechlin.

Five days ago, when we came looking for a helicopter, there was a sense of demented purpose about the place. Now there is only exhaustion. The hangars are empty and the faces that greet us are empty.

And few. The management has taken itself off to healthier climes.

We land, nevertheless, on what is still a reasonable airstrip. The general, refusing help, unloads himself from the passenger seat and walks with his crutches to the blacked-out main office block. Once he stumbles and drops a crutch, and from his feeble cursing I know how ill he is, but he won't let anyone help him pick it up.

Inside, he makes his way down the narrow corridor to what was the director's office, switches on the light and takes up a position, standing, behind the desk. He addresses us.

'I have been entrusted,' he says, 'with the command of the air forces of the Reich. I am here to give orders for their immediate mustering to attack Russian positions around the Chancellery. The raid will be carried out in conjunction with an attempt to relieve Berlin from the south. I know you will all be very heartened to know that the fight is continuing. Our aircraft will muster here, at Rechlin, and I expect them to start arriving within the next half-hour. Are there any questions?'

For a few seconds no one speaks. No one moves even a facial muscle. Then the man at the front clears his throat. His name is Pohl: I know him slightly. Taciturn but dependable, a veteran member of the ground crew.

He says, 'I'd like to say something, sir, if I may.'

'Go ahead.' The general eases himself into a minutely more comfortable relationship with his crutches.

'It's the fuel, sir. There isn't any.'

The general's face shuts like a trap.

'I don't like the tone of that remark. It smacks of defeatism.'

'I'm sorry, sir.'

'Is the radio working?'

'Yes, sir. We're picking up a lot of Russky stuff.'

'It would be surprising if you weren't, at this range. Who's your radio operator?'

A small, nervous, sandy-haired man shifts his position from one foot to the other and says that he is the radio operator. He looks like a vacuum-cleaner salesman. One of his eyes keeps closing in a tic.

'Splendid,' says the general despondently. He feels in his uniform pocket for something, fails to find it, and pulls open a drawer of the desk. He frowns, takes something out and unfolds it. It is a plan of the fuselage of an aeroplane.

'What's this doing here? Why isn't it in the safe? How many of these drawings are lying about?'

He stares at the men angrily. They look confused.

'We've just left everything as it was, sir,' says Pohl.

The general pulls open all the drawers of the desk and piles up the contents on top. There are about a dozen sets of drawings.

He fishes among the things on the desk, and brings out a pencil and a clean sheet of paper.

'Well, let's get started. How many aircraft are there on this airfield?'

'Operational, sir?'

'Yes, of course.'

'Two, sir.'

'Two?'

'Yes, sir.'

'Very well, what are they?'

'A Ju 52 and a Me 110, sir.'

The general writes on his sheet of paper.

'But there's no fuel in the Ju 52, sir.'

The pencil stops. The general lays it down. He screws the sheet of paper into a ball and tosses it into the wastepaper basket.

He swings himself round the side of the desk on his crutches.

'Show me the radio.'

He goes out of the room with the wireless operator, throwing over his shoulder that he wants to see us all in thirty minutes' time.

I drink some hot soup which they are kind enough to give me, and walk through the echoing spaces of the hangars. I speak with the ghosts of my aeroplanes. I feel the Komet behind me, proud and tiny on its towing ramp, and so strongly do I sense its presence that I would not be surprised to see it in the shadowed corner as I turn, but I turn and see only a coil of rope, a bucket of sand and a slow river of black oil seeping from a drum into a mound of sawdust dumped there to collect it.

I wander into the workshops, where ideas were given physical form without regard to whether they seemed mad or sane, might work or not, and might or might not kill pilots. Some were mad, and many killed pilots. Some were marked with genius. I tested them. I run my fingers along the top of a bench: they come up silver-black with filings. I rub the fingertips in my palm, streaking it with black. A whiff of torched metal makes my eyes sting. I walk out, gently closing the door behind me, and go back to where the general awaits us.

He is alone, sitting behind the director's desk. His face has fallen into hollows like land which has been mined, and there is a film of moisture on it which augurs ill. He is sipping a mug of soup and glancing through the papers he took out of the drawers.

He looks up at me. 'I've issued the necessary orders. There are a few things to see to. In half an hour I want to be out of here.'

'We're flying direct to Plön?'

Plön, where Grand Admiral Doenitz has his headquarters, is a lakeside town on the Schleswig-Holstein peninsula, not far from Lübeck. North of the lines of advance of the British, American and Russian armies, it is a sensible place for Doenitz to be. It is not a particularly sensible place to fly to in the last days of a war in a small, open-cockpit biplane trainer.

'No,' says the general, unexpectedly, for he has been ordered to fly to Doenitz with all speed. 'I want to see Keitel first.'

Keitel is the chief of the High Command.

'Where is he?' I say. Anyone might be anywhere, these days.

'He's moved his base again. He's on our route. I'll show you.'

I am about to leave the room, in search of a few items it would be useful to have, when he says, 'You don't have to pilot me, you know. There will be pilots here, very shortly. Any one of them can fly me north.'

'I have every intention of piloting you.'

'You'd be a lot safer here.'

'We've already had that discussion.'

He folds the drawing he has been looking at and tosses it on the floor.

'Don't you want to be safe?' His tone is curious. 'You have family, don't you?'

'I'm looking for someone.' It surprises me that I say this, although it is true. Everywhere I go, I look. But I did not intend to reveal so much of myself.

I needn't have worried. 'Half the world's looking for someone,' he says. Then (for he is not an unkind man), 'But I hope you find him.'

The subject fortunately cannot be pursued, because at that moment the others come in, the handful of men who represent the staff of Rechlin research station.

As I leave the room I hear him say, 'We have the chance to make one last, great effort for the Fatherland.'

I go in search of maps, a torch, a blanket and whatever there is in the way of food (not much: bread and some dried raisins). I check that the Bücker is all right, and return to the director's office.

The general is burning drawings in the tiled fireplace behind the desk. He is kneeling on the floor with his injured foot held at an awkward angle in the air.

I help him burn the drawings. It takes quite a long time. Then we plot our route to Keitel's headquarters in the light of the various and confused bits of information we have about the fighting.

As we taxi out, a solitary Messerschmitt Bf 109 comes in to land in response to his radioed summons.

CHAPTER SEVEN

The cage was the first thing I saw as the taxi swerved in through the gates of the Institute. It seemed smaller, and under a grey northern sky the rough wood and dyed lettering looked primitive and sad.

In the end we had not caught a companion for our vulture: there had not been time. It hadn't seemed to matter then; one was better than nothing.

I was busy all that day, meeting the people I would work with and getting acquainted with my glider. I spent the evening settling into the small flat they had found for me in the town. The following day I flew, and filled in reports. It was the third day before I managed to visit Uby.

The floor of the cage was covered in fresh straw, and the entrails were in a clean enamel bucket. He stared at me, or through me.

'They're looking after you, then,' I said.

A sort of sigh erupted from him that lifted the feathers on his neck so that I saw the pale, loose skin, like an old man's skin, and a breath of foul air filled the cage and wafted into my nostrils. The red eyes seemed to dilate with impatience; then they winked shut, slowly, a serpentine closure by the inner lid, which rose like a white shell over the eye.

I began to walk away, and then I heard him screech. The sound was outlandish and furious. It made me jump in my tracks, and echoed around the well kept trees and shrubs that surrounded the Institute's lawn.

I flew a glider crammed with instruments. Boxes with dials, nibs tracing their way over graph paper, things with pointers and needles; all connected to delicate mechanisms on the outer skin of the aircraft. I made short flights and long, at high and low altitude, in calm weather and freakish. Sometimes I was in the air all day until evening. Alone with the sky.

The peace of flying crept into me.

The peace of flying crept into me, and so did the madness which flyers have, but I didn't know it then. I only knew that when I wasn't flying I did not feel quite real. It was as if I had only to blink and my surroundings would disappear, and I would be back in the cockpit, sailing the sky on that small hard seat.

Inevitably, I saw quite a lot of Dieter.

I wasn't sure, when I went to Darmstadt, how it would work out between us. I hadn't seen him for more than a few hours since the evening when he had come to my hotel room. On the boat home he had kept at a distance. I hoped that by the time I started work at the Institute he would have got over being rejected.

To my relief, it seemed he had put it out of his mind. He greeted me warmly in the canteen the first day, and said if he could be of any help while I was finding my way around I must let him know. Our paths often crossed. We lunched together when we could, and at least once a week would spend an evening together.

This arrangement suited me very well. I liked concerts and films, and it was useful to have someone to go with. And I liked talking to him, although there nearly always came a point where the conversation ran off the rails. When it did, he never recognized that it had. Dieter lacked imagination. This was not his fault: he had not grown up in an environment where it could flourish. But it meant that he never understood our relationship. He thought what drew us together was what we had in common. He never realized that we had almost nothing in common and that was why I spent time in his company.

From time to time, Dieter tried to persuade me to join the Party.

We caught a bus into the countryside one Sunday and went walking through the fields. Dieter had been to a rally and was full of enthusiasm.

'It was wonderful,' he said. 'All those thousands of people, from all over Germany – you should have seen the banners – all those people, *united*.' His face flushed. 'It's so inspiring, Freddy. I'm surprised you don't want to be more involved.'

Sometimes I did. But I could not say this to Dieter. If he knew how strong, at times, was the tug on me to join those bright-eyed crowds, he would never let go.

I said, 'I don't feel a need to be.'

'But the Party needs your energy, your example. You have so much to offer.'

'I'm a very bad example,' I said. 'I'm supposed to be at home doing the ironing.'

He looked exasperated. 'Oh, nonsense. National Socialism has identified certain roles as being broadly appropriate to men and women, but that doesn't mean they apply in every case.'

'Oh,' I said. 'Good.'

'But *because* you're exceptional,' he said cunningly, 'there's all the more reason for you to be in the Party, don't you see? I'd even say you had a kind of *duty* . . .'

I watched a thrush pulling a worm out of the soft ground. It was a thick, strong worm and it hung on mightily, but the thrush would get it in the end.

It wouldn't get me.

'It would help you, too,' Dieter said.

'Help me?'

'In your career. Think about it. A woman who wants to do the kind of things you want to do . . . I'm serious, Freddy.'

He had answered a question for me. I never thought about it again.

Uby, when I arrived at the Institute, had not been let out of his cage. This was partly because no one was sure how to track his movements once he was free. There was a vague idea that if he was kept in one spot for a few weeks he would he would regard it as home and stay in the area. However, his woebegone appearance on the lawn, and the unpleasant nature of his diet, were becoming oppressive. My arrival precipitated things. It was decided to hold a ceremonial opening of the cage, attended by the director, the gardener's boy who had been keeping the cage clean, Dieter and myself.

We assembled on the lawn.

Uby was asleep, his beak tucked into his sack of feathers. From the cage came the odour of rottenness.

The director wrinkled his nose and fiddled with his cuffs.

'Who is going to let this creature out?' he asked.

'I will,' I said. 'I caught him.'

'Very well.'

Uby stirred as I touched the cage. I unfastened the straps that held down the lid, and pulled it right back so that the sky gaped above him.

'There you are, Uby,' I said.

Long hesitation. I held my breath with the sense of what it must be like for him. I waited for the single strong beat of the wings that would carry him upward.

His legs moved instead.

He lifted a claw, inserted it into a gap between the bars where they were nailed to a crosspiece, and climbed to the top of the cage. Then he hopped down on to the grass.

We stood there watching as he stepped with his fastidious gait over the daisied lawn.

'Well, I'm darned,' said the director.

We left the cage open. He might want to get at his food again. When we turned at the edge of the shrubbery to look back at him, he was still walking on the lawn.

It became clear after a few days that Uby could no longer fly. Or no longer wanted to.

Various attempts were made to startle him into flight. He would run a little and give an angry wing-flap, and remain earthbound.

A vet was called. He peered at Uby with distaste, said something about tendons, and left with his fee.

The sight of the vulture walking about the grounds of the Institute was soon familiar. He high-stepped along the gravel drive, slowing traffic, and paced the lawns and shrubbery, and once I saw him standing in the corridor that led to the director's office, his wings slightly spread, looking like a half-opened umbrella.

He aroused a range of emotions. In the workshops he was cursed, chased, and had spanners and other objects thrown in his direction, but the men who did this also fed him cake. They seemed to look on him as some sort of deviant child.

The women in the kitchens hated him. He was a frequent visitor to the dustbins outside the kitchen's back entrance. He would try to knock the dustbins over and, if he managed one, he would scatter its contents in all directions with his feet and then straddle the mess and bury his beak in something. When this had happened a few times, chains were put on the dustbins. Uby, thwarted, took to jumping on top of the bins and from this vantage point gazing in through the kitchen window, which upset one of the cooks so badly she tendered her notice. She said either the vulture must go or she would go.

There were many by this time who said that the vulture should go, but the director, to whom they said it, did nothing. He was an unpredictable man with an odd sense of humour. His view was reported to be that the vulture was government property, and inalienable except by its own will. Rumour said that he had a soft spot for Uby and fed him on the contents of the kitchen mousetraps.

Things remained thus. Uby went on walking around. The cook left and was replaced by someone not so good at apple strudel but better at soup.

I went to Dieter's lodgings one evening to listen to records. He wanted to play me a set of Bückner he had just bought.

Music was important to Dieter. It was important to me, too, but it had never meant to me what it had meant to him. As a boy he had sold newspapers and carried bags for tourists to get the money for a concert ticket.

'Did you have music at home?' I asked. I thought of Peter's violin lessons, my piano lessons, my father playing the cello on a summer evening.

Dieter lifted a record from the turntable and said, 'My father lost his right arm and his right eye in the war. He couldn't work, even when there was work. My mother did two jobs and brought us all up, six of us, in a three-room flat in Kreuzberg with mushrooms growing out of the walls. And do you know what she did, every Sunday? She went to church and thanked God for her blessings. Her blessings!' said Dieter bitterly. 'Hymns, that was all the music we got.'

'I'm sorry,' I said.

'Oh, it's all right. If you haven't lived like that you can't be expected to understand.'

I said, 'You hate the Church, don't you?'

'Yes. What's it ever done for the poor, except take their little bit of money from them and tell them that things will be better in Heaven?'

He lifted a record sideways to the light, inspecting it for scratches.

'Did you ever say that to your mother?'

'No, it would have upset her.'

He put away the Bückner and ran his finger along the shelf of boxed records.

'Brahms?'

'Not this evening.'

'Bach?'

He put on the fourth Brandenburg Concerto, knowing it was one of my favourite pieces. I sat back among the cushions and listened. Intricate, lovely music.

I wondered at what point Dieter, growing up in the slums of Berlin, had become a fervent nationalist. It might have been a more obvious choice for him to join the Communist Party. I asked him this.

'I hated Communism,' he said. 'I found it despicable. As if all that mattered was money, food, *things*.'

'Those things would have made your life easier.'

'I didn't want my life to be easier,' said Dieter. 'I wanted it to be *harder*.'

I looked at him curiously.

'Everything was so empty,' he said. 'So pointless. I wanted something that would make demands on me. Enormous demands. That would require everything of me.'

'I see,' I said.

'It could only be Germany.'

There was a pause.

'The thing was, of course,' he said, 'that until Hitler, Germany didn't really exist. Do you remember how awful it was, all those years? Those squabbling politicians, and half the country out of work, and Germany being a laughing stock . . . All that time, I was looking for something that was solid, that was real and wouldn't change. A sort of principle *behind* everything, that you could get back to and refer to, that wasn't a sham.'

He had pinned an old election poster to the door. One of the ones that showed Hitler gazing fearlessly into the distance. They had been all over Berlin, when I was there.

'There has never been anyone like Hitler,' Dieter said. 'No one has ever had such moral courage. He is afraid of nothing. He follows an idea right through, to the very end. Who else has ever done that? The whole of history is full of compromises.'

The record needed turning over. He got up to attend to it. Carefully he laid the needle on the edge of the groove and watched it spiral inward.

'Democracy!' he said with quiet scorn. 'Well, he rescued us from that. Other countries will follow. Democracy can't work. People *aren't* equal. Some people are completely unfit to make a political decision.'

'Who decides who is unfit?' I murmured, and realized I was quoting my father.

'The fit,' said Dieter. 'Yes, you'll laugh, but it really is as simple as that. If the fit don't decide, if they don't take the reins, you'll have collapse. It's the natural law.'

It featured largely in Dieter's discourse, the word 'natural'.

He dropped into the armchair opposite, and smiled at me.

'You don't feel that way about Hitler, do you?'

No, I didn't. I thought the adulation was grotesque, and the figure I saw on the newsreels physically unimpressive. But when I heard him speak, there was something so powerful in the speeches, so narcotic, that I understood why people surrendered to it. It bypassed reason and ridicule and ended up in some secret part of the brain that craved simplicity and excitement. I did not listen to the speeches if I could help it.

'No, I don't,' I said in reply to Dieter's question.

'Well, never mind,' said Dieter. 'There's time. You've never seen him, of course. In the flesh. Have you?'

I shook my head.

'It changed my life. When I saw him, the day he came to speak in Berlin for the first time, I knew he had complete claim on me,' said Dieter. 'I knew there was nothing I could hold back. The Party had just opened an office in Berlin. I went there the next morning. I . . .' His voice cracked, but he got it under control. 'I said, "Please take me."'

I listened to the lucidity of Bach.

I said, 'And the principle behind everything, that wouldn't change, did you find it?'

'Yes,' he said. 'The thing so strong that a new world can be built on it. The thing that doesn't lie. Yes, I found it.'

'What is it?'

'Race,' he said.

Things were starting to work out well. I had been at the Institute four months when a vacancy occurred for a test pilot to work with the design team.

I applied for the post. There was a buzz of surprise.

I was interviewed by the director, his assistant and the chief test pilot. I was asked if I realized that test flying was intrinsically dangerous. I replied that the better the pilot, the smaller the danger. Yes, they insisted, but what made me think I was up to the job?

There was no answer to this but a bold assertion that I was.

'Try me,' I said. 'There is no glider I can't fly at least as well as a man.'

They looked at me, with the look that is part amused and part curious and contains the thought, 'If she has that good an opinion of herself, perhaps there's a reason for it,' and they appointed me.

I wrote to my parents to tell them. As always, it was my mother who replied. My father never wrote to me.

I was given an amphibious glider to test. It was an excellent glider once airborne, but it did not want to take off. The only way of launching it was to tow it behind a flying boat. This made it the most expensive glider in the world, and nobody was very clear what it was to be used for anyway. It was not proceeded with.

Round about that time, Uby went away. The director had made up his mind, or perhaps it had been made up for him in some ministry office.

Uby was taken to Frankfurt zoo. It had been easy to catch him, they said: the gardener's boy had done it with a dead rabbit. I watched him leave. He stood quite still in the centre of his cage, legs braced against the swaying, as the men loaded it into the back of the Institute's covered wagon.

*

The airfield at Darmstadt adjoined a farm. One morning, as I waited for some low cloud to clear, I began talking to a farm lad on the other side of the gate. We talked about potatoes. He knew a lot about potatoes. He told me things I had never imagined about potatoes: that you could get two crops in a season, if you sowed at the right time; that there were dozens of different varieties; that if you grew cabbage between the potato rows both crops would benefit from the proximity; that if you manured too late the worms in the manure would eat the young potatoes, and much more.

I saw Dieter's motorbike turn into the space behind the hanger. He parked it and walked over. His face was dark.

'What's going on here?' he said, as if he were a policeman, or my father.

I looked at him in astonishment and said, 'We're talking about potatoes.'

'Potatoes?' said Dieter, as if potatoes were somehow disgusting.

The farmhand turned to go, having seen enough.

Dieter stopped him.

'What's your name?'

'Alfred.'

'Does your employer know you spend your working time talking to young women, Alfred?'

'Dieter!' I protested.

'No offence,' said the farmhand. 'The young lady said good morning over the gate, so I stopped and we had a chat. Nothing in it. We were only talking about potatoes.'

'Are you aware,' simmered Dieter, 'that agriculture in the Reich is in crisis because of the shortage of labour? That some of the best brains in the country are trying to solve the problems of rural depopulation and its effects on food production? And you idle your time away talking?'

The farm lad had reddened, He said, 'I don't know about that. But I know I work hard for my pay.'

He walked off, at an easy stride, over the field.

I walked off, too. I went to the hangar and found something to do, and avoided Dieter for the rest of the day.

The following morning he caught me as I walked down the corridor after a briefing.

'Freddy! You disappeared yesterday.'

I turned on him. 'What on earth did you think you were doing? I was having a pleasant conversation and you came charging into it like a bull.'

He looked uncomfortable. 'Well, perhaps I reacted too strongly.'

'Reacted to what? That poor farm boy – '

'Lout.'

In view of his own working-class origins I found this difficult to credit. I looked at the badge on his jacket. 'I thought it was the National *Socialist* Party you belonged to.'

Dieter flushed. 'He was wasting his employer's time.'

'Don't be so pompous. In any case, what he said is true: he works hard for his wages. And what does it have to do with you anyway?'

'You're very keen to defend him, Freddy. I think you really took to him.'

So that was it. How slow of me. But I had thought . . .

'Dieter,' I said, 'you are being ridiculous.'

We walked in silence to the canteen. We bought coffees, and sat at a table by the window. I thumbed through a gliding journal.

After some minutes had elapsed Dieter muttered, 'I'm sorry.' He stared out of the window, at where two mechanics were tinkering with a truck. He said, 'I didn't like to see you talking to him.'

'Dieter, what is this about? I had every right to talk to him.'

He said nothing.

'Do you mean you were jealous?'

He sipped his coffee. 'Yes.'

'But we have talked about this. I thought you understood. I just want to be friends with you. There is nothing between us that gives you any right to be jealous.'

He avoided my eyes. Then he said abruptly, as if some pathway had been cleared of an obstacle, 'That's what you say. Only I can't believe you don't feel for me what I feel for you, just a bit. I think you must, even if you aren't aware of it. I think you'll say yes to me, one day.'

That summer, something was going on which nobody talked about except in whispers.

It was the SA. There were two million of them, and they wanted something.

They were simple men; they were fighters. They had fought for the Party's victory and the Party had won. But they had not got the jobs they had been promised. Cleverer men, with cleaner hands, had got them. And they had not got the revolution they had been promised. The revolution had been and gone and left them behind.

And they were still on the streets. Parading. The streets were still their parade ground.

Outnumbering the newly augmented army by ten to one, they were – it was said – a threat to the peace. It was their ambition to replace the army. To *be* the army.

The question was what Hitler would do.

Dieter and I were both in Berlin at the end of June. We arranged to meet Wolfgang one evening for a meal. We went to a small, crowded restaurant recommended by Wolfgang for its pork and red cabbage.

Almost as soon as we sat down, the argument started.

'I hear the army has been placed on alert,' remarked Wolfgang, studying the menu.

'Where did you hear that?' asked Dieter sharply.

'Where I hear most things. The departmental grapevine.'

'Grapevines are notorious for their gossip.'

'This one isn't. It's notorious for its accuracy. Things are moving, Dieter. Do you know whose side you're on?'

'I am loyal to Hitler, of course.'

Wolfgang grinned wickedly. 'Do you know whose side *he's* on? Does *he* know whose side he's on?'

I thought Dieter was going to hit him, but at that moment the waiter came over. We all ordered pork and red cabbage to get rid of him.

'It will blow over,' said Dieter. 'He will resolve it.'

'He'll resolve it because he has to, but it won't blow over. Neither the army nor the SA will back down. And Hindenburg is dying.'

Dieter jerked his head up. He was bitter. 'Your grapevine *is* extensive.'

'Yes, it is.'

'I must say that the significance of the president's state of health escapes me.'

The wine waiter edged past with a bottle and Wolfgang dropped his voice.

'Hitler wants the presidency.'

Dieter stared at him.

'He wants it so he can merge it with the chancellorship,' said Wolfgang. 'There will then be no constitutional restraints on his power. And he can't get it without the army's support.'

'That's nonsense and it's treason. Hitler can't place the support of the army above his loyalty to Party comrades. He never will.'

'Think about it, said Wolfgang.'

'So what do you expect to happen?' I asked him.

'He'll turn on the SA, old comrades or not. The revolutionary rhetoric is cant. Our leader is a bourgeois.'

'You bastard,' said Dieter.

The waiter brought our food and, because we wanted to be friends, we talked of other things for the rest of that uneasy evening.

I was still in Berlin when it happened. The rumours had multiplied in the days preceding, and there were SS in their black plumage on the streets and crowded in the back of trucks.

On the Friday afternoon I was walking through Alexanderplatz when a group of SA men tore past me, dishevelled and wild-eyed: one was still putting on his tie. I saw more than a hundred of them a few minutes later, streaming into their barracks. They had just, that day, been dismissed on a month's leave.

The shootings began the same night. The executioners were SS squads and police. The army stayed out of it.

They took the leaders. At a Bavarian resort they took the chief, Roehm (in bed with a boy, went the story), and shot him when he wouldn't shoot himself. They shot old campaigners, lads as keen as mustard, politicians who'd intrigued too much and people who couldn't possibly have done them any harm but who once, perhaps, had seen something they shouldn't.

When the shooting stopped on the Monday, a sticky, oppressive silence began.

In that silence I took the train to Darmstadt. I saw Dieter as I walked towards the hangars. He was leaning on a fence, staring at nothing.

He turned towards me. His face was grey.

I went to Frankfurt, one Saturday afternoon, and caught the bus to the zoo.

Half Frankfurt was there. I pushed and wormed my way through audiences of children gaping at monkeys to where the birds were supposed to be. The zoo smell on that warm autumn day wafted powerfully from the cages: a smell of old fur, fleas and boredom.

I found the birds. In the parrot cage, talons gripped the bars with savagery and onyx eyes glared. Next door, bundles of feathers slept on perches. I did not see Uby. I did not see any sign of his presence.

Picking my way between dustbins and a pile of 'Keep off the Grass' notices, I walked down a path and knocked on a door that said 'Office'.

A woman in thick glasses opened it and asked what I wanted. I said I wanted to see the keeper or his deputy. She said it was impossible. I said I wasn't able to come to Frankfurt very often, had recently donated a bird to the zoo and wished to inquire about its welfare. She said the zoo received a great many unwanted donations. I said I doubted if it received many South American vultures.

She gave me a hard look, went away, came back and allowed me in.

We went down a corridor to a room which had a barred window and was largely filled with the piled-up galley proofs of a book. An elderly man in a shrunken blue suit sat on a stool correcting them. He apologized for the fact that I had been made to wait.

'We can't keep staff,' he said. 'As soon as I get a good trainee he's requisitioned for the armaments factories. Fortunately I'm retiring soon. I don't know what will happen when I'm gone. I suppose somebody will see the poor creatures are fed. What can I do for you?'

'I work at the Glider Research Institute. We sent you a South American vulture. I was hoping I might see it.'

'Ah, the vulture,' he said, and then said nothing more for a moment. He perched on his stool, listening. From outside came a series of monstrous shrieks and cries. 'Your vulture died, I regret to say.'

I sat still. The sunlight shafted through the bars and lit the dust in the air. Ridiculous that I should feel so over a vulture.

'What was the cause of death?' I asked. 'Age?'

'Oh no. This was quite a young bird. There was no apparent disease. Some birds just don't thrive in captivity.'

'We should never have caught him,' I said.

'Oh, but you did.' He gave a sigh which seemed to come from his own thoughts rather than his dialogue with me. Then he said, 'But when people are being put in cages, what does a bird matter?'

I was not sure that he had said this, and turned my head to look at him.

He smiled at me. 'Your vulture was a female, by the way. Not that it makes any difference.'

CHAPTER EIGHT

'Where the hell are we?' shouts an irritable voice in my ear.

'Near Karstadt,' I shout back.

'Where?'

'Karstadt.'

There is a silence which sounds angry. Whether he is angry because he has forgotten where Karstadt is, or because he has forgotten why we should be going in that direction, or because he got an armour-piercing bullet in his foot, I don't know.

He settles himself back in his seat, but then is leaning forward to bellow in my ear again. The Bücker rocks with the vehemence of his movements.

'When will we get to Keitel?'

I remind myself that the general is in severe pain, is exhausted and has been entrusted with a mission to save Germany.

'Can't say,' I return at the top of my voice. Of course I can't say: he knows that. It will be surprising if we get there at all, and if there happens to be an army in the way we shall have to go round it, for which we do not have enough fuel.

As if knowing himself rebuked, he settles back in his seat. But then a moment later I feel him at my shoulder once more. You can't get rid of a general that easily.

'Are you following the course we plotted at Rechlin?'

'As far as I can.' I am exasperated. I shout, 'There's a war going on, General.'

'I know, Flight Captain.'

It's a civilian rank. He is not my superior officer. For that, I suppose, I have reason to be profoundly grateful.

And so, perhaps, does he.

This is not at all what he's thinking. He startles me, for I have quite forgotten something of great importance.

'Field Marshal,' he enunciates with deafening clarity into my ear.

And so he is. In the bunker he was promoted. As soon as he came round from the operation on his foot, by guttering light in an underground room whose walls shuddered with the exploding of shells, he was raised to the highest rank of the armed forces.

Well, I shall continue to think of him as the general. He was a general when I met him, he has been a general for years. Why learn new habits now?

The SA shootings both shocked me, and seemed to be something I had been waiting for. From the beginning, the Nazis had worn two faces for me. I had been unsure which was the true face and which would turn out to be a temporary disguise.

When the SA leaders were rounded up and summarily killed, a great clarity entered my mind. I need no longer wonder what to think: now I knew what it was that ran the country.

I knew, also, what my relationship with it must be. I must keep quiet, get on with my life and try not to notice what it was doing. If I allowed myself to notice, I would in the end be forced into a confrontation that I could not survive.

Dieter and I had one exchange on the subject of the shootings. It was brief.

'Hitler had to do what he did,' Dieter said. 'Roehm was planning a coup.'

'Really?' I said. 'I see.'

After six months of test-flying at Darmstadt I got a bit restless. I would sit in my glider and watch the Lufthansa planes drone across the sky. They were big, noisy and dangerous. I wanted to fly them.

The only way to learn to fly them was to attend the government school for airline pilots at Stettin. It was run on the lines of a military academy.

I made a few inquiries. I was met with blank faces, then incredulity.

I pressed my inquiries further and the incredulity took on a note of contempt.

That made up my mind.

*

Officialdom liked me. I found this surprising, until I understood what game they were playing. I represented Germany at an international gliding event in Portugal. Shortly after that I was packed off with a team of glider pilots to introduce Finland to the sport.

In the two months at our disposal, we trained forty pilots to instructor standard, gave talks and lantern shows, put on flying displays, attended receptions and listened to speeches about the international fellowship of gliding, set a new distance record and were photographed incessantly. Then we were photographed all over again on our return.

Dazed, but feeling that I had earned my bread and butter, I went back to Darmstadt.

A fortnight later a man with a briefcase called on me. He was from the ministry.

He said, 'The government is very pleased with the services you have rendered Germany's reputation abroad, and would like to show its appreciation.'

'How nice,' I said.

'It is my privilege to inform you that you are to be awarded a decoration.'

I was astonished. I suppose I felt pleasure; I certainly recall thinking that it was thoroughly useless and why couldn't they give me something I wanted. Then a question occurred to me.

'Will all the team get a decoration?'

'No. Just you.' He smiled.

I did not smile. 'Why just me?'

'I really can't say. No doubt there were good reasons.'

'There's no reason to single me out. We worked as a team.'

He gave a little shrug. 'The decision has been made.'

'I can't accept it,' I said.

The smile dropped from his face.

I said, 'I can't accept an honour which is not awarded to the people I was working with.'

He was very unhappy. He sat upright on the sofa with his briefcase on his lap and his hands folded on top of his briefcase.

'But surely . . .' he said, and let it trail away. Then he said, 'I imagine they want to award it to you because you were the only woman on the team.'

It was some time since I had had to deal with this sort of thing; I had begun to forget about it. After a moment I said, 'You mean, a woman isn't supposed to be able to fly a glider, so if she can do it well enough to be sent abroad to do it, she deserves a medal?'

He looked as though I'd hit him. He clutched his briefcase and said, 'No, that isn't what I meant at all.'

'Then what did you mean?'

He didn't know what he meant. I felt almost sorry for him. His treat had misfired. The ministry, I was fairly sure, wouldn't like it. I wondered for an instant what I thought I was doing, antagonizing my masters at this early stage of the game, but I was too angry to stop myself.

'I don't know what they'll say,' he muttered. 'It's come from the top.' And I saw his predicament, and that he might even have reason to be worried for himself. Aviation was high politics these days. What I couldn't understand was why they should want to reward me, and only me. I had done nothing the others hadn't.

That is to say, I thought I didn't understand it. But, recalling that trip to Finland, I found certain things becoming clearer. All those photographs that had been taken of us: and whoever else wasn't in the photograph, I had to be. In a group photo, I had to be at the centre. And if only one of us could be photographed in a glider, it would be me. I had laughed and protested, and been irritated at being treated differently, but resigned myself to it on the grounds that it was the usual thing and what did it matter. But it wasn't the usual thing; it was trickier than that. And it did matter.

A girl pilot made a more interesting photograph. It was eye-catching, it was . . . I sought for what it was. A good advertisement. For what? My visitor's phrase, 'services to Germany's reputation', carried a fairly clear inference. I had been acting as ambassador for the Reich while thinking I was in Finland as a gliding instructor. And my strength in the role was precisely that I was a woman. A picture of me in the cockpit of a glider sent out two messages. One was: 'This is the friendly face of Germany.' The other was: 'See what our women can do.'

I thought of the picture of womanhood that looked out from posters all over the country. Those broad-hipped women, stirring the soup pot with a child at their skirts! When I saw them I walked quickly past, afraid in a primitive corner of my mind that if I stood and looked at that image, if I let its power fall on me, I would be drawn into it and never escape again. And I thought of the series of curt letters from Stettin which told me that, on account of my sex, I was still barred from the kind of flying I wanted to do.

Were the men who held sway over my life confused? I thought not. I thought they were completely cynical. They were simply using me.

I wandered about the room, hands in the pockets of the trousers I habitually wore, thinking about it. And an idea of such audacity and appropriateness came to me that I found it hard to conceal my grin.

I said, 'Do you think they might consider awarding me something else, rather than a decoration?'

'I suppose it might be possible.'

I said, 'I want a place at the commercial pilots' training school at Stettin.'

He was shocked. 'But that's for men!'

'Of course it is,' I said. 'That's why I need the ministry's help in getting a place there.'

If they could use me, I would use them. And I got my place. Perhaps they really did like me. Or perhaps they thought they'd teach me a lesson. Anyway, I got it.

Before I took up my place at Stettin I went home to see my parents. I had been home only once since leaving to work at the Institute, and that had been at Christmas. Christmas, of course, had its own rituals, and they, together with Peter's presence, had served to prevent any serious conversation between my father and myself.

I decided I must make an attempt to sort things out between us. At some point he must relent in his hostility to my career. Now that I was starting to do well, he would perhaps take a more liberal view. There was something else in my mind, as well.

My mother said, as we sat beside the fire and drank tea from the bone china cups that were kept for best, 'He is interested in what you're doing, you know. He keeps the newspapers if there's something about you. And he always wants to read your letters.'

'Then why doesn't he write to me?'

'Well. You know how he is.'

I saw my father alone after dinner.

'Well,' he said, with a sort of brusque affability that seemed to be masking something else, 'how are you finding it, this flying business? Is it all you thought it would be?'

'I'm loving it,' I said. 'It's everything I thought it would be.'

'Hmm.' I could tell that he had expected this reply, and that it irritated him. 'You seem to be doing quite well for yourself,' he said. 'Gliding here, gliding there. You certainly get around.' He flicked me a look I couldn't read. 'Did you like Finland?'

'I didn't see much of it. We were working very hard.'

'I don't doubt it. I don't suppose they sent you there to enjoy yourself.' He paused. 'It's in a very strategic position, of course.'

'Finland?'

'I assumed you'd realized that.'

It had not occurred to me. I was not entirely sure, in fact, what he meant. But he had shaken my confidence and, I presumed, deliberately.

I laid an envelope on the table in front of him.

'What is this?' he said.

He opened it. It contained a cheque drawn on my bank in Darmstadt.

I said, 'I promised when I took this job that I'd repay the money you'd spent on my education.'

He looked at me incredulously. 'And this is – ?'

I saw what a mistake I had made. Stubbornly, I said, 'I'm earning quite well now, I can afford . . .'

'Have you come here to insult me?' he demanded.

Perhaps I had. I didn't know. Nor, as my own anger rose, did I care.

'How can you possibly think I would accept this?' he said.

'Father, I genuinely wanted to repay that money!'

'Well, I won't allow you to. It's a father's duty to provide for his children.'

'In that case why did you say you'd thrown money away on me?'

'A father is also entitled to expect certain things.'

'You make it impossible for me to do anything right!' I flung at him.

'It is you who are impossible,' he said coldly. 'You cannot even govern your temper.'

He picked up the cheque in his strong fingers and I watched him shred it.

'I don't want your money,' he said. 'I wouldn't accept it in any case, but I may as well tell you that I don't like the source of it, either.'

The commander of the training school at Stettin was a thin-faced colonel with duelling scars and a monocle.

'The ministry in its wisdom has reserved a place for you on this course,' he said to me on my arrival. 'It is not for me to question the ministry's decisions, but I can't imagine how you'll cope. What is your flying experience?'

I told him. He listened with barely concealed impatience.

'Well, we'll see how you get on,' he said. 'Frankly, I can't see the point of teaching women to fly, let alone teaching them to fly the sort of aircraft we have here.' He pointed out of the window at a lumbering three-engined giant, instantly recognizable by its low, broad wings, its corrugated metal skin and its faintly bovine air, taxying to the runway. 'Do you think you'll ever be able to handle that? Can you even tell me what it is?'

'It's a Junkers Ju 52, Colonel.'

'Mmm. Yes, it is. Well, they are quite distinctive. Let me tell you that flying a passenger aircraft is not at all the same thing as flying a two-seater Klemm. Or a glider.'

'I know that, sir.'

'Do you?' He was staring at me, trying to stare me down. Although he was sitting at his desk and I was standing, I had the impression that he dwarfed me. 'We won't make any special allowances for you, you know,' he suddenly barked. 'You'll be treated exactly the same as the men.'

'Thank you, sir. That is how I would prefer to be treated.'

'Is it, now? This school is run on military lines. Did you realize that?'

'Yes, sir.'

'Have you considered what it means?'

'Sir?'

'It means, for one thing, *drill*. Do you think you will be able to master *drill*?'

'I shall do my best, sir.'

He surveyed me. It was clear that he did not understand how he had deserved to have this trial thrust upon him.

'Very well,' he said, and rose to his feet. He stretched out an unpleasantly long arm in a sleeve of immaculate field-grey cloth, and rang a bell on his desk. He said, 'I'll have you shown to your quarters. We've been obliged to accommodate you on the other side of the airfield from the men's dormitories. I sincerely hope there won't be any breach of discipline. If there is, young lady, you'll be out of here before you know what's happened to you. That I can promise.'

Shown to my room by the orderly, who then went round it tugging curtains and opening drawers to show me how they worked, I waited for him to leave, then unfolded the uniform which was lying on the bed. It was a basic army uniform and it looked very big.

I held the trousers against me. The waistband was almost twice the size of my waist, and the legs trailed over the floor.

I went in search of the orderly again, and explained that the uniform was much too big and I needed a smaller one.

He looked at me blankly. 'That's the uniform they gave you,' he said.

'Yes. But it's too big.'

'But that's the one they've given you.'

'But it's too *big*. I can't wear it.'

'But it's the one they've *given* you,' he said. 'There isn't another one. That's *your uniform*.'

'I see,' I said. 'Thank you.'

I went back to my room. I put the thing on. The tunic hung on my shoulders like a marquee and the trousers, having nothing to hang on to, fell down.

I thought. Theoretically it should be possible to alter these clothes to a better fit, but I had no needle and cotton, had never been very good at sewing and in any case had no time.

I attended the introductory briefing an hour later with my trousers held up with the leather belt I had fastened around my suitcase, the tunic tucked into the trousers, where it ballooned around my hips, the sleeves rolled back for about a third of their length to make a thick doughnut of fabric at my wrists, and the leg bottoms tucked into the boots, where fortunately, since the boots were also many sizes too large, there was quite a lot of space for them.

As I entered the room a silence fell. It was broken by a storm of laughter.

The instructor's glare quelled the tumult, then returned to me, disbelieving, before he motioned me to a seat.

We rose at five and began physical exercises at six. I've always been fit. I ran, jumped and vaulted. And then there was drill.

As the first command was given, to form ranks, I hurried to stand in what I hoped was an appropriate place at the end of a row, only to find that for some reason it was *not* an appropriate place. Impatiently the drill sergeant told me to stand somewhere else.

He then, at tremendous speed, rattled through the responses to the various commands he was about to give. They were familiar, of course, to everyone else on the parade ground. I could feel the sweat starting to trickle down my neck and between my shoulder blades inside the hot, prickling uniform. The men on either side of me were motionless.

The machine-gun exposition ended.

'Right,' said the drill sergeant conversationally.

There was a pause in which I felt the men around me quiver.

A howl rent the air and everyone in the two rows of trainee pilots came to attention except me. I came to attention a fraction of a second later. I tried to gauge the correct attitude without moving my head. I felt the drill sergeant's hard little eyes on me.

There followed a few more commands which I followed fumblingly. Then came a pause. He had brought us to attention again. He walked up and down, his boots clicking on the hard ground.

The man next to me stirred. It was a tiny movement, a slightly long inhalation of breath.

The drill sergeant flung himself on it. In a barrage of fluent abuse he tore us apart. I listened with my eyes wide with shock. I knew this happened, but had not dreamt it could be so violent. Why did men put up with it? They must in some way like it.

He had come to a stop directly in front of me. It had been a mistake to think about something else, even for an instant.

For a few seconds he said nothing. He moved up and down a little on the balls of his feet. The energy, the animal force, the contained fury of him just a few inches away, were terrifying. I kept my head up, my back like a board and my eyes looking straight in front, in which position they were looking at the perfect geometry of his tie.

Without a warning intake of breath, and with a ferocity which stunned me, he roared, 'And what in the name of God's mother is this?'

Fear in the air, but under it a relish.

'What is it supposed to be? Is it a man or a woman or a godforsaken nightmare?'

He stepped back, then rapped out, 'You! Whatever you are! One pace forward!'.

I stepped forward.

'Naaah!' he screamed. 'I didn't say, "One mincing, will-I-be-able-to-manage-it-or-should-I sit-down-instead little tiptoe." One pace *forward*.'

I stepped forward again, smartly, and stood at attention. He walked from one side of me to the other, his eyes raking every detail of my hopeless attire and missing no tremor in the muscles of my face.

'God help us,' he said.

He lifted his eyes to the ranks behind me and the tiny rustle of amusement died.

'Name!' he barked.

'Student pilot Kurtz, sir.' I tried to snap it out the way we had been told.

He wrinkled his nose. He looked puzzled. He turned his head and cupped his hand to his ear.

'What was that?' he said. 'What a funny noise. I thought I heard a mouse squeak.' He opened his mouth and bellowed, '*I thought I heard a mouse squeak!*'

The windows in the building behind us rattled. For a split second I closed my eyes. I couldn't help it: it was dread.

He pounced.

'God Almighty, it's *going to sleep!*'

He stood looking at me a little longer. Then he rapped out again, 'Name!'

'Student pilot Kurtz, sir.' I managed to make it louder.

He stared at the ground in apparent despair. He gazed at the sky.

'What is the proper way to address a non-commissioned officer?' he inquired of the sky at the top of his voice. 'Is it' – he adopted an effeminate, lisping delivery – 'Student pilot Kurtz, sir? Is it anything even slightly resembling' – he did it again 'Student pilot Kurtz, sir? Naaah! It is not! The proper way to address a non-commissioned officer is' – he rapped it out so fast, so staccato, mangling the words so brutally that they were almost unrecognizable – '*Student pilot Kurtz, sir!*'

He swung round and picked a man at random from the second row.

'You! Name!'

'Student pilot Rauschenberg, sir!' It was a crashing of syllables.

'You! Name!'

'Student pilot Fuchs, sir!'

'You! Name!'

'Student pilot Schuber, sir!'

'Right.' He returned to me. 'What you have just heard is not the proper way to address a non-commissioned officer. What you have heard is the beginnings of an *idea* of how to address a non-commissioned officer.'

He ordered me back to my place, and barked, 'Student Pilot Group Four, right turn!'

They turned fast, too fast. By the time I caught up his eyes were boring into me again.

There was no mercy. For an hour we marched and wheeled and formed and unformed formations and stood at attention and were shouted at, and for an hour I blundered and got in the wrong place and fell over my feet and wished to die, under the steady glare of that demonic man. Finally he dismissed us. Most of us. Me he did not dismiss. He kept me standing at attention while he walked up and down, apparently debating what to do. It seemed that I was the most appalling problem he had been faced with in all his professional life.

After some minutes he said, 'You'll have extra drill every day this week. Report to me at the end of classes.'

'Yes, sir.'

'You are the most disgusting sight ever to sully this parade ground.'

'Yes, sir.'

'Dismiss.'

I went back to my room. We had a quarter of an hour before lessons started. I needed to be alone, just for a few minutes. A few minutes were all I needed, I thought. Just to get back a sense of myself.

I sat on the bed in my uniform, and heard laughter drifting across the airfield.

Thus they thought to call my bluff.

I hadn't intended bluff. I just wanted to fly aeroplanes. But that was too simple for them to understand.

They thought I wanted to do what nature hadn't fitted me to do. I claimed equal treatment with those who were, they thought, so fitted. Very well: they would give me equal treatment.

Obviously I couldn't complain. But how could I even wish to? How dare I seek, indeed demand, equality with men and then rebel against its practical manifestations? For a few minutes I sank into such dejection that it crossed my mind to pack my suitcase and go home. For weren't they right after all? I could not cope with the equality I demanded: I was not, in fact, fitted to be in this place.

I then became aware of exactly where I was. I was sitting on my bed in a room two hundred yards away from the men's quarters. They *knew* I was a woman. This brutal equality went so far and then stopped. It stopped where it might become dangerous. It stopped when they said so.

And therefore it was going to be a contest of wits. And in this contest they had all the power, but I had David's advantage over Goliath: I was quick on my feet, and I did not accept the rules of engagement.

I saw that I must go on not accepting them. Firstly, I must never lose sight of my certainty that the ability to fly aeroplanes had nothing to do with the answer to the idiot's question. Secondly, I must avoid falling into the trap they had set for me; since neither as a man nor a woman was I acceptable in this place, I must contrive to be neither. Somewhere there was a strategy that would get me

116

through the next months. All I had to do was keep my head until I found it.

Three hours of theoretical instruction were followed by a break for coffee. During the lectures I took a lot of notes. At the end I packed up my books, conscious of the curious glances, and said to the student who had been sitting beside me, 'Are you coming to the canteen?'

It wasn't a brilliant conversational opening, but it deserved better than it got. A look of surprise, an uneasy grin and silence. He edged away.

I walked to the canteen.

I queued at the counter and got coffee and a bun. No one requested my company. I carried my coffee and bun to a table where a group of my fellow students sat talking. I put down my metal tray, drew up a chair, sat on it and said, 'Hello, I'm Freddy. I thought it was time we got acquainted.'

It isn't that hard to do. You take a breath and you've done it.

It was hard for them, though. I could see that. It was a completely new situation for them. They had no idea how to respond to it, and were angry at being at such a disadvantage.

One, at last, introduced himself and stretched out his hand. Then several others did the same.

One wouldn't give his name. He averted his head and looked into his coffee. He was a little older than the others and cultivated a handlebar moustache in the English style.

After the introductions there was a short silence. It was broken by the first one who had spoken to me: Jürgen. He was a tall young man with heavy eyebrows which were now drawn together in perplexity.

'We can't understand what you're doing here,' he said.

'I want to fly commercial aircraft.'

He shook his head. He seemed at a loss.

The boy sitting next to him said, without animosity, 'You'll never manage it. Women can't fly aircraft like the ones they've got here.'

'We'll see,' I said.

'Look, it takes strength to handle a big aeroplane. You won't have the strength.' He spoke gently. He was trying to help.

'Strength isn't the important thing,' said handlebar moustache. 'Women don't have the right mental attitude.'

I turned to look at him. He was tense with anger.

'What's your name?' I asked him.

He didn't want to give it, but saw that he had no choice.

'Werner.'

'What is the right mental attitude for learning to fly commercial aircraft, Werner?'

He reddened, under my gaze, but did not answer. Jürgen said, 'Oh, come on, it's a fair question.'

'The right mental attitude is a calm and objective one. It's a well known fact that women are emotional and easily distracted.'

'Not much distracts me,' I said.

A boy with a cheerful face and the slurred vowels of the south of Germany said that he didn't see what was the point of my learning to fly passenger aircraft, since Lufthansa would never give me a job.

I thought he was quite right.

'Someone else will,' I said, with a confidence I didn't feel. At that moment the whole enterprise seemed ridiculous: misconceived and an act of vanity. I said brusquely, 'If I can be a test pilot for the Glider Research Institute, I don't see why I can't be a pilot for an air-line.'

They exchanged glances. They knew about me: on my appointment there had been a feature in *Gliding Today* and a picture in one of the illustrated weeklies. Then there had been the publicity about the trip to Finland. It didn't help. It added another layer to the problem.

There was a silence. Then Werner lit a cigarette and tossed the match into an ashtray.

'You'll get married,' he said with contempt.

'Not if she goes on wearing that uniform she won't,' said the boy from the south with a grin.

And thus it was made possible. For they all laughed, and I smiled because the atmosphere had suddenly relaxed, and someone said, 'What happens when you roll the sleeves down?'

'The boots fall off,' supplied Jürgen.

'Not quite.' I unrolled the sleeves to their full extent. Too long by almost the length of my forearm, they dangled from my wrist like pieces of string which have been unknotted after many months and are still full of curls.

The men were fascinated.

'And how far do the trousers extend?'

'Oh, to Dortmund.' I took off my right boot and displayed the tube of trouser leg snaking over the canteen floor.

This delighted them. They made me take off the other boot as well. I stood there for a moment, feeling stupid, and then, on impulse, began to walk like a penguin around the canteen.

My audience was howling with mirth and wiping its eyes. Looking at the convulsed table, I realized I had found my strategy.

Clown, Freddy, clown. As though your life depended on it.

Fortunately you have all the materials. That wonderful uniform: who could ask for a better outfit? Your uncertain salute, your marshmallow heel-click, your voice which has been likened to a mouse's squeak. Your complete lack of instinct for the holy mystery of drill. Embrace them gratefully, they are your passport.

I did. Once I understood what my role was to be, I played it assiduously. I put it on with the uniform in the morning. I would walk into the canteen, grin at the ready, to be greeted by a good-humoured chorus of whistles, catcalls and ribaldry. I exaggerated my deficiencies at drill, recounting my latest horrible experience with the drill sergeant until my audience guffawed. I put what talent I have for mimicry to work on that drill sergeant, and within a week had caught him fairly well. It made me less afraid of him.

In a confused way my fellow students both laughed at me and wanted to help me. They would 'coach' me in drill, in sessions which had a bizarre double character. Spluttering with laughter, provoking me to ever greater excesses of self-caricature, they at the same time wished to make a better airman of me. They rehearsed me in 'the proper way to address a non-commissioned officer'. It was not enough to mangle the words, breaking them up into staccato bursts and accenting the wrong syllable: I must also drop my voice. We practised dropping my voice. I dropped it as far as it would go, I dropped it until I almost couldn't find it again, but still they said it didn't sound right. I pointed out that the lower I dropped it the more it seemed that I was making mock of the proceedings; but they

119

said it was essential to drop it, you couldn't have a woman's voice on the parade ground.

Not everyone liked what was going on. Several times I caught a look of embarrassment or shame on someone's face, but nothing that matched the look was ever said. When I saw such a look I averted my eyes, because I could not afford to have the agreement I had reached with these men upset. Werner kept scornfully aloof from the japery. He thought I was not worth making fun of, and that the others were demeaning themselves.

I could only go into the clubhouse in the evening in my role as buffoon, since to abandon that character even for a short time would raise once more the insoluble problem of my identity. Since the noise, the laughter and horseplay and the relentless demands of my role wearied me, I often preferred to go for a walk, read, or go to a concert in town. And I studied.

I studied hard. I had to, of course; there was a great deal of theory to learn and nothing but a complete mastery of it would serve me. I kept quiet about the amount of work I did, just as everyone kept quiet. No one admitted to finding the course difficult. Or perhaps they simply did not admit it in front of me.

But then there was the flying. As a buffoon, you can study or not, providing you don't learn too much. But flying is different. Buffoons can't fly. It is necessary to apply yourself with honest seriousness to the task of flying, and your success at it, or otherwise, cannot be concealed.

I stepped into an aircraft and became a pilot.

They weren't easy, those aeroplanes. Even the trainers were a long leap away from Klemms. But as the months passed we progressed to the giants. The Heinkels and Dorniers, the Junkers Ju 52 the colonel had asked me to identify. The night before I was to transfer to the Ju 52 I lay awake in a sweat of terror. How could I fly anything so huge and heavy? How could I hold it in a descent, a turn? How could I master the complex mass of instrumentation?

But when I sat for the first time in the pilot's seat, something happened. It is the thing that always happens, although never have I dared take it for granted. I sit there, running my eyes over the instrument panel, and I sink into a state of concentration which is also a state of complete receptivity. I am conscious of nothing but the aeroplane. I extend myself into it, trying to fathom its nature and its needs. And as I sit there, the aeroplane begins to talk to me.

I called to mind what I had been taught, I listened to what the aeroplane was saying to me, and I taxied my Ju 52 to the runway and lifted off with a smoothness that brought a 'Good' from an instructor renowned for the grudgingness of his praise.

Yes, I could fly. Yes, I had a gift for it. It was grossly unfair, but there it was. I knew it, the instructors knew it, and one day the colonel called me to his office and apologized for doubting my capacities, which made clear that he knew it, too. In time, even my fellow pupils knew it.

And how were they to deal with it? I was the buffoon.

The day I made my first flight in the Ju 52, a group of them were watching from the doorway of a hangar. The same group were in the canteen, arguing some point of technique, when I returned an hour later.

I got myself coffee and a sticky bun and wandered over. Most of my mind was still in the cockpit. I was pleased with myself. No, that is not what I mean. Even after a middling flight you feel exhilarated, confident. Flying does that. That's why flyers have to go on flying. That's why you can't fly and be a buffoon.

The argument stopped as they saw me.

'Hi,' said Jürgen. 'How was your 52?'

I bit into my bun. 'Piece of cake,' I said absently.

Anyone else would have got away with it.

Two of them pushed back their chairs and walked out.

Ah well, it was showdown time. Let it be. I didn't care any more. I sat down in one of the vacated chairs, and in the silence finished my bun.

Schani, the southerner, said, 'We watched you. It was a nice bit of flying.'

'Thank you.'

'We never thought you'd be able to handle a plane like that.'

'I know.' I drank my coffee.

'Why didn't you tell us?' asked someone.

'Tell you what?'

'That you could fly,'

'I did tell you I could fly.'

'Yes, but I mean . . . really fly.'

There was no possible reply to this. But I could see that several of them expected a reply: they were studying me with what appeared to be resentment.

Jürgen said, 'Yes, you have been a bit of a dark horse, Freddy. It's hardly fair.'

'I mean,' said Schani, gesturing with his big hands over the coffee cups, 'we'd have behaved differently if we'd known.'

It took a while to dawn on me. They felt I had made fools of them.

Two years, a month and the odd week after Hitler became chancellor, the wraps came off the air force.

I was back at Darmstadt, with a commercial pilot's certificate from Stettin and a promotion to chief test pilot, the day it happened.

I picked up the newspaper and there they were, all over the front page. Our aeroplanes. Fighters, bombers, trainers, spotter and liaison planes. In their proper colours, a swastika on every tail.

The Ju 52 I'd flown at Stettin was a bomber.

Everything changed, that day in March, and nothing changed at all but the paint. My work hadn't changed. I was now testing gliders for the air force: but I had been from the outset. Leafing through the newspaper, most of which was dedicated to the subject, I realized that, at least half-consciously, I had always known that. Even two years previously, my head filled with the love of flying and idealistic notions about international fellowship, I had been aware of the military interest in gliding. If I'd had any doubts, the reception our team was accorded on its return from South America would have dispelled them. It was obvious if you thought about it. Every German government since 1919 had encouraged gliding. What do you expect, if you deny a nation aeroplanes?

I wasn't sure how I felt about it. If it meant more supervision and bureaucracy, I would not welcome it. It might, on the other hand, result in a broadening of the scope of my work, in more opportunities. I hardly bothered to think of the political implications. It was inevitable that we should have military aircraft, and I thought the sooner we stopped pretending that we didn't, the better.

*

Dieter was leaving to work for Heinkel. He told me the evening of my return to Darmstadt, as we sat in a country inn to which we'd driven on his motorbike.

I was very sorry. I would miss him. I said so, and we got quite maudlin, which was a mistake because he misinterpreted my sadness and said that if I really was, after all, fond of him, then he would stay at Darmstadt a little longer while we worked things out and . . . And I had to say that I wasn't fond of him in that sense, at which his face fell and for a time it was difficult to get the conversation back where it had been.

Before he left, we went together, one Saturday, to see a flying display. Ernst had come to Darmstadt.

It was May, but it felt like high summer. The citizens of Darmstadt were in shirtsleeves and sun hats, and their children raced and tumbled on the grass.

Dieter and I, wishing to make this an occasion, had paid for seats, although I thought, as we ate our ice cream and watched the crowds, that it would have been more fun in the stands. A balloon-seller made his way along the front of the enclosure. A clown with a white face was working his passage in the other direction; and here came another clown on stilts. The clowns were collecting for Winter Relief, the state-run charity whose proceeds, it was rumoured, went as often as not towards limousines for Party bosses; but never mind, and I would not say this to Dieter.

'Would you like a balloon to remember me by?' asked Dieter wryly.

'No, thank you, Dieter. I can remember you without a balloon.'

We contributed our small change to Winter Relief, and studied the programme. Ernst was going to start with a display of glider aerobatics, and then fly the Flamingo.

'You know him, don't you?' remarked Dieter.

'I've met him once or twice.'

'I suppose you know what sort of reputation he has.'

I was irritated. 'He has the reputation of being a fighter ace and one of the best pilots in the world,' I said.

'That's not what I meant.'

'I know it isn't. I'm not interested in what you meant.'

'I'm just trying to warn you.'

'Dieter, I hardly know him. In so far as I do know him, we're friends.'

Dieter's face expressed an almost cynical scepticism that such a thing might be possible. I was angry, but there was no time to take the argument further because at that moment a hush fell over the crowd, and into the hush swooped, silently, Ernst's glider.

Good flying is like poetry. I had recovered my humour by the interval, and Dieter had gathered the grace to apologize.

He said, 'I've never met another girl like you. It's not really surprising if I keep saying the wrong thing.'

I thought this was true.

Ernst's Flamingo purred overhead. A man came out from the stands, walked towards the middle of the field and laid on the grass a white handkerchief. On each corner he placed a small object – pebbles, to hold the handkerchief down.

The Flamingo made a low pass and climbed away. In the open cockpit I glimpsed Ernst's face, unreadable in helmet and goggles. The plane banked and came in again, low.

I held my breath as he dropped down, right down, the propeller driving ripples of silver in the grass. Did any of the people here know how dangerous this was? A wing dipped, dipped further. I had seen the small hook protruding from the tip. You can't do that, I thought, you can't do it with impunity.

A flick of the wing almost too fast to be seen. His reflexes must be like a cat's.

Up came the wingtip, with the handkerchief on it.

A roar of throttle, and he was clear.

The crowd yelled. I yelled.

The band began to play a march.

CHAPTER NINE

Nine years ago I met him, this man whose brooding anxiety I feel behind me as we fly. Well, some years are longer than others. He was debonair, distinguished and covered in braid. He was an air force general and a department chief at the ministry.

Beside him stood, with his hands behind his back, Ernst, slightly less covered in braid. I was getting to know Ernst by then. He was a colonel the day I met him with von Greim, but I knew he was still really the man who could pick up a handkerchief with his wingtip.

I climbed out of the cockpit of the glider I had just dived vertically for nine thousand feet, and walked across the runway at Darmstadt to these two high-ranking officers who were smiling broadly. I couldn't decipher the smile. You never knew with the ministry. Rumour had it they would as soon stick knives into each other as produce aeroplanes any day. The smile might have meant, 'Excellent, we'll buy it,' or it might have meant, 'What a barrel of *Scheiss*, we always knew it wouldn't work.'

I came to attention and saluted.

The very tall general said, 'That was a superb demonstration: I congratulate you.'

Ernst said, 'Next time I attend a demonstration of yours I shall bring my steel helmet. Do you always level out at three hundred feet?'

Behind me the Institute's chief designer and inventor of the dive brakes hovered. I modestly stepped aside so that he could receive his due.

The praise was unstinting. Von Greim described the dive brakes as one of the most important developments in aviation for years. Ernst said the ministry had a project under way which would provide the perfect application.

Turning to me, Ernst said, 'How often have you done a nine-thousand foot vertical dive?'

'Once before, Colonel.'

'How did it feel?'

'Wonderful.'

He chuckled. 'Have you ever power dived an aircraft?'

'No, sir.'

'Would you like to?'

'Very much.'

'Come up to Rechlin next week, if the Institute can release you for a day.'

I followed them across the tarmac to the director's office, controlling a desire to dance.

Ernst, talk to me. Keep me awake. Tell me how you came to be standing at von Greim's side, covered in braid, on the runway at Darmstadt, when uniform was a thing you detested.

One's options narrow, you said to me once. It happens imperceptibly. Then one day you walk into a room and there is no way out of that room except a door you said you would never take.

Ernst stood a short distance from Milch as the brand-new squadrons roared overhead in their brand-new paint. They were a mixed bunch. This was a makeshift air force.

Never mind. However, you looked at it, Ernst thought, it was a triumph. A triumph of tenacity, cheek and financial heaven-knows-what. The Fat Man had found the money, somewhere. Money came to him. Perhaps he just took it.

The Fat Man wore a smile almost as wide as he was.

He would be commander-in-chief. His flamboyance was an asset. The make-up, the costumes, the rumours about morphine: they didn't really matter. This was a man of the flesh: people liked him.

Milch didn't like him.

Milch would be his deputy.

Milch would run this air force, as he ran everything. But the Fat Man must appear to be running it.

Milch talked about the aircraft taking part in the fly-past. The Fat Man was irritated. He compressed his lips, wanting Milch to shut up.

Next to Milch was Ritter von Greim. Quiet, civilized. You

wouldn't trust many people in this gathering, not if you had any sense you wouldn't: but you'd trust von Greim.

Within a short time Ernst couldn't go to a party without being an island in a sea of sky-blue.

Nearly all his friends were in the air force. In fact nearly everyone he knew, with however slight a connection with aviation, was in the air force. Wartime comrades, drinking companions, gliding acquaintances, old rivals in love. There they all were, in sky-blue, trying to look as if they'd worn it all their lives.

It gave Ernst a strange feeling. As if a tide had turned when he was looking the other way.

At a fancy dress party he bumped into Ritter von Greim. Von Greim was not in fancy dress.

'Had a good year, Ernst?'

'Wonderful,' said Ernst. He was wearing a clown's red nose and holding a glass of champagne. Looking at Ritter, relaxed and elegant in his uniform, he wished he had not put on the red nose.

'Good,' said von Greim. 'You seem to get about a lot. I see your posters everywhere. Hamburg last week, wasn't it?'

'That's right. Went down very well. You should come along if you're in the area. Always a bottle of something in the tent.'

'Too busy, I'm afraid. Are you still doing the pocket handkerchief?'

There was only friendly interest in von Greim's voice, but Ernst sensed contempt in the wording of the question.

'It's very popular,' he replied. He paused, then added deliberately, 'And no one else can do it.'

'That,' said von Greim as deliberately, 'is not in question.'

Their eyes locked for an instant. Ernst felt something pulling him. It was the other man's intentness, and behind it the growing gravitational demand that he could not much longer ignore.

'Ernst,' said von Greim, 'when are you going to give up all these circuses?'

'And?'

'Join us.'

'You don't need me.'

'I am the head of Personnel and I'm telling you we do.'

'Come off duty, Ritter. This is a party.'

'Your whole life is a party, Ernst. Don't you get bored with it?'

Ernst was too surprised by this frank assault to reply.

'After seventeen years, we have an air force,' said von Greim. 'And our most gifted airman isn't in it.'

'Ritter, between ourselves, I'm not the military type.'

'Sixty-two victories and the *Pour le Mérite*?'

'I am not the military type.'

'I know that,' said von Greim. 'We don't lack for military types. We need you for who you are, not for what you aren't.'

'But what would I *do*? I hate desk work.'

'How would Inspector of Fighter Pilots suit you?'

The title danced past Ernst and he liked the style of it. He thrust it away.

Von Greim said, 'We need people with new ideas, Ernst.'

That was tempting. He glimpsed how it could be, how it might even fulfil him.

He took refuge in frivolity.

'What would you pay me as an Inspector of Pilots? I'm making two hundred thousand marks a year. I can't afford it.'

Ritter's expression was sardonic. There was something in his silence which stung Ernst.

Ernst tapped his ridiculous nose, conscious too late that it might be interpreted as an insult. 'This is the uniform for me,' he said.

'Let's hope some people can see past it,' said von Greim, and excused himself.

I turn to look at him. I set the trimmer, unfasten my harness and turn in my seat. There is just enough light to see his face. It is sunk, and his eyes are half-closed.

I try to remember when his foot was last dressed, but the days and hours have run into one another and I can't remember anything in its sequence. Did he have it dressed at Rechlin? Was there time?

I look at him, proud, obstinate, obsessed, driving himself beyond the limits of endurance to perform a task which is irrelevant, and I think that he is not a bad man, but on the contrary a man in whom there was once a lot of good, but it has been thrown away.

Somewhere there must be a gigantic heap, an Alp of rubbish, containing all the things that have been thrown away in Germany.

At another party, and to the music of yet another trio playing Mozart, Ernst touched von Greim's braided sleeve.

'Can we talk?'

The only place to talk was Ernst's car.

They sat in their greatcoats in the cold, leather-smelling interior and watched the snow falling on the long bonnet, rounding its angularity into a graceful curve. Away across the lawn, at tall uncurtained windows, the party unfolded itself in golden light.

'Cigar?'

'Thank you. You always have the best, Ernst. But you spread it about, I grant you that.'

'I may not be able to spread it about much longer.'

The match flared. When it was spent, Ernst eased down his window and flicked it outside. The clean air knifed in, bringing snowflakes which settled on his face. He tasted them with his tongue.

Von Greim said, 'Have you decided to join us?'

He had practised it often, in his mind, but still Ernst held back on the edge of his reply, like a man afraid at the crucial moment to dive.

'Yes.'

There, he had toppled into it. There was not even a feeling of relief. Only, for a second, the sense of water closing over his head.

'Ernst, I can't tell you how glad I am. You won't regret it.'

'Of course I shall regret it.' Ernst tapped the steering wheel. 'I shall have to sell this.'

'You can't drive two cars at once.'

'True. Perhaps I'll sell the sports car. How much are you going to pay me, as an Inspector of Fighter Pilots?'

'Thirteen thousand marks a year.'

'Dear God, I shall have to sell the *cat*.'

'Or eat it, perhaps.'

'It may come to that. Is it a desk job?'

'There will be paperwork. But you'll spend most of your time visiting airfields.'

'A flying desk?'

'A flying desk. Seriously, you'll find it suits you. Milch will fill you in on the details.'

129

'Milch knows everything, doesn't he?'

Ernst spoke without irony. There was a pause before von Greim answered.

'Yes, he does.'

They watched as the Fat Man's bulk moved into view at the furthest window. He was making a speech. It was his birthday. The presents were lavish.

'We should be there,' said Ernst.

'He won't mind,' said von Greim.

'What is he like to work under?'

'Like a precocious child,' said von Greim. 'Never assume he knows anything. Never assume he doesn't know anything. If you repeat that, I shall lose my head.'

Ernst offered his own hostage in exchange. 'You know, after the war he was thrown out of the Richthofen Veterans' Association for falsifying his tally of victories.'

'Really? I bet the minutes of that meeting aren't in the filing cabinet any longer.'

Von Greim went on chuckling all the way back to the house, where the Fat Man welcomed them with broad smiles and a darting look, and pressed brandy upon them with his white hands heavy with gold rings.

Von Greim was right: Ernst did find his first job at the ministry congenial. He understood what he was supposed to do, and he did it. He inspected pilots by the simple method of getting into his Fieseler Stork and popping down to the squadrons to see how they were getting on. The pilots talked to him. They told him about their problems. The problems were usually the result of some bureaucratic stupidity and often he could solve them. If he couldn't, he passed them on to von Greim.

The money was terrible, but he'd never known what to do with money anyway. He sold his Hispano-Suiza and his boat.

There was a uniform. Well, of course there was: you can't inspect fighter pilots wearing a suit. He took it off as soon as he got home.

Five months passed happily. Then a plane crashed on an internal flight. On board was Wever, the chief of Air Staff. A major reshuffle took place.

Ernst was summoned to see the Fat Man at his Berlin residence, a newly refurbished villa in the grounds of the Prussian Ministry. The Fat Man was prime minister of Prussia, among other things. He was very busy but had time to attend to details of interior design. Four large rooms had been knocked together to form his study, providing four sets of french windows giving on to the terrace and gardens. In one of the gardens was a lion pit. Lions, to the terror of visitors and the Fat Man's amusement, were sometimes to be seen walking on the lawn.

The Fat Man informed Ernst that he was to be put in charge of the Technical Office.

Ernst protested that he did not have the necessary experience. The Fat Man dismissed this objection, saying that Ernst would have experts to help him and that in any case it was Adolf's wish.

Ernst knew there was nothing more to be said.

The Fat Man invited Ernst to admire a silver model of an Albatros biplane which Heinkel had given him, and for an hour they reminisced about the Great War.

The enemy fighter seems to rise out of the earth. I see it hurtle towards me long before the howl of the engine reaches my ears.

I drop as far as I dare into the folds of the land, skimming the roof of a farmhouse, seeking the shadow of the hay barn. The fighter screams above me and machine-gun fire peppers the Bücker's tail.

I fly on. The fighter vanishes behind me but, craning my neck round, I see him bank and turn in the distance. He is coming back for another try. This time he will finish us.

I am about twelve feet above a level stretch of ground between farm buildings. I yell to the general that we're going down, cut the engine, lower the flaps and pray. I taxi into the heavy shadow of the barn, rip off my harness and help the general out of his seat. There seem to be crutches everywhere. We struggle to the hay barn, and reach it just as the fighter screams over and sprays the ground with bullets. A heifer somewhere starts a terrified lowing.

The general and I sit in the hay barn and listen to the fighter.

The sound of the engine fades, then grows again.

'He'll do one more run,' says the general, 'then he'll go home.'

'What is it?'

'Mustang. I thought the Americans were further south. Did you bring the map?'

I fish it out of my pocket, along with the bread and the raisins. I halve the bread with my penknife and give him a piece, and a handful of raisins.

The fighter comes back. This time he is very low and very angry. The farmyard is hellish with flying chips of concrete and sputtering bullets. Fine dust compounded of powdered dung and powdered concrete clogs the air. The heifer lows frantically.

His wings tilt: for a moment I think he is going to bank and turn for a fourth run, but he flies straight on over the farmhouse, over the crest of the hill and away, his engine fading.

'Did he get the Bücker?' the General asks.

'I don't know.'

'Go and look, would you?'

There are holes in the tail section and fuselage, but no serious damage, and he has missed the fuel tanks.

I report back. The general is studying the map, shading the torch with his hand. His injured foot rests on a hay bale. The dressing is stained and sinister.

'Where d'you think we are?'

I point.

'Another fifty miles, then. Will the plane make it?'

'If we can take off. I don't know how much runway we've got. No room to turn round here.'

'Hmm. What is this you've given me to eat?'

'Raisins.'

'It looks like sheep droppings. Trying to poison me, are you?'

'If I wanted to poison you, I have something a lot stronger in my pocket than sheep droppings.'

'Mmm. I suppose you have. It's a pity we haven't anything to drink. I'm as thirsty as a stoker.'

He's probably feverish. 'There might be something in the farm-house,' I suggest.

There might be anything at all in the farmhouse. Neither of us says this.

I consult my watch. It's the early hours of the morning. It seems permanently to be the early hours of the morning. I am very tired and I remember that there is a blanket in the plane.

'It might be an idea to get a bit of sleep.'

'I have to see Keitel,' says the General reflexively.

I chew my raisins. In view of the fact that the war is over, except for the shooting which will go on a bit longer, that in an hour we might both be dead, and that I am piloting him, under fire, of my own free choice, I think I am allowed a question.

I say, 'Why do you have to see Keitel?'

He looks at me in astonishment, raising his head with aristocratic hauteur, and I see behind his shoulder the long line of von Greims who have been colonels, generals and perhaps field marshals.

'*Why?*'

'Yes.'

A pause. Then: 'You seem to have forgotten that I am under orders to do everything possible for the relief of Berlin. Keitel will be fully apprised of Wenck's position. It's obvious that I should see him.'

I look at the shadowed landscape and its mysteries. The relief of Berlin is a fantasy: nothing on earth can accomplish it. The general, before he went down the rabbit-hole, knew this. But the sojourn in the rabbit-hole has affected his mind.

I will fly him where he wants to go, because I have undertaken to. But to the word 'orders' I am developing an allergy. We will have to have a conversation on this subject, before it is too late, and perhaps when he is not so ill. But I fear it is a conversation for which he will never be well enough.

I ask, 'How is your foot?'

'Tolerable.'

His face has sunk to the bones. It occurs to me that there might be some medicine in the farmhouse. They might have something for the animals. Almost anything would help: painkillers, antiseptic. Why do I care? Yesterday I wanted to kill him.

'I'm going to take a look at the house,' I announce.

'Must you?'

'They might have medicine. They might have something to drink.'

'They might have something a lot nastier.'

He unholsters a very large pistol and shoves it at me. 'Take this.'

'I have a gun.'

'Take it. It'll drop a bull.'

'It's not bulls I'm worried about.'

But I take it, leaving him my small Walther, and walk up to the long, low building, keeping in the shadows. I listen for a dog's bark, but there is nothing.

Outside the door I wait for quite a long time. I am listening for any stir or vibration which tells me the house is inhabited. Nothing reaches my ears, only an owl shocks me as it swoops by.

I turn the handle and find the door unlocked. This frightens me but I go in. I have the general's bull-dropper in my right hand and the torch in my left. The torchlight sweeps over the hallway and within seconds my eyes confirm what my nose tells me, that there is nothing to be afraid of. Not unless someone even crazier than the general and myself has taken refuge here. For I have seen this before. It is what men in extremes of anger or despair sometimes do.

All over the floor of the hallway, the big flagged kitchen and the sitting room with its wrecked furniture, are small piles of human shit.

I pick my way between them and look in cupboards. The soldiers will have taken everything, but I have to look.

And they have taken everything. Every scrap of food, every shred of clothing. To find a bandage here is beyond hope.

In a yard behind the kitchen I find a pump. It has been smashed.

I return to the general, who has fallen asleep. He wakes crossly, as if it is my fault he dozed off.

The stretch we have landed on leads to an unfenced field. This will be our runway. I carry out, by foot-feel and cautious torchlight, an inspection of the ground. The best that can be said for it is that it is not actually ploughed.

We take off without incident and fly north. It's 4 am.

CHAPTER TEN

When I met Ernst in the marquee at Hamburg he'd given me his telephone number. He scribbled it on the back of a menu card and said, 'If you find yourself in Berlin, give me a call. We'll have lunch.'

'Thank you,' I said, and put the card in my pocket, not thinking he meant it.

He looked at me sternly. 'You will, now, won't you?'

'Oh yes,' I said.

I didn't. I was in Berlin several times in the course of the next year, but I didn't ring him. Sometimes I would come across the menu card in my suitcase, or propped behind the clock on the mantelpiece, and look at it. At first I hadn't got in touch with him because I was too conscious of the distance between us, professionally and socially. As time went by and I settled into my job at Darmstadt, I became more confident. I could, then, have coped with Ernst. But by then I had left it too late, or so I thought.

Then one day I bumped into him at Tempelhof. I had come back from an international gliding event and had indulged myself in a day's shopping in Berlin. I was about to fly back to Darmstadt with a colleague.

'Freddy!' exclaimed Ernst, with a mixture of pleasure and reproach. His eye dwelt on the parcels I was carrying. 'How long have you been in town?'

'Just today.'

'You should have telephoned me! Didn't I say we would have lunch? You do still have my number?'

'Yes.'

'Well, then. Next time. You will, won't you? Promise.'

'Promise,' I said, laughing, because something about him always made me want to laugh in those days; it was as if he was hardly managing to contain a laugh himself.

'Tell me about yourself,' he ordered three months later, as we sat in a small and unpretentious restaurant serving some of the best food I have ever eaten.

'What do you want to know?'

'Everything.'

His personality was compelling. He would draw out the information, but in any case he made me want to give it. Ernst could, I thought, be a man to beware of. Yet somehow he wasn't. The defining ingredient had been left out.

'Why do you want to know?' I asked.

He said, 'Most people just like to talk about themselves. They find it the most natural thing in the world that they should be asked to do so. But *you*, who really are an unusual person, unusual in your attitudes, your qualities, your lack, if I may say so, of artifice . . . you don't understand why I want you to talk about yourself.'

I said, 'You're flattering me.'

He said, 'Well, if I am I apologize, because it is clearly not what you want. But if we are to get to know each other, you will have to allow me to make occasional mistakes.'

I said, 'Oh dear, I'm sorry.'

'It's difficult, isn't it?' he said. 'But with good will, I expect we can manage.'

He grinned at me.

I grinned.

We ate our gigot of lamb. I said, 'I never knew lamb could be like this.'

'French cooking is the expression of genius,' he said. 'There are some idiots about who would have us eat nothing but *wurst* and potatoes.'

I told him about myself. He listened with complete attention.

Ernst was still flying for the crowds, at that time. He lived extravagantly; but not as extravagantly as, in my innocence, I had feared. Visiting his flat, I was struck by its modesty. It was eccentric, however. There was the cocktail bar, for instance. This occupied a corner of the sitting room, and was unlike any other cocktail bar I have ever seen. The walls behind it were hung with photographs, and the shelves were crowded with mementoes, of a trip Ernst had made to Greenland for a film. The centrepiece was a photograph of an aged Cree chief whom Ernst had flown, at his request, over his ancestral lands. The chief sat in the cockpit of Ernst's tiny biplane, his seamed face expressing calm contentment. He had died a few days later. Ernst told the story often and affectingly, and each time the chief seemed to get a little older.

Ernst didn't value possessions, except insofar as they gave him pleasure. He loved cars. Selling the Hispano-Suiza upset him and a few years later, when he could afford it, he bought another one. But it wasn't the same. It was always a mistake, he told me, to try to rekindle an old flame. He liked to dress well and spent a lot of money on his tailor (he quirked an eyebrow at my wardrobe, consisting as it did mainly of flying suits and things which looked like flying suits), but clothes did not ultimately matter to him: I think he amused himself with them. Something he did care about, apart from flying, was art. But art was fraught with political meaning these days.

On my first visit to the flat I saw a vibrant, impressionistic oil painting above the fireplace. I never saw it again. I didn't ask about it. He was working for the ministry by then, and that sort of painting simply would not have done, it would have been out of the question.

Ernst told me a lot of things about the ministry, a lot of things he shouldn't have done. There was no one else he could talk to in the same way, and he needed to talk. With his colleagues and his other women friends it would have been equally impossible.

So, within a short time I knew as much about what went on inside the ministry as if I'd worked there. It sounded a considerably more dangerous place than the cockpit of an aeroplane. I tried to visualize him picking his way between the intrigues. I thought it must be difficult for him. He wasn't cut out for that sort of thing. He wasn't naïve, but he was no politician. I think it came down to distaste in the end. And perhaps a certain innocence. He simply could not believe, in some cases, what was going on around him.

I saw him one evening when he had been head of the Technical Office for about six months. I asked him how he was getting on with the Fat Man.

Ernst laughed. 'I don't know. We hardly see him. These days he's got the economy to run.'

There was something called the Four-Year Plan and the Fat Man was in charge of it. He was also in charge of Prussia, the game laws and it frequently appeared, foreign policy. I could understand that he might not have much time for the air force.

'Milch runs the place really,' said Ernst, and turned the cat out of the chair. It was a Siamese of uncertain disposition. 'The chief doesn't like it but he doesn't have much choice. He's lucky to have Milch.'

'You're still as friendly with Milch?'

I thought there was a slight hesitation before Ernst answered, 'Oh, yes. Milch has helped me a lot. The first few weeks in the Technical Office, I don't know what I would have done without him.' He took a cigarette from a box and flicked his gold lighter. 'I wouldn't have his job for anything. He does all the work and gets none of the credit, and the better he does it the more the chief tries to undermine him.'

'But that's stupid! It's against his own interests.'

'The ministry is not the home of logic. In fact it's the closest I've come to an asylum.' Ernst tapped ash precisely into a black ashtray, watching it fall. 'The chief doesn't really care about the air force,' he said. 'You have to understand that. In the end, he only cares about one thing. He cares what Adolf says to him when he goes to the Chancellery. When he comes back from those interviews, he's like a man who has spoken to God.'

The aircraft which Ernst, on the airstrip at Darmstadt, had invited me to come to Rechlin and power dive was, of course, the Stuka.

He was mightily pleased with it, and with himself on account of it. The ministry had been lukewarm for a long time, but he had argued and badgered about his dive-bomber until one day the wind had changed and they said yes, we're going ahead with it, and gave Junkers the contract. He had joined the ministry partly, he told me, to be associated with its development. And now it was realized, it was there in the hangars, and he had designed a siren to fit over the wheel fairings so that as it dived it should scream.

I thought there was something diabolical in this.

'Yes,' he said, sketching the design on an envelope, 'but think how humane. It'll frighten everybody so much we won't need bombs.'

'Cheaper, too,' I said.

He said, 'You would go far in the ministry. Have you ever thought about it?'

A boxy, pugnacious aeroplane, the Stuka, but strong. And it could dive!

I dived it at Rechlin. The speed rocked my brain. It took all the nerve I had. The dive so flooded me with adrenalin that I wasn't in my right mind for another twenty-four hours. I couldn't wait to do it again.

'You see?' smiled Ernst.

In 1936 several things happened. One was that I went to the gliding championships in the Rhön and was told women weren't allowed to compete. No one would give me a reason.

I stormed down the hill to the village to make some phone calls. I rang Ernst at his office. He was out. He was always out.

My temper not improved, I walked, head down and hands in pockets, round the little streets, which were decked with bunting for the championships.

I collided with someone. I muttered an apology, and then found that the stranger's hands, which had buffered our impact, were still on my waist. I looked up angrily.

'Hello,' said Wolfgang.

We hugged each other. I said, 'Where have you been? I wrote to you.'

He said, 'In Sweden. *I* wrote to *you*. Where have *you* been?'

'I didn't get the letter. It must have been when I was at Stettin.'

'What were you doing at Stettin?'

'Learning to fly Ju 52s.'

He said, 'I hope you looked where you were going when you were flying them.'

We went into a café and sat at a table looking out on to the square. The sun lit the bunting and the weathercock, and my spirits rose.

I told Wolfgang about Stettin. I had never told anyone until then, and I have never told anyone since. Those five months had left a taste so queasy that I preferred not to think about them. But, sitting across the table from Wolfgang with his intelligent, hooded eyes which looked as if they had seen everything, I realized that I must tell someone, and that I could with safety tell him.

He listened in silence, with an expression of contempt hardening on his features. When I had finished, he said only, 'You're worth more than all of them.'

'Thank you.' I had needed to hear that. It was a kind of absolution. I had been treading the edge of a quicksand at Stettin; at times I had nearly lost my sense of who I was.

Wolfgang said, 'It will go on. You know that, don't you? There are men' – he smiled swiftly – 'who don't feel like men in the presence of a woman who can fly a bomber. They'll never forgive you.'

'Well, in fact . . .' I said, and as he sipped his beer I told him about my problem at the championships.

He looked concerned but not particularly surprised. He advised me to badger the daylights out of everyone on the committee, and get hold of anyone in the ministry to whom I had access. 'Most of these chaps just want a quiet life,' he said. 'And to be told what to do by someone in authority. Do you know what the reason for this piece of stupidity is?'

'No.'

'The government's putting a lot of money into training military pilots. Glider pilots are an excellent recruiting ground.'

'I know that.'

'Well, don't you see, it's a waste, from their point of view, training women to fly gliders, because women can't fly in combat.'

'But I *am* trained! They don't have to spend any money on me at all!'

'They know it's too late to stop *you*,' said Wolfgang, smiling. 'But if they let you compete, how can they stop other women from trying to take up gliding?'

'But Wolfgang, they send me all over the place gliding for Germany!'

'Of course they do,' said Wolfgang. 'You do it very well. It's another example of the total confusion that prevails here. Organizations working against each other, departments working against each other. In some cases, by design. It's really very curious, and one day I must give some time to studying it. From a distance, preferably. What will be your salvation, Freddy – it's certainly been mine so far – is that this country is run with an absolute lack of intellectual consistency.'

He finished his beer and ordered another. It came, creamy-topped and golden. He sipped it with a faraway look in his eyes.

'The trouble is,' he said, 'that this nation which has no idea how to conduct itself makes the best beer in the world.'

I followed Wolfgang's advice and badgered the life out of everyone badgerable. The telephone call which did it, I think, was the one to the director of the Glider Research Institute. I was his chief test pilot and he took the ban personally; he was very angry indeed. After three days of telephoning, arguing and refusing to go away, I was told the ban on women had been lifted.

I had dinner with Wolfgang on the second evening. He was, as always, excellent company. As usual, he did not talk much about himself, and as usual I did not realize this until afterwards. He showed me some photographs of Sweden, which he obviously liked a great deal. The photographs showed lakes and mountains, Wolfgang on skis, Wolfgang on his back in the snow, Wolfgang with friends, the Swede with whom he shared a flat, more lakes and mountains.

'Come over for a week,' he urged me. 'You'd love the skiing.'

I said I would, but I never did.

He said something else as well.

'One day you might need me,' he said.

I looked at him with a question.

'As a friend. It doesn't take a crystal ball to see how things are going to develop here, and I have contacts. If it ever happens . . .'

I wasn't sure what he was saying. The drift was clear, but why did he think I couldn't look after myself?

'I'm guessing,' he said, 'one day you may find the heat turned up. Promise me that if you need help you'll get in touch with me.'

If he wanted me to trust him, that was no problem.

'I promise,' I said.

'Good.'

'If I'm going to get in touch with you I shall need to know where you are in future.'

'The embassy in Stockholm will find me.'

'You're going to stay in Sweden?'

'If I can possibly swing it.'

I had no doubt that he would. Wolfgang usually managed to swing things. I thought of him as a sort of prince, born to have the world on his terms. He came of an aristocratic family; he had money, connections, intelligence and charm. But I also felt in him something discordant with these advantages, something which, as it were, kept him on the run, wouldn't let him come into his inheritance. What, after all, was Sweden, if it wasn't exile?

'Why do you want to stay there?' I asked.

'The Reich is not the best place for me,' he said, and I knew the subject was closed.

And it was the year of the Olympics.

I was permitted to compete on that occasion. But I remember chiefly a conversation I had with Ernst.

I had been enjoying myself, you see. I liked massed orchestras and crowds and flags, and the roar of ten thousand throats cheering. And Berlin seemed so much pleasanter that summer. It was as if the sun shone more brightly. The city was cheerful, and it was full of foreign accents.

Ernst was busy. I saw him here, there and everywhere, in the stadium, in hotel lobbies and at receptions. Chatting, smiling, cigar-waving: entertaining foreign visitors, the genial host. He was so good at it.

He picked me up after a gliding event and drove me back to my hotel. He drove too fast. His face was set and unsmiling.

'What's the matter?' I asked him.

'Nothing. Oh, it's been a vile day.'

'I thought you looked as though you were having a very good day, hobnobbing with ambassadors in the VIPs' enclosure.'

'Goddamned Games,' he said viciously. 'Banners, torches, doves. *Quatsch!*'

We took a corner with a squeal of tyres.

'Ernst,' I said, 'you aren't going to frighten me, but you are frightening a lot of harmless pedestrians.'

He slowed down, but his face remained tight.

I asked him again what had upset him.

'I just don't like it. I look around and I wonder what I'm working for sometimes. Don't you?'

'I'm working for the Glider Research Institute.'

'You're working for the government.'

'Well, yes,' I said, after a moment.

'We lead such an enclosed life,' he said.

What did he mean? I thought of the huge spaces of the sky, and of the danger that could never be eliminated no matter how skilful a pilot you were.

He said, 'They see things differently abroad, and when they come here they've got sharper eyes. They don't have fences put round their minds. We get used to it. We'll put up with anything.'

I said, with a feeling of apprehension, 'What is this about, Ernst?'

'You must have noticed that a great deal of street cleaning has been done.'

He was sneering with anger.

I could not avoid knowing what he meant. The scrubbing of slogans off shop windows, the removal of the – sometimes vilely offensive – anti-Semitic posters and magazines, from which my eyes reflexively moved away the instant I saw them, so that I almost didn't see them: yes, in several senses the city was cleaner. Look where you might, there wasn't a reference to Jews to be seen. The government was improving its image in other ways, as well. Displayed in a bookshop window I had seen a novel by Thomas Mann, whose work had been banned for years.

'What's good enough for us isn't good enough for our visitors,' said Ernst. 'In that case, why are we ceaselessly told we're right and the rest of the world is wrong? I am tired of being lied to. My God, doesn't a man deserve the truth once in a while? I am tired of having my intelligence and what little morality I possess insulted by the cause I am serving. I hate the Games, which are the most massive propaganda stunt I have ever seen, I hate this stinking regime, and I hate myself because I am not going to do a single damn thing about it.'

We drove for a mile in silence. I felt shattered. Or rather, as if a barrier I had built to protect myself had been shattered. In an attempt to stop him saying anything more, I said, 'I agree the government's gone too far in some respects, but at least the country's on its feet again.'

'Do you know what Oranienburg is?'

It was one of those camps. They were all over the country. High walls and barbed wire. Guards with brutal faces. God knew what went on in them. Nobody talked about it.

Oranienburg was north of Berlin. It was supposed to be for dangerous criminals and subversives.

'It's a KZ camp,' I said, using the common abbreviation.

'Do you know what goes on there?'

'I imagine it's pretty unpleasant.'

'It's organised sadism.'

I said sharply, 'Nobody has ever pretended this was a regime of sweetness and light. And presumably you don't get sent to Oranienburg for nothing.'

'You get sent there for disagreeing with the government.'

He stopped smoothly at traffic lights and we watched the crowds, dressed for a summer evening, saunter along the pavements. He was calm, now that he was talking. I was not calm: something seemed to have taken control of my tongue.

'All right, we have a dictatorship. A lot of people wanted that. They wanted strong government and jobs and to be able to get on with their lives. And they wanted to feel they lived in a country they could be proud of. You may not like Hitler, and I don't, but you have to agree that he's made this country respected abroad. You can't make an omelette without breaking eggs.'

I stopped, sickened by the sound of my own voice.

Ernst grimaced. 'Thank your lucky stars you're not an egg,' he said.

The lights changed and we moved forward. I sat stiffly against the leather upholstery. The words I had spoken clanged in my ears. I loathed them. I didn't know where they'd come from. But something inside me must have meant them, or why had I said them?

I wanted to unsay them, and couldn't. It was partly that I didn't know how to back down. But if I unsaid them, what was I to say instead? That I, too, hated this regime?

I glimpsed a situation in which I could lose everything I had struggled for.

People like Ernst should keep their opinions to themselves, I thought. It was all very well for him: he could stop being a general in the air force and go back to flying stunt planes. I didn't have anything to go back to except the kitchen stove.

We drove in uncomfortable silence.

'Thank your lucky stars you're not an egg,' Ernst had said.

Indeed, remarked an acid voice in my head. I felt an outsider, did I? I raged from time to time about the stupidity of Fate which had made me a woman, did I? Why didn't I look in the mirror? I with my clear blue eyes and my blonde Aryan hair. I was all right.

I curled inwardly with shame. Ernst was right, of course he was.

But then . . .

But then, what was to be done?

I said, taking refuge in his own words, 'Ernst, what *can* anyone do?'

'I don't know,' he said.

We drove on.

CHAPTER ELEVEN

The landscape has woken, and it is a confused waking. First we saw isolated vehicles nudging through the darkness. Cars with hooded lights, horse-drawn carts, the odd troop lorry or jeep. But now, with less than an hour to go before dawn, the roads are thick with traffic. It moves slowly, and all in the same direction. The direction in which we are going. North.

At road junctions everything comes to a halt. No one will give way. I see a farm cart upset in a ditch, its load of furniture and mattresses spread over the roadway, adding to the chaos.

The Russians in the east and the Americans in the west, as they approach the line along which they will meet, are squeezing Germany between them like a tube of paint, and up the tube the Germans travel, to shoot out at the top. Or so they hope. In the north there is still a piece of the Reich. Doenitz, the dour submariner, is there. And somewhere in the north is the man on whose account we have to see Doenitz. Mild-mannered and bespectacled. Beneath the high black cap with its badge of death, the face which does not fit, the face whose inappropriateness is so peculiarly frightening.

I do a mental calculation by my watch, the map on my knee over which I cautiously flash the torch, and the modest array of instruments in the cockpit. We are about twenty minutes' flying time from Keitel.

I turn my head to shout this information to the general, but I do not think he hears me.

Ernst rode high at the ministry, after his initial nervousness at being put in charge of the Technical Office. He was growing to fit the job, I thought. He might not want authority – in fact he was ambivalent about it – but it was starting to envelop him in its aura.

The cause, essentially, was the Stuka. That was the ladder on which he climbed. He had made a clever guess, and it was the right guess. Ernst's aeroplane was able to drop a considerably higher tonnage of bombs on target than any of our conventional bombers, and it cost half as much to build. It was also popular with the pilots, who liked the daring of the bombing technique. The Stuka's bombing accuracy was conclusively demonstrated by the civil war in Spain, where it was sent with the Condor Legion to prove itself. The Fat Man was delighted with his new and spectacular aeroplane, and Adolf praised its warrior spirit.

Ernst thus achieved the status of an expert.

One of the first things he did at the Technical Office was order Junkers to re-design the Ju 88 so that it, too, could dive-bomb.

The Ju 88 was a fast twin-engined bomber still in the development phase. Great hopes were pinned on it.

'It has to be able to dive,' Ernst said to me. 'Dive-bombing is the technique of the future. The Stuka proves it.'

On his promotion to lieutenant-general he threw a party. It was held in a tent in the Grünewald. Half Berlin seemed to be there. Even the Fat Man popped in for ten minutes. At about midnight a group of us went for a swim in the Havel. I enjoyed swimming in the moonlight. I could have managed without the rest of the evening. Party conversation and the drinking of a lot of alcohol were not things I was good at. Ernst knew this, but was insistent.

'I want you there,' he said. 'Please come.'

There were people there who assumed that we were lovers. I had been seen in his company rather often. He was well known to be a ladies' man. What else could our relationship be?

And there were people there who were fairly sure that we were not, but were still perplexed as to what our relationship could be. I caught their sideways glances: the women who had been, or were, or thought it would be interesting to be, involved with him. There was hostility in most of the glances.

I wondered if any of them would come and talk to me, but none did. And I made no attempt to talk to them. I could not think of anything to say. Ernst always kept us apart, his current lady love and me. I thought this was wise, and probably, in its way, considerate. For what did we have in common? Only Ernst, and Ernst was what we could not afford to talk about. The situation seemed to me regrettable, indeed silly, but there it was.

It crossed my mind, in a distant sort of way, that Ernst and I might have been lovers, that indeed there was a sort of inevitability about it, except that this inevitability seemed to be accompanied by an even greater impossibility. It was as if in another world we might have been lovers, but in this one it was out of the question. I did not know what I meant by this, but he knew it, too, and never made the mistake of trying to turn our friendship into something more intimate.

It was, of course, convenient that I experienced this impossibility, just as it was convenient that I had found myself unable to reciprocate Dieter's feelings. The last thing I wanted was to fall in love. It would get in the way of everything. I assumed that love was very enjoyable: people made a great fuss about it. But it was clear to me that if I were to hold on to my career, it was a luxury I couldn't afford.

Ernst said to me, after that party, 'Fairly ghastly, most of those people, but you have to invite them.'

It was only half true. He didn't really have to invite them. Ernst was many-sided: he was a gregarious man with a private core, a fastidious man with a taste for vulgarity. This mixture of qualities was what some of his colleagues, with a cruder cast of mind, distrusted in him. He was quite capable of revelling in a party and despising its guests. And if this meant that he despised himself, it is not the only evidence that he did.

That natural split in him was mirrored by the other one most of us had by then. The other split was never mentioned. Between Ernst and me, it was not mentioned. It was years before we spoke again of the conversation we had had in his car during the Olympic Games.

Parties, promotions. Ernst was riding high.

And so was I.

Ernst rang me one day from the ministry and asked me when I would next be in Berlin. He said he had something to discuss with me.

I was in the test pilots' office in Darmstadt writing a report. I had been testing a method of landing a glider on a net of tautened ropes.

It was hoped to use this idea for landing gliders on board ship. On my first attempt, a crosswind had caught the glider as it was landing and it had plunged at an angle through the net. My second attempt had almost severed the tailfin. I was putting these vivid occurrences into the mummified language required of ministry documents.

Ernst's call confused me. I was unclear whether he wanted to see me in his official capacity, on some loosely related but unofficial business, or even on a personal matter. The blurring of these distinctions was typical of Ernst, and he did nothing to enlighten me.

'Splendid,' he said when I told him I would be in Berlin the following Thursday. 'We'll have dinner. Then I shall have an excuse for getting away early.'

We dined at Horcher's. It was said to be the most expensive restaurant in Berlin, and was a favourite with the air force. Probably more ministry business was conducted there than on Leipzigerstrasse. Ernst was the only man in the room not wearing uniform. The food at Horcher's was excellent, but I did not share Ernst's enthusiasm for the place.

Ernst ordered champagne.

'Are we celebrating?' I asked.

'I always drink champagne when I come here,' he said, and I didn't doubt it. I had known Ernst to drink champagne in the cockpit of a glider at ten o'clock in the morning.

I sipped mine, regretting the waste. I was a complete failure as a drinking companion. I could not understand why people should want to lose their wits.

We chatted. There had been another shake-up at the ministry. The Fat Man loved these brutal reorganizations, which as far as I could see achieved nothing but to put the fear of God into everyone. The main effect of the latest one seemed to have been to push Milch into a corner by making the department chiefs report direct to the Fat Man.

Ernst retailed ministry gossip to me for half an hour. It was amusing, but I couldn't imagine that he had phoned me at Darmstadt and booked a table at Horcher's to tell me about it. I said eventually, 'Ernst, why did you want to see me?'

He grinned. He said, 'How would you like to work at Rechlin?'

149

I put down my forkful of salmon. Everything in the restaurant seemed to move to a distance. I could feel a dryness in my throat, and my heart beating a wild tattoo.

'I have just the job for you,' said Ernst. 'We're fitting dive brakes to the Stuka. I want you to test them.'

Rechlin. Ugly place, miniature town of concrete and brick, with steel hangars rising from its midst like temples, set in flat and featureless countryside. How I loved it! A pall of sulphurous smoke hung over it more often than not, which I breathed into my lungs as if it were the air of the Alps.

Clamorous air it was. It shook to the hammering and drilling of steel in the workshops, the roar and scream of experimental engines, the staccato fire of a new weapon being tested on the range. Occasionally there would be an explosion and dust would plume into the air. Then a hush would fall over the site as everybody listened. Several times in the first few weeks the alarm broke urgently into that silence, and men ran from all directions to the wire enclosure behind which stood the concrete buildings of the explosives laboratory.

I had expected trouble at Rechlin, and went prepared for it. Anyone who questioned my right to be there or my competence to do the job would be turned on with savagery. As my confidence grew, my tolerance to insults was decreasing. Soon I would have none at all, and would one day find that people were wary of me, as of an animal that had been known to bite. (I hadn't wanted that, either. You don't always get what you want. Sometimes you get what's available.)

But at Rechlin no one challenged me. They watched me, instead. For weeks their eyes followed me as I entered or left an office or hangar, and studied me with detached curiosity as I stood talking, filled in a flight sheet or strapped on my helmet in a cockpit. They were waiting for me to do something wrong. Knowing I would not get a second chance, I left myself no margin for error. With the Stuka and every other aeroplane I later tested, I learnt everything I could about the aircraft before I stepped into it. I studied drawings, talked to factory managers and engineers and squeezed information out of Ernst. On the airfield I confined my conversation to matters in hand, was meticulous over the smallest detail, and ignored attempts to frighten me with bloodcurdling stories or shock me with obscenities uttered under pretence of not knowing I was there.

In time they relaxed. In time I even relaxed a little myself.

The Stuka, Ernst's love, was a good aeroplane but I didn't like it. It entirely lacked grace, and was like a battleship on the controls. Taxying it was a nightmare. Because of my lack of height I had to sit on a cushion in order to see above the wingtips. But perhaps that wasn't such a bad thing. If, in addition to your other disadvantages, you turn up on a runway with a cushion under your arm, it reduces to zero the tests you do not have to do. I hammered that aeroplane. I put it, and myself, through the fire. I dived it and dived it, and when I crawled into bed at night and closed my eyes the bed would fall away underneath me, and I would be dropping through space with the blackness hovering at my vision's edge, deafened, half-suffocated, half-crazy, with my brain locked in icy concentration on the dials.

I found a flat in Berlin to use as a base; previously I had always stayed at the Gliding Association hostel. I was glad of the flat because from then on I seldom knew from one month to the next where I would be working. Sometimes it was an airfield that wasn't even on a map. But technically I was still employed by the Glider Research Institute, so I kept the flat in Darmstadt.

I enjoyed Berlin: its concerts, films, cafés. But in practice I spent most of my weekends immersed in a technical manual or reading briefings. If I went to see the latest film, it was usually in a group from work. From time to time I wondered if I didn't see too much of my colleagues and not enough of people who had no connection with aeroplanes; but if so, I didn't know what I could do about it. I didn't have time to make other friends.

I made time to see Dieter. He was in Berlin to visit his mother, and I had just taken the flat. It was on the top floor of an apartment building in Charlottenburg, and had a pleasant view of some chestnut trees but, at the time, not much else.

'You're going to be busy,' smiled Dieter, walking over the bare floorboards and making the loose ones spring under his feet. He

151

poked his head into the small kitchen. 'Not a lot of room here. But then, you never were a great one for cooking, were you?'

'I shall put a coat of paint on the walls and buy a carpet,' I said, 'and that's it.'

'Tables and chairs?'

'Oh, I shouldn't think so.'

He glanced at me, unsure whether I meant it.

He had put on weight since I'd last seen him, and his jaw seemed heavier. Perhaps he was just older. He was certainly more confident. The move to Heinkel had been good for him. He was doing research and test flying, and from what he said it sounded as though they thought well of him. I wasn't surprised: Dieter was a very good, very thorough, absolutely meticulous pilot. If he was also, to my mind, just a bit boring as a pilot, well, Heinkel probably wanted a boring test pilot, and I don't blame them.

He asked me about my own work.

My appointment at Rechlin had not yet been announced. I had meant to tell Dieter about it as soon as I saw him, but something had stopped me. It suddenly seemed to me that he wouldn't be pleased. If he wasn't, it would ruin the evening. Indeed it might ruin more than that, I thought.

When he said, 'And how are things with you?', still I didn't tell him.

I said, 'Never better,' and looked at my watch. 'If we don't go now we shall be late for the concert.'

I had managed to get tickets for Furtwängler conducting the Ninth Symphony.

I never fail to find that music moving. But on this occasion my enjoyment of it was slightly spoiled by a feeling of guilt. As we came out of the hall and looked for a taxi, Dieter said, 'Wonderful. Second movement a tiny bit slow, perhaps. Let's go somewhere quiet. I want to talk to you.'

'I've got something I want to talk to you about, too,' I said.

When we were settled in the corner of a rather noisy café, he said, 'I'm nervous about saying this.' He looked it, suddenly. 'We haven't seen each other for some time, and when I came to meet you this evening I thought, I really haven't any idea whether Freddy is still the same Freddy.'

I gazed into my coffee, wishing this were not happening.

'But now I feel that we haven't lost touch after all,' he said. 'So, Freddy, I am asking you again. You've had more time to think. I know you care about me; you've said so, and in any case if you didn't you wouldn't have spent the time with me that you have. You know what my feelings are. They've never changed. If you were to marry me, I could offer you most of the things I think you want. I have a good position and a good future. And you could do all the flying you wanted to do.'

'I'm sorry, Dieter.'

He lowered his head.

'It's "No", then?'

'It's "No".'

'I suppose I shouldn't have asked,' he said after a while. 'But I hoped . . .'

'Find someone else, Dieter.'

I said it gently but his eyes flashed. 'Didn't I once tell you you were the only girl for me?'

'You did say that, yes. It was four years ago.'

'Four years are nothing,' he said. 'I'm not a man to give up because a woman says no for four years.'

'Then, Dieter,' I said, 'you will be very unhappy.'

'You will never say yes?'

I shook my head.

He said bitterly, 'What kind of man would be good enough for you?'

'It's not a question of being good enough.'

'Are you still seeing Ernst Udet?'

'Dieter, Ernst has nothing to do with it.'

'You must think I'm an idiot.'

I said, 'It's a pity you have to do this. We were having such a pleasant evening.'

'Yes, we were, weren't we. I suppose you got the flat so you could be near Ernst.'

I said, 'I got the flat because I'm going to be working as a test pilot at Rechlin.'

'You – ?'

I saw, in his eyes, the information sift slowly downward.

With an effort, he said, 'Congratulations. To work ât Rechlin is a great privilege. They must think very highly of you. You deserve it. May I wish you the best of luck.'

'Thank you, Dieter. That's generous of you. I hope . . . I hope what's happened this evening won't spoil our friendship.'

'Of course it won't,' he said.

I was earning quite a lot of money. I bought a car, an Opel. I took Ernst out in it. Only once: he hated being driven.

I flew over the Alps in a glider. There were four of us, a team sponsored by the Institute, attempting the first complete crossing. When we all finished safely, the press was ecstatic: another triumph for German aviation.

Oh, the newspapers. They always spoke in chorus on any subject that mattered, and it was always the government line. But there was such a clever appearance of diversity, the headlines were so eye-catching, the photographs were so good, that . . .

That we didn't notice they were all being told what to say by the Ministry of Propaganda?

No. That we didn't care.

The newspapers made a lot of me.

I had become famous.

It is funny how quickly you get used to it. For the first few days you are nervous and disoriented. 'Can this be me?' you think as the flashbulbs pop and reporters take down your most inane remark in shorthand, and a nationally known figure strides forward with smile and outstretched hand and declares himself privileged to make your acquaintance. By the end of the week it seems quite normal and after a month you hardly notice it.

You think it has made no difference to you. You think you haven't changed. Your friends, even the most honest, may tell you that you haven't. But you have. You have lost touch with something that was never previously out of your hand, like Ariadne's thread. Now you will have to find your way back without it.

There is a moment when it is painful. That is when you realize that becoming famous has interfered with whatever activity it is you became famous for. Suddenly you cannot afford to fail at it. Your pure relationship with it has been destroyed. You have to build a new one.

You never recapture that first relationship. The new one you build, the tough capability to do the job, is the one you need in order to go where you want to go. But you hanker for the first one, locked away inside it, inaccessible.

Then there is the delicate question of your relationship with yourself. Fame is a drug. Continued doses of attention are required to keep the ego stable. It is not nice to have to acknowledge this – in fact you deny it – but you know the truth the day you meet someone who has not seen the papers and has no idea who you are.

All this assumes that you like what is in the papers. You may not.

I talked to Ernst about celebrity. After all, he should know. And it was his fault that the situation had become acute. In my early flying days, there would sometimes be a photograph of me in the gliding or national press. But when I began working at Rechlin the newspapers jumped on the story. I tried very hard to shut it out – I had problems enough to deal with in the circumstances – but the publicity had a stridently personal note that wouldn't let me shut it out. There was a reason for this. The more secret the work I was doing (and everything at Rechlin was secret, by definition), the more the story had to be focused on *me*.

'You have to become a sort of actor,' Ernst said. 'The part you play is yourself. Everybody knows it isn't really you, it's like a shadow or a reflection; but the pretence has to be kept up that it is you. The main thing is to keep the difference clear in your own mind. If you get the image right, you can live your own life quite satisfactorily behind it.'

This was sound advice. The difficulty I had was that I could never get the image right. I had absolutely no control over it. Well, you may say, of course I didn't: what sort of world did I think I was living in? Nevertheless I felt that the newspapers falsified Ernst less than they falsified me.

But then again, what could I expect? I was doing work which all the rules prohibited me from doing. My non-conformity had somehow to be explained, put into assimilable form. So they made me into a Reich heroine. It was the only thing they could do, it was the only way I would fit. And of course it was useful to them. Very useful.

And didn't I – although it was difficult, although it complicated everything, and even though it was a lie – didn't I like being famous?

Yes.

I knew it could only worsen things with my father. He had from the beginning hated my attracting the attention of the press: he thought publicity vulgar. But, for some reason, I had not imagined there would be more to his reaction than that.

I went home, as usual, for Christmas.

'I see you have a motor car,' my father said on the evening of my arrival, shaking the snow from his overcoat and hanging it on the hallstand. 'Well, you certainly couldn't have afforded that as a medical student.'

'Otto,' reproached my mother from the dining room. My father smiled, as if in apology, and planted a cold kiss on my forehead, and was cordial for the rest of the evening.

A couple of days later, I finished a letter I had been writing to Wolfgang, and said I was going to the post box to post it. My father looked up from his medical journal – it was five years old, he re-read the old ones rather than read the new ones, which he said were no longer about medicine – and asked if he might accompany me. He felt like some fresh air, he said.

Of course, I said.

The air was crystal. On the snow our feet crunched loudly. Acutely aware of his presence and that I could not escape it, I walked down the lane with him.

He said, 'I wanted a talk with you, and I'd rather not have it within earshot of your mother. She worries about the work you're doing. She thinks it's dangerous.'

'It is,' I said, 'but probably not as dangerous as she imagines.'

'That's what I told her. I told her you know what you're doing.'

It was a compliment. There was, moreover, something that almost amounted to a desire to be friendly in his tone.

'Thank you,' I said warily.

He shot me a look. 'It must take courage, I give you that. I don't like it; I can't pretend I do. But I wish to give credit where it's due, and I respect your courage.'

156

Yes, he was trying. But he had already said too much. Why, I thought in exasperation, must he always give with one hand and take back with the other? Why should he continue to assume that his approval was necessary to what I did, when I had left home long ago and was now a professional pilot? (But why, in that case, *did* I want his approval? For I did.)

'All these things they print about you in the papers,' he said. 'I presume that you go along with the publicity. You don't have to pose for photographs and give interviews . . .'

'They'll write about me anyway,' I said. 'The Ministry of Propaganda tells them to do a feature on me. If I don't co-operate, they'll just use the ministry handout. And goodness knows what that'll say.'

'Do you mean that what they represent you as saying is what you actually have said?'

'No. I usually haven't said it at all. If I don't say what they want me to, they just pretend that I have.'

'Then I don't see why you have to help them,' he said.

'It's – Father, I don't have any choice. It's practically part of the job.'

This was not the best reply. He frowned. I was with difficulty controlling a growing resentment.

'But how do you feel when you see the result?' he said. 'You can't possibly enjoy reading it.'

He was right, but I couldn't tell him so. It would go on for ever, I thought, his assumption of authority, my rejection of his authority. For both of us, it was as if life itself were at stake. He had to do it. I had to do it. I would rather be wrong than submit.

He sighed. 'Well, I suppose it's none of my business,' he said. 'You have your own life now. You've gone far beyond your family. You're a public figure.' He gave a sarcastic little laugh. 'I suppose I should be glad you come back to see us sometimes, in your motor car.'

'Father,' I said vehemently, 'you are so unfair!'

He turned to look at me.

'Am I unfair?'

'Yes.'

'Then I'm sorry,' he said. 'I would like to be fair.' His gaze moved away, over the snow-covered fields. 'But how am I to know what to think?'

I couldn't read his expression.

I said, 'What do you mean?'

He said, with quiet bitterness, 'Are you happy to work for this despicable government, and lend your support to its policies?'

We had stopped walking. I stared past him.

'Do you know what they're doing?' he said. 'The travesty they have made of science, the barbarism in the universities? Not to speak of – '

I clenched my hands. I willed him to stop.

He stared at me. He took in the look on my face. He said, 'I simply want to know whom I have for my daughter.'

I could not answer him. A torrent of words rose in my chest and stuck fast in my throat, where they choked me.

We stood face to face for what seemed a long time.

Then my father turned away and began to walk back in the direction we had come. He waved his hand curtly towards the mail box.

'Post your letter,' he said.

When Ernst said that it happens invisibly, that you don't notice, until the last minute, where you are, how trapped you are, he was, of course, talking about himself. It was different for me. I knew where I was all along; I knew I was in a room from which there was only one exit, and that it led to a closer and closer association with the ministry.

Ernst helped me into that room. Sometimes I think he lured me into it.

After I had been working as a military test pilot at Rechlin for some time, Ernst proposed that I should be made a flight captain.

This title was normally bestowed on senior civilian pilots who had a long flying record on powered aircraft and at least three years in research or test flying. Since most of my work had been on gliders, I did not qualify.

Ernst said that the work I had done on the glider dive brakes at Darmstadt, followed by the Stuka tests, had been of more importance to aviation than a dozen other projects on account of which medals had been presented. He added that I made a unique contribution to 'the flying life of the nation,' whatever that meant.

He could not have pushed it through on his own: it was obvious that I had other well-wishers in the ministry. Nevertheless there was an almighty fuss. It went on behind closed doors, some of which weren't closed too firmly, and the row came to my ears. I was a bit shaken. It's one thing to know, in the abstract, that there are people who think you have no business to be doing the job you're doing and should go back where you belong; it's another to know who they are and have to pass them in the corridor.

Well, that was the way it was, I thought. I had work to get on with, I couldn't allow this sort of thing to upset me.

I was growing a harder skin. I needed it. I could not afford to feel everything that was directed at me: envy and malice because of the publicity which I did not seek but was often assumed to seek; the resentment, never conquered however much concealed, of men at a woman in their preserve; gossip about my private life, unhindered by the fact that, in the sense which interested the gossippers, I had none. I was lonely, too, I realized, and I could not afford to feel that, either. Work kept it at bay: I was constantly occupied. But through the gaps that occasionally opened up between one activity and another, a chill wind blew.

Well, I thought, that was the way it was, too.

The Fat Man presented me with the certificate of my flight captain's rank. I had not been introduced to him before. We were in a large room with chandeliers, and he seemed to occupy the whole room. He took my hand in his hand that was like a big damp cloud, and twinkled into my eyes. He was feline and very charming. Something about him paralysed me.

I wondered if my father would notice the – for once – modest and tasteful paragraph in his daily paper. If he did, I thought it was unlikely to help matters.

I was unable to resolve the situation that had arisen between us. It should have been simple. All I had to do was write him a letter – short, and couched, for safety's sake, in terms which only he would understand.

I couldn't do it. Several times in the months after our walk to the post box, I sat down at the table and picked up my pen. After an interval, I always put it down again. I could not write that letter.

By the end of that year I had come to the notice of someone else.

'As your arm comes up, your chin must come up as well,' instructed Ernst. He was lolling in an easy chair, stroking the Siamese. 'No, not that far up, you look as if you're trying to balance something on your nose.'

'Couldn't I balance something on my nose instead?'

'No, I'm afraid not. And at the same instant, *precisely* the same instant, you click your heels.'

I practised clicking my heels. I'd been doing it for years and it never sounded any better.

'I suppose,' sighed Ernst, 'it's the shoes. They don't make shoes for ladies which click properly.'

'Something is inserted into men's shoes to make them click?'

'Yes. A special piece of iron. We start with small ones at the age of three and work up.'

'Peter never told me that.'

'It's something we don't usually talk about.'

He lifted the cat into my arms and disappeared into the bedroom, to reappear with a pair of his black patent shoes.

'Try these,' he said. 'It might give you the feel of the thing.'

I put them on. My feet slid around in them like fish in a jar.

'Now, bring your heels together.'

The click was more resonant but still lacked crispness.

'Mmm,' said Ernst dubiously. 'Maybe it's not the shoes.'

'Maybe it's the feet.'

'Perhaps you start off with them in the wrong place.'

'I always thought they were in the same place as everyone else's.'

'Perhaps,' said Ernst, thoughtfully exhaling cigar smoke into a fern, 'after you've flown the helicopter, I should come on and do the salute.'

'I don't think that would work.'

'Maybe not. Well, let's go back to the arm bit. Really, it's a very simple movement. The arm swings up stiffly but smoothly from the vertical. The trouble is stopping it at the right point. Yours goes too high.'

160

'It's nervousness.'

'Well, it looks like satire. Just do it again, will you?'

I did it again, and he walked round me, puffing at his cigar, demanding minute adjustments to my posture, and then undermining it all by making me laugh. We had been doing this for more than an hour already, and it was well into the evening before Ernst decided that my salute would pass. Under the clowning it was serious. There would be thousands of people watching me fly the helicopter at the Motor Show; the press of the world would be there. Everything about it, including the salute at the end, had to be impeccable. The smallest things mattered a lot these days. Another way of putting it was that there were no small things left.

What we didn't know was that *he* would be there.

I heard about it immediately afterwards. He had liked the show-business: he always did, it fed his vaudeville soul. And he had been there, in a specially constructed cubicle at the back of the stadium, surrounded by the SS men who at times seemed to be mere emanations of his personality.

He was there only for the duration of my flight. When I was told afterwards, my knees shook. The salute had been all right. But because of the lack of oxygen the helicopter had dropped like a stone for twenty feet before I managed to control it.

The summons came the following morning. Ernst telephoned me at my flat, bubbling, with a raw anxiety showing through his excitement.

'Hitler wants to see you.'

I swallowed. 'When?'

'At three o'clock this afternoon. A car will pick you up. Congratulations. And good luck.'

'Ernst . . .'

'Just be yourself.'

'What do I *say?*'

'As little as possible. He loves technical detail. Don't for God's sake tell him the thing nearly hit the deck.'

I remember nothing of the intervening hours until the car collected me, except the ball of fear under my heart. We drove through streets busy with traffic and garish with bunting and banners for the

Motor Show. As we approached the Chancellery the density of black uniforms increased, until there were no others to be seen.

I walked up the steps between the uniforms. I felt I was being drawn forward by some intense gravitational power which dwelt at the building's centre and had drained the reality from everything on the periphery. It drained mine, too. As I walked, accompanied on either side by black figures, through a reception lobby and across a wide hall, my faintness grew. The men on either side of me became shadowy, the great room through which we passed was blurred with blocks of light and shadow. I felt the strength being pulled out of me as we moved through halls and ante-rooms to the centre.

The door was open into a pleasant room which looked on to a garden. At a rosewood table stood a man wearing clothes which did not seem to fit him properly. I did not understand what he was doing in the room. It seemed to me, in the moment when I glimpsed him and felt the vibration of that tragic dissonance, that in some sense he did not exist. That, as it were, the boundaries of his personality had not been fixed.

CHAPTER TWELVE

The chief of the High Command, known also as 'Yes'-Keitel and the Nodding Donkey, is administering the war from a villa on the former estate of a Dutch oil millionaire. He has had to move there in a hurry, and the chances are that he will have to move again in a hurry. Indeed it has occurred to me, as I piloted the general over the shrinking corridor of land which does not yet belong to the British, the Americans or the Russians, that he may have left by the time we get there.

But he hasn't. I come upon the place suddenly, tucked among woodland, and see staff cars drawn up unconcealed on the drive. Presumably there is no longer any point in hiding anything.

Keitel is bent over a table, studying a map with an air of complete hopelessness, as we enter. He straightens up and salutes.

'Congratulations, Greim. Got news of your appointment. It should have come earlier. Then we might not be in the mess we're in.'

'Thank you.' The general-field marshal salutes as smartly as he can in the circumstances and asks if he may have a drink of water. An aide is dispatched for one.

'Sorry about your wound,' says Keitel. 'Been treated, has it?'

'Yes, oh yes. No need to worry about that.' The general shifts his crutches heavily and manoeuvres himself, with my assistance, into a chair. I take the glass of water the aide has brought and place it at his elbow, then find a seat at the back of the room.

Keitel nods courteously at me, and two minutes later they have both forgotten I'm there.

'You left Berlin early this morning?' Keitel asks.

'About one-thirty,' says the general.

'Difficult getting out?'

'No picnic. Crazy pilot, took off with the wind.' The general grins savagely. Keitel doesn't understand: he's not a flying man.

'Ivans everywhere,' the general says. 'On the buildings. In the tree-tops.'

'How near the Chancellery?' Keitel wants to know. It is all he wants to know.

'Axmann says they'll try to over run it this morning.' The general looks at his watch. Then he cocks his head, listening, as if he could hear the machine-gun fire and the running boots. He says, 'I only hope my radio message was in time.'

'What message?'

'We stopped at Rechlin. I sent out a call for all available aircraft to muster and fly on to attack the Russian positions.'

'What time was this?'

'Two twenty-five.'

'Pray God you were in time.' Keitel stares at the map. 'And how was . . . *he* . . . when you left?'

'He's a sick man, Keitel.'

'Yes, yes, but what was his mood? Was he still hoping? Still talking about Wenck?'

'It's very hard to say what he – '

Keitel cuts in. He needs to talk. 'As soon as I got here,' he says, 'I received an extraordinary wire from Berlin. Asking questions, very precise questions, founded on completely false hopes. I had to reply to it, of course. I was obliged to tell the truth.'

A shaft of pain from his foot has turned the general white. As it relaxes its hold, he slumps.

'I wanted to get him out of that place,' says Keitel. 'After all, how could he command from there? And there is Bormann forever whispering in his ear. I begged him to leave: I even thought of *kidnapping* him. Madness, of course: the place is black with SS. He refused to leave: one of his "unalterable decisions". I wired back that the only hope for them was to break out. I said I would wait for a reply. But no reply has come. I can't talk to him now. The balloon was shot down.'

'What balloon?'

'The radio telephone balloon.'

'Oh yes.'

Keitel says, 'I served him seven years. I can't believe I shall never hear his voice again.'

From the general's throat comes an equivocal murmur. For a time nothing more is said, while outside the window birds serenade the morning and a steel-helmeted sentry gazes straight ahead.

Keitel begins again.

'In all those years, he has never praised me. Did you know that? I got the blame for everything, never the praise. Whatever it was, whoever had done it. If an attack miscarried, it was my fault. If a general retreated, the wrath fell on me. I have been his desktop soldier. I represented all of them. God, how he hated the army.'

'I heard that you were . . . unjustly treated.'

'Oh, it's common knowledge. Don't they call me "the donkey"? I have had the responsibility for everything, and power to do nothing. Only to put my signature to his decrees.'

He swings round and looks out of the window at the spring day.

'Greim, some of the things I have put my name to . . .'

'So have we all, so have we all . . .'

'No, I tell you, no. Orders so far-reaching they amounted to an abrogation of law. Not just military law – God knows, that's monstrous enough – but the *idea* of law. Do you know what frightens me? That everything will break down, fragment. That there will be a universal . . . dissolution. Because of what has been done.'

'You did your duty.' The general is uneasy. 'You obeyed. You honoured your oath.'

'Oh yes, that oath. Almost the first thing he did was make us swear that oath. He skewered us on it like worms on a hook. Honour. What is honour? Once, I thought I knew. Greim, do you think it is honourable to issue decrees which fly in the face of all legal precedent, all human feeling, and refuse to sign them yourself?'

He receives no answer.

'*I* signed them. The donkey signed them. All but one. One of them I *made* him sign. That was the Commando Order. You remember it? Of course you do. An order for the murder of captured enemy servicemen.'

'If,' says the general wearily, 'you felt so strongly, why didn't you resign?'

'How can one resign in wartime? It's tantamount to desertion. In any case, who would have replaced me? He didn't trust any of the generals, even before the plot. It would have been Himmler.'

The name brings, as it always does, a difference in the amount of light contained in the room.

'Perhaps.'

'Without doubt,' says Keitel. 'Himmler's loyalty was never in question. Never has been.'

His voice is emotionless from the long checking of a profound anger.

The general pulls himself up in his chair. 'You haven't heard, then?'

'Heard what?'

'Himmler has been trying to negotiate with the West. Through contacts in Sweden.'

'*What?*' Keitel is transfixed. He stands motionless and his square, soldier's face which always seems to me to be concealing bafflement now openly displays shock. Then at the back of the eyes and the corners of the mouth there starts to glimmer something. It is a smile.

'This is certain?'

'Oh yes. It was picked up on Swedish radio.'

'What terrible news,' says Keitel without a trace of regret, and sits down.

'Hitler was devastated by it.'

'Naturally he would be.' The chief of the High Command has regained control of his facial muscles. 'Presumably Himmler didn't get anywhere, with these peace feelers?'

'Oh no, they sent him packing. They've made it quite clear that any surrender has also to be made to the Russians. I don't know why he thought he could get around it.'

'Not only that,' murmurs Keitel, 'but has he no idea of how he is regarded abroad?'

'Apparently not,' says the general, and they both shift in their chairs as if something cold has gone past.

'How strange,' says Keitel, 'that he should not know that, when it is his business to know everything.'

'Do you expect to understand his mind?'

'No. I'm a soldier, thank God, not a priest.'

'The grand simplicities of war. Yes.'

'You've found the war simple, have you?'

Their eyes communicate.

'Perhaps not.'

'I suppose he was acting in the belief that he would succeed Hitler. If the time ever comes, of course.'

'Presumably. Well, that is the end of those ambitions.'

'Do you think so?' muses Keitel. 'All those SS battle divisions, still more or less intact, in the Alps? All those secret policemen?'

There is a thoughtful silence.

The general brings his hand down on the arm rest. 'This will get us nowhere. I came here to talk about practical matters.'

'Then please do so.'

'What's the military situation in this area?'

'Chaos. Complete collapse of morale. Units hurrying to surrender to the first American who's got enough stripes.' Keitel thrusts his hands through greying hair. 'I visited the front a few days ago, trying to find Wenck again. On the way I found a battalion pulling out of a strong defensive position because they had *heard* there were Russian tanks twenty miles away! I sent the whole lot back to their positions, and threatened the officers with court martial.'

'Did you find Wenck?'

'Yes, I found Wenck. Sitting in some godforsaken forester's hut looking at the same map as I am.'

'I need to discuss his drive on Berlin with you.'

There is a pause, then Keitel laughs. It is a harsh laugh, but he seems to enjoy it. The general stares at him.

'Wenck has been told to disengage from the Elbe and advance immediately on Berlin,' says the general.

'I'm aware of that, Greim. It was I who gave him the order.'

'He will be joined by the Ninth Army, which is fighting to the south of the city.' The general levers himself out of his armchair, leans over Keitel's desk and jabs at the map with his finger. 'Here.'

'Thank you. I know where Berlin is,' says Keitel.

'All available aircraft . . .' The general runs his finger around the inside of his collar. 'What the devil's the matter, Keitel?'

'Wenck is finished,' says Keitel. 'He is bogged down among the lakes around Potsdam. He can't advance the length of his nose, and half his army is still tied up on the Elbe crossings. The Ninth has been reduced to a few battalions which have managed to fight their way through with hand weapons to join him.'

Some time passes.

The general says, 'Are you sure?'

'Don't be ridiculous, man. I saw it.'

More time goes by. Eventually the general says in a quiet voice, 'Then there really is no hope for them.'

'There's been no hope since the Russians reached the Oder. There's been no hope since Hitler insisted on fighting every battle himself. Oh, I hoped, too,' says Keitel. 'Wenck seemed the only way of getting him out: I was going to bundle him into a tank if I had to drive it myself. But even when I gave Wenck that order, and that was a week ago, I knew we were all fooling ourselves. You too, Greim. What are these aircraft you're mustering? If you've got any aircraft, you haven't got any fuel.'

The general says nothing at first. He looks at his foot, his huge, hideous, bloodstained foot, dressed twelve hours ago in a tiny room under a light which flickered like a candle with the thudding of the shells.

Then he says, dogged, as if to say it were partly to achieve it, 'I was ordered to do my utmost.'

'There is nothing more that can be done. That bunker is a place of dreams. He issues orders and thinks they can be effected by his willpower alone. I finally had to tell him it was not possible.'

The general raises his head. 'You told him that?'

'In my reply. I was telling you, earlier. He wanted to know at what time Wenck would arrive, where he would attack, when the Ninth Army spearheads would break through . . . I had to wire back that none of it was going to happen. I said there was no hope of rescue.' He gazes at the map, not seeing it. 'It was a death sentence I sent.'

An adjutant knocks at the door, comes in and hands Keitel a typed slip of paper. Keitel reads it and his mouth twists.

'A wire from Grand Admiral Doenitz,' he says. 'The bunker is still transmitting. Doenitz has received orders to proceed at once against all traitors, of whom it appears I am one. Hitler says I have been deliberately holding back the armies which were to relieve Berlin.'

CHAPTER THIRTEEN

We come out of Keitel's pleasant villa with its creeper on the trellis into bright but chilly sunshine. My eyes are sore from straining to see in the darkness, and from lack of sleep. I tax them further, staring into the white morning sky for bombers.

I check the Bücker over. It is airworthy, but the Mustang made some nasty holes in the tail section. We take off from the millionaire's croquet lawn, circle over the well kept grounds and picture-postcard castle, and turn towards Lübeck.

Easy does it, now. We'll stay low, hide in whatever is to be hidden in, and we should be over Doenitz's territory in less than two hours.

I don't know how I know this, but I know we won't.

Lübeck has been heavily bombed in recent weeks. Brave RAF, waging war on civilians and refugees and medieval architecture.

Lübeck always puts me in mind of Peter, although these days he is never far from my thoughts in any case. I feel he is alive. He has been torpedoed three times. Perhaps that's enough, perhaps they will leave him alone now.

I spent a day in Lübeck with him, in that other time before the war. His ship was there. I had a few days' holiday and travelled up to see him.

I liked Lübeck, with its winding streets and old buildings and the air that blew in from the sea. Peter and I wandered through the streets eating gingerbread. Every time we saw another naval officer, Peter hid his gingerbread in his pocket.

He wasn't happy. It lurked behind everything he said. He was out of place in the navy, with its rigid political orthodoxy. The navy was still living down the bolshevist sailors who had carried their rifles reversed in 1918. And it suffered from a sense of inferiority, a feeling that it had yet to prove itself, towards the army, the older service, repository of the nation's honour, and all that.

A naval officer had to be keener than the keenest, tougher than the toughest. Peter was just a nice boy.

I had known this for years. It was common knowledge what kind of navy Grand Admiral Raeder ran. Peter, clearly, had not known it, or not grasped what it would mean, when he joined, and no one had told him. I had never really understood why he did join: he hadn't talked to me about it. It was obviously something he had needed to do alone.

Peter said, as we walked through Lübeck, 'I think I might volunteer for U-boats.'

U-boats were still hush-hush at the time. They'd been one of the things we weren't supposed to have, under the Treaty of Versailles.

'Oh yes?' I said. 'Why?'

'It sounds very exciting. We had an address last week by the chief of U-boats, Doenitz. He's tremendously enthusiastic, he inspires you.' Peter bit into his gingerbread hopefully. 'It's new, you see,' he said. 'All of it. The boats are new, the tactics are still being developed, and it's the thing of the future. *Offensive* sea warfare. It's a far cry from sitting on the surface presenting a massive target and knowing you're as likely to be sunk as you are to sink the other fellow.'

'Yes, I can see that. But, Peter, do you remember when we went into that tunnel and you got claustrophobia?'

He looked at me under his fine dark brows (he has our mother's colouring), deeply hurt.

'I'm sorry,' I said quickly. 'I was just trying to help.'

'It didn't sound like it.' He walked on a few paces. He said ferociously, 'Why can't you be like the other chaps' sisters?'

My steps slowed.

'I never have been, Peter. It's a bit late to ask that.'

'You don't – you don't do anything normal,' he said. 'I know you're doing important work and all that, but it's still – I can't explain it in the wardroom.'

'What a pity. Why don't you just disown me? At least if you transfer to U-boats you can start again, and no one need know whose brother you are.'

My scorn made him flinch.

'It's all very well for you,' he said. 'You seem to have decided long ago that you didn't care what anyone thought. You just went ahead and did what you wanted.'

'Do you really think it was easy?'

'No, I don't suppose it was easy. What I'm saying is that you didn't *care*. You never seem to have felt that you . . . had a duty.'

'What has this got to do with duty?'

'Everything. You could never do what was expected of you. You could never give up the idea that you didn't have to obey the rules. It was only because you were a girl that you were able to get away with it. Girls have things a lot easier. And it hasn't done you any good. It's made you completely selfish.'

'You'd rather I thought only of other people's comfort and sacrificed myself to it?'

'At least you'd make someone a decent wife!'

'And sister, presumably.'

'Yes!' he shouted.

'Well, I'm sorry to be such a disappointment to you. Have you ever wondered how I feel about having you for a brother? I would have liked a brother I could respect!'

He went white.

'What do you think your upbringing has done for you?' I hurled at him. 'It crushed you. You've never recovered from it. You let Father walk all over you, and now you're nothing at all!'

I stopped. He was standing in an odd posture, stiff, like someone waiting to be hanged.

I went up and put my arms round him.

'Peter.'

After a while he moved. He sighed heavily and ruffled my hair.

'So that's what you think of me. Well, I don't blame you.'

'Peter, you're my *brother*!'

'Yes. We should have been the other way round, you and I.'

'I know. Everybody always said so.'

'Did they?'

'Yes.'

'I didn't know that.'

After a few moments Peter said, 'I'm sorry. All that was stupid and beastly. I'm really very proud of you, you know.'

'Are you? I'm proud of you, too.'

'How can you be?'

But I was, although at that moment I could not have said precisely why.

'And I'm sorry,' I said. 'Those last things I said, I didn't mean them.'

We walked on slowly. I said, 'Let's go and have lunch. I'm too old for gingerbread.'

We ate mussels and black bread in a smoky tavern, and talked. I told him more than I was supposed to about the work I was doing, and he reciprocated. And he told me about Japan, where he had been with his ship on a goodwill visit. He seemed to have spent most of his time looking at temples.

Later, when he had downed several tankards of dark local beer, Peter said, 'I should never have joined the navy.'

'You're seeing the world.'

He shook his head. 'I mean it.'

'Why did you?' I asked.

'To get away from Father.'

'Was it as simple as that?'

'I hated him,' said Peter. 'I swore I would do anything in the world to get away from him. I could only think of the navy.'

'And is it really as bad as that?'

'What I did,' said Peter, 'was just exchange one father for another. I don't think you ever get away from your father.'

I said nothing to Peter about the impasse in my own relations with Father. I didn't feel like talking about it, and in any case I very rarely did talk to Peter about my difficulties with Father. There was a sort of deference in this, an acknowledgement that, however thorny my problems in that area, they would always be of a lesser kind than his.

In the two years that preceded the war I was sent abroad on a number of missions which everyone, by then, recognized as having less to do with flying than diplomacy.

Each time I went abroad, the distance between Germany and the rest of the world had widened a bit further. It made me realize how little we were told. The union with Austria, for example: at home this was welcomed as a natural and desirable event. I had found it quite natural, myself. Were Austrians not Germans? I discovered with something like shock that outside Germany it was condemned as annexation.

Perhaps surprisingly, on our trips abroad we encountered no personal hostility. That was kept for the government. We had, it seemed, taken the prize for the world's least popular government. I was not unsympathetic to this attitude, but for obvious reasons did not say so. I did not, in fact, say much at all. I was there to fly, and I flew.

They sent me to the USA for the Cleveland Air Races. Everybody (except Ernst) had told me I would hate America. I loved it. You could crack a joke and get a smile there. There was nobody talking about blood or honour at all. But we had to pack our bags early and leave. The trouble over Czechoslovakia had turned into a crisis.

Five months later I was in Libya. Nobly, the government was still trying to promote the international fellowship of gliding.

Dieter had also been selected for the expedition. I hadn't seen him since the evening of the concert in Berlin. I hadn't heard from him, either, except a postcard to say he was now working for Messerschmitt.

He came to meet me at Tripoli airport. He was wearing the brown shirt and armband of the Party, and as I crossed the hot tarmac he gave the Hitler salute.

'Don't be silly, Dieter,' I said, 'it's me.'

His face stiffened.

In the ensuing days he gave no sign that we had been friends. His manner was chilly, and he seemed not to want to be alone with me. I tried not to let this bother me, but it did. In the end I tackled him about it.

'I am being perfectly friendly,' he said coldly. 'What do you want?'

When the gliders arrived, things deteriorated further.

There were three gliders: two workhorses and a thoroughbred. Dieter and I watched in silence as the brand new, high-performance glider was unpacked from its crate.

Then Dieter said, 'I think I'll fly it this afternoon if the conditions hold.'

173

'Do you?' I said. 'I was thinking I might.'

We submitted the issue to the team leader, who said we should fly it on alternate days and tossed a coin to see who was to have it first. Dieter won.

He came back flushed with triumph and began to tell me how to handle it.

'For heaven's sake,' I said, 'I can fly a glider.'

'You think there's nothing you can learn,' he said.

I was not in conciliatory mood. I said, 'I think there's nothing you can teach me.'

Dieter turned on his heel and walked out of the hut.

It was partly that everybody else was doing the same thing. This was supposed to be an international expedition, but the French had pulled out before the start and the Italians didn't seem to know whether they were taking part or not. As the weeks progressed the expedition came to seem more and more futile. Certainly no one believed in its ostensible purpose.

'Thermal studies!' muttered Wilhelm, the meteorologist of the team, as he plotted our day's results on his chart one evening. 'What a charade.'

'Meaning?' demanded Dieter.

Wilhelm looked up at him. '*You* know why we're here.'

Dieter cast a swift glance around the hut to check that none of the Italians was inside.

'As far as I'm concerned, we're here to continue the thermal research that was started in South America.'

'You can study air currents anywhere there are air currents,' said Wilhelm. 'You don't have to do it in areas of particular military significance.'

'If Adolf Hitler orders me to study air currents on the moon, I will study air currents on the moon,' retorted Dieter.

I said, 'Dieter, I don't think there are any air currents on the moon.'

Wilhelm swallowed his smile. I had noticed that he and Dieter didn't seem to hit it off.

'I think you miss the point,' he said.

'Oh, I understand the point,' said Dieter, 'It is you who don't understand it. We are here because we have been sent here. The reason is not our business.'

I took a long look at him. I wondered why I was surprised. But it is always surprising when someone you know well does the thing they have been giving every sign they will do, because you had thought there was more to them than that.

I returned to my book. I was reading an account of nineteenth-century travels in North Africa. I thought I might as well improve my mind.

Wilhelm picked up his pencil again. 'Well, perhaps it's a mistake to discuss this,' he said.

'It's a mistake to discuss it in the spirit you bring to it,' said Dieter. 'There's too much scepticism and intellectualism on this team.'

I saw with amazement that he was looking at the book I was reading.

In the miserable five weeks we spent in Libya – weeks in which I inwardly lamented the waste of it all, when the desert was so beautiful and the Arabs were so interesting – I only once more challenged Dieter on his behaviour towards me.

This time he admitted it. He said, 'Yes, I have decided to treat you differently from the way I did before. I have to.'

'Well, I'm sorry that you feel like that.'

'I don't know what else you can expect.'

'But, Dieter, as far as I was concerned, we never were anything but friends. It's not as if I've changed towards you.'

He said, 'I think you deceived me.'

We were standing in the shade of a palm tree, looking at the desert. Shimmering sand met shimmering sky; nothing was distinct but the movement of air.

'I deceived you?' I said.

'Yes.'

'In what way?'

'You led me to hope ... well, how do you think it looked? Everyone thought you were my girlfriend at Darmstadt.'

I flushed angrily. 'But you knew I wasn't.'

'You kept telling me I wasn't. But you were glad enough to go around with me.'

'Are you saying there is only one circumstance in which a girl is *allowed* to go around with a boy?'

'You used me,' he said. 'It wasn't fair.'

The trouble was, there was a grain of truth in it. I had found it useful to have Dieter's company. I'd known it, and guilt was one of the things that had cemented our relationship. But when he said that I had been unfair, what residual guilt I still felt on that score was blown away in a great clarifying gust of anger, and with it went, too, whatever fondness I had felt for him.

Wilhelm came round the corner, carrying a pile of record sheets, and greeted us.

I smiled at him rather vaguely. I was fully occupied by my surge of relief at having no relationship, and no obligation to have a relationship, with Dieter.

But Dieter had registered Wilhelm's arrival.

He seemed to draw himself up. He waited until Wilhelm had gone into the hut and closed the door. Then he said with contempt, almost spitting the word: 'Jew!'

The night that came to be called Crystal Night had happened by then.

I was out with colleagues from Rechlin, celebrating someone's birthday. We were having dinner at a country inn renowned for its venison. Gustav, whose birthday it was, drank a large quantity of red Austrian wine and proposed to the landlady, who was married.

We heard the glass splinter as we were drinking our coffee. The sound was as clear as if a window in the next room had shattered. As one, we stopped talking and put our cups down.

Someone joked nervously, 'Another drunk.'

'I don't think so,' said the draughtsman who had brought us all in his car.

The landlady, arranging bottles on a shelf behind the bar, said, 'There's a Jewish ironmonger's on the corner.' She stepped back to check the effect of the arrangement. 'Well, they've had it coming,' she said.

We finished our coffee, paid and went out. The inn was in a small market town. We walked down the road, round the corner and into the square. In the distance I heard a confused noise.

It was November and the night was cold. I thrust my hands deeper into my coat pockets. Under my foot something crunched. I looked down.

Shards glistened on the pavement. Behind me, inward-pointing spears of glass were all that remained of a shop window. Three windows in a row were smashed. Someone had scrawled 'Jew' and an obscenity on the door.

The confused sound in the distance was compounded of shouts and the roaring of a fire.

'Let's get away from here,' I said.

We heard more glass break in the next street; there was a cheer, then round the corner careered an open-top truck packed with swaying SA men. They shouted something jovial at our group and the truck lurched to a stop. A man jumped down from the back and ran over to us. He seemed to be asking directions. He was excited and laughing and his words fell over one another.

'What a night!' he kept saying. 'What a night!'

We said, in reply to his questions, that we had no idea where the synagogue was.

Some of what happened that night was in the papers, some wasn't. But you only had to walk down a street to see. The broken glass lay in mounds. People picked their way round it, complaining about the inconvenience.

The Fat Man was reported to be extremely angry. Insurance, you see. They claimed. Those who weren't too frightened. It ran into millions. How could he keep a grip on the economy, the Fat Man said, when this sort of thing happened?

Karinhall is somewhere in this region.

If it's still standing. I heard a rumour the Fat Man had dynamited it, rather than let it fall into inartistic hands.

I never saw it, his country seat. But Ernst described it to me. Ernst went there several times. He went there, most notably, one weekend in the early spring of 1939, when he had been head of the Technical Office for two and half years.

He had been summoned. He drove out from Berlin in his sports car. He drove through rolling heath, dotted with lakes and forested. In this region the Fat Man was establishing a vast game preserve and wildlife sanctuary. If you were lucky you might see buffalo or wild horse. The Fat Man's shooting weekends were world-renowned. Ambitious air force officers were at pains to practise their marksmanship.

After fifty miles Ernst turned off the highway, passed through a checkpoint, and took the smoothly surfaced road which wound along lakesides to the house.

On a number of counts, Karinhall inspired awe. Probably nothing so lacking in taste had ever been built. Modelled originally on a Swedish hunting lodge, it had quickly departed from this simple inspiration, spawning other buildings around a central courtyard, each of which in turn attracted statues, fountains and plantations of trees. The buildings housed the Fat Man's art collection. Under the thatched roofs proliferated antique chandeliers, rococo tables, rare tapestries, old masters, gold and silver plate. The process of accumulation seemed, to Ernst, endless. Europe was full of treasures. And why stop at Europe?

The house was a rich man's whim, named with a brutal man's sentiment. Karin had been his first wife. He had elevated her memory to a religion. Her remains lay in a pewter sarcophagus inside a granite mausoleum, its walls five feet thick, on the shore of the lake overlooked by the house. One day his bones would rest beside hers. Meanwhile he liked to swim in the lake.

Ernst parked his car on the gravel and walked to the house. He was directed inside by a well—muscled youth in medieval livery holding a machine pistol. The door took him into a hallway in which Chinese vases glimmered in alcoves, and he walked through it, shoes squeaking, resisting a temptation to tiptoe. As he walked he fancied himself covertly observed.

He wondered how many watchers watched him every day, how many listeners listened. The Fat Man had his own intelligence service. It intercepted telephone calls, anyone's telephone calls. Not even Himmler had been able to get his hands on it.

The Fat Man moved softly for his bulk. He was standing under an archway, hand outstretched and face bisected by his slash of a smile. He was wearing velvet knee breeches, silk stockings, shoes with diamond-encrusted buckles, a white silk shirt with, over it, a fur-trimmed waistcoat, and at his waist a red sash in which was stuck a jewelled dagger.

Ernst grasped his master's hand. They walked together over the polished wood and Persian rugs of the great hall to where a log fire blazed in a fireplace which could accommodate an ox. The Fat Man indicated to Ernst that he should sit in one of the capacious leather chairs, and lowered his weight into the other. A footman in doublet, green breeches and buckskin boots appeared with a decanter on a silver tray. He poured two glasses of Madeira and retreated into the shadows.

'How is Inge?' inquired Ernst's host. He had remarried, after Karin's death, and liked to play the family man. He took a cordial interest in the domestic arrangements of his subordinates. Inge was Ernst's current mistress, but had occupied the position long enough for the relationship to have acquired reliability.

Ernst said that Inge was very well and was at the moment visiting relatives in the country.

The Fat Man expressed satisfaction and began to talk about a painting he had been given, a Caspar David Friedrich, which he promised to show Ernst after lunch. He talked easily and affably, and all the time Ernst knew he was thinking about something else.

It came as his glass was refilled.

'Ernst, I'm a little worried about Milch.'

Ernst's eyebrows twitched. The Fat Man had manoeuvred ceaselessly to prevent Milch from attaining the ascendancy in the ministry which his abilities deserved and his position entitled him to; and still he was not satisfied. Milch was just too good, that was the trouble. He was tireless. He was a superb organizer. He relished paperwork. He took decisions when they had to be taken, and didn't care if they were unpopular. And, whatever was done to weaken and circumvent him, he was still the Fat Man's deputy and inspector general of the air force.

'What worries you?' inquired Ernst, as if innocent of all this.

'I don't trust him,' said the Fat Man, playing with the jewelled hilt of his dagger. 'I think he goes behind my back to the Chancellery.'

He did. He was well received there.

'If he does, can it do any harm?'

'Well, it depends, doesn't it, what he says when he's there. Milch's assessment of a situation is sometimes quite perverse. It can be dangerous, that sort of thing.'

Ernst waited.

'Particularly in view of the expansion programme.'

A five-fold (*five-fold!*) expansion of the air force had been decreed. To start immediately. Activity in the offices on Leipzigerstrasse was intense, and much of it concealed panic. A programme had been hastily drawn up. Aircraft still on the drawing board, or still undergoing major redesign, had been assumed satisfactory and fed into the projections as hard figures. Milch's eye had dwelt coldly on the lists.

'Of these aeroplanes which are supposed to be standing on the tarmac in three years' time,' Milch had said to Ernst, 'nearly eight thousand are completely unproven. That's a quarter of the total.'

Milch was right. Nevertheless his pessimism angered Ernst, who took it personally. Ernst was nervous about some of the decisions he had taken in the past year. He needed his judgement to be trusted, not questioned.

'Milch has been talking about the Ju 88,' said the Fat Man.

This was the bomber which Ernst had made Junkers re-design. It had been ordered in large numbers; it was going to be the air force's standard bomber.

'Milch says there are problems with it,' said the Fat Man. 'He says it's too heavy and too slow.'

'There are absolutely no problems with the Ju 88,' said Ernst, and felt a treacherous bead of sweat in his palm.

'Mmm. Well, I hope you're right. Certainly it won't be the first time Milch's judgement has been adrift.' The Fat Man refilled Ernst's glass, and his own. 'I've decided to carry out some changes,' he said. 'The place needs fresh air. Jeschonnek is going to be the new chief of staff. You get on with him, don't you?'

'Yes.'

Milch didn't, though. Milch and Jeschonnek hated each other.

Did the Fat Man know this, wondered Ernst, glancing at the wide, strangely softened face on which reposed a smile like a razorcut. Yes. The Fat Man knew as much as he wanted to know. The appointment was therefore calculated to increase Milch's difficulties.

'A good choice, if I may say so,' said Ernst. 'He's young and energetic.'

'Quite.' The Fat Man pushed a log, on the point of toppling out of the fire, back with a powerful thrust of his foot. He chuckled. 'And he will act as a rein on Milch.'

The log blazed up, throwing heat into Ernst's face. At his back and around his ankles he felt the chill draughts which had come from patrolling the rooms and corridors of this house, while his cheeks burned and his eyes smarted from the glory of the fire. These conflicting sensations, added to the effect of Madeira on an empty stomach, gave him a feeling of dislocation which seemed not inappropriate to his surroundings. He assumed that in time the Fat Man would tell him why he had been asked to come here. Or perhaps not. Sometimes he was summoned to the Fat Man's office and all they talked about was fighter tactics in the Great War.

'Shall we go in to lunch?' asked the Fat Man, rising with agility to his feet, and they walked under the gaze of twenty antlered stags into the panelled dining room.

Over the fish course the Fat Man said, 'I'm creating a completely new department and putting you in charge of it. It's a major office, much bigger than your present one. Don't worry, you'll have people to help you. You'll be in charge of all aspects of aircraft and air armaments production. Including scientific research.' He removed a fishbone from his mouth and pointed it at Ernst. 'Like it?'

'I don't know anything about research,' said Ernst. It was the only thing he could think of to say. It didn't matter what he said. He should feel jubilation, but what he felt was dread.

Perhaps it would be all right. Perhaps, if he was thought able to do this job, he really could do it.

'I know you don't,' said the Fat Man. 'It won't hurt you to find out, will it?' His eyes lit with malice.

Ernst took a mouthful of fish and tried to think. The sorrel sauce was exquisite.

'You can spend a couple of days next week talking to the boffins,' said the Fat Man. 'Find out what they're up to. While you're at it, tell them I want a wooden bomber.'

Ernst choked.

'Are you all right, old chap? Have some more Chablis.'

The summer of that year, I was testing a glider. It was a giant of a glider, a beautiful albatross on wide, wide wings. It was the biggest glider ever built. It had been developed as a freight carrier; now someone had decided that if it could carry freight it could carry troops. I was testing its performance with every gradation of load from empty to a dozen soldiers with full kit.

Instead of flying troops, I was flying sandbags. This was the only drawback of the assignment: the sandbags had to be loaded into the glider.

I did it myself. I could have asked for help, but that was not my way, and in any case I didn't trust anyone else to count the sandbags carefully enough and stow them as I wanted.

Every day I pitched the sandbags from my shoulder into the belly of the glider, where they landed with a dead thump. If a sandbag lands in the wrong place, you can't push it with your foot. A bag of sand is the most inert thing in the universe. My shoulder felt like Atlas's.

I had a lovely summer.

In August an appalled rumour seeped through the ministry corridors and the hangars and workshops of Rechlin.

A bombing exercise by twenty-one Stukas had been arranged on Sagan Heath. They were to dive on a dummy village and bomb with live explosive. A score of generals had been invited to observe.

The three flights of aircraft took off from their base at Cottbus just after dawn. There had been a slight haze, but it was clearing. The weather report said that a shallow bank of cloud covered the target at six thousand feet.

I picture the generals talking together, checking their watches out of habit, and focusing their field glasses on the target, palely outlined against the dense green of the forest, as they hear the growing thunder of the Stuka engines.

In the third flight, the commander checked his watch. It was half an hour since take-off, an hour since he received the weather report. The sun was climbing and its rays were already warming the canopy of his cockpit.

The leader of the first flight of Stukas, judging himself to be over the target, dived. His six companions dived with him towards the distant film of cloud.

A few moments later the second flight dived. The inhuman howl of their sirens filled the sky, and on the ground the generals smiled indulgently.

182

The commander's eyes flickered from his watch to the leading Stukas, still hurtling towards the still distant cloud, back to his watch, and back to the plummeting aircraft.

He was trained to react instantly, but horror may paralyse belief. It would probably have made no difference, the fraction of time in which his horror fought with his knowledge. Drunk with adrenalin, deafened, hell-diving, they were beyond him or anything. They had already dived far too long, they seemed to have been diving for ever, towards a cloud that should have been at six thousand feet, but was not.

'Pull out!' he screamed into his radio.

Only his own flight heard him.

The fourteen Stukas vanished into the bank of mist.

The numbed generals saw fourteen black crosses leap from the sky and bury themselves in the earth. The howling was stopped as if a great cloth had been dropped over it. There was an abyss of silence.

Then the forest began to explode.

The court martial which was at once set up established that by the time the Stukas began their dive, the cloud bank which had been over the target and was reported to be at six thousand feet had dispersed in the warmth of the sun. But that same warmth had drawn a mist from the ground, and by the time the Stukas dived the mist had thickened and hung, at three thousand feet and below, in a broad arc which completely hid the target.

Thus the pilots were at three thousand feet when they thought they were at six thousand feet, and it had to be assumed that they did not look at their altimeters. If, as they had been told to expect, they were to emerge from cloud well above ground, they would not when diving need to know their height. And as was pointed out to the court martial, in a fast dive, altimeters are not particularly accurate.

Ernst wept. He was ill for hours, vomiting.

He drank brandy to subdue his stomach, and sat in his armchair holding the cat. He stared at the wall with its smiling photographs, and saw fourteen aeroplanes slicing like knives into the earth.

'Why didn't they look at their altimeters?' he said.
He knew why.

Two weeks after it opened, the court martial was adjourned indefinitely. September had come, and we were at war.

CHAPTER FOURTEEN

Nobody had wanted this war. People in the streets were subdued. We were told the Poles had started it. The newspapers had been full of Polish atrocity stories for weeks.

France had a treaty with Poland, so France was involved. Britain had given Poland a pledge, but was not expected to declare war. She did.

I saw Ernst the following day. He turned the lit end of his cigar in the ashtray, round and round.

'It's terrible,' he said. 'We can't win it. America will come in, in the end. Nobody here understands about America. They haven't been there.'

The atmosphere at Rechlin changed. The men around me were profoundly affected. Something had happened which laid a claim on them they could not deny. I could see them straightening their shoulders under it.

The fact that war had actually come sobered me. I suppose, like most people, I had thought until the last minute that it could be avoided, that Hitler would pull another rabbit out of the hat. There were no rabbits, and there was no saying how long the war might last. One just had to take a deep breath and get on with it.

I found myself wondering what war was. Everyone talked as if they knew, as if it was obvious. I thought it was not so obvious.

It wasn't what it appeared to be, of that I was sure. The clash of shell against armour, running figures in a fog of smoke, hammering guns. That was simply incoherent. War's coherence lay in its strategy, but it was the strategy which got lost. In other words, war seemed to be more than human beings put into it: it transcended them. It seemed to be using them, rather than the other way round. I was reminded of the ancient idea of war as a god.

If it was a god, it was of course a male god.

I recoiled from this thought as if I had burnt my fingers. I made myself go back and look at it.

Here was an idea I had fought since the day I had begun to think: the idea that there are some things proper to the male and some proper to the female, with the corollary that if this distinction is not preserved a crime is committed against nature. If I had allowed that idea the dominion over me which it demanded, it would have killed me; but I could not escape recognizing that it had dominion over nearly everyone else. I was obliged to spend a good deal of my time negotiating it without coming to a full confrontation.

And now I had just thought it myself.

It was not an identification which my mind made. Like all the compelling ones, it was made by something in the stomach. How do you know you are on territory that isn't yours? It smells different; its rhythms are different. You know that you don't know how to get inside it. I knew aeroplanes, they did not mystify me. But when war broke out, something happened to my aeroplanes. Or so it seemed to me. It was as if they grew up. I was not sure I could communicate with them any longer, not sure there wasn't someone else they'd rather talk to. No one put this idea in my head: I, with repugnance, found it there. I found it as I walked under the wing and along the fuselage of a Dornier bomber I was about to take up for a test of its new landing gear. I walked close to it, smelling its smell and laying my hand on the fuselage where the black cross was painted, and it smelt and felt of war. It smelt and felt of a hard purposefulness that was in some way beyond me. I saw that bomber for the first time as part of a system which I was permitted to service but which I would never be allowed to operate. I felt a flash of the old anger at my exclusion, but after it came a different kind of thought. If I were not excluded from this system, would I really want to be part of it? Wouldn't I find it sterile, even tedious?

Meanwhile, if war was a god, here I was in its temple. How long would it be before the impiety of my presence was noticed? Or were they all too busy to notice? Had they, in fact, long ago ceased to notice me, concluded that I was a sort of man, not a very good one, but one that would do?

It then occurred to me that the longer the war continued the more they might need me. A lot of men at Rechlin had already volunteered for combat duty, and more were thinking of it. It was almost the sole topic of conversation.

Well, that was predictable, I thought, and with the thought came a rush of feeling which physically stopped me in my tracks and made quite clear to me what my desires were.

I wanted to fly in combat. I bitterly resented that I couldn't. Believing that war was ultimately futile, I nevertheless wanted to fight. This wasn't patriotism: it was the desire for an all-consuming experience. And it was a desire to test myself, for I did not know the limits of my courage. The work I did often required courage, but I was always conscious of the trade-off between courage and skill. Combat was different.

I wanted to know how I would do in this test of tests. I assumed that men felt the same way. And then I realized that that was what war was for.

The day the war began, the troop-carrying glider I had tested was given priority status. Dozens were ordered from the factories. I heard that the go-ahead had been given for operational use.

At around that time, a number of experienced glider pilots disappeared from their usual addresses.

The invasion of France we had all expected didn't come. After the lightning victories in Poland, an uneasy quiet settled down. Late summer turned into autumn, and autumn became winter. The gliders slumbered in their hangars.

One day I got a strange message. It was smuggled out to me by routes about which even now I am not sure, and it came from a gliding acquaintance I'd known for years. He wrote to me as if I were his last hope. And not only his.

The glider pilots were being kept in isolation and in conditions of absolute secrecy in preparation for a mission in the west. They had not been trained for this mission, they were not being trained to cope with anti-aircraft fire, they were not being given any practice in co-ordination with their tow-pilots, although the take-off was bound to be hazardous, and no one listened to anything they said because none of them held more than junior rank in the armed forces and many of them were technically civilians.

187

The men in charge of the operation, as was apparent, did not know anything about gliding.

It was clear that unless something was done, a lot of glider pilots were going to be uselessly killed.

The pilot who had written to me begged me to do whatever I could. There must be someone in the ministry who would listen to reason, he said.

'I can't do anything about it,' said Ernst. 'I'm sorry. Of course the situation is ridiculous. But it isn't within my sphere of authority, and everybody in the ministry is very touchy about that kind of thing.'

I knew that. I'd hoped he could find a way, all the same.

'You could try von Greim,' said Ernst. 'Really, I suppose you should go to Milch. But if you go and see Milch, don't say I sent you.'

'But who is to blame for this?' I said.

'Blame?' Ernst looked taken aback. Then he laughed. 'Nobody's to blame. It's just the way things are. What do you expect, that an operation should be run by people qualified to run it?'

Ernst was in trouble.

His new post brought him responsibilities he was unable to cope with, and a workload he had no clear idea how to delegate except to give it all to his deputy, Ploch. Or leave it on the desk and go out.

If he left it on the desk it was still there when he came back.

For three or four months, whenever I visited Ernst's office, the same set of papers was sitting untouched on the far corner of his desk. After a while he put a book on top of them. They were from Milch's office and related to the Ju 88. Another pile which never seemed to go away related to the floor space of aircraft factories. Apparently we were running short of it. Ernst's favoured solution to the problem was vigorously opposed by Milch, who sent him an unending stream of memos about production methods.

Then there was the new Messerschmitt fighter, the Me 262. Ernst kept the drawings, not on his desk, but in his briefcase, as if by continually carrying them with him he would absorb, as it were osmotically, the key which eluded him.

He had come to dread the making of decisions. He had been told he would have experts to help him; and he did, but he didn't trust them. And this distrust was well founded. His experts all had their own projects to advance and positions to secure. He would try to weigh their conflicting arguments and realize he lacked the wider knowledge which would put them in perspective; he would look at the charts and tables and pages of figures and feel baffled, and then angry. As head of the Technical Office he had got into the habit of postponing difficult decisions; it wasn't hard to do, his job so often took him out of the office. Or he said it did. Now, in his new department, this habit started to extend itself to all decisions. But, postpone them as he might, he would, in the end, have to commit himself, and then he would do it, as often as not, in anger. At least once, he flipped a coin. Once he wrote the names of two aircraft manufacturers on separate pieces of paper, screwed them up into balls and placed them in front of his Siamese cat, to see which one she played with first.

He put off a decision on the Messerschmitt fighter week after week, month after month.

I visualize him, flushed with one of his short-lived resolves, opening the stiff, smooth paper and spreading out the sheets. Drawings of wings, undercarriage, a section of the fuselage . . . The one he doesn't want to look at is the last sheet of all. He opens it out and feels a familiar tightening in his insides. It is his deepest fear. He is the director of Air Armament and everyone is laughing at him.

Messerschmitt says this plane has an engine which works on a revolutionary new principle. But Ernst doesn't understand how it works. It uses conventional aircraft fuel but there are no pistons. There is no carburettor. There is no *propeller*.

Ernst, convinced of Messerschmitt's genius, is not convinced of his sanity. Ernst's eyes tell him that he is looking at a superb new fighter plane, as sleek as a shark, with just a lot of useless metal where the engines ought to be.

Ernst had said I should go to Milch about the glider pilots, so I went. I had no great wish to; I had met Milch on several previous occasions and been sharply conscious of his disdain. However, I felt that, if I didn't. I would not have done my best.

'Sit down, Fräulein Kurtz,' Milch said, with a smile that barely touched his lips. 'What can I do for you?' His eyes flickered to his wristwatch.

The interview lasted for six minutes. As I spoke he began to stiffen in his chair. He interrupted me after the first sentence.

'Forgive me, but what has this to do with you?'

'I received a letter asking for my help, General.'

'Your *help*?'

'Yes.'

'I see.'

His tone indicated a depth of astonishment that anyone should ask for my help, or that I should be capable of giving any.

I plodded on. The lack of training for the pilots in take-off procedures and co-ordination; the lack of preparation for flying under fire.

Milch was amazed. 'An air force pilot wrote to you about that? What do you know about that?'

'General, I do have considerable experience of glider-flying, and experience with this particular aircraft.'

'So you may, but of flying under fire and of military matters generally you have, I would think, no experience whatsoever.'

There was nothing I could say. Certainly there was nothing I could say and still remain in the room.

'Very well,' he said with a sigh. 'You may as well finish.'

I had little to add, except that the pilots had asked me to take the matter up with the ministry because no one paid attention to them. In the circumstances, it did not seem wise to say this.

It was foolish to imagine that Milch would allow me not to say it.

'And why has he asked you to put your oar in? Why can't he go through normal channels?'

'He isn't listened to, General.'

'What on earth makes him think you will be?'

'I don't know, sir. Frankly, I didn't expect a sympathetic hearing. I'm just trying to do what I feel to be my duty.'

'Are you, now?' He appraised me. I had very slightly redeemed myself by my final sentence, but the idea that a woman might have duties comparable to a man's was still laughable.

'All right,' he said. 'I accept that you've come here from honourable motives, and not simply because you wish to interfere in matters which are beyond you. But that is the limit of what I'll accept. The training of pilots for an operational mission is not and never can be any concern of yours. In future will you please confine your interest to the sphere of your work.'

He stood up. I stood up, and we coldly took leave of each other.

I put off going to see von Greim. After Milch, I couldn't face another assault on my self-esteem. It was low enough already. I had been given, for the first time since I started flying, an assignment I detested. It was a towable fuel tanker, masquerading as a glider, from which it was intended aircraft should refuel in flight. The thing was completely unstable and flew like a cow, and because the whole point was to see how it behaved as a pilotless aircraft, I was not supposed to intervene to stop it lurching about the sky.

The humiliating airsickness I suffered in the tanker, together with the fact that I had begun to dread each day's flying, were enough to make me want to keep away from the ministry. Thus I postponed contacting von Greim's office for ten days after I had seen Milch. Then I pulled myself together. Milch, I realized, would have counted on just such a reaction to my interview with him.

I was told the general could see me the following Monday.

His office was light and pleasant. A vase of flowers stood on a filing cabinet, and photographs of his family occupied a corner of the desk.

He listened without interrupting as I told him about the glider pilot's letter. When I had finished, he asked casually, 'What is the name of the pilot who wrote to you?'

I said nothing for a moment.

'And are you going to show me the letter?'

I said, 'General, this man took a great risk in writing to me.'

'He certainly did,' said von Greim, without abandoning his amiable tone. 'He could be court-martialled. If the charge were divulging military secrets to an unauthorized person in wartime, which it might plausibly be, he could be shot.'

How I hated the ministry. I hated its endless identical corridors and its thousands of offices filled with people who never entertained a thought that was not orthodox from the moment they got up to the moment they lay down to sleep. How I hated the stupidity which always seemed to accompany the thing called discipline, growing alongside it as dandelions grow along a railway track. And discipline itself I hated, in so far as it was not strictly tied to the performance of a task. Unbending, unhearing, having no aim in view but its own perpetuation: the rod with which my father had tried to mould my brother, and broken him.

With this world of straight lines and boxed thoughts I had as little to do as possible, and the fact that my work flowed, necessarily, from it and back to it again was something I had decided long ago not to think about. I concentrated on my job. That was quite enough.

But the fact that I tried to ignore this world meant that when I had to deal with it I was at a disadvantage. I couldn't decipher the language. At least, I thought, with Milch I knew where I was. With the others, I never knew whether what was being said was what was meant, or its opposite.

Sitting in von Greim's office, I had no idea whether he was on my side or not. If he wasn't, I had so far done no harm by coming to see him, but I might be on the verge of a terrible mistake.

I stood up. 'It's kind of you to see me, General. I know you must be very busy.'

I moved towards the door.

'Oh, sit down,' he said. 'You knew all that when you came here. What did you expect me to say?'

'I hoped you could help.'

'Why have you come to me?'

'General Udet suggested it.'

'Oh, I see. Yes, Ernst would not be in a position to handle it. Have you spoken to anyone else?'

'Yes, sir. I've approached General Milch.'

'Milch? You've been to Milch? What did he say?'

'He told me to confine my interest to my work.'

Von Greim's mouth twitched. 'And notwithstanding that, you've come to me?'

'I felt I had to, General. If something isn't done these men are going to be killed.'

'They may well be killed anyway,' he said. 'However, you're

192

right. But you can hardly expect me to take action on a matter like this without being in possession of the evidence.'

Of course I couldn't. I brought out the letter from an inner pocket of my jacket and sat with it in my fingers.

I said, 'General, will you give me your word – '

'Will I *what?*'

He looked amazed. Then a few moments later he laughed. He held out his hand for the letter. I gave it to him.

The amusement left his face as he read it. He made a few notes on a pad, and handed the letter back to me.

'It's yours,' he said, seeing my surprise.

'Thank you.'

'Thank you for coming to see me. I appreciate your straightforwardness. However, allow me to warn you that it is not advisable to try to bargain with senior officers of the air force. I wouldn't try it with the army, either.'

'No, sir.'

'I'll find out what I can about this,' he said, rising from his chair and going to open the door for me. 'Your correspondent will not be court-martialled.'

I looked up – he towered above me – and met his eyes.

'That is not a bargain,' he said. 'That is a piece of information.'

'Thank you, General.'

As I left the ministry, I thought there probably weren't more than half a dozen people in the whole building I would trust: but I'd trust von Greim.

On the Wednesday morning of the seventh week of the tanker tests I walked into the briefing office with my now fixed, bright smile.

'Right,' said the briefing officer, looking at a sheet. 'No work for you today.'

He was always friendly.

'They've cancelled it,' he said. 'That flying wheelbarrow of yours: they've struck it off the list. Scrap metal.'

The joy rose in me slowly, from my feet. When it reached my face it would spread out into a smile that would illuminate the whole of Rechlin.

He leafed through his papers. 'On second thoughts, there does seem to be something here for you after all. Agricultural machinery.'

The troop glider was making one final appearance in my life.

It was a hard winter, and the gliders might have to land on ice. Some means had to be devised of preventing them from skiing into the nearest obstruction if they did so.

The designer had come up with a set of fearsome-looking brakes which would dig into ice like ploughshares. These were what had to be tested.

I took the glider up into a pale blue sky. Below, the earth sparkled like a frosted cake. Only one circuit was necessary but I flew two, the second for joy of not being in the petrol tank. The brakes were over-efficient and I broke a rib on my safety harness, and no one believed me when I said I didn't mind at all.

Some weeks after my interview with General von Greim, I received a cryptic letter from him. It stated that, 'arising from the matters discussed between us', a training programme had been drawn up 'for all personnel involved in the project'. It thanked me for my assistance, and was generous in its praise of my sense of duty.

A long time later I heard what had happened. After speaking to me, von Greim had demanded that a full-scale rehearsal of the planned glider operation be carried out. The result was chaos. Serious training was begun that week.

And in May they were used, those gliders. They swooped out of a dawn sky blossoming with fire on to the concrete carapace of a fort in Belgium.

The war was on again, and roaring.

Then, almost as suddenly, it seemed to be over. For a few weeks we watched, in the flickering dark of the cinemas, the stunning, shattering advance of our troops. Holland fell, Belgium capitulated. Outmanoeuvred and driven back to the Channel, the British army took to fishing boats. The French . . .

How strange that was. The ancient enemy, the bogeyman of Versailles, was made of straw.

By the middle of June the German army was in Paris.

CHAPTER FIFTEEN

The Bücker coughs daintily. Then it hiccups. Then the engine cuts out, starts again, and cuts out.

There isn't time for anything fancy. Thank God for a flat landscape and thank God there isn't much growing in it. I land in a field directly ahead, a field of short grass bordered by scrubby, unkempt hedges. I switch off the engine, jump out and fling up the engine cowling.

You always get a blocked fuel supply when you least want it.

The general struggles with his crutches, rattles his door furiously and eventually disengages himself from the aircraft. I don't help him. I am fully occupied in detaching the fuel pipe from the carburettor in such a way as to lose the least possible amount of petrol. You always get a blocked fuel supply when you don't have a surplus of fuel.

He labours up to the front of the aeroplane and stands beside me.

'I'll soon have it fixed,' I say.

He looks at the sky. Twenty miles to the west, the guns are thundering. Less than twenty miles away, the bombers drone. I can see them, black insects abroad in the pale morning. So far they haven't seen us. Or perhaps they have something more important to do. But it is a bad place to be sitting on the ground, trusting to one's camouflage paint, messing about with a fuel pipe.

'Can I help at all?' he asks.

'Yes. Could you just hold this bit of tube so it doesn't drip?'

He makes no move to take it. I stand there irritably, holding it, waiting for him to take it from me so that I can have both hands free for the carburettor.

In what has suddenly become silence, I hear the click of the bull-dropper's safety catch.

I turn my head and see them. In the hedge-shadow at the edge of the field, they are almost a part of the earth, with their exhausted stillness and grimed, sunk faces. The rags of uniforms hang on them.

'Who are you?' demands the general.

They do not reply. He levels the pistol.

'Don't shoot, sir. We aren't deserters.'

'What are you, then? Come forward where I can see you.'

There are five of them. Four are sitting with their backs against the hedge. The man who spoke is on his feet and has a cigarette sticking like a gun barrel out of the corner of his mouth. He comes forward two or three paces; the others remain still.

'All of you!' barks the general.

The four begin slowly to get to their feet. Only the man who is standing has his rifle.

'What's the matter with you? Wounded?'

'No, sir.'

Their faces are expressionless. They walk a little way forward over the grass as the general has ordered, with a sort of thoughtfulness, as if considering his reason for it.

'Then why aren't you with your unit?'

'We lost touch with it, sir.' Belatedly the spokesman takes the cigarette from his mouth, wipes his mouth with the back of his hand, and looks at the cigarette he is holding.

'How?'

'In the fighting at Lauenburg, sir. We were ordered to pull back and take up a new position, but the Tommies came over the Elbe like – '

'Lauenburg's nowhere near here. Why haven't you managed to join up with your unit again?'

'We couldn't find it, sir. We got a lift on a truck coming this way. We reckoned if we could get to Lübeck . . .'

I avoid looking at them. I hope the general will not press the trigger. Part of him wants to shoot them, I can feel it; and part of him knows that this is a perfectly pointless conversation and wants to go to bed.

'You still haven't told me what unit you belong to.'

They tell him. I can see that it means nothing to him. Naturally. He knows only about the disposition of air force personnel. For the same reason, when he asks, and is given, the name of their command-ing officer, that means nothing either. And all this they know.

'Well, you aren't making much of an effort to get to Lübeck at the moment, are you? Skulking in a hedge.'

'We were just resting, sir.'

This sentence, with its barest suggestion of insolence, hangs in the air. But the longer it hangs there the more it demands attention. The insolence in it grows like yeast. In the end something must be said to overlie it, or it will become too dangerous.

I say to the man with the rifle, 'Do you happen to know the name of this place?'

And he doesn't, but one of the others remembers, or thinks he remembers, the name of a village they came through ten miles back, and this passes a few minutes harmlessly while I plug the fuel pipe as best I can with a bit of cloth and investigate the carburettor. There is enough grit in it to kill a chicken. Rinsing it out with a few precious drops of the reserve fuel in the can behind the general's seat, I ask them a few more questions ostensibly designed to find out where we are, but in fact aimed at distracting the general from the righteous anger I can feel seething within him.

In the end the soldiers walk away. It is the simplest thing to do, and they do it. If we had a car, they might shoot us and take the car, but they can do nothing with an aeroplane. They will walk until they are out of sight, and then they will sit down somewhere and wait for us to go, and then they will sit a bit longer and wait for the Americans. Or the British, whoever gets here first.

I finish cleaning the carburettor, reconnect the fuel pipe, pour the reserve fuel into the tank, and help the general back into his seat.

He grunts, 'Those men were deserters. I should have shot them.'

'What good would that have done?'

'None at all, but it was probably my duty.'

'Why didn't you?'

'Hasn't there been enough of it?' he says.

We take off.

The bombers to the west of us are Mosquitoes. When the Fat Man saw the first shot-down Mosquito he went into a rage the like of which had not been seen for years. The Mosquito has a wooden fuselage.

'A beautiful aeroplane,' howled the Fat Man, 'which every piano factory over there is turning out!'

In 1939, the Fat Man had told Ernst to commission a bomber made of wood. Ernst did nothing about it.

Ernst in his new department did nothing about many things. Usually it was because he did not know what to do. Then, seized by an idea, in a whirlwind of determination he would implement some profound administrative change which brought about chaos. There was no one he could trust: he was surrounded by men building their own empires, and by an all-pervasive corruption. Out of his depth, he lost confidence in his judgement, and to compensate trusted it when he should not have done.

Poor Ernst.

He had enough problems, without making himself the laughing-stock of the ministry by ordering a wooden bomber.

Ernst had seen Professor Messerschmitt at a display of air force equipment at Rechlin. The display was the Fat Man's idea, laid on to impress Adolf.

Messerschmitt, thin and obsessed, stood beside his record-breaking fighter, the Bf 109. He appeared to have lost interest in it. It was said that he became bored with an aeroplane as soon it was out of the design phase, that he was only interested in designing new aeroplanes.

Some of the exhibits were correctly explained to their guest by the Fat Man, and some were not. From time to time Milch would attempt to interrupt, and be stopped by a barrage of ice from the Fat Man's blue eyes. The party came eventually to an item which Ernst, who had a bad headache, privately considered a disaster. It was the world's first rocket-propelled fighter plane, designed by Heinkel. It was not going to be demonstrated because everyone was afraid it would crash.

Excusing himself to visit the lavatory, Ernst found Professor Messerschmitt morosely surveying the scene through a small opened window in one of the cubicles. He was having to stand on the seat to look.

Ernst coughed.

'Oh, it's you,' said the professor. He was rarely polite. 'That plane's no good,' he said.

'I'm inclined to agree with you,' said Ernst.

'You promised me fighter development,' said Messerschmitt.

'I did no such thing,' said Ernst, unbuttoning.

'You promised me fighter development using new technology.'

It came back to Ernst with uncomfortable clarity that he had said something like that, one evening when the brandy was flowing.

'Heinkel doesn't understand fighters,' said Messerschmitt. 'He should stick to bombers. I don't try to design bombers, do I?'

'No.'

'There you are, then,' said Messerschmitt. He stepped down from the lavatory seat. 'When are you going to make a decision on my 262?'

'We need more time to study the drawings,' said Ernst.

'You've had them three months already.' The professor washed his hands under the tap, smoothed his receding hair back from his domed intellectual's forehead, and departed.

It was the Fat Man who, without knowing it, rescued Ernst from his plight.

I went to Ernst's flat one evening in late autumn. He was in a funny mood. He was up and down these days. Just after the Stuka crash, he'd looked terrible. He had refused to talk about it. All September he had been miserable. He had perked up in October, and sunk again at the beginning of November.

There was a half-finished cartoon lying on the sitting-room table. He often drew these cartoons: his office was hung with a selection of them. I suspected that several had been drawn there while more official business languished on the desk. He had a real talent. He unerringly caught the likeness and somehow exaggerated without malice. Indeed, most of his drawings were affectionate. However, they were so well observed that sensitive souls found them too close for comfort.

The one he was working on was a drawing of himself. I looked at it and found nothing to say. It showed Ernst asleep at his ministry desk amid piles of paper. From his head came a dream bubble in which a beaming Ernst, cigar in hand, was flying a glider among fluffy clouds. The caption was, 'Dream of a Department Chief.'

'How are things, Ernst?' I asked.

'Things are fine. D'you know, I think this damned war might be over,' he said.

A lot of people were saying that. However, it surprised me that Ernst should say it.

'The chief's put out a directive that any project which won't be bearing fruit by next year has to be cancelled.' said Ernst. 'So obviously *he* doesn't expect the war to last long.'

'I shall be out of a job!'

'No, you won't. This is long-term research we're talking about, and a lot of it is frankly a waste of resources anyway. It's given me the opportunity to bring down the chopper on something I never liked the look of in the first place,' he said. 'Some fantasy of Messerschmitt's.'

His face was hard. He looked like a man under stress, not like a man on top of his work.

I said, 'Ernst, have you thought of taking a holiday?'

'*Quatsch!*' he said, and picked up his hat. 'Let's go out. I can't stand this flat tonight.'

On the way down the stairs he said, 'There's something top secret coming up on the fighter front. Are you interested?' He didn't tell me what it was.

Messerschmitt strode into Leipzigerstrasse a few days later.

'I have come,' he told Ernst, 'to demand the reason for the cancellation, not only of the airframe of my Me 262, but also development of the Jumo engine. It may have escaped your notice, but that engine is revolutionary. It is the engine of the future. We have the lead in this research, and we must keep it. General, you may cancel what else you like, *but you cannot cancel a jet engine!*'

Ernst, pale, said, 'I will take what measures I see fit.'

'I shall go to Milch.'

'Milch has no authority to over-rule my decision.'

'Then I shall go to someone who can.'

'Do so. The commander-in-chief has given me a free hand.'

'You have thrown away the future of German aviation,' said Messerschmitt.

Ernst said, exasperated, 'We are not talking of cancellation. I have merely ordered the suspension of work on the project.'

200

'You may as well scrap it. We shall have lost our lead. May I remind you that there is a war on?'

'It is precisely because there's a war on that I am forced to do this. We have to make economies. Do you know,' said Ernst, referring to a recent highly secret ministry expedient, 'that half the bombs in the stockpiles are filled with concrete?'

'Is that any reason why the aeroplanes have to be driven by rubber bands?'

Ernst went to the door and shouted for his adjutant. 'Coffee,' he ordered. 'Strong.'

He placed in front of the professor the carved African box in which he kept cigarettes. Messerschmitt took a cigarette, lit it, and walked around the room, exhaling smoke at the pictures. He paused in front of the cartoons. Ernst was glad his drawing of Messerschmitt was not on view.

'You're an artist,' said Messerschmitt. 'I'm an artist. Both of us are in the wrong job.'

'I'm an airman,' said Ernst.

The adjutant brought the coffee, and the professor sat down. He balanced the little cup on his long bony knee and tapped ash into the saucer.

'The idiocy of it is,' he said, 'that the Me 262 can win this war.'

'It won't be ready in time,' said Ernst.

'You seem very sure it will be a quick war.'

'How far are you from production?'

'Eighteen months.'

'Too long,' In any case Ernst didn't believe him.

'You have no imagination,' said Messerschmitt calmly. 'What is more, you don't understand my aeroplane. I know you don't. I've watched you looking at the drawings, and I thought, there is a man who doesn't understand what he's looking at.'

He put his coffee cup down and stood up. He produced a notebook and a pen from an inside pocket, flipped open the notebook on Ernst's desk and began to draw.

'This is how a jet engine operates.'

'Get out of my office,' said Ernst.

Messerschmitt raised his head, stooping over the desk, and looked at him. That penetrating stare, directed upwards at close quarters, numbed Ernst. Unconsciously he backed away.

Messerschmitt folded up his notebook and put it in his pocket.

'A pity,' he said, 'that the future should be in such hands. What are you going to do next? Cancel the high-altitude version of the Bf 109?'

'Of course not.'

'The 109 was ahead of its time,' said Messerschmitt.

'Yes. It's a fine aeroplane.'

'The 262 is its natural successor. I haven't failed you yet. Let me do it, General.'

'No,' said Ernst.

There was a pause. Then the professor picked up his coat and nodded curtly.

He couldn't let him go, Ernst realized. He must offer something, soothe the vain feathers.

'Professor,' he said, 'your contribution to our victory is crucially important.'

'Now you make me a speech. What use is that?'

'The ministry will be issuing many new contracts in the next few months. Short-term projects, conversions and so on. There's a lot of scope for us to work together.'

'Co-operation requires mutual understanding,' growled Messerschmitt.

'Exactly. I'm asking you to understand my position. Looking to the future, I think I can assure you that in tendering for future projects, you will find this office sympathetic.'

A silence. Then Messerschmitt's eyes met his, and Ernst had the sensation of drowning in a cold bath from which the cold handshake could not rescue him.

Ernst pinned his faith on the Griffin. He had ordered it from Heinkel in 1938. It was to be our much-needed long-range strategic bomber. Ernst had taken great trouble talking it over with Dr Heinkel; it was the aeroplane that would vindicate him. He flew down to the factory as often as he could to see how it was coming on.

He made one such visit shortly before his interview with Messerschmitt.

The Griffin loomed enormous in its cavern of a shed. High up under the roof, men in overalls were working with welding torches on the fuselage. The sparks skipped and skidded over the curved steel. The shed was incandescent with noise, heat and industry. The aeroplane at the centre of it all kept its silence.

'It's beautiful,' said Ernst to Dr Heinkel.

'Yes.'

Ernst stood among sawdust and metal filings and gazed at his creation. At the far end of the shed the massive tailfin rose like a sail. Below the rudder was the cutaway section where the rear turret would fit. As Ernst watched, a workman with a coil of electrical cable in his hand lowered himself into this space and disappeared from view. Ernst tingled.

'Are you on schedule?' he asked.

'Yes. Barring accidents, she will fly in four months' time.'

Ernst turned his head. The thrust of the great wing was interrupted by a huge cavity.

'Don't worry,' said Heinkel, 'the stresses have been worked out. I've told you, we have done this before.'

'But the aircraft on which you did it before is not in service!'

'No, it was experimental. Trust me, General. Coupled engines will work.'

They walked through the din of the workshops back to the cool pleasantness of Heinkel's office.

Meanwhile. Ernst's relations with Milch were deteriorating steadily.

Early in 1940. Milch went to see him.'I've been on a tour of some of the bomber squadrons,' said Milch. 'Do you know that the crews are still worried about the Ju 88?'

'What is it now?' said Ernst. 'Do they want their hands held before they take off in it?'

He was ashamed of saying this, but could not retract it.

'Shall I tell you what's wrong with it?' asked Milch. He ticked the points off on his fingers. 'It's heavy. It was supposed to weigh six tons. It weighs twelve. Because it's heavy, it's slow. It has the same speed as the Heinkel 111, which is practically obsolete. Because it's slow it's vulnerable, so it needs more armament, which makes it even heavier. And because it's heavy, it has half the range it was supposed to have. *Half!* And this is our standard bomber!'

'All right, it's departed from the specifications,' retorted Ernst. 'What aircraft doesn't?'

'And it is dangerous. The pilots gave me a list of faults as long as my arm. Thirty-one, to be precise.' He felt in his pocket. 'Shall I read them to you?'

'No, thank you.'

'Any one of those faults could cause the deaths of a crew on a combat mission.'

'And has it?'

'I beg your pardon?'

'Milch, the war is over!'

'It's hardly begun. The air force hasn't been tested yet.'

'I hope you will say so to the families of the crews who have died.'

Milch said, 'Ernst, when this war starts to become serious, we shall find we aren't prepared. We have shortages of virtually everything, there is nothing in reserve, and our standard medium bomber is a disaster. What are you going to do about it?'

Ernst passed in a fraction of a second from defeat to rage.

'I am sick to death,' he shouted, 'Of your damned interference! Will you get out of my office!'

Milch did not move a muscle. Ernst rested his head in his hands. He was feeling dizzy.

Milch said, 'We have to increase production of the Heinkel 111 and the Dornier 17, and stop production of the Ju 88 until the problems are sorted out. You must go to the chief.'

A vision of the Fat Man, looming behind his desk filled with gold and silver aeroplanes like Jove behind his altar, caused Ernst's hand to tremble as he lit a cigarette.

'Why don't you go to him?' he said.

'He won't see me.'

It must cost Milch dear to make that admission, thought Ernst. But there was no sign of it.

'He'll have to see you,' said Ernst, hypocritically. 'You're inspector-general of the air force.'

'You well know,' said Milch, 'how the land lies.'

Ernst tasted a small, mean triumph.

Perhaps Milch saw it. Or perhaps he would have said what he said next in any case.

'There is another reason why you should go to him, and that is that these problems with the Ju 88 are your fault.'

'*Mine?*'

'Yes. They are all the result of your demand that it be redesigned. It was a perfectly viable aircraft before that. Since then, God knows what has been added to it – air brakes, structural reinforcement, the thing is a flying barn door – all because of your crazy insistence that it should dive-bomb. Since the Stuka, it's been the only idea in your head!'

Ernst did not trust himself to reply for a time. Then he said, 'Conventional bombing in Spain had very poor results. A medium bomber has to be able to dive-bomb if it's to be any real use.'

Milch said, 'A medium bomber that can't dive-bomb is a lot more use than a medium bomber that can't fly.'

But Milch was in a minority in his assessment of the situation. To all appearances, the air force was doing brilliantly. Adolf certainly thought so. In July, following on the victories in France and the Low Countries, there was a rash of promotions.

The Fat Man was made Reich Marshal. This was a new rank, created for him, and rendered him the superior of any other officer in the German forces. He had a new uniform designed for himself, in dove-grey.

Milch became a field marshal, and made sure everyone knew it.

And Ernst became a colonel-general and was awarded the Knight's Cross to his Iron Cross.

The Fat Man informed Ernst that, so high had his star now risen, he must move to a more suitable address.

Ernst protested. He was deeply attached to his flat with its exotic clutter, draughty windows and silly Greenland bar. He told the Fat Man that it was his home.

The Fat Man appeared not to understand the word. All the air force chiefs lived in houses befitting their status, he said. All except Ernst. He intimated that enough exceptions had been made for Ernst since he joined the staff, and it was time Ernst conformed to a requirement.

He had found just the house for Ernst. It was a big house in spacious grounds in the Grünewald district. Almost country. Ernst went to see it and disliked it. It was so large he would have to have servants. Ernst didn't want servants. He said he wanted his privacy. The Fat Man laughed at him.

In grief, Ernst packed up his possessions, put the cat in a basket and said goodbye to Pommerschenstrasse. He drove to the new house.

His key jammed in the lock. He had to wrestle with it for several minutes before it turned, bruising his fingers. Glancing behind him as he went in, he saw the tasteless wrought-iron arch above the gateway with its funereal cross in the centre, and made a mental note to have it taken down.

In August, Operation Eagle was launched.

The squadrons roared towards England. The Fat Man, directing the battle in his bathrobe from a hotel room, was confident. He thought that two or three weeks would see the end of the RAF and the first four days destroy its southern defences.

The first four days saw German losses at least twice as high as the defenders', and a use of communication systems by the enemy which the Fat Man did not understand. He shrugged it off. The important factors, he said, were the superiority of German training and the German warrior spirit, and soon these things would tell.

The battle entered a second week, and a third, with no lessening of its ferocity. Our pilots were becoming exhausted: it was little consolation that the RAF must be exhausted as well. Then in the last week of August something which should have been impossible happened. The British bombed Berlin.

Reprisal raids on London were at once ordered. Newsreels dwelt with relish on the inferno of the docks, the smashed streets of houses. Amid the excitement, only a few men at the ministry, to whom no one listened, noticed that our air force had stopped bombing the RAF airfields, which was the only possible way in which the battle could be won.

Milch was one of those men. Milch at the moment was taking little comfort in his field marshal's baton. He had been voicing grave forebodings about Operation Eagle from the outset. For never mind the training. Never mind the warrior spirit. Look at the equipment.

The Ju 88 was fulfilling Milch's worst prognostications. In a conflict in which speed was of the essence, the Ju 88 was mortally slow. Night take-offs were hazardous in it, its dinghy was almost impossible to release – it had all the faults Milch had thought it had, and several more.

Then there was the Messerschmitt Me 110. Messerschmitt, darling of the ministry, had slipped up badly over the Me 110. It was supposed to supplement the Bf 109 in the role of fighter escort, since the 109 barely had the range to reach London. The 110 had the range but nothing else. It was a sluggish aeroplane which in the first few days of Operation Eagle was given such a terrible time by the RAF fighters that it needed its own fighter escort. There not being much point in this, it was taken out of the battle, and Messerschmitt was told tersely to update it.

And then there was the Stuka. Milch is reported as saying that the less that was said about the Stuka the better, since far too much had been said already. He had always maintained that there were circumstances in which Ernst's fêted dive-bomber would be a lame duck. It had now met them. When not in a dive, the Stuka was slow and clumsy, an easy target. After heavy losses, it, too, was withdrawn from the battle.

As for RAF communications, the efficiency of which had come as such an unpleasant surprise on Leipzigerstrasse: 'Why,' demanded Milch, 'don't we have radio contact between fighters and bombers?'

Nobody answered him. The true answer, had he received it, might have had to do with the fact that in Germany nobody had been supposed to talk to anybody for years.

In November, the Fat Man announced that he was going to his hunting lodge in East Prussia for a holiday, and handed over command of the air force to Milch. By this time the invasion of Britain had been officially called off and the bomber raids were winding down in the late-autumn murk. Everyone knew that Operation Eagle had failed.

Ernst had been keeping his head below the parapet for three months. His relations with the Fat Man were uneasy, his relations with Milch were glacial. He was smoking heavily, and his drinking, although he denied it, was slipping beyond his control.

As Operation Eagle unfolded and lips in the ministry grew tighter, I was testing a device for cutting the cables of barrage balloons. These eerily beautiful things, like dinosaurs abroad after their time, were proving a menace to our bomber pilots. They floated above the British cities, their steel anchor cables, invisible until you were almost on top of them, waiting to slice through a wing or shatter a propeller.

The backroom boys devised a fender to deflect the cable to the wing, and a steel blade to be fitted there to cut it. A Dornier 17 was equipped with these, some barrage balloons on the British model were made, and I spent several weeks flying the bomber at the balloon cables. We attached strips of bunting to the cables to make them easier to see. The fender affected the aircraft's manoeuvrability, so after a time we took it off.

One day there was great excitement. An enterprising pilot had managed to capture a real British balloon which had snapped its cable and was drifting. We arranged to use it for the next test.

At this point Ernst decided he was going to pay us a visit.

On the day of the test with the real balloon, there was a strong wind. The cable, having already snapped, was shorter than the ones we normally used, which meant that I would have to fly low. But I would also have to cut the cable at an angle, since the wind was blowing the balloon at a slant. No one was quite sure how this cable would behave even in ordinary conditions, since it was differently constructed from the ones we had been using: it had fewer strands, but they were thicker. In short, the test should have been called off. But here came Ernst's Stork, dipping down to the runway, and out of it stepped Ernst, beaming, holding the briefcase he was never seen to open.

'Everything all right, Flight Captain?' he said.

He was going to the Chancellery that afternoon. He was going to report, there, on this test.

'Everything in order, General,' I said.

I took off, and flew towards the glint of steel.

Usually the cable parted cleanly. There would be a slight shudder imparted to the control stick.

As my wing touched the cable, the overstressed strands of steel exploded, shearing the blades from the starboard propeller. The cockpit canopy shattered as the broken pieces of propeller crashed through it and just past my head. I shut off the engine and tried to right the aircraft. Seconds later, with a visceral roar, the damaged engine tore itself free and fell out. The wing thrashed and bucked and the aircraft tried to roll over.

I fought with the demented control stick, and managed to keep the Dornier just above the hilltop at which the nose had pointed itself.

Somehow, on one engine and not much more than one wing, I kept the bomber in the air long enough to get it over the hill and bring it down in an approximation of a landing. I sat quietly, hearing the loosened sheets of metal in the wing sigh and bang in the wind. I took a peppermint out of a paper bag of them I carried for emergencies, and popped it into my mouth. Then I felt for my pencil and jotted a few notes on the pad on my knee.

There was the sound of a small engine behind me, and Ernst's Stork put down daintily twenty yards away. I got out of my cockpit as he got out of his.

His face was as white as flour. With his hand still on the cabin door, he stood and simply stared at me.

In the end, because someone had to say something, I said, 'I'm all right, Ernst. It's all right.'

He went on standing there. It was as if it was he who had escaped death.

Ernst's illness started that year. Perhaps it was his only way out of an intolerable situation.

He walked into his office one morning to find the desk more than usually covered in stacks of paper. He yelled for his adjutant.

'How dare you litter my desk like this? There isn't room to put down a pencil! What is all this rubbish?'

'It's been accumulating for several days, sir. You haven't been in the office.'

'No, I've had more important things to do. Take it away.'

'Sir?'

'Take it *away*.'

'But what shall I do with it, sir?'

'Good Lord, I don't know. Burn it. What is it, anyway?'

'Reports, mainly, sir. Some correspondence for you to sign.'

'Which is the correspondence?'

The adjutant indicated a pile.

'Very well. Leave that, and take the rest to Ploch.'

Ploch would deal with it. He was sound. Ernst didn't know what he would do without Ploch.

Left alone, Ernst glanced listlessly at the correspondence.

At the bottom of the pile was a contract. It was an order for one thousand of the new Me 210s. The Me 210 was the improved version, ordered by the ministry, of the unhappy 110 which had performed so badly in Operation Eagle. Or rather, it wasn't. Professor Messerschmitt had taken the drawings out of his designer's hands and re-drawn them himself. It was a new aeroplane. Professor Messerschmitt only really liked new aeroplanes. The first Me 210 hadn't even flown yet.

Ernst signed an order for one thousand aeroplanes of which the prototype hadn't flown yet, and pushed it aside. He tipped some pills into his palm and swallowed them with a mouthful of brandy from his hip flask. He presumed that Messerschmitt knew what he was doing, and in the light of the relationship between them it was a presumption he needed to make. But sometimes a giddy exhilaration took him, like the thrill of a fairground ride, and he didn't care. For, wasn't it a fairground? Everywhere he looked there were the flashy lights, the cheery mechanical music, the painted grotesqueries, and the endless, triumphal movement in circles.

In late spring, Ernst was summoned to the Fat Man's office in the grounds of the Prussian ministry.

The Fat Man's face was clouded. With none of his usual affability, he motioned Ernst to a chair on the far side of his plateau of a desk. He did not offer Ernst a cigarette, a cigar or a drink, or talk about fighter tactics in the Great War. He came straight to the point.

'I want some production figures. Showing fighter and bomber production for the past three months and a reliable forecast for the rest of the year. I want them on this desk first thing tomorrow morning.'

Perspiration drenched Ernst's shirt, and his ears began again their painful throbbing.

After an interval, the Fat Man thumbed open a box of Turkish cigarettes and pushed it towards Ernst. He leant back, a Jove troubled but magnificent in his white bemedalled uniform.

'Look, old man, you put me in a spot. Adolf wants the answers to certain questions. I send for you, and I ask you how many bombers we're going to have coming out of the factories in six months' time. And you come back with some figure which sounds satisfactory, and I give this figure to Adolf. And six months later I look around for these bombers and they aren't there. Why not? You can't tell me. You produce some convoluted explanation which wouldn't convince a nun of the Virgin Birth.'

His eyes rested on Ernst. There were in them anger, coldness, perplexity, an infinite capacity to take pleasure in others' suffering, and a regret that he had to do this.

'It won't do,' said the Fat Man. 'It looks bad. And it's not the way to win the bloody war. I might as well tell you that we shall be invading Russia in a matter of weeks.'

Ernst dropped his cigarette on to the carpet, and scooped it up again in frantic haste. Then he sat still for a few moments, trying to collect his thoughts.

The Fat Man toyed with one of his aeroplanes. Gold rings encrusted with diamonds and rubies sat heavily on his fingers. 'Would you like to tell me about these problems with production?' he suggested.

'We'll soon get on top of them.' Ernst heard himself talking. It seemed effortless. He didn't know where it had come from, this talent to evade, obfuscate and invent. It had crept out of the walls of the ministry and taken up residence in his soul. But it was not effortless, it drained him.

The Fat Man cut through Ernst's elaborations with a brutal gesture.

'The reason we have half the number of fighters we should have is that you have run down production of virtually everything in favour of two Messerschmitt planes, both of which are behind schedule. The reason we have half the number of bombers we should have is that there are still, unbelievably, problems with the Ju 88, and you've run down other bomber production to create capacity for the new long-range bomber, the Griffin – and damn me, there seems to be something wrong with *that* as well!'

'Teething troubles,' said Ernst, dully.

'I don't think so,' said the Fat Man. 'That aeroplane smells funny.'

Moments passed. Sunlight shafted through the tall windows. There was a lion walking on the lawn.

'I suppose I shall have to fly down to the Heinkel works and look at it,' said the Fat Man.

'No!' exclaimed Ernst in fear, before he could stop himself.

'What,' asked the Fat Man, and his eyes were cold but dreamy, 'is wrong with the Griffin?'

'A spot of overheating with the engines.'

'Why don't you want me to look at it?'

Ernst was quick in a corner. 'In the circumstances it might suggest you don't have confidence in me.'

'I suppose it might. And I don't.'

This came like a blow. But at least the Fat Man had been distracted from his train of thought.

Ernst listened as he pursued the new one.

'I've decided to bring Milch back to oversee production. He'll be working *with* you: your assistant, as it were. We want to preserve appearances. But he has my authority behind him. Understand?'

CHAPTER SIXTEEN

Where are we? Over the great flat rollingness of the north German plain, enamelled with lakes, furred with forests. Beyond the horizon its northern fingers stretch and slip into the Baltic, a half-land of islands and inlets, grotesquely shaped, knobbly like the interiors of caves, but soft. Shapes of sand or mud, not shapes of land.

I know it well, that pure, melancholy coastline. When I was at the training school at Stettin, I flew above it every day the weather was fit for flying. Heinkels, Dorniers, Junkers I flew. Now here I am in a little flea that could tuck into a Heinkel's armpit.

We are flying low again. I feel horribly exposed. There is a perpetual cold sensation in my stomach and legs as if they were naked, because that is where I expect to be shot. It's bad weather for flying, the wind has turned and is blowing from the north, driving before it a wall of cloud, driving the bombers home to their bases. But not all, not yet. High up, to the west of me, drone the Mosquitoes, winking their beady eyes over Schleswig-Holstein, where the British will be in two or three days, drinking their tea and eating their corned-beef sandwiches in the squares.

The wind is bad. It gusts, snatching at the wings, and I have to fight the controls, which is dangerous at this height. I want to climb, but then the aeroplane will be visible for greater distance, and silhouetted, a clear target, against the sky.

It wasn't the mounting chaos in aircraft production, or the necessity to work side by side with Milch, who could barely restrain his scorn at what he saw, that tipped Ernst over the edge. It was the invasion of Russia. He seemed to see in it, magnified, an image of his personal disaster.

Stories of his behaviour at this time reached me: how he would leave the office, shouting at his adjutant, and fly from one place to another, turning up at factories with demands to see production figures, turning up at conferences with these same production sheets under his arm and showing them to people, almost thrusting the papers in their faces, as if they had been demanded as proof of his right to existence. Stories of how he smoked incessantly, and was swallowing pills like sweets.

No one had any idea what to do. After all, the problem was really quite simple, and so was its solution. Ernst was doing a job he was unfitted for, and he should resign.

I spent an evening with Ernst just after the invasion was announced. He was in command of himself, but strained.

We dined at Horcher's. I disliked Horcher's more and more. I never had the heart to tell Ernst this. The walls were covered in leather, which I found faintly disgusting. Since the start of the war it had ceased to pretend to be anything other than a high-class dining club for the air force. But Ernst, surprisingly, liked it. Or perhaps he just liked its familiarity, the being acknowledged.

We talked. We talked about gliding, about mutual friends, about the nearly disastrous flight of the helicopter at the Motor Show, and many other things of no particular import. We talked like this all through the soup and the main course, and when we came to the dessert Ernst laid down his spoon beside his untouched sorbet and said, 'It's all over.'

I laid down my spoon, too.

'What is?'

'It's all over for Germany.'

The tanks had crossed the border that morning. The radio was jubilant with the victory cries of Goebbels. I hadn't noticed that many people wanted to listen to the radio.

'It's an insane adventure,' said Ernst, 'and it will end in ruin.'

I hoped no one had heard him. There was a string quartet playing Haydn.

'It's a circus,' he said, 'and the ringmaster is mad. He will keep us here for ever, galloping in circles on our horses, somersaulting through hoops, throwing knives and swallowing fire and being shot out of cannon, until the tent falls down and buries us all.'

'Ernst, for God's sake!'

'What does it matter? What does anything matter? Oh, I shouldn't be saying this to you. You have a life ahead of you. At least, if they don't kill you in one of their crazy experiments you do.'

'Those crazy experiments come out of a research station run by your department.'

'They do, that's true. One day it's quite possible that I shall put my signature to a project which will cause your death. How do you feel about that?'

I tried to smile. 'If I'm going to be killed, I'd rather be killed by my friends.'

He thumped the table. 'How I hate that! The acceptance of Fate. The embracing of death.'

'I don't. I assure you.'

'Why do you do that job?'

'Because I want to fly!'

'Is that all? Is it as simple as that?'

He had calmed down. He looked at me in apparent surprise, as if he really hadn't thought of it.

'Of course it's as simple as that.'

'I see.' He studied his sorbet. He said, 'Do you mean that that's all that matters to you?'

I tensed slightly. 'People matter.'

'Of course they do, or you wouldn't be human. Though I have had my doubts about that.'

'Ernst, that's a terrible thing to say!'

'Oh, I'm sorry. I'm making a mess of this conversation. All I meant was that you seem so self-sufficient. The rest of us stumble around in the dark looking for a friendly hand, most of the time.'

I had nothing to reply to this.

'Don't you mind,' he said, 'flying for the mad ringmaster?'

'Ernst, if you don't stop this you will get both of us shot.'

'Oh, I don't think so. They need us. We're both protected. You must know that.'

I couldn't eat my dessert. I pushed it away. He pushed his away, too, and lit a cigarette.

'I suppose I'm asking you these questions because I think it might help me to understand myself,' he said. 'I don't know how I got where I am. I don't know how I can go on doing what I do. The difference between us is that what you do, you do well, and what I do, I do badly.'

'The difference between us,' I said, 'is that my work has freed me, and yours has trapped you.'

He considered this. I had thought it often. There lay at the heart of my relationship with Ernst a mutual incomprehension, and this was the cause of it.

He said, 'But in another way you're as trapped as I am.'

'I don't feel it.'

'You don't allow yourself to think about it. That's part of the trap.'

'What, exactly, don't I allow myself to think about?'

He gave a long sigh, whether at my obstinacy or his own thoughts I didn't know.

He said. 'Don't you know what's going on in this country? What Germany has become?'

His words opened a gulf at my feet. In the gulf I glimpsed, before I wrenched my mind away, the barbed-wire camps, the starved prisoners, the strange silence where the Jews had been.

A shiver went through me. Not now. I could not deal with this now.

But he was gazing at me. He was asking me to confront it with him.

I said, 'You asked me something like that once before.'

'Yes, I remember it.'

'I asked you then what anyone could do about it. You said there was nothing.'

'I said I didn't know. I still don't. With Himmler's men in every nook and cranny and children schooled to denounce their parents. We just have to wait for the tent to collapse.'

'Well, then . . .'

'Freddy, that's not a reason for denying that what's happening is happening. Is it?'

I looked into the gulf. For a few seconds of shame and disgust I made myself hang over it, and see what was in it.

Recoiling, I said, 'If you live in an abattoir the only way to get by is hold your nose.'

'That's more like it.'

216

He poured wine into his glass. He was drinking steadily.

'Ernst,' I said, appealing to him, 'one has to live.'

'Yes,' he said. 'You're right. But there's no dignity in it, is there?'

'Are you looking forward to the tent's collapse?'

'It will be catastrophic.'

'That doesn't answer the question.'

He laughed, without amusement. 'Both of us are directly employed in holding it up.'

I had to tell myself that his comment was entirely fair. I said, 'Well, if I don't hold it up . . .'

'Someone else will?'

I was silent.

'But it's true,' said Ernst. 'Someone else will.'

I was grateful. I decided to try to explain something to him. 'I've always felt I was outside things,' I said. 'That I didn't belong, and therefore the rules didn't affect me.'

He smiled. 'That would account for certain aspects of your career.'

'But,' I said, 'if you feel that, you also feel that nothing that goes on is anything to do with you either. You feel it's all the same thing. The rules, the assumptions, the obsession with discipline, the different roles for men and women which have to be observed or the sky will fall . . . the clothes, even. And the politics. It's all part of something I don't believe in.'

'I see.'

'And I came to an accommodation with it because I had to. Because I have to live. And I came to an accommodation with *all* of it because it all seemed to be the same thing.'

'But it isn't,' Ernst said simply, 'is it?'

I didn't answer. I had become half-seduced by what I was saying and hoped he would try to analyse it, not see straight through it.

'Why did you say "you" and not "I"?' he said.

'I didn't.'

'Yes, you did, to start with. You said, "If you feel that . . ."'

I toyed with my dessert.

'God knows,' he said, 'I'm not judging you. How could I?'

'Ernst, if I really allowed myself to think about what's going on I'd . . .'

'What?'

'I'd have to stop flying.'

He stared at me. 'Flying? My dear Freddy, you stand to lose your life!'

'It comes to the same thing.'

He gave me a long, thoughtful look. 'Funny,' he said, 'you can know someone for years and think you understand them, and you don't at all.'

I thought I heard bombers. My hearing was often in advance of the warning system. I turned my head to listen.

'They don't know you're outside all this,' said Ernst drily. 'They'll bomb you with the rest of us.'

He listened with me. Or I thought he was listening, for his face had that intentness. Then suddenly he said, 'They crashed in perfect formation.'

It was a moment before I caught up with him. The Stukas on Sagan Heath.

He said, 'I hear the howling sometimes, and then I hear it stop.'

The faint drone was distinct to me now. Urgently he said, 'Why didn't they look at their altimeters?'

'In a fast dive – '

'*Quatsch!* An altimeter will tell you something. And an altimeter is not the only instrument in a cockpit! They *knew* how long it takes to dive a thousand feet. Why did they go on diving? Would *you* have gone on diving?'

I had been through it in my mind, over and over.

'No.'

'Neither would I. So why did they?'

He stubbed his cigarette out in the ashtray and reached for another.

'They believed what they'd been told, that's why. They'd been told by their commander that the cloud was at six thousand feet, therefore it had to be. And in that you may read the entire tragedy of this country.'

The air-raid warning screamed across the night, drowning the strains of Haydn and spinning waiters on their heels to take back to the kitchen the dishes they had just brought from it. We rose and made our way to the cellar, to spend an hour among the pick of the German army's loot from Paris while the earth shuddered above us.

Karinhall was covered in dead leaves and fungus, and its walls stirred in the breeze. It had become a gigantic barrow, a heap of decomposition rising from the Prussian plain.

Ernst steadied himself. He picked his way through the camouflage netting and found the main door. It was guarded, as usual, by a beautiful youth holding the latest in weaponry, and it seemed to Ernst that the boy smirked in the gloom of the shrouded doorway as he slipped through into the Fat Man's palace.

Inside, little had changed except in the way of further elaboration, the further piling of goods on goods, gold on gold. Accumulation had become a law. The Fat Man could not stop. Two ante-rooms displayed the presents he had over the years been given: they were called the Gold and Silver Rooms, and that was what they contained. Ernst glanced through the doorways. 'Loot,' he murmured, and passed his tongue over dry lips, and walked on under the crystal chandeliers.

He was shown into the Fat Man's study, but the Fat Man wasn't there. His throne-like green leather chair stared at Ernst from the far side of a desk like a tennis court. How, with such a desk, was there room for the dozen tables which also occupied the study? Leather-topped, marble-topped, polished wood. Ernst counted them. There was plenty of room. There was room for many more green leather chairs, of scarcely smaller dimensions than the Fat Man's: he sat in one. Medieval wood carvings – lovely, violated – hung in alcoves. There was, he knew there was but he could not think about it, there was a Leonardo on the wall facing him.

Nothing, Ernst supposed, need be denied a man who wanted the world, if he accepted no rein on his appetites and no rule of law, and was born into an age of dissolution.

A liveried servant came in and informed Ernst that the Reich Marshal was 'on the upper floor', and had asked that Ernst be shown up. The 'upper floor' was the attic of Karinhall about which many stories circulated. Ernst would be permitted to observe the Fat Man, perhaps even join him, in a favourite pastime.

He walked behind the servant up a rustic staircase and through a plain pinewood door.

The attic was well lit and smelled of thatch. You could see the thatch, shadowy and cobwebbed but glimmering like summer, far up above the rafters. It was warm and spacious here, like childhood.

The train set occupied the entire length and breadth of the attic floor, which was so extensive that at its furthest point the small locomotives with their carriages and trucks were almost out of sight. You could hear them, though, ticking and purring along the shiny track, clicking over the points, rattling through the tunnels and making the miniature fir trees, which were made from real branches, shake as they passed.

There were two passenger trains and two goods trains. As Ernst watched, the Fat Man, wearing a crimson silk dressing gown and standing at a control board, switched the points on one section of track to take a goods train down a siding, where he halted it. From a shed in a forest clearing he brought out a fifth locomotive and rotated it on a turntable so that it was facing backwards. Then he reversed it along the track, deftly switching points to avoid the other trains, into the siding where it attached itself to the front of the engine of the stationary goods train. Pulled by two locomotives, the train careered at speed in loops and figures of eight, and two fir trees fell over with the vibration of its passage, and the Fat Man chuckled.

But there was more to the game. The Fat Man loved elaboration, and technology had put delightful toys into his hands. One of them was in his hand now. A flat rectangular box, in size like a small cigar box, with an aerial projecting from one corner of it. He seemed to gesture with the box, or point it. There was a whirring, somewhere in the attic, deeper than the whirring of the locomotives, and out of the shadows above the roof beams darted a tiny, brightly painted aeroplane, and flew low, swooping, above the goods train.

'Watch,' said the Fat Man.

The little aeroplane began to bomb the little train. A door in the belly of the fuselage popped open and from it dropped a red ball, then another and another. The red balls struck the side of the train and bounced off across the track, except for one which lodged right in the open top of a goods truck. The Fat Man was a good shot.

He looked at Ernst, expecting applause.

'Bravo,' said Ernst.

'Sometimes I use bombs filled with flour. The effect is quite dramatic. But it gets in the works. Drink?'

'Thank you.'

Drinks were set out on a table. Ernst poured himself a brandy. The aeroplane was – apart from the bomb-hatch – a perfect miniature replica of a Fokker D V II, and it was painted in the colours and markings of the Richthofen Squadron. Ernst did not know why this should cause him pain, but it did.

'Recognize it?' asked the Fat Man.

'Of course.'

He couldn't cavil: the markings were legitimate. The Fokker D V II had been flown by the squadron in the last months of the war; it had been flown by the Fat Man. Naturally Ernst flew it, too. By that time, Ernst recalled, the Richthofen Squadron had become the Richthofen Wing, comprising four squadrons. Had that been the Fat Man's doing? No, it was general policy, a tactic to hold back the encroaching disaster; yet Ernst could not help thinking of it as the Fat Man's first experiment in expansion, a stepping-stone to an empire.

'Here, you can have one, too,' said the Fat Man, and out of nowhere buzzed a second little aeroplane, an Albatros this time, which circled prettily above the circling trains.

'This is how you use the controls.'

Ernst put down his brandy and took charge of a remote-control box. After a minute or so he got the feel of the thing and could make his Albatros zoom and dive, spiral and roll gratifyingly.

'Will it loop?'

'Wouldn't advise it. I wrote one off that way. It went into the rafter. They're quite fragile, you know. Man in Kreuzberg makes them for me. Jew. I have to look after him, of course. We'll never get rid of them, they're too damn useful.'

Ernst concentrated on perfecting his handling of the Albatros. It would not do to have an accident with the Fat Man's toy. The Fat Man had called in his Fokker for re-arming and was now buzzing the trains preparatory to another attack.

For half an hour Ernst and the Fat Man made war on the Fat Man's train set. Then the Fat Man asked casually, 'Why did you want to see me?'

It had receded. The fatigue, the deadness. The sense of unreality. It came back.

'I want to resign.'

'I won't hear of it.'

'Chief —'

'Call me Hermann.'

He had never been able to. 'My health . . .' said Ernst.

'Then go into hospital. God knows, you look like a sick rabbit.'

'It is not just my health.'

'What is it, then? The production figures?'

Ernst brought his Albatros to a shaky touchdown between the tracks. The Fat Man watched cruelly.

'I'm in the wrong job,' said Ernst.

'Are you forgetting that I chose you for it?' The voice was hard. 'I didn't choose you because I thought you were particularly fitted to do it,' said the Fat Man, 'although I didn't expect you to make the shambles of it that you apparently have. The last report I got from Milch doesn't bear reading. I had to put it down after page two before it became bad for *my* health. What on earth possessed you to allocate a quota of aluminium per aircraft which is four times what a fighter weighs *fully equipped*?'

Ernst didn't know. He remembered signing something. There was so much corruption in the ministry and among its suppliers that, once he began to glimpse its extent, he realized there was no point in trying to do anything to stop it.

'You're welcome to inspect my personal accounts any time you like,' he said, lifelessly, and then there came before his mind's eye the Gold and Silver Rooms, and the booty of half a continent, in the house below.

'You're a fool,' observed the Fat Man.

'I don't deny it.'

'Mmm. You know, I like you, Ernst. Always have. Man of flesh and blood, like me. It's a pity you had to be such a damn fool.'

'May I ask, then, why you did appoint me to this post?'

'To neutralize Milch. I'd have thought anyone could see that. You on one side, Jeschonnek on the other . . . Perhaps *I* was the fool. Jeschonnek's starting to look a bit green about the gills, as well.' He laughed. 'Milch's tougher than the pair of you put together.'

'Probably.'

'Oh, for heaven's sake stand up to me, Ernst. I can't stand boot-licking.'

It was a belief of the Fat Man's – sincerely held, Ernst thought – that he liked his subordinates to challenge him. Several had done so and been posted to obscure or dangerous places.

'I'm not boot-licking,' said Ernst. 'I'm ill, I'm suffering from severe depression and I am not able to discharge my duties. I want to resign.'

'Well, you can't resign and that's that. Impossible. Out of the question. As for your being ill, I'm sorry to hear it and I'm telling you to take some leave and seek treatment.'

Ernst visualized Milch's well-directed industry in his absence, rationalizing, re-ordering, shining light in dark corners, ruthlessly amputating.

'Milch will run the department while I'm away?'

'Naturally.'

'Then I can't go on leave.'

'That's preposterous. If you resign, you'll hand over to him permanently!'

'After a few months there wouldn't be any place for me there.'

'Well, that's your problem. If you can't assert your authority within your own department, don't look for sympathy from me. In the wild' – his teeth flashed – 'this wouldn't happen. The weakening leader is challenged and killed by a fitter rival. But I can't afford to let things take their natural course. Nor can I grant your request. If I allow you to resign, Adolf will want to know why and the entire country will want to know why. When things start to come out, doubts will be cast on the ability of the air force, on the way the ministry is run, perhaps even on me personally. The whole damn house of cards will fall down. Oh, no. Take a rest, Ernst. Take as long as you need. There's a sanatorium near Wiesbaden: book yourself in and don't worry about the cost. All right?'

Ernst was silent. But the Fat Man read all he needed to know in Ernst's defeated face, and after a pause he turned his bulk again in the direction of the tiny trains that whirred tirelessly around the track he had designed for them.

CHAPTER SEVENTEEN

If you look at a Komet head-on as it stands on the runway, you are looking at a glider. You can tell it's a glider because it has no wheels. It jettisoned them just after take-off. What you are looking at, necessarily, is a Komet which has just landed. At no other time can you have this viewpoint. Most of the time you can hardly see the tiny aircraft for its towing ramp. (The Komet cannot taxi, it can only take off and fly.) And once a Komet stands, fuelled up and ready to go, on its runway, you will not be allowed anywhere near it.

From this angle, the shape is perfectly cruciform. There are the two short verticals of landing skid and tailfin, and the two long horizontals of the wings. There is not, as you would see on every other aeroplane in the world, a smaller horizontal behind the wings: the tailplane. The Komet has no tailplane. The wings are very broad, are swept back and taper so sharply that they almost form a triangle.

Because the Komet has no tailplane, it has no elevator: that is incorporated with the ailerons. The combined control surfaces are called elevons. It sounds tricky, but it isn't. That part isn't. The Komet is not difficult to fly, in the normal sense. And it loves to fly. When released, it hurls itself into the sky like . . .

Like a devil, I always thought. Hurling itself up out of the Pit.

Two things more to notice. One is the minuscule propeller on the nose, just big enough to beat an egg with. This has nothing to do with the propulsion of the aircraft, but drives the turbine just before take-off.

And lastly . . . Strange to leave this until last. It is the first thing anyone notices. And yet, talking about the Komet, we never referred to it: the fact that the test Komets were bright red, the colour of poppies, the colour of blood.

*

The letter telling me I had been selected for the Me 163 test team based at Regensburg took me by surprise. It was more than a year since Ernst had mentioned 'something top secret coming up on the fighter front', and asked if I would like to be considered for it. Since I had heard no more, I had assumed that the project, like so many others, had been cancelled.

Regensburg is in Bavaria. The journey took twenty-six hours. The train I intended to catch was rescheduled three times before it finally arrived, without a restaurant car. Trains had become rare and unpredictable things. It was said that most of them had been sent to the East, those that weren't used for ferrying Party bigwigs about.

We swayed and rattled through Germany, with long and unexplained stops between stations, for the rest of the day and all night. I slept in my seat and woke desperate for coffee, even the kind that didn't contain any coffee, but there wasn't even that. At Nuremberg I had to change. There was a two-hour wait. Periodically the station would fill with soldiers on the way to the Front or on their way home. At one point I saw – and thought I was dreaming – a squad of Russian prisoners of war, carrying shovels, and couldn't take my eyes from their stubble-grown, famished cheeks.

I arrived at the test base on the second afternoon of my journey. The first thing I saw as I got out of the car that had been sent to collect me was a blackish-purple cloud, which seemed to contain within it a dart of flame, hanging just above the runway. Then the roar reached me and rocked me back on my heels. Something small and brightly coloured shot at an incredible angle into the sky. Within seconds it had vanished.

I walked up some rough concrete steps into a makeshift-looking wooden building labelled 'Office'.

'Welcome,' said Dieter. 'We're delighted to have you with us.'

My eyes travelled round the spartan, spotlessly clean room. He had been sitting at a typewriter: he rose to shake my hand.

'Thank you,' I said. 'Who's in charge here?'

'I am,' said Dieter.

The Me 163, or Komet, had started life as an ultra-fast glider. The decision was then taken to fit it with a rocket motor, which would take it rapidly to an altitude from which it could glide back to earth.

A motor was developed, and the project was handed over to Messerschmitt for further refinement and testing.

Nothing like the Komet had been seen before. Launched on a detachable undercarriage, it would climb to twenty-five thousand feet in a minute. Flying it was like riding a cannon ball. Its operational ceiling and its maximum speed both far exceeded what the pilots could actually do with it. On an early flight a Komet approached so close to the speed of sound that it went briefly out of control. At that speed, the air starts to solidify. The pilot wasn't believed: it was faster than the instruments in the ministry wind tunnel could measure.

The Komet's fantastic speed was its *raison d'être*. It was expected to create havoc among enemy bomber formations, into the midst of which it would hurtle like an avenging Fury.

This was the creature we were asked to test. For all of us, it was the greatest challenge of our flying career. Naturally, it was reckoned a high privilege. But it didn't stop there. The Komet demanded everything. It wasn't the aeroplane that was being tested. It was the pilot.

The problem was the fuel. There were two different fuels, and since their composition was secret they were known by their code names of T-factor and C-factor. The C-factor was stored in the wings, the T-factor in small tanks on either side of the pilot's seat and a large tank behind it. Pumped by the turbine into the regulator and then piped into the combustion chamber, they produced, on meeting, the controlled explosion which propelled the Komet like a mad flea down the runway and flung it into the sky.

But the explosion was not always controlled. Rocket fuel, naturally, is volatile. This was so volatile that the tiniest quantity of it was apt to explode. Cataclysmic in their meeting, the fuels were just as lethal kept apart. The T-factor was liable to ignite on contact with any organic substance. Its feedpipes were made of a special artificial fibre, and it had to be kept in hermetically sealed aluminium containers since it caused steel and iron to disintegrate.

The C-factor, on the other hand, corroded aluminium and had to be kept in enamel or glass.

The risk at take-off was therefore very high. A fault in a feedline spelt death. A fireman always stood by with a running hose at take-off, because one good thing, the only good thing, about C-factor and

T-factor was that they were both neutralized by water. But no amount of water could stop an explosion after the first critical fraction of a second: the fireman was really there for something else. And when this fuel exploded, it did so with a ferocity that could not be imagined until you had seen it. There was nothing left. Nothing. A stain on the ground. Some distance away, a scrap of hair.

Landing was as hazardous. The Komet was supposed to have exhausted its fuel by the time it returned to earth, but often there were a few drops left in the tanks, and a few drops were all it took. Sometimes there would be quite a lot left because the engine had cut out prematurely. It would do this if bubbles formed in the fuel lines. After numerous fatalities a fuel cock was installed which allowed emergency release of unspent fuel, but it never really worked properly.

In view of all this, of the Komet's alarmingly high landing speed, and of the fact that it *had* to land on its runway because any unevenness in the ground greatly increased the chance of an explosion, it was, I thought, a shade too much that the landing skid, which was retracted in flight and had to be extended just before touchdown, sometimes refused to extend and dislocated the pilot's spinal column.

There is something I've left out. This is the worst thing. After all, if you're blown to bits it will upset the people who find the bits, but what will you know about it? But the other thing ... We never spoke of it.

The fuel is corrosive. It attacks anything organic. It works very quickly.

Because of this, you are provided with an acid-proof protective suit. Because of this, the fireman stands by with his hose of running water. But the fireman cannot be there the instant you land, when a spill of fuel from a ruptured feed pipe is all too likely, and he cannot be with you in the cockpit at twenty thousand feet as you watch the fuel pressure gauges and know that something is wrong. But you have your acid-proof suit. And it is useless. It is not acid-proof. Ask any pilot, ripped from the cockpit by someone's reckless heroism seconds after his flesh has begun to dissolve.

And this is the fuel which the manufacturers of the aeroplane, finding more space than they expected in the cockpit, have stored in two neat thirteen-gallon tanks alongside, respectively, your left and right thigh. In addition to the 200-gallon tank right behind your back.

I slipped my feet into the grips of the rudder pedals and ran my eyes over the Komet's instrument panel. Compared with some, it was simplicity itself. However, there were things in this cockpit you wouldn't see in any other aircraft, things which had more to do with plumbing than flight. Pressure gauges. Valves. Taps. Pipes. The motor was ten feet behind me, but I was encircled by its veins, pumps and arteries. And its smell, that implacable corrosive smell, hung in the air.

I flicked the switches on and ran through the pre-flight checks. I found myself doing them aloud, a thing I hadn't done since I was at Stettin. The sound of my voice steadied me.

I snuggled the radio headset on to my ears. Rudi, the senior ground crewman, lowered the canopy and gave it a double tap with his finger, for luck. I grinned at him, locked the canopy shut and saw him walk away.

I set the engine control lever, and switched on.

Everything happened at once. The turbine howled, fuel sprayed with an metallic 'crack' into the combustion chamber behind my seat, the aircraft shuddered like something possessed, and dimly I heard the roar.

My gaze on the dials, I moved the engine control lever to its furthest point.

The aeroplane seemed to waver, almost to float on its own shock waves. Then, like a dancer, like a swimmer pushing off from the poolside, it moved forward. It was bounding, skipping, the runway was suddenly flowing very fast towards and under me. As the wings snatched air, I brought the stick back.

The next few seconds were the most dangerous. If the fuel pressure fell, I would have to abort the flight. And within thirty feet I must jettison the wheels, or their presence would endanger the aircraft. But if I did this too soon, they would bounce back from the runway and perhaps strike a fuel tank.

I pulled the release lever.

As the wheels dropped away an invisible hand shoved me back in my seat and the Komet shot upward like a bullet. We were climbing at an angle that seemed nearly vertical. Within a matter of seconds the speed was over 500 mph.

I sat strapped in the seat of my rocket and looked at the heart of the sky into which I was rushing. So high, so deep. Like falling, I thought: this vertiginous ascent was like plunging into an abyss. So this was the Komet's secret.

The pressure change was telling on me. I felt the sweat gathering on my forehead, an ache in my skull, the air in my bowels and stomach expanding until it threatened to explode. We were trained for this, we were prepared, but nothing helped you through these first moments. I gritted my teeth, knowing it would pass, and then a few seconds later had something else to worry about as the bitter vapours from the engine began to irritate my eyes. After another half a minute they were streaming.

Time to level out. Level out while you can still see the altimeter.

The fuel should be nearly exhausted: it was enough for only four minutes' flight. I had to hope, as I pushed the stick forward, that I had judged correctly and would use up the last drops before I gained a dangerous amount of speed. The fuel gauges weren't critical enough. In this aircraft nothing worked as well as it ought to, and some things didn't work at all.

Yet what an aeroplane it was! What joy and terror were in its climb! With what superb impudence it hurled itself at Heaven!

Its fuel spent, it changed its nature. As I began the series of long, descending sweeps and spirals that would bring me back to earth, I felt the beauty of it come alive under my fingers, the cold beauty of a glider imagined among pure shapes and symbols, and I knew that I loved it, and would love it whatever it did to me.

It was difficult for me, when I was at Regensburg, to get to Berlin, and during that time I only saw Ernst once. In any case, for much of the time he wasn't in Berlin, or wasn't there for long. There were times when no one seemed to know where he was.

The inevitable collapse had come in the summer. Two days after his visit to Karinhall, he went into hospital. He was there for less than a week. In the course of that week Ploch, his second-in-command, sent him a telegram, on receipt of which Ernst discharged himself from the sanatorium and returned to Berlin. A month later, when Ernst was too ill even to keep up his sporadic attendances at the office and was staying at a hunting lodge belonging to von Greim, Milch dismissed Ploch from his desk at the ministry and sent him to the Eastern Front.

The gist of Ploch's telegram is not hard to guess. Once he thought Ernst was out of the way, Milch reorganized the department from top to bottom. Projects were weeded with a ruthless hand. So were people. Mass-production techniques were introduced. Industrialists were brought in to manage ministry offices.

By this time the full extent of the disaster which had taken place under Ernst's management was becoming clear. The worst things, the two unforgivable things, were the Me 210 and the Griffin.

The Me 210 was the fighter that Professor Messerschmitt had decided to redesign, and of which Ernst had ordered a thousand without waiting for it to fly. The plane went straight into full production. As soon as the test pilots began to fly the models coming out of the factories, terrible things started to happen.

Aeroplanes spun out of control, or sideslipped and dived into the ground. The undercarriage collapsed. Messerschmitt refused to accept that there was anything wrong with the plane. But the managers of the plants where the aircraft were to be assembled knew it, and stopped the production lines. All around the country Me 210s stood about half finished, while rusting wings, tail sections and engines piled up for hundreds more.

The Griffin, our long-awaited strategic bomber, was now also in production. There were two fit for service.

There had been rumours about the Griffin for a long time. It was said that on some aircraft the wings had buckled. An even grimmer fault was reported. On a perfectly routine flight, a Griffin would suddenly blaze like a firework. The engines had caught fire again.

I heard stories about Griffins blazing up and falling out of the sky. I asked Ernst. He wouldn't tell me. It was too bad to talk about. It was one of the ground staff at Rechlin who told me. He was present in the hangar when the Fat Man, hearing that a Griffin was undergoing tests at Rechlin, fulfilled his threat to Ernst and went to see it.

The Fat Man had never had sight of this aircraft before, or even of the drawings. When he was ushered into the hangar, followed by a flustered retinue of managers, officials and engineers, he came to a dead halt just inside the door while his sharp eyes roved indignantly along the wings.

'It is supposed to have *four engines*!' he bellowed.

'It does, Reich Marshal, it does!' Heinkel, dragged from his office by a panic-stricken phone call, almost fell over his feet to explain. 'They are *coupled*.'

'What the devil does that mean? Two engines drive one propeller?'

'Exactly, sir, yes.'

'Damn silly idea. No wonder it overheats. How d'you get at the engines?'

'Reich Marshal?'

'How d'you service them? How do you change a sparking plug on them? God in heaven, man, this aircraft has to be *used*!'

At which a pallor descended on those present who knew anything about the Griffin, because in fact it was not possible to take out a sparking plug without stripping down the entire engine. Nor was that the only problem. Connecting rods broke and punched holes in the crankcase. The coupling of the engines had involved inverting them, which meant that fuel dripped from carburettors on to red-hot manifolds. These things accounted for the Griffin's incendiary habit. And because everything was jammed tight against everything else, it was impossible to put in fire walls.

'Why,' howled the Fat Man to his ashen-faced subordinates when enough of this awful truth had been extracted from them, 'do the engines have to be coupled?'

The answer was in mathematics. He cut it short.

'In plain language, it reduces drag on the wings. Why is it so important to reduce drag on the wings?'

Heinkel looked surprised. 'But, Reich Marshal, if it is to dive-bomb . . .'

'If it is to what?'

'To dive-bomb, Reich Marshal.'

'Who said it had to dive-bomb? I wanted a conventional four-engined bomber. Are you telling me that all this hocus-pocus with coupled engines is because it is supposed to *dive-bomb*?'

He stared round at them, rage mottling his heavy face, then back again at the majestic, useless aeroplane.

My relations with Dieter were polite and cordial. In the circumstances, of course, they had to be. I was relieved to find that there did not seem to be tension between us. At the same time, I realized that we spent very little time in each other's company. If we saw more of each other, I thought, it might be a different story.

One evening when I had been at Regensburg for several weeks, he invited me to have a drink with him in a local inn.

'Well,' he said as we sat in the high-backed settle by the fire, 'what do you think of our Komet now?'

'The Devil's sledge,' I murmured ruminatively. The Komet had a variety of pet names among the pilots: most of them made some reference to the diabolic.

'I don't like to hear it called that,' said Dieter seriously. 'It's an unforgiving aircraft, yes. But to give it a name like that is irresponsible, I think.'

'Irresponsible?'

'It's bad for morale.'

I told myself that he had always been rather humourless.

'It matters what things are called,' he said, apparently reading levity in my expression. 'Morale is all-important on a project like this.' He paused. 'But then, perhaps you wouldn't understand that.'

'What is that supposed to mean?'

'Women think differently from men,' he said.

'The aeroplanes don't seem to notice a difference.'

He took a pull at his beer. 'All right,' he said at last. 'You're a good pilot, nobody's ever said you weren't. But women do think differently, and frankly I believe that this is not a suitable project for you to be employed on.'

I knew then that a quarrel was unavoidable. I said, 'Why on earth not?'

'It's not a suitable aeroplane for a woman to fly.'

'What rubbish! What does "suitable" mean? I *can* fly it! What else matters?'

I saw that I had hit the nail on the head: I could fly it, and that was the trouble.

'Dieter,' I said, 'I've had to put up with this sort of thing ever since I started flying, and I'm about sick of it.'

He said primly, 'I don't know what else you can have expected.'

'I expected rather better of you!' But then, I thought, why should I?

It seemed he agreed with me. 'Why?' he said. His anger had surfaced. 'Everything you do, every idea you express, runs directly contrary to the National Socialist idea of womanhood.'

'Really?'

It was a mistake to mock him: he couldn't deal with it.

'You have no respect!' he shouted. The inn went quiet and I felt people's eyes on us. He felt them, too, and calmed down, reddening.

'If I had respect for all the things I was supposed to have respect for, I'd be sitting at home making potato salad and blackout curtains.'

'Perhaps it would be better if you were,' he said. 'Your elevation into some sort of heroine by the newspapers has given false ideas to women all over the Reich, who think they ought to be able to fly aeroplanes and drive trucks and work in industry instead of being at home to support their husbands and look after their children.'

I said, 'There's a shortage of labour because all the men have been called up for the Front. If there weren't women in the factories, the factories would close down.'

'It's not true,' he said. 'That's a lie being put about by anti-social elements. There are thousands more women out at work than there need be, and it's a very bad thing for the country. And I blame – '

I thought he was going to say he blamed me, and I laughed.

'Your frivolity in political matters is deplorable,' he said.

He drank his beer. He said nothing for a time. Neither did I. Then he began talking about morale again. He seemed to think it was bad for morale to have a woman on the Komet team. I demanded to know in what way it was bad.

He said, 'Your presence confuses the men. It . . . saps something.'

'Have standards fallen since I arrived?'

'The atmosphere has changed. There a softening. Something's gone, something abrasive. And it worries me.'

'I don't understand. What is this abrasiveness useful for?'

'If you were a man you wouldn't need to ask,' said Dieter. He seemed to think this was sufficient reply.

I had to say, after a time, that I was not a man and would like an answer.

'It hardens us,' he said. 'That's what it's for. It makes us hard to ourselves and hard to each other, and if we're going to fly the Me 163 day after day, hard is what we need to be. Human life doesn't matter. National Socialism says so, and it's the truth. But it's difficult to remember. The presence of a woman on the airfield makes it that much more difficult.'

'I see.'

'There's nothing I can do about it,' said Dieter. 'I didn't make the appointments to the team. I wish you weren't on it, but without a very good reason I can't remove you.' He paused, tracing the beer-mug's pattern with his finger. 'And the fact that, in spite of everything, I still care about you makes the situation worse. If you're going to test-fly, this is the last aeroplane I'd want you to be assigned to.'

It happened two days later.

I was in the recreation room playing table tennis with Heinz. Heinz had joined the test team the same day as I had, and we had trained together. We played a lot of table tennis.

In the fourth game we had a prolonged rally. The bluish-white ball skimmed over and over the net, like a glider. I imagined a glider covered in that taut translucent skin.

There was a roar and the building shook. A vase of wild grasses fell off the mantelpiece and broke. The table tennis ball bounced three times on the spot where Heinz had hit it into the net, and finally rolled to the edge of the board and fell off.

Heinz and I laid our bats on the table and made for the door. By the time we reached the corridor we were running.

Outside, the air had changed. It was difficult to breathe and it hurt the lungs, and at the back of its stinging foulness was a taste to make you retch. It tasted of blood.

Over the runway hung a thick, viscous cloud of clotted purple-black. It clung to itself, globular and heavy, like a cloud of flies above a carcass.

Below it was nothing. A scrap of metal, about two feet long, twisted out of recognition. A stain on the ground.

Dieter spoke, his voice stretched and dry. 'Who was preparing for take-off?'

'Düschen, sir.'

Düschen was a squadron leader who had been posted to the base from the Eastern Front. He had arrived eight days previously, grumbling about being taken out of the fighting.

On either side of the runway was a grassy field. The grass was kept cut with a scythe. It was thick, lush grass, even in autumn. As I looked at it, its lushness grew obscene.

We walked into the grass to search. We found some objects which it would later be possible to put into a coffin. I found something. I do not want to think about what it was.

Dieter summoned me to his office that afternoon.

He said, 'I don't want you to carry out any more sharp flights.'

By 'sharp' flights was meant fuelled flights. He was telling me I could only fly the Komet as a glider. Flights were often made in it that way because it still needed testing in that capacity.

'May I ask why not?'

'I would have thought that after what happened this morning you wouldn't need to ask.'

'Is the whole team suspended from sharp flights?'

'No, of course not. Only you.'

'Why? What have I done?'

'Nothing. I just don't want you to fly it fuelled up. The risks are too great. I simply can't take the responsibility of anything happening to you.'

'You're no more responsible for me than you are for any other pilot on this base.'

'Nevertheless – '

'Are you questioning my competence?'

'No.'

'Then how dare you single me out like this?'

'How dare *I*? I am the commander of this test station and I will make what arrangements I choose!'

'You aren't fit to be the commander,' I said between my teeth, and he jerked his head as if I'd struck him. His eyes were wide with shock, and I saw in them hatred, at last acknowledged.

He said, 'If I had it in my power I'd remove you from the team, but you were wished on me from above and I have to put up with you.'

'My commiserations.'

'I have enough on my hands running a station on which the test aircraft explodes whenever it feels like it, without the additional problem of a woman on the base, and a woman, moreover, who is habitually insubordinate.'

'That's really the problem, isn't it? You can't get it into your head that I'm not a woman, I'm a *pilot*!'

'Don't be ridiculous, of course you're a woman!'

'On this base, on any airbase, I'm a pilot. That is what you've never been able to understand. Always going on about your cherished feelings for me, when all I want is to be allowed to get on with my job. Or rather, what you *say* your feelings are, which in fact is not what they are at all.'

'What would you know about feelings?' he said. 'You have none.' His lips had tightened to a bitter line.

'Perhaps. Dieter, you aren't the person to arouse them.'

'Have you ever cared for anyone? Cold, hard and ambitious, that's what you are.'

'I thought hardness was a requirement for being on this team. You made me quite a speech about it the other evening.'

'In a woman it's unsuitable. Everything about you is unsuitable.'

'Some people might consider that your attitude towards me was unsuitable.'

'You don't even dress properly when you're off the base! You go into town looking like a . . . like a mechanic. It shames the whole unit.'

'I would have thought the unit had more important things to be ashamed of. Like the character defects of its leader.'

There was silence for a few moments. We rested, facing each other across his bare wooden desk.

Then I said, 'I was appointed to this team to fly on the same terms as every other pilot. I intend to take this up with the ministry.'

'And just whom do you intend to run to at the ministry?'

'I shall speak to General Udet.' It seemed my only recourse.

236

The effect on Dieter was dramatic. His face twisted. He hissed. 'I wondered when you'd bring your boyfriend into this.'

'Make up your mind, Dieter.'

'He's finished, your General Udet. He's on the scrapheap. He can't help you.'

I turned and walked to the door.

Dieter's arm shot up in the salute. 'Heil Hitler!' he crowed.

I went out and closed the door behind me.

Where are we?

I don't recognize the feel of this land. This land feels ominous. Below us I see wrecked farmhouses and burnt villages. We fly over a hamlet and I see what looks like a row of bodies lying in a field.

The general leans forward to shout in my ear. I can't hear the words, but the message is plain. Get us out of here.

I can guess where we are. There is a strong headwind blowing, and as we try to make our way westward it has blown us off course. We are too far east. Nearer Stettin than Lübeck, north instead of north-west of Berlin. We are right over the area into which the Red Army is pouring, hellbent on its demarcation line.

Then I cross a wooded rise and there it is. I catch my breath with the suddenness. A Russian spearhead, an armoured column, headed by tanks, camouflaged with netting and branches, is moving fast down the wide, straight, dusty road.

I fly directly across the middle of them: I have no choice. They are as surprised to see me as I am to see them, and react slowly. Machine guns spit as the column falls behind me, and the Bücker trembles and dips. I go into a climbing turn as steep as the aircraft will manage, relieved that it answers to the controls. When I have levelled out at a little under a thousand feet, I turn my head to check whether there is damage to the tail section, and as I do so my eye is caught and held by an outlandish sight.

Behind the brutal spearhead, and spread out over the surrounding fields, from which it has the air of having sprung, moves an army from the Middle Ages. Foot-soldiers in flapping greatcoats push carts piled high with objects. Others ride ponies, or walk beside wagons pulled by oxen, also heaped high with goods. On the carts are bedding, cooking stoves, bicycles, saucepans and chairs. Among these ambling Red Army soldiers, a few vehicles bump along – looted civilian cars, a motorbike and sidecar.

The cars and motorbike are not being driven. They, like the carts, are pulled by oxen.

The whole advancing tide drives in front of it an assortment of cattle, sheep, pigs, goats and chickens, and more chickens hang in bunches by their feet from the saddle girths of ponies and the wooden sides of carts.

Over this army hangs a yellowish halo of light, where the sun's glare, deflected downwards by the leaden cloud, is filtered through the haze of dust thrown up the armoured column.

It was a dank November night when I went to see Ernst. As I opened the gate, raindrops showered on me from the wrought-iron arch. I picked my way over the slippery paving stones, which in the light of my shaded torch shone greenish, to the shrouded, silent house. All I could hear as I stood on the steps was the drip of moisture from the eaves, and my own breathing.

I rang the bell. It jangled, setting my nerves on edge. After an interval the door was opened, a laborious process involving much rattling of locks, and Ernst's manservant, Albert, peered at me from the gloom. He seemed to take a while to recognize me, although I had come to Ernst's uncomfortable mansion several times.

'Come in, Flight Captain, I'm sorry, it's the light. The general is in the drawing room.' He lowered his voice. 'You'll find a change in him.'

Ernst looked up as I entered, and at once all thought of involving him in my dispute with Dieter vanished from my mind. There was indeed a change in him. His eyes had gone dark, like shot-out search-lights.

He was sitting on the carpet in front of the coal fire. A pack of playing cards was spread out, face down, in front of him. A bottle of brandy and a glass stood at his elbow. The cat dozed by the fender, rapping the tip of its tail on the cards.

'Well, hello!' exclaimed Ernst with ghastly joviality, 'Would you like a drink?'

'No thanks. I just need to get warm.' I sat in the armchair nearest the fire and held out my hands to the blaze.

'I'm reading my fortune,' he said. 'My mother was a gypsy, you know.'

His mother had not been a gypsy at all. It was a strange thing to say. It was not courting disaster quite as surely as saying that your mother was a Jew, but it was on the way.

'What's in the cards?'

'I'm going to be rich, but give all my money away. I'm going to be famous, but it will be my downfall. I'm going to be loved, but never for very long or by anyone with the smallest amount of discrimination.'

'Ernst . . .' This was painful. 'You have a lot of friends, and they are very discriminating.'

'Where are they, then? They don't come to see me. When did you last come to see me?'

'I'm sorry. I'm at Regensburg. It's difficult.'

'Ploch came to see me,' he said, pushing the cards around with his finger, 'but I wish he hadn't.'

'Why?'

Ernst didn't answer. He stared into the fire. My gaze followed his, and was held there. Beneath the darting flames glowed the pale purity of the fire's heart. Its beauty was so alien, and so dangerous, that I longed to touch it. Away from that intolerable intensity flickered crumbling red caverns, and small fields of downy ash. Could anything live in fire? Salamander, phoenix. I wished that I could live in fire.

'You can see anything in a fire,' said Ernst. 'Anything you want to see.'

'Yes.'

'What do you see?'

'Salamanders.'

He smiled. 'Are they pretty?'

'Lovely.'

'What it is to be at peace with oneself. One looks into a fire and sees salamanders.'

'What do you see?'

'Hell,' he said.

He laughed, as I sat rigid, and poured himself a drink.

'I'm sorry,' he then said, 'I haven't offered you anything. How unforgivable.'

'Yes, you have.'

He got to his feet. He looked exhausted. 'What would you like? No use offering you brandy. Some coffee? Cocoa? Someone's given me a tin of cocoa: it's Dutch, I haven't the faintest idea what to do with it. But I'm told it's good on a cold evening.'

'Thank you, I'd like some cocoa.'

He rang for Albert, and gave instructions for a mug of cocoa to be brought.

'I can't get used to having servants,' he said. 'They make my flesh creep. They're always there.'

'I suppose that's the point of having them.'

'What a hideous place the world is,' he said, and turned over a card, and then another, and then shuffled the whole pack together and started spreading the cards face down over the carpet again.

'What is the matter, Ernst?'

'I can't tell you,' he said.

After Albert had brought the cocoa, Ernst lit a cigar and grinned at me, a strange lopsided grin as if only half of him wanted to do it and the other half wanted to do the opposite.

'You're looking at the last of the flying clowns,' he said. ' "Professor" was putting it too high. I was never more than the dunce. I could fly, though. Couldn't I?'

'You can still fly, Ernst.'

'Shot down,' he said. 'I'm finished.'

I didn't know what to say to him. 'You need a rest, that's all,' I said.

He shook his head fiercely. I couldn't understand what was consuming him. I couldn't understand his need to despair.

'There's no way back,' he said. 'There's no way back. There can never be any way back from this.'

I assumed he was talking about himself, his predicament. I said stupidly, 'That isn't true. In a few months you'll be on top of things again.' Not that I believed it. But how can you acquiesce in someone's statement that he is finished?

'Oh God,' he said hopelessly, 'you just tell lies like all the rest of them.'

It silenced me. I had to wait for him to speak again. The fire sighed and settled. The cat muttered in its sleep, and rapped its tail on the cards.

240

When he was ready, Ernst began to talk.

'I thought it was a game,' he said. 'I thought, what does it matter if I put on a uniform, I can always take it off again. But you can't, it sticks to the skin. It becomes the skin. Do you know that?' He looked at me, and his gaze was terrible. 'There are people whose uniform has become their skin. And I thought, I will create an aeroplane because it is an aeroplane that needs to be built; and if it happens to be a bomber, well, that doesn't matter. I never thought about what a bomber was. I thought it was all a game, and in time it would stop and we would all go home. But we're never going home. And it isn't a game, it's a nightmare.'

He drained his brandy, poured himself another one and turned the glass slowly in his hands.

'Ploch came to see me,' he said. 'He was on leave from the Front. He came to see how I was. He didn't look too wonderful himself. We had a drink. I got maudlin: I started talking about the last war and how much simpler it was, how much clearer, to be in the cockpit of a fighter plane; how you knew what you had to do and why you had to do it. I said that things were now so bad with me that that was all I could think of: to go on a flight over enemy territory and find . . . some honourable solution. And Ploch said . . . Ploch said . . .' Ernst frowned down at the carpet, frowned intently. 'He said, "War as you knew it no longer exists."'

'What did he mean by that?' I asked.

So Ernst told me. He told me what Ploch had said. I listened without moving as Ernst spoke quietly to me about horrors which are beyond the mind's grasp. He spoke of people killed like cattle, systematically and not in anger, because they were of the wrong racial stock. He spoke of ravines used as graves, of the landscape itself become a vast cemetery, of the meaning of individual death lost in multitudes. He spoke of bulldozers levelling and re-levelling the ground because the dead, in their putrefying hosts, would not lie down. He spoke of the men who had to do this work, some of whom were Himmler's men but some were from the regular fighting forces. He said it had been made clear to him by Ploch that this was not some monstrous aberration from the plan. This was the plan.

I heard him out, with my brain locked.

There was a long silence.

Ernst stood up. 'Forgive me, if you can, for telling you that,' he said.

I found I could not speak.

'Time to go,' said Ernst, and kissed me on the forehead.

CHAPTER EIGHTEEN

What do you do with information you cannot process, information which paralyses whatever it comes into contact with? You do with it what your body does with poison. You throw it out.

I threw out everything Ernst had told me in the last hour I spent with him. It wasn't difficult: it required only a single, cleansing act. What Ernst had told me wasn't true because it *could not* be true. Beside that impossibility, other impossibilities – the impossibility of Ernst's having invented it, of Ploch's having invented it, of my having imagined it – were all as nothing.

I went back to Regensburg.

I was feeling rather unwell. Perhaps it was stress: there seemed to be a permanent tension in my stomach. It wasn't only Ernst who needed a rest, I thought.

I had done nothing to help him. But then, what could I do?

I got on with my work.

I would have liked to defy Dieter's order that I should not fly the Komet fuelled-up, but that unfortunately was out of the question. Not only would it have cost me my place on the team, but it was impracticable because I could not take off without the help of the ground crew. I resigned myself to being a glider pilot again. I had a full schedule of flights. There was still a lot of testing to be done on the Komet which had nothing to do with its rocket motor. Numerous problems, some quite intractable, resulted from the aircraft's high gliding speed. After a fast turn, for instance, the compasses spun so much they were unusable for several minutes.

'Let's be honest,' said Heinz as we ate together in the pilots' mess, 'the thing's a death trap.'

'Yellow, are you?' grunted Max. He had just joined the team as a replacement for Düschen. He was nervous and aggressive and wanted to prove himself.

'Of course I am,' laughed Heinz. 'Every time I get into that crate my guts turn to jelly.'

Max sneered. But Heinz was eating his lunch, and Max wasn't.

'My cockpit filled with steam yesterday,' mused Heinz. 'At five thousand feet. Couldn't see a damned thing. Bit much, really.'

'The Devil's kettle,' I suggested, and we both laughed, to the disgust of Max.

'I'd give anything,' said Max, when Heinz and I had finished laughing, 'to fly this plane in combat.'

'You would, would you?' said Heinz tolerantly.

'Think what it could do on the Eastern Front!'

'The main problem on the Front,' remarked Heinz, 'is snow.'

'That's a rumour!'

'It's true.' Heinz laid down his knife and fork. He never walked away from an argument. 'I've got a brother out there,' he said. 'The war's ground to a halt. The gun turrets jam, the diesel's frozen in the trucks.'

Max had gone red to his hairline. He said, 'I'm amazed to hear such unpatriotic talk on a base of this kind.'

Heinz said, 'If you had anything between your ears but a wind tunnel – '

I left them to it. I lay on my bed and read *Twenty Thousand Leagues under the Sea*. The base library was not wide in its scope: it was Jules Verne, the Westerns of Karl May (said to be Hitler's favourite author), or SA marching songs. After half an hour I put on my boots, went outside and climbed into my Komet.

An Me 110 towed me up. The big wheels of the Komet gave it a slight bounce on the concrete. Approaching thirty feet, I released the catch that held the undercarriage, and the Komet gave a little jump of pleasure and rose into its element.

Ten minutes later I was dropping the tow cable and letting the nose fall to the gliding position. She settled at once into a long, clean sweep like a hawk's. The tailless body on its broad, backswept wings seemed made to fly for ever. Turning, sweeping, rolling, looping, I would not have been surprised to find I could do impossible things in this aeroplane, like flying backwards, because this turbulent red creature which flew like a hawk and climbed like a cannonball had also the properties of a hummingbird. Together we soared, my Komet and I, testing the nature of flesh, metal and air; and as we flew lower I saw, in a burst of sunlight, our strange shadow scud across the fields.

I made my final turn and, as I did so, something jumped at my attention. I blocked it out, because landing required one to concentrate fully. Once down, with the canopy released and Rudi welcoming me with his ragged smile on to the runway, I turned my head to look again. I had been right. The flag inside the entrance gate was flying at half-mast.

Dieter called me to his office as soon as I reached the reporting room. He looked solemn.

'I have some bad news for you,' he said. 'In the circumstances, I regret saying what I did the other day. Perhaps you would like to sit down.'

Ernst.

He takes the pistol from its drawer. He loads it, round by round. How many times has he done this, and emptied it again? And why this pistol? He has many newer and more convenient: magazine-loading, automatic. But this revolver went through the last war with him, strapped against his thigh.

War as you knew it . . .

He is sitting on the bed, his big oak bed which was the first thing he bought when that war ended, although he had no money and no job, because he considered a good bed, a good suit and a few bottles of good wine a man's indispensable base in life. It has seen many adventures with him, this bed: it has been a good friend. Recently he has slept alone. Inge can't cope with his moods. His state of mind frightens her. He can't talk about it.

There isn't anyone he can talk to. Once he was surrounded by friends. Or he thought he was. Now they keep away. He has the plague.

He rotates the cylinder with his finger. Six rounds. Why six? One will suffice. He doesn't usually miss his target: he isn't going to miss now. He could have put in one round and turned it into the firing chamber. Why has he put in six?

245

To make the mathematics inescapable.

He holds the grip of the pistol lightly in his right hand, and rests the barrel on the fingers of his left. The metal is cold.

When he's fired it, it will be warm, and there will be a tang of something acrid in the air. But he will not be able to smell it.

He lays the gun carefully on the unmade, chaotic bed, and walks from the bedroom to the top of the stairs. He listens. The house appears completely silent. It is just after four in the morning. Albert sleeps at the other end of the house. He snores heavily. Ernst knows this, having once tiptoed down the corridor to listen. But it is a large house and several heavy doors are at present between Ernst and Albert.

Albert will look after the cat.

Downstairs, the cat sleeps in the armchair, the clock ticks and the embers of the fire shift downwards. Ernst feels an impulse to go down the stairs and look at these things – the cat in the armchair, the clock on the mantelpiece, the still-warm ashes of the fire. He doesn't. It is sentimentality. These things can't help him. All they can do is cling round his ankles and get in the way of his resolution.

How many times has he been here, peering into the abyss? But this time it is different. This time he has not made his own way here to reconnoitre the terrain and see if in the darkness, which of course is impenetrable, he can perhaps glimpse a familiar shape. This time, something has brought him here. This is the only place for him to be.

He has made a will. It lies, scrawled on a sheet of air-ministry paper, on the table of the drawing room, held down by a brass candlestick which he found in the pantry. It says, this will, that anybody who comes to the house can take anything they like. He wonders who will take the bed.

They will have to give him a state funeral. They will tell some lie or other.

It's cold. Ernst clutches his arms around himself, the need to die temporarily forgotten in the need to be warm. He is in his shirt, trousers and waistcoat. He took off his jacket three hours ago to go to bed, and then realized that the time for that was over.

He goes back to the bedroom and puts his jacket on, and then stands there, motionless.

What next?

There is nothing next.

How strange, this feeling that nothing comes next. That this is the very edge of the world. In the blinding light or darkness that streams over that edge, everything shrinks and recedes.

The edge dizzies him. He retreats from it, and goes and sits on the bed.

The rumpled bedclothes – did he get into bed? with his clothes on? he can't remember – bring him back to a consciousness of how concrete is the failure of his life. The dented pillows and tormented sheet fill him with self-pity, so that his eyes overflow; then disgust with himself returns and he gets up and begins to walk back and forth across the floor. His foot crunches on something: a piece of charcoal once used for drawing. It must have fallen out of a pocket, he hasn't drawn anything for months. He picks it up and tosses it on the bed.

In the opened wardrobe his uniform hangs like a spectre. He sees again Ploch, bleak-visaged, in that same uniform, putting on his gloves in the room below in a silence which neither of them could break.

There is nothing ahead of him and no way back. This is the place. And now he is afraid.

Perhaps someone can save him from this. Perhaps, even, there is someone he should give a chance to save him from this.

He picks up the telephone and dials Inge's number.

He hears the phone ringing in her flat, three miles away. It rings for a long time. He waits. She will be asleep.

The phone rings and rings, and is not answered.

He remembers that she is somewhere visiting relatives. He replaces the receiver.

Such isolation.

He has been used. In what a cold game of chess has the Fat Man moved him here and there! And others have used him. Friends have spent his money and turned their backs on him. Once, women wanted him for his glamour. Now he has none left.

He reaches for the piece of charcoal. With it, on the wall above the bed, Ernst writes his farewell message to the world.

He writes two names: the Fat Man's and Milch's. Below them he

draws a line. Then underneath the line he writes, in staring capitals:
I HAVE BEEN BETRAYED.

He stands back. He is breathing heavily. He looks at what he has written on the wall and feels drained, drained of everything.

An incident in the Great War comes back to him. It was his first aerial combat and he had the quarry in his sights. A French Spad. He had his thumb on the firing button and he couldn't fire. He was afraid to. The Spad got away. He told no one and for three days hugged his misery to himself. Then he was sent up again. Emerging from cloud, alone, he found himself above a formation of twenty-four French bombers. He selected one and dived on it, firing. It went down.

He was no hero. He simply knew that if he didn't do it, he would have to kill himself.

That blinding darkness.

Time to go.

Ernst lies down on the bed. He picks up the gun, places the muzzle where it has to go, and pulls the trigger.

Rudi settled me into the cockpit, checking the straps on the harness with his knobby fingers. He closed my canopy and tapped it for luck. I locked it, and signalled ready for launch.

We moved forward over the patched concrete. The wheels of the Me 110 lifted, and on either side of me the thick, yellowing grass dropped away.

Moments later, the radio crackled and went dead.

I cursed. It wasn't the first time it had happened. The radios were like everything else in this the-pilots-will-sort-it-out aeroplane.

At between twenty-five and thirty feet, I pulled the lever to release the wheels.

Something was wrong with it. It felt stiff and wouldn't move the whole way. I pulled it again, as hard as I could. Still it didn't work properly.

A few seconds later the aircraft started to vibrate. A shudder passed through it from nose to tail, followed by a series of vertical tremors which seemed to originate from under my seat.

The undercarriage had not dropped, and was interfering with the airflow.

Ahead of me the co-pilot of the tow plane made urgent signals from the rear of the cockpit. Presumably they had tried, and failed, to contact me by radio.

Shuddering and trembling, the Komet allowed itself to be towed to a thousand feet. It seemed to be trying to shake itself to pieces. How I loathed that undercarriage, clumsy affair with its childishly big wheels. In my imagination it had grown enormous and parasitical, it was as large as the Komet itself.

The tow plane banked gently to the right and began a wide circuit. The Komet's control surfaces reacted unpleasantly to this further disruption of the airflow. The stick seemed to have a massive weight behind it. The rudder pedals kicked angrily under my feet. The Komet was a hawk no longer. This was like flying a mattress in a high, wind.

Below me on the airfield fire engines and ambulances were moving about. Very lights had been sent up. Poor Düschen, I thought, had never got this much attention.

I tried the release lever again, without result. I had now tried it at least a dozen times.

Once, twice, we circled the airfield. The co-pilot of the Me 110 stared beseechingly at me from the rear of the cockpit, waiting to see me drop the tow cable. I shook my head, unable to do more because I dared not take my hands from the control stick. I wanted to be towed up higher, so I would have as much height as possible in which to rid myself of this encumbrance.

Finally they realized what I wanted. The engine note of the Me 110 deepened, and it began to climb. Shuddering like a beast at the slaughterhouse, the Komet laboured after it. The trouble with something going wrong at the beginning of a flight, I reflected, was that it gave you the entire flight to think about what was likely to happen at the end of it.

At ten thousand feet I cast off the tow and began the long descent. I would not get another chance. Every second had to be used, because every second brought me nearer to the height at which I must land.

I used every second. I coaxed and hammered the release lever until my hand was numb. I tried working the lever in conjunction with carrying out certain manoeuvres which might jerk the undercarriage loose. This was very risky, and the undercarriage remained as firmly fixed as ever.

Inexorably, I lost height.

At four thousand feet I considered my options. There was still one thing I could do. The parachute was underneath me on the seat. I could bale out. I was probably expected to. Our instructions on the point were that test pilots mattered more than aeroplanes.

On the other hand, if there was a chance of bringing this aeroplane down safely, any self-respecting pilot would try to do so.

How big does the chance have to be?

What was most likely to happen was that as I came in to land the airflow around the elevons would become so chaotic that I would finally and irrevocably lose control. If I didn't, if I somehow managed to fight the aeroplane down to the runway in a level attitude, I would still be going too fast – because of the extra weight – and committed to landing on an undercarriage which was not designed to take the shock of landing and which would probably choose that moment to detach itself. In other words, a crash of some kind was inevitable.

But it might not be that serious. And at all events, the tanks were empty so the aircraft could not explode.

Three thousand feet. On the airfield they were staring upwards.

For the next minute or so, I applied myself systematically to trying the lever. At some point it *must* give. All I needed was that fraction of a second when metal shifted a fraction of an inch.

It didn't shift even slightly.

Two thousand feet. How long this was taking. I tried the lever once more, and then decided to abandon the attempt because there were more important things to be done.

Suddenly I wanted to get it over with.

I checked that the sky was clear all round me. I was on a wide loop, which was bringing me into a tighter circle which would be my last circuit of the airfield. The Komet was still shuddering and leaping like a dying fish but by now I was used to that, and I was concentrating on losing height at the rate which would bring me down to six hundred feet just before I crossed the southern perimeter fence of the airfield.

Flying downwind she is fairly steady. I get a glimpse of the staring faces. A ninety-degree turn on to base leg: the control surfaces don't like it, the plane jumps and skids and tries to slip away from me, but I hold it, icy and sweating with the effort of concentration, and now everything is happening very fast. I have run out of time, I have to make my final turn and the perimeter fence is racing towards me and I am *too high* because the speed is too fast, and the only way to lose height quickly enough is to put the wing down and sideslip, so I put the control stick, which is bucking like a mule, to the left and kick the left rudder and she goes down, but she is going down in a horrible lurching movement which, when I try to stop it by returning the stick to centre, becomes uncontrollable, and now there is no air beneath the wings or at least none that's any use to me because the control surfaces have become insane and the stick thrashes uselessly in my hands.

Here it comes.

Brown earth, shockingly close.

I will not die.

CHAPTER NINETEEN

General, old soldier with a shattered foot still waging a lost war.

Which war is it? Which war do you tell yourself, at this moment, that it is? Is it the war Ernst thought it was, until Ploch told him otherwise?

But you were there, you knew. I know you knew.

You, too, would have liked to go on a flight over enemy territory and find some honourable solution. And until five days ago, who knows, you might have managed it. But you can't fly a plane with a shattered foot, and I am not interested in heroics.

Poor Ernst. Everybody used him, including you. The Fat Man wanted him in the air force to please Adolf; you got him into the air force to please the Fat Man. Did you really care what happened to him?

It was you who got his bed. I couldn't believe that anyone could bear to have it. But you asked for it, it seems.

Perhaps a good bed is not to be sneezed at.

You went to his funeral. He got the full treatment. The flag-draped coffin, the march. Every holder of the Knight's Cross was there. He had been killed, it was announced, testing a new weapon.

(They kept the newspapers for me.)

The Fat Man, in dove-grey uniform and with gold spurs on his boots, gave the funeral oration.

'I have lost my best friend,' he said.

I was in hospital for five months after the crash. The Komet had hit a ploughed field at 150 mph, bounced, lost one of its wheels and turned over. Most of my injuries were to the head.

A surgeon rebuilt my face. The pain ... what is the point in remembering it? For a time it is the universe, there is nothing else. The pain and the fear of more pain, the fear of being touched, the terror of further mutilation. You are animal, and you know it at last. You must creep back up, out of it, back into your human skin. It takes a long time.

Pain changes you.

Visitors, flowers and letters came. Dieter came. He seemed upset.

'It's been in all the papers,' he said, although he hadn't brought me a copy. Not that I could have read it anyway. 'It hasn't been very good for morale, all this publicity.'

I thought he said, 'At least when a Komet *blew up* the ministry kept quiet about it,' but I was still very ill, barely conscious after the anaesthetic, and perhaps I misheard him.

My mother and Peter both came to see me. My mother took a room in the town for several weeks while the worst of the surgery was being done, and came every day. I was both glad of her presence and wished she would go home: I had never got over my feeling that I must protect her, and attempting to do so in the circumstances was exhausting.

She brought a letter from my father, and a tonic which he had made up himself and said I must take twice a day as soon as I was able to. It tasted horrible, but I noticed that after taking it for a week I was starting to want to eat again. He could not visit me himself: he could not leave his patients. This was the simple truth, my mother said: with so many doctors drafted into the army, he had become the community physician, and he was working all the hours there were.

But he had found time to write to me. I was touched. It was the first letter he had written me since I left home. It was a brisk, down-to-earth letter about practicalities, and included much sensible advice about rest and diet, but the concern in it was unconcealed. Perhaps by nearly dying, I thought, I had finally resolved the problems between us.

Peter brought his wife, Marie. I thought he had chosen well. Marie was a plump and lively girl, with a pragmatic turn of mind and a ready laugh. She seemed devoted to him. They showed me a photograph of my niece. She was four months old, and lay on a rug almost as swathed in wrappings as I was.

People I had never met sent me gifts. I was touched, and wrote to thank them as soon as I was well enough. The gift for which I was most grateful was the most difficult to write a thank-you letter for. It was a bottle of pure fruit juice. Fruit juice was unobtainable. It had come with a handwritten note: 'With admiration and sincere wishes for your recovery. Heinrich Himmler.'

I was told I would never fly again.

He stood by my bed, the doctor, with his face composed in the look of authority. I know about that look, how it masks ignorance, powerlessness and the wish to have nothing to do with the matter. He was the surgeon's younger assistant.

'Fräulein Kurtz.'

I looked at him without turning my head. It hurt to turn my head. It hurt to look at him.

'You have been asking what your prognosis is.'

Indeed I had. I'd been asking for three months. I suppose it was unreasonable of me to ask on the day of admission, as I came up the stairs, my knees buckling, handkerchief clapped to the hole in my face, the ambulancemen I would not allow to hold me up two steps behind me.

'And what is it?'

Moving my lips was still difficult, it felt like moving dough. Sometimes whistles came out instead of consonants.

'You will not fly again.'

'*Quatsch!*' I said indistinctly.

'I beg your pardon?'

I repeated it.

'I'm sorry, but you must accept the fact. Fighting against the inevitable will only retard the healing process.'

What was the fool talking about? I had always fought against the inevitable. It was the only way I could live.

'Why are you so sure?' I asked.

'Your skull was fractured in six places.'

I knew that. When they told me, I had been frightened. My skull, irreplaceable bone cage for the fragile brain. By now I was rather proud of its ability to survive six fractures.

'Yes,' I said.

'The brain was compressed.'

'It doesn't seem to have done it much harm.'

His eyelid twitched with annoyance. 'It will not have done it any good. There has also, as you know, been severe damage to the bones of the face, including displacement of the upper jawbones.' He looked at me with something like hostility. 'That would have presented a major trauma to most women. We've been surprised – '

My stare stopped him.

'As a result of the damage to the brain and middle ear, you will be subject to nausea and fits of vertigo for months to come, probably years. Your balance may never return fully. Normally, a pilot who sustained these injuries would not be expected to resume operational duties.'

I made an impatient movement.

He said, 'Have you found your concentration impaired? Your mind wanders?'

'Not much. On the whole, it remains fixed on the desire to get out of here.'

'You will find that concentrating is less easy than it used to be. I think I'm right in saying that concentration is essential to the kind of work you were doing?'

The kind of work I was doing. The Komet surged again under my feet.

'Won't my concentration come back if I train it?' I asked.

'Train it?'

'With mental exercises.'

He looked surprised, as if a child had asked him a question in theoretical physics.

'Well, I . . . ah . . . I suppose it might, to some degree. But it will never come back fully. You must resign yourself, *Früulein* – he smiled without regret – to being grounded.'

He looked at my chart, and began to walk away.

'Doctor,' I said.

He turned, irritated.

'Do you wish me to address you as "Doctor"?'

'Of course. That is my title.'

'My title is Flight Captain,' I said.

I went to convalesce in a cottage on a mountainside where people would leave me alone.

They did, on the whole. The village was curious, but kept a polite distance from the stranger with the not-quite-right face who was reported by the postman to do some bizarre things. I discouraged visitors by saying that my mental recovery depended on complete solitude, until in the end even the atrocious Herr Menke with his troop of drilled little boys kept away. The only person who came to see me regularly was Gretl, wife of the neighbouring farmer, who by arrangement brought me a hot meal every day. Often she brought me something for breakfast as well, a couple of home-baked rolls under a napkin, with a knob of farm butter in a dish. I would pour her a cup of coffee (I had real coffee, I had brought a big box of it, it was the only thing I could give her) and we would sit together at the scrubbed kitchen table and look out over the valley.

Gretl would talk. She talked about her life, which seemed to have an enviable roundness to it, and about the village. She was mother, aunt or grandmother to a good portion of its inhabitants. She had a sharp eye for unkindness and pretence. Of Herr Menke she said, 'When the milk is being skimmed, sooner or later something you don't want will come to the top of it.'

Gretl interpreted the village to me, and me to the village. What she said I don't know, but it satisfied them.

My balance had gone. Sometimes it was as much as I could do to walk across a floor.

To get it back, each morning I climbed the steps at the gable end of the house.

The cottage was built on steeply rising ground. In front of it the land fell away to a wooded valley, behind which rose the peaks of the next mountain range. In the mornings the valley was scarfed with mist. From the valley a brown dirt track wound up to the cottage, and on past it to the crest of the hill and down to the next valley, Päsebühl. Behind the crest, at times seeming many miles distant and at other times so close you imagined you would reach it in an afternoon's stroll, rose the tall snow-capped peak which the villagers called 'Grandfather'.

Into the gable wall of the cottage, rising to the ridge, a rough ladder of stone steps had been built. They were weathered slabs, grey, thick and smooth. They were like seals. Frosted and treacher-

256

ous in the early morning, they would be dry and slightly warm after the sun had been on them for an hour. An iron handrail protected the outside edge of the steps.

The first morning, I stood by the bottom step with my knees shaking. Then in one movement, as if boarding a boat. I put my hand on the iron rail and my right foot on the bottom slab, and stepped up. Then I brought my left foot up beside it.

It was ridiculous, but I was already breathing heavily.

On the second step, a wobbly feeling which had no physiological justification appeared in my right ankle.

The third step was hard. Both ankles were wobbling, my knees were shaking again and a familiar drumbeat had started inside my head. I was acutely conscious of the space around me. I dared not think about it. Once I did, it would start to rock.

Hand on the rail, I pulled myself up to step four, and drew air deeply into my lungs as I did so. That helped.

But then I was stranded.

It was horribly high, I was going to fall. On this tiny bit of stone I perched, clutching the rail, besieged by space beneath, around and above me. In vain did I tell myself that I was only a few feet above the ground. The delicate, deranged mechanism of my middle ear shrieked otherwise.

The longer I stood there, the more terrifying my disorientation became. I shut my eyes. Behind my eyelids, the landscape moved un-hindered.

As I opened my eyes I glimpsed the pearly buds of the creeper which grew up the walls of the house. This I saw with one sober part of my brain. But the rest of my brain had abandoned observation and reason. It screamed that the ground below me was alternately rising and receding like a heavy sea, that the house was leaning over like the mast of a ship, and that I, at the top of the mast, pitching and rolling with the motion, was on the point of falling like a stone into the midst of the heaving fields.

Herr Menke was a small man with a nasal voice, sandy hair and eyes like little green pebbles.

He called on me the second evening and asked me if I had any waste paper which 'his boys' could have. It was the weekend of the

Jungvolk's monthly paper collection: as village schoolteacher, he ran the local group in his spare time. They had the best record in the district, he said, and the previous year had come second for Winter Relief.

I said that I had no newspapers. He said he would send his boys around all the same, because I might find something in a cupboard, and began to talk about the Mothering Sunday parade. He wanted me to attend and make a speech. I refused.

He was annoyed, but tried to conceal it. He said he hoped I would soon have my strength back. He said my presence in the village would be an inspiration.

Space had changed its nature for me. Every bit of it now had to be negotiated and tested over and over again.

For a week I climbed each morning to the fourth step, until I could do it without any difficulty. Then I decided to venture higher.

I stood on the fourth step and felt the determination drain out of me. The distance from the step on which I stood to the next one seemed an immense gulf.

More in exasperation than courage, I launched myself into the void. I found myself trembling on the next step, with my sweaty right hand gripping the guard rail so that the knuckles shone.

It was a small triumph. I did not have long to savour it. My mind now focused on something which I had not previously thought about. Between the steps themselves, there were gaps.

No sooner had I seen this than a strange thing happened to my legs. They went cold. They felt entirely lacking in strength, and as if they were being pulled. The space between the stones was pulling at them.

I tried to go further. I couldn't. I rested for a while. The mountain peaks across the valley glistened white.

Before me rose a ladder of stone I dared not even look at.

When Herr Menke came the second time. I had had a bad day. I was depressed, unable to stop thinking about Ernst. The weather had been too bad to go for a walk. The progress I was making with the steps did not render me immune to vertigo in the most unthreatening of circumstances. That afternoon I had been sitting in an armchair trying to read one of a parcel of books my mother had sent from home; I got up, and the floor got up with me.

'Our boys are heroes,' sighed Herr Menke, gazing into the Alpine night. 'How I wish I were out there with them, fighting the Bolshevik hordes.'

'Why aren't you?' I was too tired to observe the rules that evening.

He looked at me reproachfully. 'I have a weak heart.'

'Oh? I'm sorry to hear it.'

'You can't be more sorry than I was, Fräulein. I begged that army doctor, I even – you'll think this foolish of me – tried to offer him money, but he wouldn't look at me. A heart like that is no use in combat, he said. I would be a danger to my comrades.'

'Quite true.'

'Well, I flatter myself that I make no small contribution on the home front. Someone must prepare the young for Germany's future. We fight a war here no less than they do there. This little village has seen its own battles for racial purity.'

The nausea hit me without any warning at all, and I had to catch the arm of my chair in an attempt to steady myself as the floor lifted and rocked around me. I clung to the chair arm, concentrating on my breathing, willing the diabolic thing the floor was doing to stop.

Little by little the undulation subsided, until there was only movement in my peripheral vision. Weak, and feeling a dampness under my clothes. I turned my attention at last to Herr Menke, who had gone pale and was staring at me.

'Can I get you a glass of water?'

I would have laughed if I had had the strength, so terrified did he look. I nodded instead. He went to fetch the water.

Soon, I imagined, he would leave. I was wrong. Within a few minutes he had recovered from my indisposition and had begun to explain to me the military situation in North Africa. After that he proceeded to the naval war in the Atlantic, the inferior fighting quality of American troops, and the catastrophic effect on enemy morale of the first German bombs on New York, which, according to certain information he possessed, were due to be dropped any day.

*

259

Gretl apologized for the humbleness of the fare she brought me. In fact, my appetite sharpened by the mountain air, I found her casseroles and stews delicious. I did, though, realize how spoilt I'd been. The meat ration was now three hundred grams a week. As a test pilot I had been able to eat meat or eggs whenever I wanted, and at Regensburg protein was compulsory.

Gretl often stayed with me for a few minutes while I was eating, but one evening she stayed until I had finished. She had begun to talk about her nephew, her sister's youngest son: a gentle boy, she said, who 'would be eighteen now'.

Was he dead, then? I didn't want to ask. He had been wonderful with animals, she said. He would put his hand on a trembling, panic-stricken ewe, and it would calm. And at the same time, said Gretl, something would happen to him. He was a nervous boy, and ordinarily was clumsy, but when he saw a sick or frightened animal he would become sure of himself, and his hands would know what they were doing.

'He always wanted to help,' she said.

She was crying. I pushed my plate away and tried to comfort her, but she blew her nose and told me to take no notice.

I felt helpless, as I always did when confronted with grief. And there was so much grief around. Gretl's nephew had been killed. I presumed, on the Eastern Front, which was swallowing lives like a quicksand. Amongst so many, what does one matter? But it does. A death is irreducible.

'I'm sorry, Gretl.' I said, and thought of my brother, who was somewhere in the Atlantic. The oil on the black water, the silent torpedo.

It took me two months to climb to the top of the stone staircase.

On the morning I did it, a cold wind was rustling the trees. There would be snow.

I made my way up the stone ladder. I no longer needed to rest on each step, but could walk up, left foot on one step, right on the next. But I was conscious of how slowly I must do it, of how my heart laboured and my knees gave warning of mutiny.

The higher steps were more difficult than the lower ones. I had to fix my attention firmly on a point in the distance and concentrate on that. Even so my legs trembled and I had the notion that the steps were going to fail under me, fall out of their anchorage in the wall.

I stood on the twelfth step, and faced the last three. They went up into nothingness.

I must not think of it like that. They were just steps, as rooted in the fabric of the house as the ones I had climbed.

I clutched the rail. It was firm, and as cold as a snake.

I made myself look calmly at the steps. They rose to the ridge. That was what they were for: to give access to the roof. The last step was about three feet below it. Here the rail curved round and went into the wall of the house, its intrusion marked by a circle of pale cement. To stand there at the rail would be like standing on the bridge of a ship.

Gretl – no, it was the postman – was coming up the lane. I felt stupid, dithering half way up a wall. I must get up these steps, and down again.

But the steps went up into nothing.

I began to feel ill. I rested my head against the harsh stone wall. The house moved against the sky.

You can do it. You've done it before.

I put my foot on the thirteenth step and grasped the hand rail.

I started to pull myself up to stand on the thirteenth step, and the world shifted. The house began to tilt over into the valley, which seemed to be both moving away from me and rushing towards me like a runway, and the stone step pressed upward on the sole of my foot as if rising and moving outward, taking me with it on a hideous flight over this whirling landscape. I clung for my life to the rail.

Gradually, very gradually, it passed. At some point I found that the fields and woods, the track and the distant houses, had modified their movement. They undulated in a current which was not too bad at all as long as I didn't look directly at it.

I found, too, that I was standing on the thirteenth step.

With both hands on the rail, I pulled myself up again. I pulled myself through terror and emptiness on to the fourteenth step.

I pulled myself on to the fifteenth step. My legs were buckling under me but I stood at the rail like a captain on his ship, and inside me I was singing.

With my left hand I touched the rough terracotta of the tile at the end of the ridge.

Then I began carefully to go down.

Letters came for me in my retreat. I welcomed them, but they unsettled me. They reminded me pungently of the world I had left, the stages of my return to which I planned every day, my absence from which was – I told myself – the sole cause of whatever unhappiness I felt.

I had one letter from Dieter. In view of how relations had been left between us, it was quite friendly. I replied, but he didn't write again.

I heard the next bit from Heinz. He had come to see me in hospital, and written me several letters which were full of irreverent gossip and pilots' slang. One day I received a letter from him saying that Dieter, flying the Komet as a glider to test some new instruments, had landed it on a retracted skid and injured his spine. He was in the same hospital as I'd been in.

Poor Dieter, I thought, and grinned. I wrote to him, to expiate the grin.

Heinz's next letter contained the news that he was going to the Eastern Front. I never heard from him again.

Gretl's nephew had not been killed in action. He had disappeared while in police custody.

She told me about it as we drank coffee on the little paved terrace. She suddenly put down her cup, almost banged it down, reached for her handkerchief and burst into tears.

It would have been his birthday that day. It was two years and three months since they took him.

'He'd been helping with the lambing at Püsebühl,' said Gretl. 'He had ridden over on the pony, and he'd just got back. It was dark, and he was tired. He hadn't eaten, or even washed. He hadn't had time. He came in, sat down in the chair by the fire, and he asked if he could have a drink of goats' milk. He used to like that. He never drank beer or spirits or anything like that, just goats' milk, and sometimes he'd have some milky coffee. Anna', his mother, 'gave him some, and he was drinking it. Then the police banged on the door.'

She drew in her breath painfully.

'There was no reason. He never harmed anyone. But they must have him. We knew at once. The way they looked at him, standing in the doorway with their guns, and him sitting there, poor lad, with the muck and the blood still on his shirt, drinking his goats' milk. They weren't local police. We'd never seen them before. They asked him his name and said they were investigating a crime and they wanted him for questioning. He said could he go up and change his shirt, and they said no. And then at that moment his father came in through the back door and stopped dead, and one of them said, "If you move a step we shoot the boy." So of course he didn't move. So then they took him, they took Stefan, and as he went out of the door Anna managed to put some bread and sausage into his hand and they let him take that. They put him into the sidecar of their motorbike and they drove off.' The tears rolled down her cheeks. 'None of us ever saw him again.'

I looked down the narrow track that led to Gretl's house and the other houses of the village, and the little Catholic church, and to the school and the Party headquarters and the small police station which was only distinguishable from an ordinary house by the flag planted in the front garden. It looked so undramatic.

'Do you know what happened to him?'

'Oh yes.' It was said almost with disgust.

'It was five months before we heard anything. Anna was ill with it. He was the youngest, you see. And besides, he was ...' A complex expression crossed her face. 'He was a bit simple, as people say. You had to tell him what to do sometimes, because he wouldn't know. Everyone kept an eye on him.

'We went to the police, of course, the police in the village. They said they knew nothing about it. Perhaps it was true. There was one person in the village who knew about it, all right. But no good asking him. So we just had to wait for news.

'After five months we got a letter from the government. It said that Stefan had been taken, "in the interests of society", to somewhere called Grafeneck, in Wurttenberg, where he had died' – she paused – 'of a contagion. It said his body had been cremated and that we were not to attempt to visit the place. It said he had been suffering from an incurable disease and we should be grateful for his release.'

She lifted her head and gazed at the mountain peaks across the valley. She looked proud.

'Except for the fact they told us he was dead,' said Gretl, 'every word on that filthy piece of paper was a lie.'

I held her work-worn hand in mine, and tried to say how sorry I was.

She turned, angry.

'Früulein, why must they do this? He never did any harm. Why must they creep about murdering children?'

I had heard of Grafeneck. Rumours. A few death notices in the papers which were strange in their wording, in the impression they gave of a stifled tragedy.

'He wasn't clever enough,' said Gretl. 'That was the crime they were investigating.'

I could think of nothing to say that might comfort her.

'Früulein, you know some of these men, the important men who make decisions.'

No. No. I didn't.

'Can't you explain to them that the ones who are being killed are just children, who've never done any harm? They don't know what's happening, they can't know. Früulein . . .'

She grasped my arm and her fingers transmitted to me her terrible urgency. 'I can talk to you because you are a woman and you understand, and at the same time you work with these men and they respect what you say. They'll listen to you.'

Go away, Gretl. Leave me alone. Please.

'Früulein, when you're better and you go back to Berlin, will you tell them what is going on?'

CHAPTER TWENTY

I turn through ten degrees, correcting my course, and as the wing lifts after the turn I see something which is not there.

A line of people walking naked in snow.

I shake my head to dispel the image. It goes, but not entirely. Something lingers, the ghost of a ghost, and I have the sense of sitting in a cockpit surrounded by a transparent canopy which allows me to see what is below me.

I have been flying too long without a break. This flat, frozen countryside, these thoughts, the mad, sick man behind me.

The general's hand grips my shoulder like a vice and he shouts in my ear.

I shake my head. I can't hear him.

He shouts again. This time I catch it.

'Did you see them?'

My stomach jumps.

'Take her to the left,' he yells.

He's as lucid as I am.

I move the stick and the wing dips, and as the nose swings west there they are. But not the ghostly procession of my dream: these are real people, sunk in the misery of flesh.

They are country people, farmers, by the look of their wide wagons and the horses that pull them. The horses are thin and the wagons are almost empty of possessions, and in them ride huddled, blanket-wrapped figures.

As I fly further up this column, I see what has been thrown away by those ahead of them. Armchairs, bedding and carpets line the sides of the road. A suitcase has been dropped from a wagon and has burst open, its contents spilled on the ground. People walk past it without a glance. Someone has thrown away a red dress. Not far from it is a kitchen stove. Then, dropped one by one like stepping stones, I come to six brilliant rectangles of colour. Someone loved paintings enough to bring them on this journey, and despaired enough to throw them away.

The travellers have the look of people who have been on the move for a long time. They and their wagons have the look of the east, of Hungary, perhaps Romania. They are ethnic Germans, making for the one place they can think of where to be German does not carry an automatic sentence of death.

I climb, and return to my correct heading. The terrain is featureless and wintry.

More and more it is like flying over Russia.

They gave me an Iron Cross. First Class.

For the crash? For surviving it? For climbing up to the roof? Or for impenetrable reasons of their own?

I crossed the halls of Byzantium, again, to receive my reward. The emperor had a new palace. Speer had designed it. It was vast and felt like a vault. There were tapestries of stallions everywhere. I hadn't realized our leader was a horse-fancier. Had he ever sat on a horse? Impossible. That figure with its look of a railway official, standing with its hands crossed in front of its vulnerable parts. How could it have entrusted itself to the otherness, the passion, of a horse?

Here and there on a patch of wall was a green stain. Mould. He'd moved in in a hurry, he'd insisted the place be ready on a certain date. Dates were very important, they were part of the magic. It was the anniversary of the day he came to power, or something. Alas, the time taken for plaster to dry is profane time and unaffected by magic.

What happens when reality conflicts with magic? Magic wins. And you get a green stain.

I went home, in the last stage of my convalescence, to see my family. Peter was with his ship, but Marie came for a week with the baby. The baby was big now, nearly a year old, and was trying to walk and was falling over. I spent quite a lot of time with her. There were still moments when I thought I was falling over, myself, and it was nice to have understanding company.

266

My parents were looking older. It was with a pang that I saw this, and in particular how much my father had aged. He was now quite grey, and thinner; he seemed diminished, and the iron had gone out of him. As soon as I saw him I knew that the balance of power between us had shifted. And I was sorry, because I had not wanted to win through his weakness.

Not that he was defeated: he was simply working far too hard. He did nothing but see patients. He had no time for his books, his walks or his music. He would have allowed himself Sundays, but he was always called out.

'Do you have to do it?' I asked.

'Yes. There is no other doctor for thirty miles. What am I to do? Turn them away?'

He had that afternoon delivered a baby, visited a patient dying of pneumonia, certified a death by drowning and another from cardiac failure, attended to the needs of two amputees invalided home from the Front, and performed an emergency operation on a child who had been crushed when a haycart overturned. He had seen a number of 'routine cases' as well. He looked exhausted.

'One cannot abdicate from a responsibility,' he said, 'no matter how heavy it is.'

I sat by him. I said, 'It won't do your patients any good if you're too ill to look after them.'

'I know, but meanwhile will you kindly tell me what I am supposed to do? What would you do?'

I toyed with the lacy fringe of the tablecloth.

The same thought occurred to both of us at the same moment.

He smiled wryly and said, 'Well, we know what you did, don't we?'

He had never before referred with anything approaching humour to my giving up my medical studies.

I said, 'Have you forgiven me yet?'

He thought about it. 'Yes,' he said after a time, and the slight shock with which I heard this answer revealed something to me.

Although I had spoken seriously, there was a sense in which I had not meant the question. I had never considered that in abandoning my medical studies I might truly have done something unforgivable. The idea that my father had truly not forgiven me was therefore –

although I had lived with it for years – somehow not real. It was as though we had been playing a subtle game with each other.

'Yes,' he said, 'I have forgiven you, but I still don't understand why you did it.'

'Why I gave up my studies? But I never –'

I stopped myself. How could I tell him that at no time had I been serious about medicine? Yet for some reason, and obscurely, I had imagined that he knew it. He was my father: he was supposed to know.

'I never imagined I'd make a good doctor,' I said.

He laughed. 'I had my doubts about that, too. But then why did you take up medicine at all? It surprised me, I can tell you.' He paused. 'You wanted to get away from home, of course. Like Peter. I knew you wouldn't marry. Your mother always thought you would. She doesn't understand why you're doing what you're doing.'

'And you don't either.'

'It seems . . . such a harsh thing for a woman to be doing. And I suppose I find something childish in it. The wish to fly.'

'That isn't your real objection.'

He paused. 'If you're referring to a conversation we had one Christmas . . .'

'I wouldn't answer a question you asked me.'

'It seemed to me afterwards that I had no business to ask it.'

'I think you had every right to ask it. I just couldn't answer it, at the time.'

'Well, let's leave it at that, shall we?' he said. 'I have my own opinions, you have yours. We have to live together on this earth.'

'Father, listen to me. I am not a Nazi.'

He raised his head. His eyes lit a little.

'When you say that . . .'

'I detest this government,' I said. 'I have as little as possible to do with politics. I just get on with my job and hope they'll leave me alone.'

He looked delighted and bewildered, 'Why on earth didn't you say so?'

'I have now.'

'I can't tell you how . . . relieved I am.'

'I'm pretty relieved to have told you.'

268

We smiled at each other.

'We're very proud of you, you know, your mother and I,' he said, and I knew that he meant he was.

'But you'd still rather I'd become a doctor.'

'Yes, I would.'

Of course. He never really deviated from any position he had taken up. And he was talking of what he loved.

'It is a noble profession,' he said. 'The noblest. The most exacting, too. Its rewards are the greatest of any profession's, because its responsibilities are the greatest. You save life, you give life, you are sometimes judge over whether or not life should continue. And you know things. There are times when you wish you didn't know them. But the knowledge you have is knowledge of a thing so marvellous, so intricate, so *intelligent*, that the more you know of it, the humbler you become in the face of it.'

I didn't know whether he was talking to me or to himself. Certainly he had never revealed so much of himself to me.

I said, 'You mean, the humbler you *should* become. Not all physicians are like you, Father.'

He laughed, with a measure of irony. 'Then they must be bad physicians.'

Once, I would not have thought him capable of that joke.

'So you see,' he said, getting up and going to pour himself a glass of wine, 'it was hard for me to understand why you made the choice you did.'

'There was no choice,' I said.

He lifted his head quickly.

I said, 'I never really wanted to become a doctor. When I had qualified I was going to apply to be a flying missionary doctor in Africa. It was a way of flying.'

He stood still, the wineglass in his hand, framed against the light of the window.

'It was a way of *flying*?'

I nodded. I suddenly couldn't speak.

He said, 'You let me believe . . . oh, but that is despicable. How could you?'

I had tricked him, yes. Betrayed him. And how could I not have seen, all these years, what I'd done?

He went and sat in a chair on the opposite side of the room, and gazed out of the window. He looked stunned.

He said in the end. *'Why?'* as if he could have understood all of it but for this last, heartbreaking conundrum.

The vehemence with which he spoke that single word released a flood of feeling in me. I raised my hands to my head, holding the skull bones. The doctors had told me to avoid excitement.

'Father, try to understand. *I had to fly!'*

'You pass my comprehension.'

'You aren't trying to understand. You have no idea what it's like to be barred from the one thing in the world you care about. It feels like exile.'

'Didn't you care what anyone else felt?'

'Why should I? None of you cared what I felt: you dismissed it. You all had your lives, you'd survive whatever I did to you. If I couldn't find a way to live my life, I wouldn't have a life.'

'You can't possibly mean that.'

'Oh, but I do mean it. I know you don't understand a word I'm saying. But I mean it.'

My father looked very sad.

Then a ghost of a smile crossed his face. He said, 'You don't believe in making things easy for yourself, do you?'

'Father,' I said, 'I'm sorry I lied to you. I really am. But I didn't know what else to do. It made me feel wretched.'

There was quite a long pause. Eventually my father gave a heavy sigh. 'I forgive you,' he said. The faint smile returned to his face. It grew a little stronger. 'You're so stubborn,' he said. 'I suppose you get it from me.'

I had to start flying from the beginning again. I began where I had begun more than twelve years before: with a training glider.

I knew without putting it to the test that my hands had become stupid and my thinking had slowed. But what made my stomach hollow as I sat in the cockpit waiting for the tow cable to tighten was the fear that the giddiness would come back.

The first flight was unpleasant. The cockpit felt strange, and as I put my feet on the rudder pedals a small shock ran through me. It was part excitement, but part apprehension.

The launch alarmed me: it seemed very fast. Once I was free of the tow plane and gliding, things were better, but I knew I was not in sympathy with the glider. I seemed to have a new body, not just a new face. I hated this new body, which didn't know how to settle itself in a pilot's seat, did not instinctively respond to movements of the aircraft, and couldn't anticipate.

I brought the glider down and sat in rueful contemplation on the runway. The commander (it was a gliding school for Hitler Youth) strolled over.

'How did it feel?'

'Terrible,' I said. 'I don't think I could fly a kite on Luneberg Heath.'

'What nonsense. You did a perfectly good circuit and the landing was excellent. And if you can land you can fly, as you well know. Launch was a bit rough. Tell you what, let's go up again.'

He walked towards the tow plane.

He was right, of course, and I went up again, and could feel a communication start to establish itself between the glider and my sluggish senses. The new body was not completely hopeless. I thought I could probably manage to get along with it for lack of anything better, and assumed that with practice it would improve.

In the course of the next few weeks I worked my way from gliders to sports planes and military trainers. With all aircraft requisitioned for military use, I had to fly what was available, begging favours among my contacts and hoping no one would ask to see my medical certificate, which stated that I was not fit to fly. I intended to demonstrate that I was, and then return to the surgeon who had issued it and ask him for a different one. I was stuck on the Stork for a while because there wasn't anything else, but then an Arado biplane turned up, and a week after that I was flying an Me 110.

After I'd been flying for two months, I spoke to the friendly briefing officer at Rechlin and asked if he had anything nobody would miss for half an hour. He offered me a Focke-Wulf 190 in for testing.

A lovely aeroplane! Fast, agile, good-tempered. For half an hour I rejoiced in it and in my return to flying. I started on my landing circuit resolved to go back and see the surgeon within the next week.

I made my final turn into the runway.

As the starboard wing dipped, I saw the horizon tilt and had the horrifying sensation that it was rising and pushing me upward. I strove to hold the plane at the correct angle, against the gigantic movement of the earth and sky. The instruments were reading normally. Everything else was insane. Forcing myself to believe what was on the dials, I pulled the wings level, lowered the flaps and dropped down towards a runway which rose towards me with a sickening swaying motion. I taxied to the hangar and sat drenched in sweat and shaking.

It was going to take longer than I had thought.

The telephone at my flat in Berlin rang one weekend. I wasn't expecting a call.

An unfamiliar male voice asked if I was Flight Captain Kurtz and, when I said I was, requested me to wait. As I waited, the line seemed to go dead. Then it became so clear that I could hear the creak of a chair at the other end.

A second voice, precise, but with a Bavarian softness to the vowels, came smoothly on to the line.

'Flight Captain Kurtz? Good evening.'

'Good evening.'

'This is Heinrich Himmler speaking.'

How well he must know the momentary silence that ensues, the listener's world drops away like a trapdoor. I see him, sitting upright in his black uniform, holding the black telephone receiver, smiling a little with the pleasure of a man who believes in his work, as he says, 'This is Heinrich Himmler speaking.'

'This is an honour, sir,' I had the presence of mind to say.

'Tell me, are you fully recovered from your accident?'

'I've made a very good recovery, thank you. It was kind of you to send the fruit juice.'

'Not at all. I'm glad to hear you're better. And I believe you're flying again?'

I wondered who had told him that. 'I'm trying to get fit for duty, sir.'

He said, 'Your country is proud of you, Flight Captain.'

I tried to think of something to say, other than 'Thank you'. I said, 'Thank you.'

'Courage is one of the qualities which distinguish us from the lower races,' he said. 'I have been an admirer of yours for a long time, and have wanted to make your acquaintance. Unfortunately I have a lot of calls on my time. However, I have an evening free on 17 October. Will you give me the pleasure of dining with me?'

I held the receiver in my hand. I stared at it.

'Are you there, Flight Captain?'

No one says no. No one can ever have said no.

'It will be a great honour, sir.'

'Good. My car will pick you up at seven.'

His aide rang back five minutes later to ask if I had any special dietary requirements.

The man most feared in Germany received me, smiling, at the door of a modest suburban house. I didn't recognize the district: the car journey had taken a long time and I suspect had been circuitous. The short gravel path to the door ran between trees, but there were bright lights shining on it. The occupier did not intend to be surprised.

A flurry of wind blew a dead leaf on to the shoulder of his jacket. I'd known he would wear uniform: there had never been a photograph of him wearing anything else. I'd wondered how I could sit all evening across the table from the belted black tunic, the little deaths'-heads, the dagger. But he was wearing field grey, in his capacity as Commander-in-Chief of the Fighting SS. Somehow it didn't make any difference. It looked black.

I had dressed for the occasion, breaking an otherwise invariable rule. My discomfort with myself for doing this increased the discomfort of my clothing: a blue taffeta creation that cramped my elbows and made my neck itch. I felt ridiculous in it, and vulnerable. I was hoping, unreasonably, that as the evening progressed I would forget I was wearing it.

Himmler raised my hand to his lips, bowing over it. His own hands were small and quite dainty. The sides of his head were shaved and the hair on the crown was cropped straight across. It made his face look narrower than it was. The shape of his head did not conform to the Aryan norm; it was said that he worried about it. There were specks of dandruff in his hair.

273

He took my coat, handing it to his adjutant, and led me into a fussily furnished drawing room. On the patterned cream and blue wallpaper hung a multitude of inharmonious pictures – German landscapes, fraternity and sporting photographs, family snapshots, a framed text which said, 'Prepare for war with peace in thy soul', and a picture of a tall stone standing in a forest clearing. Over the mantelpiece was the room's focus: a signed portrait of Hitler. 'To my trusted Heini, in comradeship,' was written across the corner.

A log fire burned in the grate. It was warm in the room: indeed, it was stuffy. The heavy brocade curtains were of a deep red which clashed with the orangey-red of the carpet, and the sofa and armchairs were expensively upholstered in an unpleasant sage green. Knick-knacks stood on every surface; there appeared to be no coherent taste behind the collection. There was a large bookcase against one wall, completely filled with leatherbound books, not one of which was even slightly out of alignment.

Himmler moved a chair closer to the fire for me and asked what I would like to drink. I asked for something non-alcoholic. This delighted him.

'How wise you are! I only drink in moderation myself. I have something rather special. A mineral water from the Czechoslovakian Protectorate: the source was discovered by one of my geologists.'

He rang for his adjutant, who shortly reappeared with a carafe of sparkling water on a tray, and two glasses.

Himmler poured it. The light flashed on his thick spectacles as he offered me my glass.

'*Heil Hitler!*' he said.

I shot to my feet.

The serious conversation then began. He had no small talk, only a pedant's delight in erudition. In reply to my question, he said the photograph on the wall was of a rune stone in a Norwegian forest. This prompted him to talk about the runic alphabet and the Germanic culture which had produced it.

'We should never make the mistake of thinking that our forefathers were primitive,' he said. 'They knew things about which we are completely ignorant'

He instanced the properties of plants. The knowledge of herbs had largely been lost, he told me. It was a subject of the greatest importance. He had himself established a herb garden as a first step towards its study.

I asked him if he found much time to pursue his interests actively.

'Only at a distance,' he said. 'I can order research to be undertaken, but I rarely have the time to pursue it myself. Although, in fact, later this evening, if you'll be so patient, I will ask you to co-operate in a little hobby I do have. It's really the reason for this house, which is a small indulgence of mine.'

'Is this hobby connected with your work, Herr Himmler?'

'Yes, I confess it is. Everything I do is connected with my work. But that is the way I am. Everything is serious, for me. But I have certain pet projects.'

'Where is your herb garden, Herr Himmler?'

'A place called Auschwitz. I don't suppose you've heard of it.'

I hadn't. We went in to dinner.

Over the soup he asked me about my work.

He said, 'Do you believe that courage is a genetic matter?'

'I hadn't thought about it.'

'It is a male characteristic.'

'Women have courage, too.'

'Yes, but in women it's related to such matters as the protection of the young. It is limited.' He darted a look at me. 'Do you regard yourself as abnormal?'

'No, I don't.' I tried not to betray my shock.

'Perhaps that was the wrong word. It's my habit to think in scientific terms, and the language isn't always appropriate.'

He changed the subject, drawing my attention to the plainness of the food. It was indeed plain, in the sense that it had not been elaborately prepared or presented, but it was food of a quality and quantity which no ordinary table in Germany had seen for years. The main course was a baked ham surrounded by glazed apples. Side dishes contained a variety of fresh vegetables not one of which was easily obtainable in Berlin.

'One does,' my host said, 'hear of certain excesses, but I will not allow it in my own domestic sphere.'

He began to talk about religion. He had been unhappy to find that most people believed him to be an atheist. He said that he had a firm belief in a guiding Power. But this Power had no special interest in human beings. 'That is the mistake the Christians make,' he said, 'and hence arises most of their foolish pseudo-morality. Man is an animal among other animals. And the strongest animal wins the struggle for existence. *That* is the divine law.'

His eyes behind their thick glasses glittered as he said this, and he seemed to sit straighter in his chair. How his body must torture him, I thought: his short, soft mouse of a body. The near-sighted eyes, plump waist, weak chin.

I said, to see what he would do with it, that since Christianity had survived for so long it must itself, for that time, have been the strongest animal.

He thought about this. He seemed to find it interesting.

'The Church has survived for eighteen hundred years,' he said. 'That is true. But what is this Church? It's the church founded by St Paul. Paul was an enemy of life, as the Jews always are. He took the religion he found, the primitive Christianity, which was a form of Bolshevism, and corrupted it, which again is a typically Jewish activity, to make of it a world faith. He saw the Jewish core in it, the thing which would prevent it from being acceptable to civilized people, and he removed that, and substituted for it ideas taken from Greek and Hindu sources, Aryan sources; and then he served up the resulting broth as a new religion.'

I said I hadn't realized there were Hindu elements in Christianity.

'Oh yes, certainly. There are echoes of the Kshatriyas, the Hindu warrior caste. "I come not to bring peace, but a sword": you are familiar with that saying? It's in the New Testament. Similarly many sayings about casting away what is unfit, and the seed having to die before it rises again: that is all Aryan and Germanic. St Paul, like all Jews, plundered Aryan culture to infuse life into his creations, since he had no life to give them himself. Let me offer you another baked apple.'

'Thank you.'

'So the fact that Christianity has survived for so long is largely due to the leavening of Aryan principle in its teaching. You might say, the iron hand in the velvet glove. Incidentally, I noticed you looking at the text on the wall in the drawing room. That is from one of the Hindu scriptures. I like to read them, when I can. So I would say the Church's survival is at least fifty per cent due to that. And the rest is due to terror.'

'I'm sorry, did you say "terror"?'

'I think that is an appropriate word for it. Priest-rule by terror. We must remember that the priests had absolute power over the people because they were believed to have power over their souls. That is impossible, of course, because the soul is not something that can be rewarded or punished, it is simply something which is reincarnated within the tribe or clan. I am myself a reincarnation of Heinrich I of Saxony. But the lie was clever. Imagine a society in which, if you offend against the laws, you *must* either confess, which consolidates the power of the priests over you, or face the prospect of everlasting punishment. In a society like that, I think there wouldn't have been much work for Heinrich Himmler to do.'

He smiled with approval.

'They employed other forms of terror as well,' he said. 'But if I am to speak of these things I must be blunt. Will you permit me?'

'Please.'

'Well, then. The Christian priesthood, in its denigration of women, its insistence on celibacy, its all-male communities ... what do we have here but a homosexual fraternity? Internally, it would exert pressure on individuals to conform to its perverted norms. In monasteries, needless to say, you would get this in an extreme degree. As a homosexual fraternity the priesthood would be very cohesive: and that would give it great power. You're familiar perhaps with the Greek idea that an army composed of such men would be invincible? The natural comradeship being strengthened by the other, unnatural, bonding? And indeed in a military corps there is a constant danger that this will arise, and one must be constantly on one's guard ... Mineral water? It is Jewish, of course, this propensity. I believe in some cases they actually resorted to kidnapping. Our forefathers had a straightforward method with homosexuals: they drowned them in a bog.'

We had by this time reached the dessert. It was stewed pears.

'I am very fond of these,' said Himmler, 'I hope you like them?'

'Yes, I do. We used to have them on Sundays when I was a child. My mother cooked them with cinnamon.'

277

'Do you see much of your family now?'

'I have seen them recently, but I don't often get the chance.'

'A pity,' said Himmler. 'Family life is so important. How is your brother, do you know?'

I hadn't told him I had a brother.

I said I had last heard from Peter four months previously; that he was on a destroyer somewhere.

'He joined the navy young?'

'He wasn't much more than a boy.'

'The navy is a fine service, particularly now that Grand Admiral Doenitz is in charge, but nowadays the natural choice for an ambitious young man would be the SS.'

'Peter wanted to go to sea,' I said.

'Did he? A romantic. Well, there's no harm in that, in its place,' said my host indulgently, and helped me to pears.

'Presumably,' I remarked, 'you don't have room for romantics in the SS?'

'None at all. My men have to be as hard as iron and as cold as ice. But, beyond that, if there is something of the visionary in them, that I welcome.'

'And do you often find it?'

'The visionary? Quite often. I am heartened at how often we are understood, when it is so easy to misunderstand. I know how it is. People see the black uniform and they're afraid. It's human. But there is a job to be done. We are charged with the spiritual defence of Germany. Sometimes I have to be rougher than I would wish.'

We ate our pears. His little triangle of moustache moved up and down as he ate.

I heard myself say, 'Herr Himmler, a lot of people have been concerned about the mercy killings.'

'Ah, the mercy killings. They are what their name indicates. The children are not normal.'

'But if there is a place for them in the community, Herr Himmler?'

'What place can there possibly be?'

'Perhaps looking after animals, or something of that sort.'

He smiled tolerantly at me. 'What is the point? Anything they can do, a normal person can do better. And if we allow them to live, they may breed. There are measures one can take, of course. But, I say again, what is the point? Being subnormal, they cannot be happy. Why prolong their misery?'

I turned my glass in my fingers. He deadened me: he deadened thought. All that was left was a furious, inarticulate protest. Normal, abnormal. Natural, unnatural. The theology of the kindergarten. His mind was a tunnel which curved back on itself. I felt his birdlike eyes on me, and wondered whether the tunnel was a torment to him, too. But through some power the source of which I could not guess at, some ravenousness rooted in his pedant's nature, he had induced tens of thousands to share the tunnel with him. They wore the black uniform, and all of them were was hard as iron and as cold as ice.

He said, 'To put compassion, so called, for a racial defective above compassion for one's healthy comrades is immoral. The race cannot afford it. We are farmers, we are stock breeders. We take what is healthy and breed from it, and that which is unhealthy we do not breed from, and we do not suffer it to occupy the living space and eat the food of the healthy stock.'

He had been a farmer. I tried to think of him loading hay, shovelling dung or holding an animal down for the vet with those typist's hands.

'We'll talk of this no further,' he said, after the cheese had been set down on the table. 'Now, may I offer you some of this very good cheese? It's a mountain cheese, made in a region of Bavaria which I happen to know rather well.'

The cheese was tasteless and acid. I praised it highly.

We returned to the drawing room for coffee, which he poured himself from an elaborately chased antique silver pot. When I admired it he said it was Italian and had been presented to him on an official visit to Rome.

I said I supposed he had not had much time for sightseeing.

'We drove past the Coliseum,' he said. 'The ruins are impressive. However, on the whole I would rather read about things like that than visit them: one gets a clearer perspective. You yourself have travelled quite widely, haven't you?'

'I've been lucky, yes.'

'Yes. Brazil and Argentina in 1933, Finland in 1934, then Portugal, then a second trip to Finland, followed by the international air show

279

in Switzerland. You spent a week gliding in Britain, if I remember rightly, in 1936, visited the United States in 1938 and, at the beginning of 1939, spent five weeks in Libya.'

My mouth was as dry as sawdust.

He said, 'Are you surprised that I know so much about you?'

'I'm surprised you find it worth your interest, Herr Himmler.'

'Oh, surely not. You're a remarkable person. Naturally I take an interest in you.'

Why should it have frightened me so much, the completely predictable fact that he had a file on me? Had I thought I was exempt?

Yes, I had.

For no reason, with no possible justification, had I thought this. Just that I had got away with so much for so long. I had broken so many of the rules. So much that should have touched me, hadn't. I had known it could not really be true, but it was how I felt. I seemed to myself almost beyond jurisdiction.

And now the reckoning was in. I had never broken any rule that mattered, and everything important I had ever said or done was in a file kept by Heinrich Himmler.

The room was stifling and I felt like a prisoner in my silly dress. Involuntarily I glanced at the door.

He said, 'It's strange. People who would say they are entirely in agreement with the keeping of a card index which records the name of every individual in the Reich, if this is the only way to have an orderly state, are very upset to find that their *own* name is on it.'

'That would be illogical. But, Herr Himmler, I have not said that I am in agreement with it.'

'No. But perhaps you don't remember disorder. You must have been very young at the end of the last war, when the Bolshevist sailors mutinied and for a few weeks Bavaria was in the hands of something calling itself a *Soviet*. Believe me, Flight Captain, those were dreadful times.'

'You were in one of the Free Corps then, weren't you, Herr Himmler?'

This was contemptible: I was trying to placate him.

'Yes.' he said. 'That is how I became involved with the Party. We were in the same fight. It was the happiest time of my life. But it

280

was a terrible time for Germany. None of us who lived through it, and fought for Germany through it, will ever forget it. And that is why I started my card index. To begin with, it was small. But as Germany's needs have grown, it has grown.'

He stood up, he almost sprang to his feet. 'Flight Captain, will you do me a great favour? Will you let me take the measurements of your skull?'

'My skull?' I could connect the word only with death.

He laughed. It was the only time I saw him do it. His face was lit, transformed and made older by laughter. Other people's faces become younger when they laugh; his lost its look of adolescence and became a man's.

'For my collection,' he laughed.

It lasted only a few seconds, I suppose, the normal space for which a man laughs at a joke. Then his face was as it always was again, the immature, earnest features given weight by heavy brows.

He said, 'You're a most unusual woman. I want to take your head measurements so they can be analysed and preserved for posterity.'

I concealed my revulsion as best I could. Probably he would not in any case have understood it.

I said, 'My skull was fractured in six places in the crash, Herr Himmler, and my face has had very extensive plastic surgery. I think I should tell you that.'

'You mean that the measurements may not be the original ones?' He looked like a boy who had put his hand into a bird's nest and found it empty.

He did it, none the less. He led me down to his basement. We went down stone steps, the chill of which struck up through my shoes, and through a grilled door which he unlocked.

He pressed a switch at the bottom of the stairs and lights came on in a room surgically tidy. Whitewashed walls, a scrubbed linoleum floor. Against one wall was a bare wooden table, next to which were two cane-bottomed chairs. There was shelving around the walls.

There were things on the shelves.

Bottles and jars of things. Whitish, bloated things in foul-coloured liquid. Things whose stink reached out to me through the glass. They possessed eyes and arms. Each had its label. I read some of the labels. Their Latin was opaque and had a grotesque ring. I was looking at a boiled egg with feet.

281

I turned away from the things and saw the skulls. Two long rows: sixty sockets gaping. Regularly spaced and, like the jars, labelled in a careful hand. On some of them, across the dome of the cranium or from front to back of the head, a red line had been painted, and against this line was written a measurement.

'Please, sit down,' said Himmler.

He had pulled out one of the cane-bottomed chairs for me and positioned it a few feet from the table. I sat down. From a drawer in the table he brought out a large bound notebook, two pencils, a tape measure, a ruler and a pair of steel calipers. He walked to a wastepaper basket in the corner, took a small penknife from his pocket and sharpened both the pencils. He returned and set them down on the table, precisely parallel to the ruler and notebook.

'May I?' he said, and with his hand turned my head a little to the right.

The touch of the calipers was cold on my skin. The tape measure made me want to scream. I thought it would tighten and tighten until the fissures in my skull opened up again. He measured and wrote, measured and wrote, He spent a long time on the sides of my head just above the ears, which he palpated with hard, inquisitive fingers before grunting and writing a sentence in the book.

We didn't speak. There were just our breathing and the sounds of his absorbed labour.

How cold it is in this cockpit. The cold gnaws through my leather gloves and awakens an old, deep ache in the bones of my remade face.

Snow covers the ground. The wind blows from the north, and we must fly into it. In this landscape everything looks the same, and until we get to the coast I do not know where we are.

CHAPTER TWENTY-ONE

I got the general's telegram that November. What a year it was for invitations.

He had requested an operational command, and they had given him an air corps somewhere on the Eastern Front. His men were cold, hungry and dispirited and he thought they would benefit from a visit from me.

I had not yet resumed my flying duties. It seemed a good idea to visit Russia: later, I would not be free to.

I flew out, with a suitcase of borrowed furs, in a battle-scarred Dornier flown by a nervy pilot not out of his teens. The flight, stopping twice to refuel and take on supplies, took many hours. The temperature in the cabin dropped steadily. I put on my furs and went for a walk.

I found the navigator eating a bar of chocolate over his maps. He was a wiry lad with close-cropped hair that looked like a wheatfield. When I appeared he tried to hide the chocolate in his pocket. Then he grinned sheepishly and offered me a piece.

I said, 'Where did you get chocolate?'

'Swapped a watch for three bars of it. Gave a bar to my mother, a bar to my girlfriend, that left one for me.'

'Oh, and now I've eaten a piece of it.'

'That's all right,' he said. There was a watch on his wrist, a good one.

There were stories about watches. The stories had a funny taste to them. The point was that there were so many watches, used ones, all at once. Peter had told me a story about a chest full of watches – a *chest* – being sent to the crew of a U-boat as a reward for bravery.

I looked at the map on which he was plotting our course. 'Where are we?' I asked.

'I'm not supposed to tell you.' He pointed with his pencil tip. 'We're here.'

We were over the northern part of what used to be Poland, approaching the border with what used to be, and was fast again becoming, the Soviet Union.

'I suppose I shouldn't have asked,' I said.

'I'd want to know where I was if I were you,' he said. 'In this crate, being flown by this pilot.'

'What's wrong with the pilot?'

'He's just got a screw loose. He goes a bit crazy sometimes and imagines one of the engines is on fire. He had a mate who went down in a Griffin like that.'

'What happens when he imagines one of the engines is on fire?'

'Well, what would you do if you had an engine on fire?'

'Shut the engine down and look for somewhere to land.'

'Yes, well, that's what he does. But he hasn't done it these last couple of trips. He's flown too many missions, we all have.' He consulted his instruments, made a quick calculation and moved his pencil on the map.

'I don't know why you want to come out here,' he said. 'It's not a place for a woman. It's not a place for a human being.'

As we flew further east it was apparent that we were entering a combat zone. The vapour trails of fighters criss-crossed the sky. Through the transparent roof of the cockpit I saw three Focke-Wulf 190s pass two thousand feet above us and bank away to the south. On the rim of the horizon, where the land stretched away flat like a table and the dusk came down like a fine powder falling, bright lights glowed and darted: the lights of war.

We came under fire once: a rattling hail on the starboard wing which I felt in the bones of my feet. I had never been under fire before, and a hitherto unknown, longed-for fear caught at me, leaving me exhilarated.

I descended from the bomber on to a mud-caked runway lashed by rain. The red marker lights of the airfield, furred by mist, illuminated cascading needles of ice and vanished, long before their lines converged, into a flat darkness.

Von Greim, on the airstrip to meet me with a handful of officers, was welcoming but brisk.

'The weather's filthy,' he said. 'Everything's a quagmire. We'd better get you indoors before you catch pneumonia.'

I could hear the guns. I asked how far we were from the Front.

'About twenty miles.' said von Greim, startling me, 'if it hasn't moved since lunchtime.'

In a staff car we skidded and squelched through the mud to a compound of wooden huts. Two sodden sentries with faces pinched from cold presented arms as von Greim led me up the few steps to his own quarters. Inside, in a cramped space piled with maps and papers, he turned to face me, unbuttoning his greatcoat and distributing muddy water around the room with uncharacteristic carelessness.

He said, 'I should never have invited you.'

'I beg your pardon?'

'The situation's changed radically. The Reds have been pushing us back along the southern half of the front ever since July. Now the offensive has spread to the north. They've re-taken Smolensk.'

'Where is that, in relation to where we are?'

'We're here.' He pointed with a white, wet finger at the nearest map. His fingertip was poised towards the left-hand edge, over a contourless area cut by rivers, marshy and forested. Smolensk was near the opposite edge of the map, a little to the north. It was about seventy miles.

'They're over the Dnieper,' he said. 'They'll be at Minsk before we know where they are. Your stay will have to be short, and certainly you mustn't go any closer to the Front.'

'Are you telling me I've been freezing to the observer's seat of a Dornier for ten hours for nothing?'

'I'm sorry, but I can't take the risk.'

'*Quatsch!*' I said.

He was taken aback. We did not know each other well. I could see him wondering whom he had invited.

'How are the men out there going to feel if I'm sent back home again? It won't do a lot for morale.'

'Have you any idea what the front line is like?' he said.

'I've come here to find out.'

'You heard the shelling when you got off the plane? That is what you will be in the middle of.'

I stuck out my jaw.

'It's no place for a woman,' he said.

'General, I insist.'

The wind had risen, and was driving rain through the gap at the bottom of the door.

He took off his cap, slowly, and ran his fingers through his hair. It was grey. There had hardly been a grey hair in it when I'd last seen him, eighteen months previously.

'Very well,' he said.

I was astonished by the suddenness of his capitulation. I think now that he was utterly wearied by a situation which was corroding him. He had no surplus energy for arguments with me.

I was taken to the Front the next morning.

Von Greim himself flew me, in an air force Stork, to a tiny airstrip about fifteen miles to the east. We flew low, skimming treetops and the roofless hulls of buildings. The air thickened with smoke and dust as we approached the firing zone, clearing occasionally so that I glimpsed what was happening below us. Once we flew fifty feet above a horse pulling a rocket launcher out of a ditch. The straining, mud-spattered men looked up as we went over. A moment later an explosion flung the Stork sideways like a paper glider.

On an airstrip in the middle of a cabbage field we transferred to an armoured vehicle driven by an army sergeant. The ground was shivering. We began to drive towards the trenches.

Much of the land was forested, or had been. Groves of trees stood white and blasted. The ground was churned, torn, and viscous with mud. We drove through an uprooted, roaring, quivering landscape and, at the end of a twenty-minute journey which seemed to have taken many hours, stumbled out on to pitted, smoking ground. I was clutching my steel hat like a talisman. The sergeant snatched it out of my hands, rammed it on my head and pushed me into a bomb crater.

He and the general landed beside me, and a fraction of a second after that the shell landed. The ground heaved like an animal, and earth rained on us. I thought I had lost my hearing.

The sergeant was mouthing at me to put my fingers in my ears. How, in this chaos, could you know when a shell was coming in your direction? They screamed through the sky every few seconds. Pounding their percussion in my head were the screech of shells and the crump and roar of their landing, the bass thunder of the guns, the drumming of aircraft, the rattle of machine-gun fire, and, piercing everything, a dreadful demonic whoop-whoop-whoop which was the most sinister sound I had ever heard.

'Rocket launcher,' mouthed the sergeant.

The general was looking at me. 'Are you all right?' his lips said.

I nodded. I was frightened out of my wits.

The sergeant scrambled out of the crater, and the general and I followed him.

We began, in the rain, the mud and the shelling, a tour of cold, exhausted troops huddling in holes in the ground.

For nearly two weeks I toured front-line positions. Sometimes I visited infantry or artillery units, sometimes I was at the makeshift airfields a few miles behind them where the front-line squadrons were.

I was there to cheer up the men, and I knew I could only do this in my own way. I was supposed to remind them of the women they had left behind. I suspected (correctly) that I was not in the least like the women they had left behind; nevertheless I was a visitor from home and could tell them about it. So I took them magazines and pictures and gossip, and news about the latest shows, and said practically nothing about the effect of bombing on the cities or about the miracle weapons we were constantly told would end the war; and for these crumbs they were distressingly grateful.

Conditions were bad on the Front. The fight was vicious, and it was going the wrong way. The weather was cold and getting colder, and the men in the trenches were constantly in wet clothing. They lacked medical supplies. They lacked food. Their rations were harshly calculated as the minimum on which a man could live and fight. They were perpetually hungry.

And there was the mud. It was ubiquitous. It turned up inside boots, inside drinking mugs and saucepans, in one's hair and between the bristles of a toothbrush: it got into beds and food. Half of what could be seen beyond the steamy, cracked windows of the huts was mud. The other half was the lead-grey, water-laden sky.

The weather badly affected the spirits. It affected mine. It affected those of the men I had come to visit. They made an effort

287

for me, but I could see what an effort it was. They were having to reach deep inside themselves to find the bit of life to welcome me, to behave as their minds told them was required: to find the place where all they had left behind and were supposed to be fighting for had been put away, and was now walled up and nearly inaccessible.

I thought about the other reasons for their state of mind. Our armies had invaded these lands with dazzling violence. Victory seemed assured and easy. But, pursuing a vanishing enemy across seemingly endless plains, the troops had plunged into a vastness which one day turned on them. Winter. They were not prepared for winter. It was supposed to be all over by then. They had no winter clothing. Their equipment failed. First the rains bogged them down, then the blizzards froze them. They began to die from cold. And then the enemy came back. Well clothed, well equipped, and fighting with bitter fury.

It was two years since the glittering advance had sunk to its axles in the Russian mud. Since then there had been successes, but small ones. Moscow had remained elusive. The oilfields had not been won. The industrial regions had been grasped but had slipped away again. And Stalingrad ... That huge wound was still numb. An entire army lost, thrown away, three hundred thousand men, for nothing. For an idea that there must be no retreat.

And now came the retreat that nothing could stop. It was soldierly and hard-fought, but in its nature it was ignominious. The German Army was back where it had been two years earlier, and moving backwards every day.

And the air force, who were my hosts?

Selected no longer from an elite but from what could be found, hastily trained, supplied with the results of Ernst's tenure at the ministry, given spicy promises of wonder weapons which never appeared, fighting an implacable enemy defending his homeland, and living daily with the shame of its failure to supply the beleaguered Sixth Army at Stalingrad – the less said about the air force the better.

Add it all together: the huge failure, the mud, the knowledge that after the mud would come the snow, the miserable rations, the longing for home, the exhaustion, the fear of the terrible Russians ... it was enough, quite enough, to account for the state in which I

288

found those airmen, a state as it were of something frozen inside, of their living on the surface above it.

Was there something else?

If there was, I clearly wasn't supposed to know it.

On the fifth day of my visit to the Front, I saw, from the cabin of the Stork, something that gave me an unpleasant feeling. The general was piloting us from a forward position back to our home airfield, but a pocket of heavy fighting had forced him to detour to the west into a sector he seemed to want to avoid.

The light was beautiful. The rain had stopped but, high up, thick wisps of greyish cloud hung like the tatters of a scarf. The afternoon sun, already low, tipped them with gold. In the pores of the sky the moisture was collecting again. There would be rain within an hour.

I looked at the ground. We were at less than a thousand feet.

In the distance were pinewoods and the metallic blue of a lake. From this height I could see two villages. One had been all but demolished by the advancing Panzers, but the other, which we were now approaching, was intact and the focus of considerable activity.

You can see so much from a Stork.

A lorry was disgorging troops into the square in the centre of the village. There were other troops in a field. The troops in the field were guarding a group of prisoners. But what was inexplicable, what my mind recoiled from, was that the prisoners were naked.

I said to the general over the radio, 'What's going on down there?'

'Down where?'

'In the village we're almost over.'

'I can't see anything.'

He couldn't fail to see it! He hardly needed to turn his head.

'It's just to the left of the port landing strut,' I said.

A moment passed. 'Well, I'm afraid,' said the general, 'that from where I sit it's completely obscured by the port landing strut.'

I began to think he didn't want to see it.

'What's the name of this place?' I asked.

'I think we'd better observe radio silence from now on,' said the general.

The junior officers threw a party for me at the end of the first week. The weather had worsened by now. Snow was lying outside, and drifting against the windows. Inside, the hut was festive. They had made brightly coloured paper streamers and brought in fir branches. On the tables stood little vases of greenery or paper flowers. Pictures cut from magazines were stuck on the wall. The pictures didn't make the hut look more cheerful, they made it look more forlorn.

I was told to close my eyes. Something was set down on a table. When I opened my eyes I was looking at a large iced cake.

I could not imagine what, in the circumstances, might have been involved in collecting the ingredients for a cake.

They asked me to make a speech. I found it difficult to say anything. The simplicity of the occasion, its generosity, the knowledge that even in a few days some of these men would be dead, affected me strongly. Fortunately they only expected a few words. I thanked them, and said I hoped that one day, when the war was over, they would be my guests. I said I would not offer to make them cake, because they had been through enough already. (They laughed a great deal at this.) I said they must never doubt that they were constantly in the thoughts of the people at home, and I told them that the sacrifices they were making would never be forgotten.

There was enthusiastic applause, and then I cut the first slice of cake and the chef, to my relief, cut the rest, and we washed it down with mugs of tea.

Some time later I found myself at one of the tables, talking to a shy lieutenant called Pauwels, a gunner in a Heinkel, who wanted to show me photographs of his girlfriend.

In the past week I had been shown many photographs of girlfriends. It was remarkable how similar these photographs were. The girl, with fair, braided hair, stood smiling, sometimes holding the hand of a younger brother or sister, against the background of a modest house. I wondered that these men never photographed their sweethearts in cars or canoes, or on mountain tops or with their hair down. I supposed they did, but that these other photographs had no talismanic property. It was the photograph with the braided hair and the family home in the background which promised that the world would return to order, and the photograph's keeper return to the scene depicted.

'She's very pretty,' I said to Pauwels. 'What's her name?'

A man in field grey joined us at that moment. He pulled up a chair and sat on it with a casual movement, as if it were his. The men nearby glanced at him, but no one greeted him.

Pauwels continued talking to me. 'Her name's Helga. We're engaged. We'll get married on my next leave.' He arranged in a row the three photographs he had taken from his wallet – Helga in front of the house, Helga in the park, Helga with her parents in the garden.

The man sitting on the other side of him, a bomber pilot rather older, had been leaning silently with his arms folded on the table. He moved the photographs so he could look at them.

'She's a nice girl,' he said.

'She's the best.'

'They're all the best.'

Pauwels's face suddenly lit up. 'Will you come to our wedding?' he asked me.

'Yes, if you invite me. And if the trains are running.'

'Will you come to mine, too?' A cheeky-looking Austrian had drawn up a chair opposite mine and was taking photographs out of his wallet. The procedure began again.

'You don't know how much it means to us that you've come out here,' said Pauwels. 'It feels like the ends of the earth, this place.'

'It is the ends of the earth,' said the Austrian.

'That's no way to describe our future colonies,' said the man in field grey. He was smiling: the reprimand was intended lightly. I saw that it wasn't army field grey, it was SS.

The airmen looked at him with a dislike which none of them seemed willing to articulate.

Then the Austrian challenged him with. 'Come to check up on us. Meissner?'

'No,' said Meissner, easily, 'I've just delivered a message to your commanding officer. I thought I'd join the party. Don't mind, do you?'

He turned to me. 'I'm afraid you've fallen into bad company,' he said with a smile. He smiled often.

'Oh, I've no complaints,' I said.

'If you don't like the company, find another table,' said the Austrian in a low voice to Meissner.

Meissner did not react.

The bomber pilot said, 'Take it easy.'

Pauwels shifted uncomfortably and rearranged his photographs. He said, 'We might have a singsong later, if Rainer brings his accordion.'

The Austrian got up and walked to the other side of the room.

The bomber pilot followed him with his eyes, then returned his attention to me. 'I'm sorry about that,' he said.

Meissner leant forward. He said seriously, 'You can't walk away from it, you know. What do you think you're fighting for?'

Pauwels's face tightened. He held up one of the photographs of Helga between his thumb and forefinger. 'I know what I'm fighting for,' he said.

'That's juvenile,' said Meissner. He stood up, clicked his heels to me and left us.

The bomber pilot made a face and began filling his pipe.

I thought it was time to talk to someone else.

I began to move around the room, meeting as many of the men as I could. The atmosphere was getting livelier: schnapps was served, a crate of beer – a gift from the general – had been brought in, and bottles of something nameless, in thick green glass, were passing from hand to hand.

After an hour or so, someone remarked that we ought to take the general a piece of cake. I volunteered to take it.

He was on the telephone. The walls of the hut were thin and I could hear his voice clearly. Standing on the step, I heard him say, 'No, you may not assume so. That sector is under air force control.'

I was going to knock, but something in his voice stopped me. I stood there and listened.

'I have only your word for it. I imagine Himmler has more weighty matters to worry about than a minor piece of housework behind the lines.'

A pause. Then: 'Be damned to your weekly reports, Major. I am trying to fight a war here. You take my men for your special operations, you tie up my communications, you limit my area of manoeuvre, and now you are proposing to carry out a task two miles from one of my airfields before I have vacated it.'

I heard papers being moved around on the desk, and then the

final, angry, 'No, I am not withholding my co-operation. I am not able to, am I?' The phone was banged on to its rest.

I waited a little longer and then knocked. The general was sitting at his desk, frowning at a map. He looked up, and his eyes fell on the cake as if he did not have the faintest idea what it was.

I returned to the party. Round the rim of my skull I could feel a headache starting, one of the blinding headaches I had had after the Komet crash.

Back in the hut there was music. Rainer had brought his accordion. We sang folk songs, love songs and songs about home as night fell and the snow drifted against the windows.

Rainer played a dance tune, and someone asked me to dance. Nothing could have been more natural, but it brought home to me the terms on which I was there. I had been pampered, flattered, given cake and not allowed near the controls of an aeroplane ever since my arrival, and I was finding it suffocating. Only the obvious misery of the conditions in which the men were living, and the fact that my presence was, visibly, cheering them up, prevented me from rebelling.

However, to dance was little enough, and certainly they deserved to have something done for them. So I whirled around the floor in the arms of one and then another well-scrubbed airman who wanted to show me photographs of his girlfriend, and it was out of the question to tell them they should have kept their cake and streamers for a better cause.

A field-grey uniform claimed me and I found I was dancing with Meissner.

He said, 'I'm afraid I wasn't very popular with your companions earlier. I'm sorry if I caused you embarrassment.'

'Not at all,' I said.

'Their attitude is understandable,' he said. 'But childish.'

I felt indignant. A bond had grown between me and these air force boys. I respected them, I cared about them.

I said, 'I don't think you should call them childish. They're doing a man's job.'

'Yes,' he said. 'But the SS is doing the more difficult job.'

I glanced up into his face. It was calm and confident. I felt a need to shake his assumption of superiority; or at least call him to account for it.

I said. 'This difficult job. You mean the spiritual defence of Germany?'

He did not hear the quotation marks in my voice. He did not hear the irony. Perhaps, after all, they were not as audible as I'd intended.

He lowered his eyes to mine. He said, 'But exactly. How wonderfully well you put it.'

He could not more effectively have stopped me.

Lamely. I said, 'But you believe in what you're doing?'

He laughed. 'Indeed I do.'

'Then why is it more difficult than what these men are doing?'

I asked this question out of hostility, without thinking. Not until a few seconds had passed, and he had not replied, did I realize what the question actually was.

It never occurred to him that I could be so stupid. He thought I meant something else altogether.

He said, thoughtfully, 'Forgive me. I was on the point of forgetting who I'm talking to. You would understand, yes. You would have the necessary courage.'

We waltzed, under the lights and the streamers. My skin felt cold. I had the sensation of a rock in my throat which I could neither spit out nor swallow. I had another, quite separate sensation: that I was on a train I couldn't get off, that wouldn't stop, that would carry me steadily to the end of this conversation.

'Is it a question of courage?' I asked. I had to ask it, it was part of the conversation that had to take place.

'Of course,' said Meissner. 'We walk alone. Although we have help with the practical tasks, we carry the moral burden.' His shoulders lifted in a shrug. 'Even the practical help we are grudged. They work alongside us, you know, on some operations, and still try to dissociate themselves. I have no respect for that.'

'Do you get commanders withholding their support?'

'Well, they can't withhold it, but I think some of them would like to. General von Greim . . . ah, but I must mind what I say. He's your host.'

'He is, and he's a very considerate host.'

'Has he been taking you round his airfields, showing you the war?'

'I've seen a lot of airfields, and I've seen something of the war.'

'The war the SS is fighting,' he said, 'is the real war. But of course the other one is necessary. The territory has first to be won.'

There was a terrible clarity in this. It invaded my mind and I could not keep it out. My headache now was very painful and I felt I might soon be sick, but I could not abandon this conversation.

I said, 'Why do you take their clothes away?'

'I beg your pardon?'

'When you round them up, why do you take their clothes away?'

'It's part of the procedure,' he said.

After a few more bars of accordion music, I said, 'It's called "housework", isn't it?'

'Who have you been talking to?'

'It was an expression the general used.'

An airman approached us, wanting to dance with me. Meissner shook his head. The airman went away.

Meissner said, 'I could show you something of our war, the real war, if you're interested.'

I felt my eyes dilate.

'Oh, I'm sorry,' he said at once, 'I shouldn't have presumed . . .'

'It's all right,' I said.

'No, it's quite improper. You are, after all, a woman.'

'What are you proposing?' I asked.

'Well, we have visitors on our special operations sometimes. We're rather proud of the efficiency of our procedures. I could arrange . . . but it's really quite unsuitable.'

'Thank you. I accept,' I said, and the train had arrived.

Meissner smiled with pleasure. Then a doubt appeared in his eyes. 'I'll have to get von Greim's permission,' he said.

'Do you?'

Meissner studied me. I was challenging him to a serious breach of protocol. He liked it: his mouth curved up.

'Well,' he said, 'in view of who you are, I don't see why there should be any problem. I'll see what I can do, shall I?'

It was almost a week later that he returned to the base. I was due to fly home in three days' time, and was sitting over a not-very-serious game of chess with the navigator who had been on my flight out. I had not forgotten about Meissner: indeed our conversation had never been absent from my mind for longer than a few minutes. But it had developed an air of the fantastic, and I was no longer quite sure that it had taken place.

I felt someone come in and stand with his back to the closed door, looking at me.

I glanced up, and saw the square-chinned face and the calm, light eyes. He strolled over to one of the tables and picked up a newspaper.

Unsettled, I tried to concentrate on my next move. The game had completely gone from my head.

'Excuse me,' I said to the navigator, and went to speak to Meissner.

He said, 'Are you still interested in my invitation?'

A sort of giddiness caught me. I said, 'I'm flying back to Germany in a few days.'

'I know you are. There'll be a unit operating thirty miles from here the day after tomorrow. Someone can pick you up early and get you back to the base in time for lunch.'

I felt horror. I also felt helpless. Whatever this was, now that I found myself so near it I had to know it. Therefore I would go. But what I found out . . . Things Ernst had said, huge shadows, moved on the edge of my mind. I could not contemplate what finding out might mean.

'What are the arrangements?' I asked.

'Be at the gates at six. Someone will pick you up there. Dress as warmly as you can, you'll be standing about a lot. That's all.'

The only possible thing to do was refuse.

'I see,' I said. 'Right. I'll be there.'

Something else was required. 'Thank you,' I said.

The headlight glimmered through the dark at precisely six o'clock. An SS motorcycle. Fur-wrapped and fur-booted, I climbed into the narrow sidecar. We drove for more than an hour, bumping over rutted, icy roads. I could see nothing from my sidecar, which was not unlike an aircraft's cockpit, but the dim gleam of the reflected headlamp on tyre-marked snow, and to my left the dense black bulk of the rider, leaning forward into the night.

296

Then we rounded a bend and there was before us what looked like a star blazing on the ground. As we drew closer I saw that a dozen or so vehicles had been parked in a circle with their headlights facing inwards. In the centre of this circle of light stood small groups of uniformed men.

The motorcycle stopped and its rider dismounted. I climbed out of the sidecar. There were streaks of light in the sky. A short distance away a group of officers were talking, laughing and hitting their gloved hands together for warmth. One of them detached himself from the group and came towards me. It was Meissner.

'I hope the journey wasn't too uncomfortable,' he said.

I said it hadn't been.

He walked with me to the circle of officers. I found myself next to an army major who was holding a briefcase and looking at his watch. Hearing that I was with von Greim, he said in an undertone, 'Goodness knows what you want to come here for.' Then he said, 'I'm sorry, that wasn't very polite of me. You rather lose your bearings, doing this sort of thing.'

I said. 'Do you do much of it?'

'No,' he said, 'thank God.'

Then, as if at a signal, all the regular army officers in the circle turned and saluted each other, and saluted the SS officers, and got into cars and drove off.

The signal, I thought, might have been the arrival of a large lorry with high wooden sides which parked itself a short distance away from the others.

Things now began to happen quickly.

One of the remaining officers – an SS lieutenant, there seemed to be no senior or even middle-ranking officers left – shouted a command, and troops jumped down from the backs of two canvas-covered transport trucks which were facing into the circle.

In the growing light, I could now see the outlines of a large building, a barn or church, about a hundred yards away. The troops spread out to form a corridor between this building and the back of one of the other lorries. A sergeant unlatched the door of this lorry and banged on the side with his rifle butt.

People began to come out. They were mostly women and old men. There were a few children. They were all humbly dressed and clutched bundles of belongings. They seemed disoriented. They stared around them, and at the soldiers, who pushed and bullied them down the corridor towards the stone building.

We had moved from the space between the lorry cabs to a position outside the circle from which we could see what was happening. I was standing with Meissner, the lieutenant and another man, a tall, stooped, bespectacled man who was wearing civilian clothes with a Party armband.

The man in civilian clothes said, as if to himself, 'There are so many of them.'

The lieutenant looked at him sharply. 'That is precisely the problem.'

'Yes, I know. I just wonder when we'll get to the end of it. Comparatively speaking, this is inefficient. Other means are in use elsewhere.'

'We are using the means prescribed here. I merely follow orders.'

He broke off to shout at a trooper who was lounging in the doorway.

'Shall we walk down?' suggested the man in civilian clothes.

Inside the building – it was a barn, empty except for a few small tables and chairs – the men and women prisoners had been separated by herding them on either side of a wooden partition. Meissner indicated that I should go into the section which contained the women, and himself went on the other side of the partition.

The women were being made to take their clothes off. They were told to do this in a particular order, depositing skirts in one place and shoes in another, and leaving their jewellery on a table at which an SS man sat. Beside each women's jewellery, as she left it, he chalked a number, and told her to remember it.

The women were undressing hurriedly, not talking, eager to placate the guards. Some of them helped each other, with fastenings and buttons which had suddenly become difficult with the trembling of their fingers.

I found myself unable to watch more of this. I went outside. I stayed out there in the clear, icy dawn, stamping my feet to warm them. The sun hung in mist over the tips of the forest.

After about a quarter of an hour the first batch came out. Women. They were naked. I stifled what rose in my throat, and watched.

The guards had strung themselves out quickly between the barn and the high-sided lorry that was not parked with the others. With their heads lowered and hands held to shield their privacy, the women walked along the line of guards to the back of the lorry, and up the ramp which had been placed there for them.

The door was closed behind them. Bolt after bolt was shot home, then a flat iron bar was lowered across the centre of the door.

The guards relaxed and joked.

Meissner had joined me. He said, 'Do you feel all right?'

'Yes,' I said.

He nodded and went to speak to someone else. The guards went back to the building. One of them had sneaked round the back of the truck, out of sight of the lieutenant, and was having a cigarette. Just by his right boot, in front of the rear wheel, a lever was sticking out from the truck's chassis.

I walked a little, over the snow, to keep warm.

After an interval two more SS men came out of the building and walked towards the truck.

Meissner, holding a black attaché case under his arm, came up to me and said, 'I'll have to leave you here, I'm afraid. I have to take a message to Divisional HQ. The rider who brought you here will take you back.'

'Thank you.'

'He'll be leaving at 11.15,' said Meissner, checking his watch. 'You can decide what you want to do until then. There'll be coffee shortly. I don't imagine you'll want to go with them.' He indicated where the two SS men were getting into the cab of the high-sided truck.

'Where are they going?' I said, in the frozen voice in which I said everything.

He said. 'To do the second half of the job.'

There was a pause before I said, 'And what is that?'

'What d'you think?' he said.

His lips were curled. There was a tension in him as if he might snap.

I said, 'Do you mean . . . ?' and couldn't finish the sentence.

He said, 'I thought you knew.'

I said, 'I didn't know anything.'

He said, 'Then you have no business to be here.'

There was another pause. Then I said clearly, 'What is going to happen to these women?'

A tiny shock went through the muscles of his face, as if something had been detonated miles away.

He began to say something, but his lips drew back, exposing the teeth. He said, with what seemed to be anger, 'If you want to know, you'd better find out.'

He walked to the cab in which the men were sitting and banged on the metal with the flat of his hand. The door opened.

Meissner beckoned to me.

I got into the cab. The door slammed and we set off.

They were drunk, I realized almost straight away. The cab was full of the sweet, oily fumes of whatever had been in the green bottles at the party. How had they got drunk so quickly? Or were they pretending to be drunker than they were? The van swerved and skidded on the road, and the driver and his companion laughed uproariously, while from behind us in the body of the truck came a succession of thuds.

I sat by the window, staring out.

They felt they should engage me in conversation.

'Well, what d'you think of the East, then?' said the driver's companion.

'I think it's a terrible place.'

'There you are, the lady thinks it's a terrible place,' said the driver. He changed gear and the noise of the engine became deafening. He waited to change up again before saying anything else. Then he said, 'I expect she thinks we're terrible people.'

'She will in a minute, if she doesn't already,' said his companion, and they both laughed a lot.

The driver pulled a bottle from under his seat. He thumbed the cork out of the top and took a swig. He handed the bottle to his companion.

'What a pig you are,' said the second man, 'what a bloody pig, excuse my language, lady.' He wiped the rim of the bottle with his cuff and offered it to me.

'No, thanks,' I said.

'Sure?'

'No thank you,' I said. 'I don't drink.'

He put the bottle to his lips and tipped his head back. His face flushed with the alcohol.

'Wonderful stuff.' he said.

'It's goats' piss,' said the driver. He swung the wheel and we skidded again. 'No, it's goats' something-else, I won't say exactly what.'

'You watch your manners, you ignorant swine.'

'She doesn't mind us. She wouldn't be here if she did.'

We drove erratically past churned fields and roofless cottages, keeping always parallel to the forest. Finally, at a fork, we turned off towards it. We slowed down at the edge of the trees, then drove in among them. There was a road, newly made: I could see the fresh gashes on the tree trunks where machinery had been brought in.

We stopped where the road stopped. To the left of us was a long, deep trench, which at first I thought was a tank ditch. The excavated soil was piled up on the far side of it.

We all got out. The driver went down his side of the truck towards the back, and his companion sauntered off with the bottle, knocked the snow off a tree stump with his foot, and sat down.

The driver had left the engine running.

I walked round the front of the cab so that I could see what he was doing.

He was trying to manipulate the lever which stuck out at the side of the truck just in front of the rear wheel. It seemed to be stiff, and he was grunting and crouching down so that he could put his shoulder into moving it. He shouted for the other man to come and help, but by the time his companion reappeared the driver had straightened up and succeeded in moving the lever by a thrust with the sole of his boot.

I heard the lever lock into its new position, and the note of the engine change. I could not define what was different about it except that it now sounded muffled.

Almost at once a terrible noise began. I cannot get it out of my mind.

Hammering, frantic hammering, on the inside of the truck.

The driver looked at his watch. He seemed to have gone pale. He went and joined the other man on the tree stump. They passed the bottle from hand to hand, and smoked and looked at the sky.

The hammering continued. I noticed, at some point, that no exhaust fumes were coming from the tail pipe.

I walked into the darkness between the trees until I fell. Then, raising myself on my hands and knees, I vomited like a dog on the clean earth.

When I went back, the driver's mate was just throwing away the empty bottle. He threw it into the trench.

The hammering had stopped.

The driver got up and walked down the side of the truck to the lever. He got behind it and pushed it hard with his foot. The exhaust from the engine began to cloud the air again.

I saw then that a car had drawn up not far away. It was a black Volkswagen. Two men sat in the front, smoking.

The driver of the truck went to the back of the vehicle and drew back the bolts. I heard him lift up the heavy iron bar and open the doors.

Stench filled the air.

The men sitting in the Volkswagen could see inside the back of the truck. I could not; I was standing near the cab with my back against a tree. But I could see their faces. I could see, at the moment the doors were opened, their incredulous fascination. Then their faces closed, they became like walls.

The two men got out of the car and threw their cigarettes away. They were wearing overalls. They went towards the back of the truck.

The driver's mate, who had remained sitting on the tree stump, now got up and went to the cab. From behind the seats he took out a wooden pole with a large, rounded hook on the end. He walked, carrying this, to the back of the truck.

All of them looked at their watches. Then they went into the back of the truck.

CHAPTER TWENTY-TWO

I don't see the coast until we are over it. The metallic lid of cloud cuts off sunlight. It has become very cold.

The dark water opens unexpectedly below me. I have the sensation of flying over the edge of the world into space, as the men who sailed with Columbus must have expected to do. I am disoriented for a moment. There is something wrong with the coastline. Then I see what it is.

Ice webs the knotted fingers of land. Ice, green-white, unearthly, Ice where the sea should be.

People are standing on it. They have walked out on to it with their possessions in blankets, their handcarts and children, and are waiting in a long and patient line as if queuing at a bread shop.

They are waiting to be taken off by the boats.

Out on the water are three battered ferries, making for the bay. Much further out, near the limit of my vision, is a larger ship, perhaps a destroyer, steaming hard in the other direction for the safety of Lübeck.

The people on the ice look up. Not at us.

I have grown slow with tiredness, and of course cannot hear above the engine's noise.

Two Russian planes streak past a hundred feet ahead of me, and the black bombs fall from under their wings. They are carrying out what must be a practised manoeuvre. They do not bomb the refugees. They lay their black eggs in the pale air, and the eggs fall down, down and through the green-white ice, so that eyes spring in the ice, and the darkness comes up out of them and spreads. The darkness eats at the ice until the web of ice is broken into islands, and on these ice-islands people huddle until the islands themselves begin to sink into the water.

The planes climb away at the end of their run and sweep out to sea, where the ferries labour in the swell.

I turn west, hugging the coast, seeking what shelter there is from this numbing sky.

I was found a place on a bomber returning to Germany twelve hours earlier than the one on which I had been scheduled to fly.

I spoke to no one on my return. In fact I hardly noticed there were people around me. The ones I saw moved past my vision like figures on a screen. When I heard them talk, it surprised me. I looked at them and thought, if you knew what I have seen, you could not go down the street so casually, you would not find it worthwhile to argue with the newspaper vendor.

I had been walking for years on the thinnest crust of ice. Thousands walked with me: it was all we could do. But below our feet there dropped away a frozen darkness. Immeasurable. Unimaginable.

I had said to von Greim, 'I have just seen something taking place thirty miles west of here which I would like you to explain to me.'

He was putting on his coat to go out. He stopped with one arm half way into a sleeve and said, 'You had no business in that area.'

'Nevertheless I was there. I wish I hadn't been. General, are you aware that the German Army is herding civilians into vans and gassing them?'

'My God,' he said, 'oh. my God,' and he took off his coat and flung it on the desk and turned to face me in fury.

'*Why* can't you mind your own business?'

It seemed to me that I had never seen him before.

'You know about it, don't you?' I said.

'That sector is under the jurisdiction of the SS. The air force pulled out of it days ago.'

'What does it matter whose jurisdiction it's under?'

'That's ridiculous. If it's an SS-controlled sector I'm not responsible for what goes on there.'

'Do you *know* what's going on there?'

'How am I supposed to know whether I know? The SS does what it likes, you're well aware of that. It's accountable to nobody but Himmler.'

'And to whom are your men accountable?'

304

'I beg your pardon?'

'Men under your command serving in those Special Duties squads. Are you responsible for what they do, or not?'

'It does not involve me.'

'It *does* involve you! You are working with the SS!'

'I am not working with the SS! I am commanding an air corps in combat, and you are at this moment preventing me from carrying out my duties.'

'General,' I gripped the back of a chair, because I really felt I might faint. 'Do you know what I've just seen?'

He flinched. I saw in his eyes the depth of his fear.

'No,' he said, and his features were rigid. 'No, and I don't want to.'

Back in Berlin, with my life waiting for me to resume it, I felt a great lassitude. The simplest actions seemed to require disproportionate effort.

I turned my mind after a day or so – reluctantly, it was reluctant to fix itself, it wanted to drift in a void – to the matter of flying. I must get myself fit for work.

A nausea began in the pit of my stomach and travelled upward. I walked to the bathroom and was sick. I lay on my bed for most of the afternoon, facing the idea that I could not go back to my job.

I could not dissociate it from what I knew. All aeroplanes were contaminated by the ends for which the air force was being used in the East. I had once thought aeroplanes were non-political. Later, when I learnt better, I still had thought that they were innocent. I could no longer think that. And the Komet, most alluring of all, was the worst of all. That pride, that shattering speed, that steepness of ascent. That insistence on death. I knew what they were now. At the heart of Dieter's 'hardness to ourselves' was a soft, disgusting secret.

For days I did little but wander about the flat, pick up books and put them down again, and stare out of the window.

One evening I found an unopened bottle of plum brandy in the sideboard. It had been there three years. I opened it and drank it. How much of it, I don't know. When I came round the following morning, recumbent on the carpet, the bottle was lying on its side, unstoppered, on the edge of the table, with a sticky brown pool below it on the floor.

I cleaned up, observing that the headache was no worse than the one I had had for months after the crash, but was of a different kind, having a sort of dessication to it. There were other, very unpleasant, effects. I went for a walk, after which I was so disoriented that on returning to the building I tried to let myself into the flat below mine, to my intense embarrassment and the amusement of its occupant, who was at just that moment coming up the stairs. Then, since there was nothing else to do, I went to bed for the rest of the day.

I had never done any of these things before: got drunk, mistaken where I lived, or gone to bed in the daytime when not ill. As a trio they were quite an achievement, but at the time they merely consolidated my wretchedness.

Most of the city had been bombed, and much of it had been levelled. Berlin was being reduced to the elements from which it had arisen: brick, stone, timber joists, exposed pipes, the open ground. To achieve this, the RAF came over every night and the USAAF came every day. Raids lasted two or three hours, sometimes even longer. People sat in shuddering, dark caves which might at any moment collapse and bury them, and tried to hold their minds together. They emerged into newly wrought devastation and went to work, if the premises were still there, or home, if that was. Or they went in search of friends or family, hoping not to find, when they got there, a pile of smoking rubble and the fire brigade trying to extricate someone from the ruins.

Walking one day through the destruction, I realized that the tenacity of ordinary people was amazing. No one got enough sleep. No one had enough to eat. Often there was no water. But they carried on.

Admittedly there wasn't much alternative to carrying on. Even so, I found it admirable. A desire to do something to help stirred me out of my apathy.

The nearest camp site for people bombed out of their homes was three miles from my flat. There were no buses because of a heavy raid on the Tiergarten, so I walked.

A number of streets on the way were occupied by furniture. Kitchen cupboards, cooking stoves, beds, tables and chairs stood amid a litter of wood and plaster in the roadway, and among them wandered, with dazed expressions, people who were presumably trying to identify their own household goods. A horse and cart stood at the end of one street, piled with the contents of a sitting room. A pinched-looking man with a plaid scarf around his neck was pushing a pram full of books round the obstructions, and talking to himself in a frenzy of grief.

On the walls of the bombed houses, messages were chalked. They said things like: 'Everyone in this shelter got out alive', and 'The Schmidts are staying in Potsdam', and 'Greta, where are you?'. Further on, a road was under water. In the water, ragged children played. A policeman shouted at them to clear off, but they ignored him. These children who didn't seem to belong anywhere were starting to appear in the bombed cities. Presumably, until rounded up by some welfare body or other, they lived in the ruins, on their wits.

The camp site covered about ten acres. The rubble had been cleared away to the perimeter and the ground was already becoming a sea of mud. Straw had been dumped on it here and there in an attempt to halt the process.

The tents were heavy bell tents, large enough to house a family. They stood in rows, each covered in a camouflage patterning which made it look like a toadstool wearing a hairnet. In the open space between the tents wandered hundreds of Berliners. They all looked lost or baffled, as if they did not know how they had come to be in the middle of a muddy camp site, holding a papier-mâché bowl of soup, dressed as if to go to the office.

I traced the sweet smell of woodsmoke to a bonfire between a row of tents and a marquee. It seemed the fire was not a permitted fire. A burly man in some uniform or other stood pointing an accusing finger at the fire and berating the family who had lit it.

I went into the marquee. Trestle tables occupied its length, and behind them sat men sifting through documents. On the other side of the table, waiting their turn, stood the people to whom the documents belonged.

One official was saying to the man across the table from him. 'But *why* did your grandfather change his name if he wasn't a Jew?'

'Because it was Hungarian and no one could spell it,' said the man. He looked bewildered.

'Name?' barked an official at me.

I said. 'I've come along to see if there's anything I can do.'

'About what?'

'Do to help.'

'Help?'

'I thought perhaps you could do with an extra pair of hands. Putting up tents or something.'

'We have contractors who put up the tents. This site is run by the Nazi People's Welfare Organization. Do you belong to it?'

'No. But surely with all these people to provide shelter and food for, you must be able to use extra help!'

'I daresay we could, but we can't have just anybody coming along here and helping,' said the official. 'You'll have to go through proper channels.'

He scribbled an address on a piece of paper and gave it to me.

As I left, the man with the Hungarian grandfather was protesting, 'But I have six children, and you cannot refuse to re-house them because the name on a document has been changed!'

Outside, I wandered over the trodden straw towards the soup kitchen. A bald man with a paunch was manipulating the temperature controls of a steel vat. Steam and a strong odour of turnips were coming out of the vat.

A few paces further on, women were cutting bread under an awning.

There were eight of them. One brought loaves from the open back of an army truck and put them on the table. Two others took the cut bread on trays to a counter where people queued. The remaining five were cutting. They all cut the same way. They held the loaf against the chest and sliced it horizontally with the almost casual movement of a very sharp knife.

I watched them for a little while. Straight-backed, firm-jawed, their greying hair closely braided, their eyes fixed on what they could do well and resolutely turned from what was not their business. They were the women of the Nazi Women's League, and they were cutting bread for Germany.

I started to walk home.

The sirens wailed after ten minutes. Someone beckoned me into a shop I was passing and I went down to the cellar. It was a sitting-cross-legged shelter. Since neither the flak nor the fighters nor God could stop the bombing, people had reverted to magic. In some shelters you had to hold hands and count. In some you counted backwards. In some shelters the buckets of water represented more of a hazard than the bombs. In some shelters you weren't allowed to touch the walls. In this shelter you had to sit cross-legged.

It was a short raid, less than an hour, but by the end of it everyone was ready to kill the child who in a nasal singsong had been intoning nursery rhymes since the first bombs began to fall.

We stumbled out into the light, the smells of burning, of powdered brick, or exposed sewage and gas.

A bomb had fallen in the middle of a building, crashing through all four of its floors and blowing out the wall fronting the street, while leaving the others intact. A rail of green dresses swayed on the edge of a cliff, and from a full-length mirror my surprised reflection looked back at me.

I was at the end of the street when the first floor, and the green dresses with it, fell. I heard the roar, and then someone scream. I turned and ran back and, with others, began to pull at the mounds of brick, plaster, splintered wood and smashed tailors' dummies.

After a while some ambulancemen came and helped us. We got a child out: it was the child who had been singing nursery rhymes in the cellar. Three rafters had fallen together in such a way as to make a protective tepee over his head, and he was suffering from nothing worse than a cut finger.

His mother was dead.

We dug out an old man as well, swearing vilely because the falling plaster had broken his artificial leg, from which we had to cut him loose with my penknife. The ambulancemen didn't have a knife, only a shovel and a syringe, and there was nothing to put in the syringe. The ambulancemen and I carried the dead woman, the child, and the old man, who had a nasty head injury which he didn't seem to have noticed, into the ambulance, and took the last two to an emergency hospital set up in the crypt of a church and the woman to a place set aside for the reception of those who had failed to survive air raids. It was a high-rooted building like a railway shed.

'We could do with someone like you on this bus,' grunted the driver as we got back into the ambulance.

'Wouldn't I need medical training?' I said.

'Know any first aid?'

'Yes.' All pilots learnt first aid.

'That's all you'd want. We don't carry drugs: the army's got) em all. Bit of first aid and a strong back.' He looked at me closely. 'Don't I know your face from somewhere? You ever been in the news-papers?'

'No,' I said.

And that is how I became an ambulance auxiliary.

Any work you aren't used to is hard on the body to start with. My back ached from lifting, my arms from the painstaking piece-by-piece removal of rubble from human bodies. Until they hardened, my hands were cracked and dry, and the nails tore down to the quick.

One evening I reached the staircase of my apartment building almost too tired to climb it. I hauled myself up with a hand on the stair rail, reached the landing, groped for my key in the pocket of my blackened overalls and inserted it into the keyhole. It didn't work.

Things always behave thus when you're too exhausted to cope with them. I fiddled with the key ineffectually, my temper rising.

The door opened from the inside.

'Oh, not again!' laughed the woman who lived downstairs.

After a moment's bewilderment, I realized that I had made the same stupid mistake as before, and that this time it was inexcusable.

Stammering apologies, I retreated.

'Why don't you come in?' she said. 'You obviously want to see inside this flat. Come in and have a cup of coffee.' She surveyed me. 'You look as if you could do with it.'

'No. I don't want to bother you – I really am terribly sorry – perhaps some other time . . .'

'Come in,' she said. I don't know why I went in, but I did.

Places hold so much of a person that I have often wondered that people let each other into their homes at all. I walked into a warm, bright sitting room full of the carelessly displayed evidence of a life.

Family photographs, some of them faded and cracked: an assortment of interesting bric-à-brac on the mantelpiece, including a piece of coloured glass, a postcard of Constantinople and a carving that looked African; an ostrich feather; a theatrical poster for a left-wing cabaret of twelve years ago (risky, this: didn't she care who saw it?).

'Sit down,' said my hostess, and without hesitation I collapsed into a chair. The chair was rickety but comfortable. I closed my eyes in the warmth of the fire.

She was holding a cup of coffee in front of me and grinning. I pulled myself awake.

'You are tired,' she said. 'Would you like to lie down?'

'I only live upstairs!'

'Yes, but the first time you came to my door you looked so dazed I didn't think you'd make it up the next flight, and this time you're so tired I'm not sure you'll make it.'

There was an openness and energy about her which I liked. I felt myself responding to it, with some surprise. I hadn't taken any pleasure in another person's company for what seemed a long time.

'My name's Paula,' she said.

'I'm Freddy.'

'Is that short for something?'

'No,' I said, 'it's my name.'

'I see.' She waited for me to smile, and in the end I had to.

'I was christened Frederika,' I said.

'That's a pretty name.'

'I never liked it.'

I stretched out my feet in front of the fire, like a cat. It was comfortable here.

She smiled with amusement. Instantly self-conscious, I interpreted the smile, drew my feet in, sat up straight and looked at my watch. It was covered in brick dust. I wiped the dust with my thumb and then didn't know what to do with the brick dust on my thumb. It was half past seven. I wiped my thumb on my overalls. To hell with it.

'Sorry,' I said. 'I've had a long day. I mustn't stay long.' I took a gulp of coffee and burnt my mouth.

'Stay as long as you like. I'm not doing anything this evening.'

After a pause I said, 'I've dug fourteen people out of the rubble today.'

'That would account for your tiredness and the fact that you have plaster in your hair. Why are you doing it?'

'Someone has to.'

'Yes, but why are *you* doing it?'

'I'm on sick leave from my usual job, but I'm not actually sick, if you follow me.'

'Perfectly.'

'And I need to do something, I can't just sit around. Or I *will* get ill.'

'You're a test pilot, aren't you?'

I set down my cup on the tiled fireplace.

'I told people at work that you lived in the flat above me, and they didn't believe it.'

I laughed. There was irony in the laugh, but not too much. Harshness seemed out of place.

'I wondered if I'd ever meet you,' she said. 'You seemed to be away so much and for such long periods. And when I did catch a glimpse of you, you looked so aloof. As if you wouldn't *want* anyone to say Hello to you.'

'Not true.'

'No, I suppose not, but I didn't want to take the chance. We all protect ourselves against rejection, don't we?'

'I don't know. Do we?'

'Perhaps that isn't what you protect yourself from.'

'Do I have to protect myself from anything?'

'Is that a boast?'

People did not usually challenge me in this way. I found I liked it.

'I suppose,' I said, 'it might be.'

'Is it hard for you to accept there might be things you're afraid of?'

Afraid? It was too big a question. I said, 'Not at all. People who are never afraid are a danger to themselves and everyone else.' This sounded smug.

'That isn't quite what I meant.'

'What did you mean?'

'Never mind. I shouldn't have asked. It's not my business.'

I wanted her to ask. I could have sat there all evening answering, or parrying, questions.

'Would you like a schnapps?' she said.

'Thanks, but I don't drink.'

'Not at all? Not ever?'

'Oh, occasionally. A glass.' I thought with shame of my solitary orgy.

'Have a schnapps. Join me.'

Hard liquor these days was strictly a black-market commodity, and to be offered it was not a casual gesture. I accepted.

She poured two measures into small, green, frosted glasses, tipped hers down her throat and gulped it. I did the same with mine. In the mouth it was quiescent, warm and oily. In the throat it turned to fire.

I assimilated it, slowly, and let it add its glow to the firelight, the russet brown of the velvet curtains, the mantelpiece crammed with photographs and arcane objects, the cabaret poster and the mandolin on the wall, her face, framed between the bookcase and the edge of the kitchen door. (A pointed face. A chin with a hint of pugnacity, a small and slightly upturned nose, clear observant brown eyes.)

I said, 'Do you live alone here?'

'Yes.'

I felt pleased.

'Drop in again,' she said, when I left, 'I'm in most evenings.'

It was nearly a week before I did.

There were several reasons for this. Russia had put a curtain between me and other people. Instinctively, I avoided personal contacts. I would pull people out of the rubble, and resuscitate them if I could, but once they were breathing I had no wish to talk to them. I did not want to hear their life stories, or tell them mine.

I found that I did want to talk to Paula. But here something else intervened: an uncharacteristic loss of confidence. Why should she want to see me, I thought. She had other things to do.

Since Ernst's death I had seen little of other people. First there had been the crash, the spell in hospital, my convalescence; then, trying to pick up the threads of my life again, I had – as always – given the over-riding priority to flying, and left friendship to find what room it could.

Ernst's death had affected me deeply. It was not simply the gap he had left in my life, or grief for the waste of his. I reproached myself bitterly for not trying to help him, for not seeing until right at the end how ill he was, and for allowing into my head the useful and persuasive notion that he was stronger than I was, when my instinct had told me that the reverse was true. I reproached myself, most of all, for the selfishness of my motive the last time I had gone to see him. Fortunately he had never known that I had gone to him only to ask him to help me. Or had he? Perhaps he had sensed it.

I did not, in short, think highly of myself. I did not expect to be liked, and perhaps did not want to be. The encounter with Paula arrested me in what had become almost a conscious pursuit of loneliness. It was like a voice calling, when you are walking through mist. Perversely, at first I rejected it. But then I had to answer.

I knocked at her door with an armful of flowers. They were late roses, heaped on me by a florist whose small daughter's life we had probably saved after a cellar wall collapsed on her.

Paula stared at the flowers, then at me.

'Perks,' I said.

'I'm in the wrong job.' She worked at the munitions factory. 'They're beautiful,' she said. They were: the colour of peaches, and only slightly the worse for brick dust.

We sat by the fire, and talked.

'I got a letter from the town council,' said Paula. 'Apparently I'm occupying too much space. They want me to move to a smaller flat or take a lodger.'

'Really? That's bad luck.' Mentally I compared this dismayed reaction with my attempt to help the homeless.

'I wonder why they haven't written to me.' I said. 'My flat's at least as big as yours.'

'You have certain privileges.' She registered that I didn't like this. 'Well, they wouldn't want you to share your flat with someone else, would they? You're doing secret work.'

'I'm not any longer.'

'But surely you're going back?'

I said nothing.

'I'm sorry, is that something I shouldn't have asked?'

'It's all right.'

'I ask too many questions.'

'You do ask a lot, yes.'

'But you don't give much away. You're very guarded.'

'It's training.' I despised myself immediately for saying this. 'No,' I said, 'it's a habit. I always keep my distance.'

'I do, too.'

'That's how I come to be sitting here, is it?'

'Well, it looks like it, doesn't it? We must have recognized each other. Would you like a schnapps?'

'Um . . . yes. Please.'

She poured two measures into the frosted green glasses.

'I could get a taste for this.' I said.

'Well, don't. It may be a long time to the next bottle.'

'May I ask where you got it?'

'Complicated. I did someone a favour. And the someone for whom I did a favour has a sister who has a boyfriend in the army catering corps.'

'That isn't very complicated.'

'It's a ridiculous way of getting hold of a bottle of schnapps.'

'What was the favour?' This was bold of me. It would necessarily be illegal.

'I introduced her to someone who could give her an abortion.'

Her eyes stayed on me to see how I would react. The official line on abortion was that it was sabotage of Germany's racial future. Doctors got fifteen years in jail.

I said. 'I imagine if a woman wants an abortion, she has a good reason for it.'

'She was raped. By an SS officer. So of course they would force her to have it. I hate all this business about breeding and purity. It makes me feel sick.'

'I hate it, too.'

'That's why my marriage broke up,' she said. She had already told me she was divorced. It was increasingly common. The divorce rate had climbed steeply as soon as the laws were relaxed.

'I'd quite wanted children before it became a duty,' said Paula. 'But somehow . . . I don't know, everything they touch becomes *dirty*. On me it had exactly the opposite effect, all that fanfare about motherhood. And Karl was keen for us to have children: he was ambitious, he said it would help him. That made me angry, too. So I refused to have any.'

'You refused?' It hadn't occurred to me that one could refuse.

'Not openly. Goodness knows what that would have provoked. He was ready enough with his fists as it was.'

'He *hit* you?'

'Sometimes. I just made up my mind I wasn't going to get pregnant. I mean, that's about all you can do, isn't it, if the man's determined not to use anything?'

She looked at me. I avoided her eyes. Yes. I knew what she was talking about. I knew just enough about what she was talking about to know that there was a lot I didn't know. Conscious that, at my age, such ignorance was unusual. I felt embarrassed, and then defensive.

'Hey,' said Paula, 'what's the matter? Have I stepped on a land mine?'

'No. It's nothing.'

'I offended you by saying that.'

'No, you didn't. It's just that I'm not used to this kind of conversation.'

She gave me a searching look. Then she said, 'You don't actually . . . know that much about men, do you?'

I felt horribly let down.

'Well, you haven't missed much,' she said casually.

I wasn't the only one who had needed someone to talk to. Paula had been renting the flat for nearly a year and had made friends with only one other person in the neighbourhood, a woman with two young children who lived in the next street.

The bombing and the shortages had produced a communal feeling, but something strong and insidious worked against it. On every street and in every building the government had its spies. You could be reported for almost anything. For saying that the war was lost, for instance. People said it all the time, but it was disloyalty to the regime. You could be shot for making a joke about Hitler. People did that all the time, too, particularly in Berlin, where the humour ran in a savage vein. But every now and then, word came that someone had been picked up for it. And shot.

You had to be careful. So everyone was. As a result, friendship was just about the most precious commodity in the Reich.

It never occurred to me not to trust Paula. After a couple of weeks, my 'dropping in' became a habit. I would tap on her door as I came home, to say Hello if not to go in, although nearly always I did go in. We talked about families, schooldays, youthful ambitions, my relationship with my father, her marriage, Ernst.

Talking about Ernst led me naturally to talk about my work for the ministry. I was not, of course, supposed to discuss this with anyone. By that stage, members of the same family were not supposed to talk about their day's work over the supper table, even if they worked at the shoe factory.

I talked freely. I couldn't close off that part of my life from her, because it had been more important than any other part, and if I were to start shutting gates I wouldn't know where to begin or stop. But the deeper reason was the disgust I felt for the machine that had used me. If I could sunder myself from it by any means I would do so, and a potent means was to betray its secrets. The betrayal was purely symbolic. I had no secrets of importance, beyond possibly the Komet, and so far the Komet had proved itself of considerable value to the enemy in reducing the number of Germany's pilots. All the same, talking about it made me feel better.

I didn't tell Paula about Russia. Once or twice I veered towards it, and then drew back. It was enough that it dwelt in my mind: I did not want to plant it in hers.

Our relationship settled into a stride. It felt steady, built to go a long way. After a while the conversations all merged into one. They became the same conversation, picked up and continued whenever we were together, and continued in my head when we weren't. The conversation rooted itself into my life. After a while I could not imagine my life without it.

I studied, one evening, a gilt-framed photograph of Paula's mother and father. He, stout, whiskered, in the Sunday suit of a respectable bourgeois but with an anarchic gleam in his eye, stood with his hand on the back of his wife's chair. She was tall and slim, and had a pensive face framed by dark curls. I knew that Paula's mother had died two years previously. She had been beautiful. I said so.

'Yes,' said Paula. 'That was before she had seven children. But her face was always beautiful.' She picked up another photograph. 'This is Grandpa, my mother's father.'

Grandpa looked interesting. The photograph had been taken in the tropics. In the background, palms waved and there was a hut of exotic appearance. Grandpa, in tropical kit, held a rifle in a casual fashion and gazed into the distance in the manner of an explorer. Something about him also suggested the buccaneer.

'Taken in Africa,' said Paula. 'He went out to be a colonist, but he wasn't much good at it. He wasn't much good at anything, really, except losing money.'

'Did you know him?'

'A little. He died when I was six. I thought he was wonderful. So did a lot of women, apparently.'

'What about your grandmother?'

'She died before I was born. Her health was poor. And he dragged her all over the world. She died in Baghdad. All he really wanted to do was travel. When he died he left trunks full of stuff, none of it worth anything – some of it's here.' She indicated the collection of objects on the mantelpiece. 'I remember these trunks arriving on a cart, and the carter and my father bringing them into the kitchen. They took up the whole kitchen. My parents had a row about it. We were living in a tiny cottage. I remember my mother saying, "They are all that's left of him and this is where they belong." She was his only surviving child. There'd been a son, my uncle, but he was killed at Passchendaele. It was unlike my father to make an issue of that kind of thing: normally he was very easy-going. But it was a hard time, it must have been the time of the inflation. My father was a cabinet-maker: the business just collapsed. He said, about these trunks arriving, "It's the useless baggage of a lifetime, and it's not enough that *his* life was encumbered with it, now ours has to be encumbered with it as well!" But he did accept that we had to have them, after that. They went under the bed, and in various other places. There was always one on the landing which you had to walk around. He was a Communist, my father.'

It took a moment to register.

'He was a *Communist*?'

'Yes.' She laughed at my consternation. 'They don't have horns, you know. Or perhaps you think they do?'

I had been brought up to think so. Then, one day, out of curiosity to see just what sort of diabolical material it contained, I had taken down a copy of the *Communist Manifesto* from the shelf in a bookshop, browsed through it and found it to contain a peculiar mixture of the boring, the incomprehensible and the surprisingly true, but nothing devilish. That was before such books were burnt. When the Nazis came to power, the more stridently the government insisted on the evil nature of Communism and the subhuman characteristics of Bolsheviks, the more clearly I had perceived these claims to be fantasy. I recalled seeing the SA and the Red Front fighting in the streets of Berlin and thinking there was no difference between them. But something remained from my childhood: it was not a fear of Communism, but it was the shadow of one.

I said, 'What happened to him?'

'He was taken to a KZ camp in the round-up after the Reichstag fire.' The Nazis had claimed that the burning of the Reichstag building in 1933 was a Communist plot. If it was, it had been a very stupid one: it had turned every Communist in Germany into a hunted animal. 'He was a fool,' said Paula without emotion. 'He never hid his politics, he never even considered changing sides. I don't think it was that he was a particularly brave man: he was stubborn. He couldn't bring himself to do what thousands of others did when, as he put it, the thugs got into the driver's cab. And he didn't take them seriously. All the speeches about destroying Bolshevism and destroying Jewry. He thought it was rhetoric.'

I watched the flames flickering in the gas fire.

'My mother tried to tell him,' said Paula. 'She knew nothing about politics. She tried to keep out of political arguments, they upset her. But she knew what was happening. She knew it wasn't rhetoric. And he, with all his years in the German Communist Party, and his dialectics of this and historical necessity of that, poor father, he had no idea. When they came for him, he looked . . .' she smiled – 'so *outraged*!'

'Were you there?'

'Yes. I was there. I was living in lodgings, and studying for my exams' – she had studied fabric design – 'but I was at my parents' house that evening. I was so glad, afterwards, that I had been. Not that we had time for goodbyes. They knocked the door down, and then they knocked him to the floor, and then they started pulling the books out of the bookcase – he had all the Marxist classics there. God he was a fool! – throwing them on the floor and kicking them around the room. Then they got tired of it and took him away. They took the books as well, all they could find.'

I tried to think what I would have been doing at the time. Sitting in a glider, probably, sure that all this did not concern me. I thought of my own father and that, for all their differences, he had a quality in common with Paula's.

The light and shadow moved on the surfaces of her face with the gas fire's flickering.

'It's all right. I got over it. He's dead, of course.'

She was sitting back on her heels in front of the fire with her head held up, looking straight in front of her. Her face was still, and absorbed in thought. In profile her features were delicate, and at this moment vulnerable. I wanted to move to comfort her, but the self-contained quality of her sadness stopped me. Instead, I sat and looked at her. I saw how small, elfin almost, was the uptilted nose, how perfectly scrolled the ear, I saw the alert poise of the neat, dark-curled head and the alarming delicacy of the throat. I studied this profile unaware, at first, of how intently I was looking at it.

She turned her head and I felt as if I were falling. I flinched back in my chair, away from the unguarded gaze of those eyes. What was this? My heart was thundering. She saw the shock on my face and came out of her introspection at once.

'What's the matter?'

I shook my head and mumbled, 'Nothing.'

She placed a hand on my knee. 'I think we need some coffee,' she said, and went to the kitchen to make it, and I went with her, because I could not bear to let her out of my sight.

Can you know something, and not know it? Of course.

I assume, now, that I didn't want to know: that the answer I would have got, if at that stage I'd clearly asked myself what I felt, would have frightened me. But I don't really remember. I have certain luminous memories. All the rest is muddle, an amiable heaping-up of days and weeks, of walking to the ambulance station with a spring in my step, and coming home and standing at her door with my hand raised, unable for a moment to knock because of the happiness that flooded me: of talking by her fireside into the small hours, under the spell of an enchantment that would not let me leave and would not let her send me away; of shared shopping trips as exciting as a childhood Christmas although there was nothing in the shops to buy; of sitting beside her in the shadows of the air-raid shelter, where with trepidation and triumph I held her hand. I don't recall what happened at what time, only that it happened; but I recall with crystal clarity the Saturday evening we were going to a concert when a gas main, or something, exploded nearby and the blast knocked me back against a wall and her straight into my arms, at last.

What I felt, the devastating assault of what at that moment I felt, succeeded finally in concentrating my mind.

I'd never been much good at doing what I was supposed to do. At times I had managed to turn this to advantage; indeed, I had made a career out of it. But this was in a different league. Nothing, nothing at all, gave me permission to be in love with a woman. Everything I had ever heard of told me it was aberrant, impossible and wrong.

It felt like dawn on a spring day.

I tried to be analytical about what seemed to be happening, to rationalize. It was hopeless. My thoughts went round in circles. My attempts to be more detached in my relations with Paula faltered after the first thirty seconds. I did not want to be detached. I did not want to be rational. I loved her.

But how did she feel towards me? This question, utterly crucial, I had left until last because it had to be left until last; and when I considered it my heart sank into my boots.

I went to look in the mirror. I had had one of the best plastic surgeons in the country. Now that the contours of my face had settled, I could see how brilliant his work had been. There were just two fine white scars, one above the right eyebrow and the other on the opposite temple.

Looking at this face, you would have no idea what had happened to it. Or would you, I thought, and was I the only one who didn't know?

And did I seriously imagine that my face was the only problem?

I must speak to her. There was no other way to find out.

The simplest things are the things you can't do.

I lay awake most of the night, looking at the reflected glow of the fires on my ceiling.

The following evening I stopped at her door. My knees were shaking and my throat was tight. This was worse than the Komet.

I knocked.

Paula had her back to me when I made my stumbling, terrified opening move.

'There's something I need to talk to you about.'

She was pulling the curtains against the sombre sky. Above the line of rooftops opposite, a white pencil of searchlight probed. The wind blew rain against the windows.

She paused, leaning across the table with a handful of the heavy fabric. Then with a firm movement she drew the curtains together, and the room was almost dark, illuminated only by the gas fire and the line of light from the stairway which showed at the bottom of the door. She faced me, in that near–darkness, and although I could not see her eyes I felt them on me.

How do we dare to do these things?

She walked past me, her nearness suddenly a torment, and switched on the wall lamp in the alcove. A quiet light filled the room.

'What is it?' she said.

She was standing behind me. Her voice was level and wary.

'I'm in love with you,' I said.

There was a silence which stretched out and out, like an immensely long carpet.

'But,' she said with a small laugh, hardly interrupting the silence, and then did not continue.

'I know what I feel,' I said.

She came from behind my chair – it was always the high-backed, overstuffed, broken-winged chair I sat in, and perhaps, I thought, I would never sit in it again. She wandered around the room, then leant against the edge of the table.

'How long have you felt like this?'

'I don't know.'

322

'The evening we were going to the concert?'

'Before then.'

'I see.'

How dispassionate she was. It was like being in a doctor's surgery.

I said, 'I think about you all the time. I've never felt like this before. Half the time I don't know what I'm doing.'

She said nothing. The rain drummed against the window. My spirits sank lower.

Then she said, 'What do you want to do about it?'

My heart skipped and thundered, aghast, excited, finally despairing. I gazed mutely at her.

'Perhaps we ought to stop seeing each other.'

'Paula, *please!*'

'All right,' she said, with a smile so quick I almost missed it. 'But it's better if I don't see you for the next few days.'

I told myself that a few days were nothing.

'You have rather sprung this on me. I need time to think.'

'I'm sorry.'

'Don't apologize.'

I put down my coffee cup and stood up. 'I'll go now.'

'Yes. I'll see you on Friday.'

This was Monday.

I went up the stairs exultant at having staked all, and numb with the fear of loss.

Tuesday, Wednesday and Thursday passed. I traversed them like an automaton. On Friday I prepared myself for the worst.

I knocked. It seemed a long time before Paula opened the door. She was smiling a little nervously. 'Come in,' she said.

I went in. We were both trying to pretend nothing had happened.

'Sit down,' said Paula. 'I'll make some coffee in a minute.'

I sat again in the high-backed, overstuffed chair.

She stood behind me and her hands were on my forehead. The world stopped.

I found that happiness was a state of stillness. The seeking, the filling up of time, cease. Moments are endless, days are oceans. The room in which you sit with your lover is the whole world.

And I found that you don't say this. It's unnecessary. And you have become inarticulate. There is only one thing you can say. Indeed you have to say it. It is torn out of you, it tumbles out of you. Each time you say it, it is a cry of triumph, a tenderness that shakes you apart, and an act of submission. You must say it. But the words burn.

Stillness? I found that love is a storm. Love is such pain I do not know how the mind withstands it. It is a rack, a precipice. I am speaking of requited love.

So where is the stillness? At the heart of it. And sometimes you are in the heart of it. and sometimes you are in the storm.

CHAPTER TWENTY-THREE

We are over Doenitz's bit of the Reich, and within sight of Lübeck, when the Bücker coughs again.

The fuel gauge registers empty. It has been registering empty for some time.

I throttle back and lower the flaps. The engine cuts out at fifteen feet. It's a bumpy landing.

We are on a patch of heath. I help the general out of his seat and go to look in the fuel tank. It is the emptiest thing I have ever seen in my life.

'Well,' says the general, 'I suppose we have to walk.'

'Can you walk?'

'I can't stay here.'

'There's a road,' I say, 'about a quarter of a mile away.'

'Yes, I saw it. The air force has a regional HQ in Lübeck; if we can get there we can get transport to Plön.'

Nothing, clearly, is going to stop him seeing Doenitz.

I begin to walk, then freeze in my tracks as out of the corner of my eye I see him unholster the bull-dropper.

He flicks the safety catch and takes aim at the Bücker's engine.

'No!' I shout.

He drops his arm and stares at me.

'Please don't do that!'

'I'll do what I damn well please. It's air force property.'

'It's brought us all this way,' I say, conscious how it sounds, how ridiculous it is, with all that's happened. But I hate destruction. And I hate ingratitude. 'It got us out of Berlin.'

'Sentimental nonsense. I'm not going to leave it for the enemy.'

'It's hardly a strategic bomber.'

'Irrelevant what it is. It's a piece of equipment.'

'General, the war is *over*.'

'Field Marshal. And it may be over for you,' he says.

'It was over for you yesterday. You said there was no point in leaving the bunker.'

Oh, he's angry with me. But then something shifts in his head, the way I have seen it happen often in the past five days, the centre of balance shifting from one part of his mind to the other, and he raises his arm again and puts two shots into the Bücker's tyres. A compromise, acceptable to us both.

We begin to walk towards the road. Ahead of us, the smoke is rising from the latest RAF raid on Lübeck.

We don't talk as we make our way over the heath. Talking is too much of an effort for him, while hauling himself along on the crutches. Well, I don't mind silence.

Paula said one morning, 'I got another letter from the council.'

I didn't want to talk about letters from the council. It was another half an hour before we had to get up and go out into the world. It was a very precious half an hour. I moved my lips against her hair.

'What did it say?' I asked eventually.

'Someone from the Housing Committee is coming to see me tomorrow evening.'

'Tell them your bedroom regularly has a second occupant.'

'This is serious, Freddy.'

'Listen,' I said, 'if you've got to have someone else living here, why don't you come and live upstairs with me?'

She held my hand against her. 'You're crazy,' she said softly into the pillow.

'No, I'm not. I'd see more of you.'

'We're practically living together as it is!'

'Is it too much for you?'

'No,' she said.

I raised myself on my elbow and looked at her. She was so beautiful. There were times when it was almost too much, when I felt so intensely I didn't know how I could go on living.

'I still can't believe this,' I said when, nearly half an hour later, we had not yet got up.

'You thought all there was to life was aeroplanes, didn't you?'

'That's right.'

'Do you miss your aeroplanes?' Her finger traced a line down the side of my face and along the chin. I had to meet her eyes.

'A bit.'

'Perhaps aeroplanes are safer.'

'I'm sure they are.'

We said nothing for a time.

Then I said, 'Do you think we are safe, in fact?'

'I had a friend,' said Paula. 'He was a barman. He disappeared. If we were men, we'd be in a concentration camp by now.'

'Do they think women don't matter?'

'Of course we matter. We're the brood mares. It just suits them better to pretend this doesn't happen. Doubtless they have their reasons.'

'What will be our salvation,' I said, 'is that this country is run with an absolute lack of intellectual consistency.'

'That doesn't sound like you.'

'It isn't me. It's Wolfgang.' I had told her about Wolfgang. 'I think he might be in the same boat himself,' I said. 'It's only just occurred to me. It's why he can't come back.'

'He's lucky, then. To be where he is.'

'Yes. And we're lucky, too. I never thought I'd be glad to get different treatment, but I really don't want to be drowned in a bog.'

'Don't kid yourself,' said Paula.

'Meaning?'

'They *don't* like it. They'll get you for something else, if they want you.'

'Like what?'

'Oh, left-wing sympathies or something.'

She lay very still after she had said this. So did I.

I said, 'I'll make the coffee,' and at once regretted it, because the only thing that mattered was to go on holding her.

The housing official came the following evening and pronounced that Paula must take in, not a single lodger, but a family.

'That settles it,' I said. 'You *must* move in with me.'

'What am I going to do with all my things?'

'Bring them upstairs. Well, not the furniture, obviously. But you can pop down and keep an eye on the place, can't you? You can explain to this family that you're moving out for their convenience, but you want access to the flat.'

'I'm not moving out for their convenience, I'm moving out for mine! Or is it yours?' Her chin jutted. 'I'll tell you what, Freddy. I'm not moving out!'

We had a row. It was very upsetting. But we made it up. A few days later we moved Paula's portable belongings, in bags and suitcases, from her flat to mine. The photographs and pictures, ostrich feather, books, cracked teapot ('it was my mother's and I'm *fond* of it!'), several armfuls of clothes and shoes, a plant or two, the green schnapps glasses.

I deposited the last load on the bed, went to her and put my arms around her from behind. She was dusting a shelf and turned her head into mine, affectionate but a little impatient.

'I want you to be happy here,' I said.

'I will be happy here. When did you last dust?'

We left all the furniture except an item Paula refused to abandon: a child's desk with a fold-down lid and attached bench-seat. It was battered and ink-stained and the seat was loose. It had lived in a corner of her sitting room with a vase of flowers on top of it. Her father had bought it for her when she was at school. He had believed strongly in equal education for girls. 'And considering he couldn't afford it and we didn't have room for it, I'm certainly not leaving it behind now.'

'You were very fond of your father, weren't you?'

'Yes.'

Paula emptied the desk of its contents – some letters, a book, a wooden paintbox, all of which she locked in a drawer of the sideboard – and we carried it upstairs.

The following day the Kargs arrived.

Herr Karg was a stocky man in his fifties with oiled brown hair, a bristly moustache and light blue, protruding eyes. He wore a suit, tan shoes which still had a polish to them, and a trilby planted squarely on his head. As he came up the stairs he looked aggrieved. I soon learnt that this was his habitual expression. Perhaps it was the result of being bombed out of his house, but I suspect that he had looked aggrieved since infancy.

Frau Karg had a pinched, pale face that looked dried out, and a nose reminiscent of a shark's fin. Her hair, which was of no particular colour, was drawn back in a braid of squeaking tightness from which a few strands attempted escape across her forehead. She would push at these crossly with a finger. She had flinty little eyes which darted about a great deal as if it might jeopardize her survival not to gather every possible scrap of information about her surroundings. Her voice was high and insistent and made everything she said sound like a complaint, but then it usually was a complaint.

Their daughter, Hildegard, was twelve and had imbibed her parents' sense of perpetual injustice. She combined this with the zeal of a keen member of the German Girls' League, the uniform of which she was wearing when they arrived.

Herr Karg carried his cardboard suitcase through the open door, set it down on the carpet, took a quick look around the flat and said, 'Well, this isn't what we were led to expect.'

'Looks very bare, doesn't it?' commented his wife, casting a glance around the sitting-room walls, and went to check that there was cutlery in the kitchen drawer.

The daughter went to the window, stared out, and languidly traced her initials in the condensation on the pane.

'There's no teapot,' announced Frau Karg. 'Well, I'm not buying one.'

Herr Karg had been testing the bedsprings with one hand. He came back with an aggrieved look.

His daughter said, 'How am I going to get to Girls' League from here? It's miles away.'

'You'll have to set off earlier,' said her father.

'I *can't*!'

'There's no milk jug, either,' said Frau Karg.

Paula and I went upstairs and shut the door.

What the Kargs had expected, apparently, had been a room for themselves with a separate bedroom for the daughter, and shared use of the kitchen and bathroom. That they had an entire flat to themselves did not appear to compensate them for the fact that their daughter had to sleep on the sofa. Or for the absence of a teapot and milk jug.

Paula raged.

329

'Beastly, mean-minded people! How can they be like that? They've been living in a *tent*! Wouldn't you think they'd be grateful?'

'They've always been like that,' I said. 'Can you imagine what they said about the tent?'

'That man gives me the creeps! Did you see that his shoes were polished? What sort of man lives on a camp site and has polished shoes? He's some wretched minor official. I bet he's in the Party. That's how they got rehoused so quickly.'

'How do you know they got rehoused quickly?'

'Of course they did. Can you imagine them being on a camp site longer than a few days, complaining away like that?'

'Paula, my love, you are not being very logical.'

She came and laid her head on my shoulder. 'Do you expect me to be?'

'No.' I stroked the head. It was warm and heavy and full of awkward thoughts and of things I had no inkling of.

'They know who you are,' she said.

'No, they don't.'

'Yes, they do. I've seen Frau Karg looking at you. She's not stupid. And I bet she's got a memory like an elephant for what's been in the papers.'

'Well, if they do,' I said, 'does it matter?'

'I wouldn't think so.' She sighed. 'If only it wasn't them in the flat. I feel they degrade it.'

I said, 'Would it make you happier if we brought some more of your things upstairs?'

'What could we bring?'

We brought out the overstuffed broken-winged armchair. They didn't need it. We hauled and pushed it up the stairs. Herr Karg watched it go with incredulity. His wife stood with her hands on her hips and an expression of I-told-you-so bitterness on her face.

'There won't be anything left here in a minute,' she said.

'You don't have the right to take that armchair, you know,' said Herr Karg. 'We're entitled to properly furnished accommodation. It says so here.'

He waved a piece of paper at us.

Paula said, 'There's another armchair and a sofa in the flat.'

'It belongs here. It's part of the furnishings. You're in contravention of the regulations.'

'They are,' said Frau Karg. 'They're in contravention of the regulations.'

'Listen,' I said, fighting my temper. 'You have got something you are *not* entitled to, and that is a whole flat to yourselves. Isn't that enough for you?'

'And that's another thing,' said Frau Karg. 'The property-holder is supposed to be in residence. It could put us in a very awkward position. Why *isn't* she living here? That's what I want to know.'

'I don't *want* to share my flat with you!' Paula spat.

'Not good enough for you, eh?' said Herr Karg.

Behind him his daughter picked her nose and smirked.

'You're pretty difficult to please, aren't you?' I said.

We were holding the chair on the tenth step above the landing: I had a strong impulse to drop it on them.

'I require things to be done in the proper manner,' said Herr Karg. 'I always have done and I always shall. I've a good mind to make a report.'

'What on earth d'you think you've got to report? That you have more accommodation than your piece of paper allows you?'

Frau Karg's eyes darted to her husband, who walked ponderously back into the flat. She returned her attention to us. Her eyes moved from me to Paula, back to me, then back to Paula.

The only thing to do with the Kargs was forget about them, so we tried to. I climbed the stairs past their door trying not to hear their voices, which were usually raised in complaint or anger, and hoping the door wouldn't suddenly open and force us to confront each other. I recalled the many times I had stood outside that door, and hated them for besmirching my memories. I hated them for their destructiveness and their insatiability. But I attempted not to think about them except when physically in their proximity: I would not allow them that much of my life.

Once a week Paula went down to collect the rent. The amount they were to pay had been fixed with precision by the council: fifty-five per cent of the total. Gas and electricity costs were to be shared 'in a manner to be agreed'. They weren't doing badly. But inevitably they resented paying. They seemed to think, or pretended to think, that Paula was lying about what the rent was. She produced her rent book, but they shook their heads cynically and paid up – since they had to – with self-pity.

Further trouble then arose over the gas meter. They said she had done something to it so that the gas cost more than it should; when their backs were turned, she would get the money out. In vain did Paula protest that she had no key to the meter, and in the end call in a man from the gas company to confirm that the meter had not been interfered with. They refused to listen. Then they came out with what was really on their minds. She should be putting money in the meter herself. It said, on their piece of paper, that gas and electricity costs should be shared. They weren't going to say anything about the electricity. But the gas she should pay towards. It was keeping her flat and the contents aired, wasn't it?

'They're mad,' I said.

'Perhaps they are, but that doesn't make it any easier.'

After one altercation in which Frau Karg had physically threatened Paula, I accompanied her when she went down to see them.

At times it seemed to be a sort of nightmare, lapping away at the edges of our life and seething away under our feet. But it was only at the edges. It was only once a week. The rest of the time we didn't have to think of them, we were alone in our castle.

Who could want anything more, I thought, and wondered at the restlessness of the human race, and the ambition to fly every aeroplane ever built which had once consumed me. I had, of course, had only myself to live for.

'Don't leave me,' I said.

'I won't.'

From time to time I tried to think about the future. I was now unofficial relief driver on the ambulance. I couldn't go on doing it for ever, and the ministry wouldn't go on giving me sick leave for ever. But then, the war surely couldn't go on much longer. The Americans and the British were in Italy, hurling themselves against Monte Cassino; the Red Army was slowly and bloodily pushing our divisions back to where they came from. No one doubted that when it reached the place they came from it would exact the most terrible revenge. However, by that time Paula and I would be somewhere else. I didn't know where, but I'd get us out. Perhaps there would be a plane. Or there was Wolfgang. Wolfgang had made me promise that if ever I needed help I would get in touch with him. I had written to him already, a long letter almost entirely about Paula, described as a close friend with whom I was sharing my flat. I'd felt he would understand. If he didn't, it didn't matter. He had not yet replied to this letter. When he did, perhaps I would write again, asking him if he remembered a promise I had made him in a restaurant at the Rhön gliding championships.

There was a knock at the door one evening. Paula answered it.

I heard Herr Karg's pompous delivery, and his wife's accusing treble. I heard Paula's voice, first careful, then angry.

I put aside what I was doing and went to the door.

They had come about the hot water. Hot water was a luxury these days. Quite frequently there was no running water at all, and it had to be fetched in pails. However, the Kargs, taking hot water as their due, had lit the boiler so that their daughter could have a bath. It had 'exploded' in front of them. They said they were lucky not to have been seriously injured.

The boiler was old and unpredictable. Paula had warned them about it when they moved in. The way to deal with it was to turn the gas off and try again ten minutes later when you had recovered your nerve.

Paula said this. I told them that the boiler in my flat behaved in exactly the same way, and perhaps their daughter should resign herself to not having a bath this evening, like most of the population of Berlin.

They weren't listening.

'We're just about tired of it, I can tell you,' said Herr Karg.

'That we are,' said his wife.

'Tired of *what?*' asked Paula and I together.

Frau Karg extended a finger and pushed it at Paula, not quite touching her.

'Of being expected to live in a flat which is half stripped of furniture and the things it ought to have, paying through the nose for rent and gas, and now we're expected to put up with a dangerous boiler.'

'Compensation, that's what I'm thinking of,' said Herr Karg. 'I intend to go into it. There are a number of things I intend to go into.'

'Why don't you just go away?' I said. 'Go back downstairs, to the flat you are lucky to have, and leave us in peace.'

'Peace?' Frau Karg tittered. 'Oh yes, I expect you'd like to be left in peace, wouldn't you? You and her.' She let a moment elapse. 'I know who you are, you know.'

There was a pause before anyone said anything more.

'Well,' challenged Herr Karg, 'what are you going to do about it?'

'About what?' asked Paula icily.

'The boiler.'

'Oh, for heaven's sake.' Paula, I could see, as she set off down the stairs, intended to be done with the wretched business in a couple of minutes. She would light the boiler and leave the Kargs to fester.

But I saw the glance of triumph that flashed between them.

'Things could be sorted out if you took a more reasonable attitude over the money,' said Herr Karg as we trooped down the stairs.

'Yes. that's what it comes down to,' said his wife.

The implication of blackmail was unmistakable. But if – I thought as my fists clenched – they imagined they could blackmail us with . . .

No. They were not such amateurs.

I was the last into the sitting room and all I could see as I came in was the sideboard with its wrenched-open drawer hanging down.

But Paula, flanked by the Kargs, was looking at the table.

On the table was a thick, strongly-bound book, much handled, with worn gold lettering on the spine. It was by Karl Marx. The title was *Grundrisse*.

Her father's, of course. Foolishness runs in families.

She could have said that it was his, that she had kept it only out of sentimentality, even – possibly – that she had not known it was there.

She said none of these things. I shall honour her for ever for what she said.

'That book is mine, and you are not fit to touch it.'

She picked it up and went back up the stairs.

The general and I walk and rest, walk and rest. Progress is slow. From time to time we stop and eat a bit of the bread I brought from Rechlin. The raisins are all gone. There is nothing to drink. It's cold and the day is far advanced.

334

The road we walk along has been bombed. Some craters are big enough to hold a horse and cart. It's still negotiable, though, should any vehicle wish to drive along it and rescue us, but no vehicle does.

The RAF is raiding Lübeck again.

The general, at one of our bread stops, begins a conversation.

'I intend to give myself up to the Americans, when the time comes. With this foot I am hardly a combatant.'

'It's the only sensible course,' I say.

'I'm worried that they may interrogate me.'

'I'm sure they will.'

'Yes. Well, what am I going to say?'

I stop chewing. What, indeed, is he going to say? He is going to have to say he didn't know what was going on behind the Eastern Front, and they will not believe him. Or he will say he was not in any way involved, and they will not believe that either.

'It weighs on me,' says the general. 'But I will have to tell the truth as I see it. There are limits to loyalty.'

He has the expression of a man who fears he will have to disappoint a grandchild on its birthday.

'General.' I say, 'what are you talking about?'

'Goering's mishandling of the air force, of course. Incompetence, laziness, favouritism. He lost the war for us.' The general sighs. 'I knew it was going on, but what could I do? I was pledged to carry out my orders. We all knew about it, really. None of us did a thing.'

The Kargs made no further move after the confrontation in which Paula had taken back the book. Probably they were waiting to see what we would do. Paula, who at first had expected the arrival of the Gestapo hourly, and went dead white when one evening unfamiliar footsteps approached our door (it was the fire warden), calmed down after a few days and stopped referring to the incident.

I was extremely worried, and did not know what to do. For once in my life, I had a problem which could not be solved by sheer determination. It even occurred to me to give the Kargs money, since that was what they wanted (I would have got it from somewhere); disgust, combined with the knowledge that a blackmailer is never paid off, stopped me.

Thus preoccupied, I drove the ambulance, empty, past a park one morning on the way to pick up the rest of the crew, and saw a crowd gathered to look at something. Over the tops of their heads I glimpsed a familiar blunted curve.

I could not drive past it. I pulled on the brake and jumped out.

A Focke-Wulf 190 had crash-landed. Most of the tail had been shot away and the port wing was badly holed, but the pilot had got his aeroplane down in one piece. A policeman was standing guard until the reclamation crew arrived.

I pushed to the front of the crowd and, disregarding the police-man's shout, laid my hand on the engine cowling. It was warm.

I felt dazed as I climbed back into the ambulance cab. A painful nostalgia flooded me, and made my eyes sting. What had I lost, when I gave up flying? To be in the presence of an aircraft made my pulse beat faster. The smell of oil, the smell of metal, the electricity latent in the dust of a cockpit . . . Flying is not a job. It is passion.

I gazed at the rounded blade of the Focke-Wulf's propeller against the sky, and thought that an aeroplane was an aeroplane. Who owned it, or for what it was used, were things for which it could not be held accountable.

An excitement began to gather in me. I let in the clutch of the ambulance and drove away, thinking furiously.

Within no time at all I was back on a familiar merry-go-round. No, the aeroplanes were not accountable, but I was. I could not fly without flying for the government. For one thing, the government owned all the aeroplanes.

It was not possible to square this circle. My mouth filled with a sour taste.

At some point during the day, a quite different idea dropped like a meteor into the to-ing and fro-ing of my thoughts. Here was a possible solution to the Karg problem! I was still, in theory, chief test pilot at the Glider Research Institute and entitled to a flat in Darmstadt. My previous flat had been requisitioned, but the Insti-tute would help me find another one. And Paula could live in it with me.

There might be bureaucratic difficulties, and Paula's presence might even have to be concealed, but anything was better than living above the Kargs; and surely the war would soon be over.

I would have to move fast. But first I must sound Paula out on the prospect of my returning to flying. I decided not to say anything about Darmstadt until I had found out what the possibilities were.

'Of course you must go back to flying if you want to,' said Paula. She was looking very tired. She worked long hours at the munitions factory. 'I never really understood why you behaved as if you didn't intend to. But don't you have to get a medical certificate first?'

'Yes, I suppose so.' I'd hardly thought of that. I'd assumed that if I wanted to fly, I could fly. I decided now that I had to make that assumption, or I'd never get anywhere. 'It'll be all right,' I said vaguely.

'What will you do, write to the ministry and tell them?'

'Um . . . yes. The ministry or Darmstadt.'

'You seem to have made up your mind about this without thinking about it much.'

'Oh no, I have thought about it.' I toyed with my potato dumpling. What would they give me to fly? In a sense it was all the same thing. Did I imagine I could test even the most modest aircraft without being part of the war? A few months previously I could not have considered it: was it that what I had seen in Russia now mattered less to me? No, but it was becoming unreal. Acknowledging this, I shivered slightly. But the war would soon be over. And then all of this would stop.

'It'll sort itself out,' I said.

'*Freddy!*' Paula shouted.

I gazed at her in astonishment.

'This is a very important decision which affects *us*, and you are talking about it as if it's a question of whether to buy rice or potatoes! What is the matter with you?'

'I'm sorry, I didn't think . . .' Indeed, what was the matter with me?

'If you want to go back to flying then you must, I will not try to stop you, because I know what it means to you and I know in any case that if I try to stop you then that will be the end of our relationship. But I think you might at least have considered what it involves for me. I shall see much less of you, your job is dangerous . . .'

'Oh, God,' I said, and got up from the table and went to her. I said, 'You could come and live with me in Darmstadt.'

'You've just thought of that, have you?' She held her hands over mine and stroked my thumbs with hers, which never failed to enchant me. 'Come on,' she said, 'let's eat. This food's getting cold.'

I telephoned the ministry the next morning. A letter would have taken days to arrive, and might not have arrived at all, such a state were the postal services in. I said I was ready to resume work, and had a medical certificate. I would deal with the surgeon later.

The response I got surprised me. I was told to wait for a minute or so, then Milch's adjutant came on the line and asked me to come for an interview at the ministry offices the following day, with Milch himself.

There had been another heavy bombing raid. The air when I came out of the station was hot, gritty and foul. People held wet towels to their faces to make breathing easier. A lot of fires were still burning.

The ministry headquarters had been demolished in a previous raid, and Milch had a temporary office in a requisitioned villa some three miles away. The bombs had not spared this building, either: broken glass was still being picked up as I arrived, and several rooms were ankle-deep in plaster. Here and there a ceiling was propped up with a length of wood.

Milch's office was calm and tidy. He rose to greet me with his usual frigid smile

'I'm glad to see you recovered,' he said. Then he came straight to business. 'I can't pretend we have a surplus of test pilots. The project I have in mind is top secret and will be ready for testing in a few weeks. You may not like it. You have the right to refuse without its being in any way counted against you.'

It was an odd preamble.

He took a photograph from the drawer of his desk in such a way that I couldn't see the picture, and laid it face down in front of him.

'Have you heard of a project codenamed "Cherry Stone"?'

'No, sir.' This was untrue. There had been much mirthful speculation among Komet pilots as to what 'Cherry Stone' might be.

'Cherry Stone is a pilotless aircraft, a flying bomb,' he said. 'I initiated it myself a few years ago. The principle is fairly simple. The aircraft is launched from a ramp; it has an automatic guidance system which controls the course, and when it has flown a predetermined distance the motor cuts out. It then goes into a dive and detonates on impact. It's been designed primarily for use against southern England. It is not a precision weapon, obviously. Its purpose would be to lower civilian morale.'

He looked at me to see if I had followed his exposition. Milch expected women to be stupid. If they were, they aroused his contempt. It they weren't, they aroused his hostility.

'I see,' I said.

He turned the photograph over and pushed it towards me.

I saw a thing like a fish, but with stubby wings, carrying on its back a bulbous tube which tapered towards the tail.

'That's the propulsion unit.' Milch placed the tip of a pencil on the tube. 'It flies on a mixture of paraffin and air. Cheap to make. So cheap, in fact, that we've held it back in case the enemy manage to capture one and start making their own. But now, well . . .' His mouth set in a line. 'We expect an invasion of the French coast in the course of the summer.'

Even Milch knew the war was lost.

I said, 'Field Marshal, did you say this was a *pilotless* aircraft . . .'

'We're working on a manned version.'

It took a while to sink in. I had been too long away from them. I had been living in the normal world.

'Sir . . .' Careful. But his rigid posture told me all I needed to know. 'A manned version of this would be a suicide weapon.'

'Correct.'

A wave of repugnance rose from somewhere deep inside me. I was unable to prevent it from registering in my face.

'That's a common reaction,' he said. 'Personally, I sympathize with it. I did not initiate this development. However, I have taken responsibility for it. The pilots will all be volunteers and will all fully understand what's involved.'

His voice was dry. He might have been talking about the introduction of a new filing system.

Then he said, with a short laugh, 'Naturally we are not asking

339

you to volunteer for a suicide mission. Matters are not yet so desperate. But I have to make clear to you the context in which you would be working. What we would want you to do, initially, is test the converted aircraft. The piloted version will be flown as a glider, launched from underneath a Heinkel 111. Then, when the pilots have been recruited – recruitment is going very well, which may surprise you – there will be a need for instructors.'

He took back the photograph and returned it to its drawer, as though the interview were over.

'I shan't attempt to persuade you,' he said.

He had stung me, and I would not be so easily dismissed.

'May I ask a question?'

'Certainly.'

'What is the purpose of a piloted version?'

'Accuracy. It would be used against military targets associated with the invasion. Munitions depots, dockyard installations, and so on. We hope to force the enemy to change his plans.'

I said, 'It's a desperate measure.'

'I agree. One imagines, however, that that very fact will have a certain psychological effect on the enemy.'

I wondered in whose brain this idea had originated. Certainly not the Fat Man's: he was a lover of life, it would have horrified him.

I couldn't possibly do it. I had prepared myself for a mental tussle over the work Milch might offer me, even for finding that I could not after all go back to flying for the ministry; but I had never thought of anything like this. Yet something about it fascinated me.

'Why have I been approached, Field Marshal?'

'I wasn't in favour of your involvement. I must tell you that. But others have pointed out your experience in glider-related work. As I say, we don't have a surplus of test pilots.'

'I see.'

'Think it over,' said Milch, rising. 'If you decide against it, I expect we can find something else for you. Meanwhile, get some flying in.'

I walked out into the shattered city.

I remember a brilliant light striking my eyes as I came through the door. It was the sun striking a mirror, that was all, a mirror somewhere in the shell of a building.

I don't remember anything else about that morning, that part of my life, just the sun dazzling me and the envelope on the sitting-room table.

A white rectangle, my name on it in the handwriting that moved me, just as her voice and her step moved me.

In the emptiness of the flat I stared at the white envelope. Then I picked it up and tore it open.

'Dearest Freddy, I love you. But I can't stay here, and I will bring you trouble. Don't look for me – P.'

I rushed back into the street. I ran up and down as if possessed. I stopped people and demanded of them if they'd seen her. For hours I spun and blundered like a fly that has stunned itself on a window. Then I went back to the flat and began to let my loss come home to me.

Of course I looked for her.

I went to the factory at which she'd worked. They hadn't heard from her. I visited the friend with the two young children in the next street; she hadn't seen Paula for a fortnight and had no idea where she might have gone.

I had the address of a younger brother in Neuruppin. I went to see him. He had lost a leg in Norway. He was affable but could not help except to give me the address of another brother in Wittenberg.

I wrote to the address. There was no reply. Travelling by this time was extremely difficult; the railway system had all but broken down under the continual bombing, use of cars was restricted and petrol was almost unobtainable. Eventually I managed to get to Wittenberg. The street in which Paula's brother had lived no longer existed.

This was all I had, except the name of a cousin whom Paula hadn't liked, who was married to a brigadier and lived in Potsdam. I went out to Potsdam. The cousin hadn't had any contact with Paula for eight years.

There was one remaining possibility. I was loath to contact him and thought it out of the question that Paula would have sought his help, but I couldn't rest until I'd done it. He was easy enough to find, with the aid of the letters and documents she'd left behind. I telephoned Karl, her ex-husband, and asked for a meeting. To make sure he'd see me, I told him who I was, and invited him to lunch at the Adlon Hotel.

I wanted to intimidate him. But when I met him, it seemed irrelevant. He was a small-town bully with a sneer for his inferiors and a toadying smile for anyone who might do him good, a blusterer who had evaded war service by buying his way into a war-essential industry (he manufactured gunsights). He had married again and had children, two sons for Germany. He was bitter about Paula. She 'had not been a wife' to him. He implied, crudely, that she had been unfaithful, and then apologized obsequiously for offending my sensibilities.

He had not seen her since the divorce. That I had expected. I had hoped from the meeting, though, to gain a few clues. Perhaps in the six years of her marriage to him she had made friends to whom she might now turn?

It seemed not. All my probing elicited only two possibilities. One was a woman much older with whom Paula had for a while contemplated going into business. ('Nonsense, and I told her so. I was earning plenty of money for us both.') The other was the wife of one of Karl's partners. It was hard to tell from his contemptuous references to 'women's outings' and 'women's gossip' whether this had been a friendship, or merely a tactical association into which the women had been forced by their husbands. Neither sounded as if it would lead to anything, but I wrote both names down and thanked him.

I had told him that Paula, on being obliged to take in lodgers, had deposited some documents with me for safe keeping, and that I was concerned about her disappearance because I was sure she would not voluntarily have gone away without letting me know. He asked, naturally, why I hadn't been to the police. I said that, in the light of her father's politics, I had been afraid of stirring up trouble for her; if they had no interest in her, an inquiry on my part might arouse it. This wasn't a particularly logical answer, but since he wasn't interested in what I said, but only in what he was saying, it passed.

He wanted to talk. He had carried this hurt around for years. I let him talk, listening at first for anything that would help me, and then, when I realized he had told me all he could, switching off my anger as he spoke of Paula from the depths of his resentment.

As I listened, my feelings towards him began to change. He was

342

unhappy, if ever a man was: trapped in his bombast, isolated from his current wife, friendless, not stupid enough to escape knowing that he was a coward. What had Paula seen in him? There might once have been a certain humour there, an appealing zest for life. And before the beer and the sedentary habits began to tell on him, he would have been good-looking. I wondered how she had appeared to him. What had *he* seen, when he asked her to marry him?

This thought, the picture it conjured up, hit me so painfully that I gasped aloud. He looked at me in surprise, then went on talking. But from that moment I saw him differently. He was a fool and a bully, but at some time, as best he could, he had loved her.

And thus we were confederates. Was that what this lunch had really been about? For I longed for the company of someone who had known her, I longed to hear her name. I longed to speak sentences which contained it. And with whom else could I do this, who else would share, to the point of not even noticing it, my obsession?

We parted with expressions of mutual gratitude. I went back to my flat, and at some point in that endless afternoon wept like someone plunging over the edge of a precipice.

I have not ceased to look. In every street, every public place. All the faces are the same, they are all not hers.

Herr Karg turned up with a piece of paper in his hand.

'Pay the rent to the landlord,' I said.

I started to close the door. He put his foot in the way.

'Herr Karg,' I said, 'get out of here or I swear to God I will kill you.'

He went.

Towards the end of the second week of Paula's absence, I informed Milch I would accept a post on the manned flying-bomb project. With its sombreness, it appeared to me now in a light almost consolatory.

The day is paling from the sky when I hear the roar of a lorry behind us.

The general turns laboriously and stands in the middle of the road. The lorry might or might not stop. There are many reasons, these days, for not stopping when signalled. With the bull-dropper in his right hand, the general waits in the lorry's path.

It comes to a halt with the bonnet a foot from his chest. The muzzle of a Luger stares at us from the driver's window. The general, pistol levelled, identifies himself and asks to be taken to Lübeck.

The passenger door opens, and an S S corporal with a machine pistol jumps out.

The general repeats his demand. In order to face the S S man he has to move a pace backwards, and in doing so he stumbles. I move to help him, and the Luger barrel jerks and a voice from inside tells me me to stay where I am.

'Identification,' says the corporal.

'I'll have you court-martialled,' says the general. 'Can't you see my rank?'

'Your papers, please.'

'Papers,' growls the general. 'Yes, I'll show you a paper.' With his left hand, clumsily, he unbuttons his greatcoat and searches the inside pocket. He brings out an oilskin pouch wrapped round with tape, and holds it out to the S S man.

'Open it.' The general is too encumbered to do so. The S S man nods at me. 'Open it.'

I untie the tape, take out the thick envelope inside, and from the envelope withdraw the letter which bears the Chancellery crest and is signed at the bottom with a despairing scrawl.

The S S corporal stiffens as I hold this letter towards him. He does not touch it. His heels slam together and his arm shoots out in the robot salute.

'My apologies, Field Marshal, sir. The area is full of deserters. How can we assist you, sir?'

'You can take us to air force headquarters in Lübeck,' the general says, with surprising mildness. 'As quickly as possible.'

So the general is helped into the back of the lorry, and I climb in beside him. There is just room for us behind a stack of long cylindrical objects which I cannot see clearly in the shadow and avoid touching until the S S corporal tells me what they are.

'Carpets.'

'Carpets?'

'Oriental carpets, property of the Gauleiter of somewhere or other. Being taken to Lübeck for him, for shipment somewhere

where the gentleman thinks he'll be safe.' With one eye on the general, the corporal spits.

We set off. The lorry is heavily laden, and the road bad. We proceed at not much more than walking pace. After a while, I become aware of a peculiar quality in the general's gaze as he looks out over the tailboard of the truck. I follow it.

The sky is full of threatened storm. Sunlight slants from a rift in a purple cloud.

And purple is the face that lolls beneath the leafing branches of a tree. The slack disjointedness of the neck jars with the unnatural stiffness of the body. A white placard hangs round the neck. It reads: 'I was a coward who refused to defend German women and children.'

It is only the first. All along the road they hang, for a distance of a quarter of a mile. Their feet dangle hopelessly; their feet are the saddest thing in the world.

It was mid-April when I began to test the piloted version of what later became known as the V-1. We referred to it as Project Reichenberg, after the name of the conversion factory. 'Cherry Stone' was clearly too frivolous, in the circumstances.

The converted aircraft looked very like the photograph Milch had shown me. The queer-looking propulsion tube mounted on top of the fuselage was still there, retained for balance, although it would not be used. Just forward of it was a small cockpit. A glider's landing skid had been fitted.

The aircraft reminded me a little of the Komet. Both were a nightmare to land; both had a vendetta against pilots. The principal problem with the V-1 was that it wasn't designed to land, only to fly and crash. Crashing was therefore what it liked to do.

The flight of mine that went most dramatically wrong concerned a tank of water. The landing skid had been built to take the weight of an instructor and pupil, but not the weight of a large quantity of explosive. This was stupid, because it overlooked the necessity to test the flying qualities of the aircraft with the weight of the explosive and pilot together. An ingenious solution was found to the problem: the weight of the explosive would be simulated by a tank full of water, and before landing the water could be emptied out by means of a lever-controlled plug.

I was flying my tank of water at eighteen thousand feet and the plughole froze.

I felt I was living through the Komet crash again: the dangerously fast approach, the frantic working of a suddenly inert lever. At five hundred feet the ice melted and the water flooded out in a delirious release which hit the ground like a storm behind me. Sitting on the runway undoing my straps and grinning like a loon, I wondered what made me think I wanted to die.

As we were getting to the end of the testing, the volunteers turned up. Young, very young, scarcely out of their Hitler Youth uniforms and yearning to be brave and die laughing for Germany. They were all glider pilots.

Training began. Since there was quite a lot of time for training, and since the bureaucratic mind abhors time not fully used, an order came through from the ministry for the pilots to have several hours a day of pistol practice and a programme of physical exercise. Inevitably, they ended up spending more time on physical exercises and pistol practice than learning to fly the V-1. It was noted that the commanding officer, who had reaped considerable personal prestige from being in charge of the project, declined to put his own name on the list of volunteers. An air of less than complete certainty began to pervade the pilots' talk of their mission.

Then the Allies landed in Normandy.

We had known it was coming, but it was a shock. I was shocked because it meant that the end of the war was *real*. And what would come after it I could not imagine.

The pilots were devastated. Where were the targets they were supposed to be attacking with their bombs and lives? Irrelevant, suddenly. On the wrong side of the water. The important targets now were concentrations of troops and armour, all in constant movement. Quite unsuitable for a glider crammed with high explosive.

Perhaps that was why the Fat Man interfered.

He had done nothing for so long that his name had become a byword for inaction. Jokes about him had always circulated, but now they had turned vicious. He was blamed, and rightly, for the fact that there were no fighters to challenge the enemy bomber fleets which droned above our cities day and night. Adolf no longer had time for him – but, curiously, would not replace him. He was still sometimes to be seen in public, a bejewelled and powdered mountain of flesh in a pastel-coloured uniform, but he was never to be seen when there was a crisis.

But after 6 June the Fat Man stirred himself. Not to repel the enemy landings, no. (The news that filtered through to us from that front suggested sheer chaos in the command levels of the air force.) The Fat Man stirred from his torpor and decreed that the suicide pilots should commit suicide, not in the V-1, but in a version of the Focke-Wulf 190.

They were profoundly upset. Naturally. You cannot tamper with the dream of self-immolation. And in any case they were glider pilots, and they didn't know how to fly a Focke-Wulf.

From this point a downward slide began which could not be halted, even by the replacement of the commander. The pilots were asked to sign a declaration that they were willing to commit suicide in any aircraft assigned to them and against any target. Many of them were reluctant. This was not what they had meant at all. A training programme began to convert them into Focke-Wulf pilots.

Then Adolf heard what was happening and said he didn't want the Focke-Wulf 190 to be used. For once I agreed with him. It was too good a plane to be used as a flying bomb.

By that time the original Cherry Stone had been launched against London. The papers reported that London was ablaze from end to end, that buildings had been blown down like card houses and food stocks destroyed, and that the population was hysterical with terror. Nobody took the slightest notice of the papers any more.

By that time, too, Goebbels had invited the pilots to a buffet lunch at the Ministry of Propaganda and made them a speech on the subject of heroism. And by that time, Himmler also had spoken. He was deeply disturbed by the proposal to sacrifice good German youth. He wanted the pilots for this mission to be chosen from among criminals and the incurably diseased. He offered to supply candidates.

The summer dragged on, amid confusion, gloom and pistol practice. In the west, the Americans, Canadians, British and French chewed their way towards the Rhine. An army plot to assassinate Hitler failed and numerous generals were hanged from meat hooks. We lost Paris. The Red Army was in East Prussia, it had reached Warsaw, it had recaptured the Romanian oil fields. Project Reichenberg drifted, sank, was rescued, drifted on once more and finally was scuppered. The pilots went to the front, to be sacrificed in a more orthodox manner.

What was I going to do? The war was nearly over, but its dying throes were taking a very long time. It seemed that the world itself was nearly over. The countryside was filling up with refugees and deserters, the towns were full of charred ruins, flooding water mains, hollow-faced civilians bartering for the essentials of life and wild children living in caves in the rubble. Winter came and there was no coal. There was no food. There was only the noise of the bombing and the hysteria of the Propaganda Ministry.

The German army made a bold attempt at breakthrough in the west. By January it had failed. And in January a tidal wave began to roll from the east. It was the last great Russian offensive. Nothing could stop it. It rolled through Poland, East Prussia and Silesia and brought the Red Army tanks to within a hundred miles of Berlin.

In those months I did what I could, and what I was told to do if there was anyone to tell me. I had stopped thinking about what should and what should not be done in a war, and what I should do. Too much had happened that the mind could not cope with. Without respite the horrors accumulated, the numbing tales piled up of people baked alive in their shelters in Hamburg, of skin melted in Dresden, of G I's singing *God Bless America* in the graveyard that was Cologne. After Dresden I concluded that Ernst had been right about uniforms. They all did the same thing to their wearers.

I carried on flying because I had to do something and nothing I did would make any difference. And because one day, somewhere, in another part of Germany, I might see Paula's face. By that time, in any case, I had no home. The flat in Berlin was destroyed by bombing. With it went all the things of mine and Paula's I had not crammed into two suitcases and taken to my parents. And with it I hope, but I do not imagine, went the Kargs.

I flew messages, and sometimes silent generals. As the armies slugged it out closer and closer to home, I helped evacuate wounded. Sometimes I am fairly sure I was evacuating terrified soldiers who just wanted to get out of the path of the Russians.

I was in Munich, looking for landing grounds for hospital planes along the Austrian border, when I got the message from General von Greim asking me to fly him to Hitler's bunker.

CHAPTER TWENTY FOUR

The sides of the stairwell, as we descended, were intermittently lit with candles in holders which had been crudely hammered into the plaster. The flames guttered in the shell-blasts, and some went out as I looked at them. All the stairs were covered in a whitish powder which crunched under our feet.

A sound grew in my ears as we went downward: a deep rumbling and thumping. The generator. At the same time there came up from the depths into which we were descending a faintly rotten darkness, as if the air had decayed.

There were three long flights of stairs, narrow and steep. The general swore heartbrokenly as one of the SS boys stumbled and jarred his foot.

Breathing heavily, they brought the general down to a small landing. Facing us was a wall: to the right a narrow passage led a few yards and then turned a corner. We went round this corner, and into a further long passage. At the end of it, a flight of concrete steps could be glimpsed leading upward to a second entrance.

Half way down the passage, we had to manipulate the stretcher through a doorway into another corridor. We had reached the inhabited part of the bunker. People came silently to the doors of tiny rooms, and searched our faces, as we went by.

A curving flight of steps led down to the lower level of the complex. The noise of the generator now rose to its peak, and I glimpsed, on one side of me, the valves and pipes of the bunker's mechanical heart, and on the other a net of cables. Further on we passed white-tiled washrooms.

The corridor we were now in was presumably used as a sitting room, because we had to negotiate our way round three armchairs. In one of them an Alsatian dog was curled up, on the seat of the second lay a Western adventure yarn with a lurid cover, and in the third, staring stiffly ahead of him, sat the minister of Propaganda.

He swivelled his eyes towards us as we went by, but said nothing.

Off the next corridor opened rooms which were larger than the others. Here the SS boys halted, and one of them called out loudly, 'Doctor Stumpfegger!'

At the door on my right, filling it, appeared a huge man with a pleasant face. He took in the group of us and his gaze dropped to the general's foot, where it lingered for a fascinated moment. Then he opened the door wide.

We went through a tiny ante-room into a white-walled surgery in which were a camp bed and a scrubbed table. Dr Stumpfegger indicated that the general should be laid on the table, then, turning to wash his hands, he dismissed the young soldiers and said to me, 'You can stay and help.'

He opened a box, took out needle and phial, and in a fluent sequence of movements upended the phial, filled the syringe and plunged it into the general's arm. He rolled up the blue trouser leg, took a knife and cut away the blood-soaked scraps of boot leather. Then, picking up one of a set of shiny instruments, he began to remove from the general's flesh all the objects which did not belong to it but were intimately embedded in it.

For an hour I held things, passed him things, and watched.

'First case I've treated in this room,' he said.

He told me that he was Hitler's personal surgeon, but that, since there was nothing for him to do in that capacity, he had set up a casualty station in one of the other shelters.

'One of the soldiers I treated yesterday was twelve years old,' he said, as he stitched the general's flesh.

He laid over the purple wound a strong-smelling ointment, and on top of that a pad of lint, and began bandaging. We lifted the general from the table and laid him on the bed.

About ten minutes later, as the general was beginning to turn his head and groan, there was a shuffling tread along the corridor.

Into the room, his left foot dragging and his face betraying the enormous effort by which he now drove himself forward, came Hitler.

He greeted me, and asked me to wait outside.

I sat in the corridor while the semi-conscious general was made commander-in-chief of the air force.

At that time I still didn't know the reason for our journey. I had hardly bothered to speculate about it: orders from Berlin had long since ceased to be rational. But as I sat, beginning to feel my exhaustion, in the armchair next to the dog's, people materialized out of the corners and passageways of the place and surrounded me. It seemed they were trying to tell me a story, but they all talked at once. Gradually I made out what they were saying.

The Fat Man had done it at last.

Some two weeks previously, he had departed with his entourage for the Bavarian Alps. Forty-eight hours ago, from that place of safety, he had sent a telegram to Hitler asking for permission to assume the leadership. He had always been second in line, and it was the thing which had made him unassailable.

Presumably he had thought it was all over for Hitler, isolated in his hole in the ground with the Russians at the door, and who could blame him? But to Hitler the telegram could only be a declaration of treason. The worst of it was an implication that the Fat Man would use his powers to negotiate for peace.

Hitler, in an outburst of rage which still caused my informants to pale as they spoke of it, had ordered him to be stripped of his offices and placed under arrest.

That left the command of the air force vacant. And Ritter von Greim was one of the few remaining generals not to have disgraced himself in the opinion of the Chancellery.

As I walked back towards the surgery I heard Hitler's voice, painfully hoarsened, raised in denunciation.

'This is the man I named as my successor, the man to whose manifold failures I turned a blind eye! He would perform such wonders with his air force! He has destroyed Germany with his junk shop of an air force!'

He was dragging himself around the small room. Behind his back, his hands jumped like cats in a sack.

I slept that night, and succeeding nights, on the floor of the ante-room to the surgery, on blankets I had found in a cupboard. There wasn't anywhere else.

The bunker was noisy at night, as noisy as it was during the day, with people coming and going, the throb of the generator and the incessant thud of the shells into the fabric of the Chancellery. No one seemed to make much distinction between night and day there, and after the first twenty-four hours I no longer had any sense of time myself. The lights burned with a wavering yellow dimness, when they were not extinguished altogether; when they went out, in the cramped darkness you could hear the breathing and feel the thoughts of the thirty other people in that concrete tomb. Food appeared on the tables at irregular intervals; but there seemed to be a shame attached to eating, no one wanted to be seen doing it, and so you would come across people eating in corners with their backs to you, or see them stuffing a piece of bread into their pockets as you approached. Sleep also appeared, in the circumstances, irrelevant, or perhaps disrespectful; and so no one was either fully asleep or fully awake. Hitler himself had for years been in the habit of retiring to bed at five o'clock in the morning, and rising at noon. They said he now hardly slept at all.

My own sleep that first night was interrupted by the general's groans as the pain of his wound consolidated its hold, by an intensification of the shelling, and by a voice which broke through the mists in which I was wandering and dragged me back to wakefulness. I had known that voice for years. For nearly half my life it had promised, threatened, exhorted and sneered. It was a clever voice. It made you doubt what you had thought was certain. It made you understand things you had thought too difficult. It made you believe the unbelievable.

Because it was so clever, it made you rather afraid. You hoped it would not decide to sneer at you.

In the end it drove you to the edge of your reason and all you wanted to do was get away from it. But that you could never do.

I lay and listened to the voice of the minister of Propaganda, on the other side of the partition.

He was talking to himself. As he talked, he walked around the confined space of his room. I could hear, each time, the fractional hesitation before the deformed foot was put down.

It sounded as if he was trying to work something out; as if, when the rhetoric attained clarity, so would his thought.

I crept from under my blanket and went in search of something to read.

The Western in the armchair had gone. So had the dog. Where the dog had been sat a sunken-faced SS major. I spoke to him but he didn't seem either to see or hear me. I left him and went to the washroom for a drink of water, but there was no water in the taps, so I went back to bed.

The voice was continuing its search for meaning.

I awoke in damp air that tasted of plaster dust, and went to look at the general. He was fretful, and wanted to be up and about. He insisted on being helped to one of the armchairs in the corridor. After half an hour he asked me to help him back to bed again.

The bunker was full of the Fat Man's disgrace. It was not hard to detect satisfaction behind the shocked tones. The Fat Man had run out of rope a long time ago. It was something to talk about, too. I was made to tell the story of our flight into Berlin and the armour-piercing bullet that got the general's foot, but after I had told it half a dozen times interest flagged and conversation reverted to the former topic. The Fat Man was, as it were, more substantial. There were only two topics of conversation in the bunker which could be endlessly recycled: the Fat Man, and the progress of General Wenck.

Keitel had been dispatched from the bunker the previous week to find Wenck and order him to come to the relief of Berlin. Wenck was now awaited: daily, hourly. And daily, hourly, opinion in the bunker shifted. Wenck would never come; rescue was beyond hope. Wenck was almost here: the armoured spearheads of the Twelfth Army had been sighted.

Before long I had had enough of both topics.

A grim-looking Hitler Youth commander strode past me in the corridor as I went to the sickroom. He walked towards the far end of the bunker, knocked on a door and disappeared inside. From that direction a few minutes later, I heard Hitler's voice raised in violent excitement.

Von Greim was receiving a visit from the minister of Propaganda. The minister was sitting on the end of the bed swinging one foot: it was the crippled foot in its heavy boot. He looked, as always, spry, alert and intelligent. With his aura of energy and hatred and his bright eyes and neat ears in a bony skull, and with his thin child's body, he made me think of a rat.

He was saying, 'The enemy coalition is going to break up; nothing can stop it. Britain is in crisis, you know: they're desperately short of food. Churchill can't control the situation.'

The general regarded him dully.

'In America the population is turning against its Jews. In Britain schemes are being laid to oust Churchill. Starvation in France, massacre in Poland. In Rome, there is an epidemic of syphilis.'

'Oh?'

'It's only a question of time. We *must* hold them off. I have great hopes, Greim. Great hopes. And so does Adolf.'

'Does he?'

The general wanted his visitor to go away. His visitor arranged himself in a more comfortable position on the bed.

'He's very tired, of course,' he said. 'He only gets two hours' sleep a night. It isn't enough, even for a man of his extraordinary powers.'

Conversation lapsed. The minister turned in the end to me, but before he had said much we heard Hitler's step in the corridor outside.

He limped into the sickroom. He was holding a tattered street map and a handful of coloured buttons.

He spread his map out on the general's bed, obliging the minister of Propaganda to get off it. The map was food-spotted and starting to disintegrate. It was an ordinary street map of Berlin, of the sort you used to be able to buy at news stalls.

Hitler's trembling hands hovered over the orderly configuration which represented the stone fields above us, and he said, 'Wenck will come this way.'

The general heaved himself up on his pillows.

'This is the route I want him to take. Look.'

The yellowed finger traced a path from the city's southern outskirts towards its centre. 'He will skirt the concentrations of Russian armour. Axmann has just given me a report on their positions.'

He began placing buttons on various parts of the map. 'They are here. And here.'

The ceiling shuddered and plaster fell from it on to the map. He brushed it off irritably.

In mid-afternoon a rumour started and ran through the bunker in minutes.

'Fegelein's disappeared.'

Fegelein was the SS liaison officer. He had not been seen for a time. He had missed two conferences, telephoning in for a report.

Hitler had sent out a squad of police to find him.

Speculation followed smartly upon rumour. Fegelein was planning a getaway to Argentina. He had had false passports prepared. He had a bag of diamonds. He was involved in secret negotiations with the enemy.

These speculations proceeded to a certain point, and then stopped. The speakers would lower their voices and say, 'But, of course . . .'

Of course what? Of course, you have to remember that he is EB's brother-in-law.

No one was sure what weight that might carry. Eva Braun did not, as far as was known, attempt to influence Hitler. The idea that anyone might in fact influence him was ludicrous. It was not known whether she even had any liking for Fegelein, or whether she was as aware as everyone else that he had married her sister in order to be near the throne. Nevertheless . . .

Nevertheless it was something to talk about. They were avid for news down there, desperate for news that wasn't the only news there was.

In the evening the Hitler Youth commander, Axmann, came again, with more of that news.

EB was the most exotic of the bunker's inhabitants. Her quarters, naturally, were at the far end of the corridor next to Hitler's, and from them she emerged several times a day to sit in one of the arm-chairs.

I had never even glimpsed her before. Once, I had seen her face in a photograph, and then the person showing it to me – it was Ernst, and goodness knows he told me enough he shouldn't have – hesitated before answering my, 'Who is that?' She was not supposed to exist. Our leader was supposed to be above the need for a woman. Only the inner circle knew about her and, from what I gathered, they didn't know much. Most of the time she was not even in Berlin. She would appear occasionally, to play hostess at a tea party.

Perhaps, I thought, there wasn't much to know.

Yet she had turned up here, in the last weeks, of her own accord. Even – said gossip in the bunker – against his orders. He had told her to stay in the south, where she would be safe. When staff officers and department chiefs in their hundreds had deserted Berlin in the middle of April and streamed in convoy to the mountains (including, notoriously, the Fat Man), she alone had made the reverse journey.

I admired this. I looked for something that matched it in my conversations with her.

'Poor Adolf!' she said, picking dog hairs from the skirt of her blue dress and dropping them to the floor. '*Everyone* lets him down, even the people he's been kindest to.'

She began a story I could not really follow about Speer.

'Adolf was like a *father* to him, and they had so much in common, both being architects,' she said. 'Do you know Speer?'

'Not personally.'

'Adolf had such a high opinion of him.' She sighed. 'And won't they all be sorry!'

This last sentence was delivered with a spite which startled me. I waited for her to amplify it.

'When the end comes,' she explained.

'Very sorry,' I said.

'It's wonderful that you've chosen to be here with us,' she said. She reached across and clasped my hand. 'This will be the greatest moment of our lives.'

She gave me a brilliant smile which rendered her face lifeless, as if it were a doll's.

A man with a sour expression and a notebook, who was often to be seen asking people what Hitler had said to them and writing it down, joined us at that moment, and I did not have the chance to ask her what she meant.

*

I was sitting in an armchair eating a bit of sausage on my third day in the bunker when someone sat down beside me.

'We haven't met,' he said. 'Reinhardt. I'm with von Below.'

Von Below was the air force liaison officer, and frequently in and out of the general's sickroom. I offered Major Reinhardt a portion of sausage.

'No, thank you,' he said. 'I've just had some nourishing vegetable soup. No wonder the Reich Marshal couldn't stick it in this place. Mind you, it's just as well. When he was in the conference room, no one else could get into it.'

Since I had only just met him and we were already talking about the Fat Man, I asked him if he had been here when the telegram arrived. He told me something very interesting.

'Hitler was in a temper,' he said. 'An assault he'd ordered hadn't taken place. It hadn't taken place because there weren't the men to carry it out, but you can't tell him. He said the Reich was doomed, and he was going to stay here and die. Everyone protested. We'd been trying to get him to go to Obersalzburg for weeks, but when he's made his mind up . . . Anyway, Keitel asked him how he thought he could command from the bunker, when most of the troops we do still have are in the Alps. And he said there were no further orders to give in any case. If they wanted orders, he said, let them apply to the Reich Marshal, who was better at negotiating.'

I chewed my sausage slowly.

'And this,' I said, 'was reported . . .?'

'Of course. Quite properly. It was reported at once to the Reich Marshal, who then sent the telegram.'

The Fat Man had been sacked for efficiency.

'You may laugh,' said Major Reinhardt, 'but when that telegram arrived I thought Adolf was going to have a seizure. It was quite terrifying. I hope I never see the like again.'

I'd heard of those rages. I could never quite believe what was said of them. Surely words are only words?

I asked him whether he was quartered in one of the other shelters. He said he was living outside; it was now very difficult to move about, but he preferred it to the confines of the bunker. He estimated that we had three days left.

I asked him, carefully, whether he had any plans.

357

He said, with matching care, 'Plans? No. But I am not of the mind which seems to be prevailing here.'

I assumed he meant the wild veering of opinion over General Wenck.

He took out a cigarette and turned it between his fingers, not lighting it. Smoking was forbidden in the bunker. Lowering his voice, he said, 'The only sensible thing is to give oneself up to the Americans, but first one has to find them.' He paused. 'Nothing can be done, of course, until . . .'

'Until?'

He declined to finish the thought. 'And you?' he said.

'I'd like to get out of here at the first opportunity.'

His eyes widened a little. He said, 'In that case, I'm surprised you didn't get on the Ju 52 that flew in this morning.'

I felt my heart skip.

'What Ju 52?'

'Ah.' He straightened his cuffs. 'It flew in about ten o'clock, landed near the Brandenburg Gate. It had come in to fly the two of you out.'

'What happened to this Ju 52?'

'Von Greim sent it away again. I'm sorry, I thought you knew. I naturally assumed he would have told you.'

The general's face was sunk and yellowish-grey, and had the look of an old flannel. I felt no pity.

I said, 'Why didn't you tell me a plane had come for us?'

'You weren't here.'

'I was just down the corridor!'

'Don't shout.'

I walked round the room. I wanted to kill him.

'General – '

'Field Marshal.'

I would kill him. I thrust my hands deep into my pockets. I drew the stale air deep into my lungs. I said, 'I do have rights.'

'You do, that's quite correct, and I should have consulted you.'

He closed his eyes and lay back on his pillows. That was all I was going to get.

I said, 'If you had consulted me, I would have said I wanted to leave.'

'No doubt.'

'Is that why you didn't?'

'You must draw your own conclusions.'

'I conclude that you wanted to stay here, for reasons of your own, and thought that what I wanted was not of any importance.'

'It isn't,' he said. 'We're all going to die anyway.'

I went and sat on the operating table. I swung my legs and studied the ceiling, which had assumed a complicated appearance owing to the amount of plaster which had fallen off it. I said, 'If I'm going to die, it's not going to be in this warren.'

'There are many people who will count it a great privilege to die in this warren, as you call it.'

I thought that he had said 'will' and not 'would', but I couldn't be sure. There was noise all the time – the shelling, the generator, the coming and going in the corridors, the shouting that periodically came from the far end of the bunker and brought a certain look into people's faces.

I said, 'Do *you* want to die here?'

He said, 'It's not a matter of what one wants. Since there's nothing I can do outside, I have no duty to leave. In any case I'm in no state to travel.'

When would he be, I thought. Despite my anger, I couldn't blame him for preferring anything to the ordeal of another flight. But it was a miracle that the Ju 52 had got through, and when would there be another chance?

'How is your foot?' I asked.

'Just remembered, have you? Hellish. Where's Stumpfegger?'

'D'you want me to get him?'

'No. He'll be busy. He'll come when he has time. Just do something about these pillows, will you?'

'What do you want done with them?'

'Make them comfortable. It's like lying on a heap of marrow-bones.'

I applied my fists to them. He yelled.

'Oh, for God's sake leave them alone. What did I do to deserve you for a nurse?'

'I'm not your nurse, I'm your pilot. Speaking of which, why *did* you ask me to fly you here?'

He turned his head into the pillows. 'You can fly a helicopter.'

'Was that all?'

'Why else?' he said irritably.

'I just thought there might be something you had to say to me.'

'I don't have anything to say about anything,' he said, closing his eyes, and he looked so ill that I went to fetch Stumpfegger.

Fegelein had been found. Competing versions of his arrest said that he had been found with his feet up on his mistress's bed, that he had been found disguised as a nun in the western suburbs, and that he had been apprehended by some Hitler Youth whom he had tried to bribe with a gold watch to let him across a bridge.

What Hitler would do was eagerly debated. He sometimes surprised people by his loyalty to erring subordinates. And in any case there was still EB. She might yet, said some in the bunker, come to the aid of Fegelein.

I did not think so. I detected no susceptibility to another's plight in the rehearsed movements of those endlessly tended hands, the watchful blue eyes, or the soft voice which slid easily into bitter denunciation but was more normally employed in lamenting the unkindness of the world to Adolf. I thought Fegelein would do better enlisting the support of the dog.

At some time during the day he was brought back. I saw him being marched capless through the corridors by a squad of hard-eyed policemen. They disappeared in the direction of Hitler's quarters.

Later I heard that he had been stripped of his rank and was being held under guard in one of the other shelters.

In the late evening the shelling of the Chancellery rose to a new pitch. The walls of the bunker seemed to ripple, the plaster loosening and running in rivulets to the ground.

The hour at which it is normal to go to bed approached, but no one gave signs of doing so. The Propaganda minister took up a position in the corridor, standing with his hands gripping the back of a chair, as if to make a speech, but remained quite silent. The two secretaries, the telephone operator and a policeman sat in other chairs, talking in subdued voices. People stood in doorways, as if waiting for something. Stumpfegger, in the sickroom, with pedantic thoroughness, was re-bandaging the general's smashed foot, criss-crossing the strip of cloth to make precise angles which all three of us took comfort in contemplating.

In the end I lay down on my blankets and drifted into a half-sleep. I was roused by a hand gripping my shoulder. It was Stumpfegger. Hitler had summoned us all to a meeting in his private quarters.

He sat in an armchair covered in some flowered fabric. There was a shadowiness about him. As the territory of the Reich crumbled, so had he. If you looked away and then looked back quickly, I thought, he might not be there.

The dog lay at his feet. There was a low table beside him, and on it was a wooden box with a brass keyhole.

On his left sat E B.

I wondered what it felt like, being his intimate companion, the repository of his confidences. I could not imagine those confidences. I studied her pretty, conventional dress, the face that never expressed anything but vicarious emotion. They said she had a sports car, but that he would not allow her to drive it fast.

The small room was crowded: I counted twenty-two people. The man with the notebook was sitting on the other side of the low table. Beside me, exuding suffering, sat the general, his foot propped on an upturned waste paper basket.

The Propaganda minister spoke first. I had a curious impression that he had been set in motion by a movement of Hitler's hand.

He said that since there was no way of knowing when the Russians would break through to the bunker, the meeting had been called to make sure that nothing was left to chance. The final act must not be left until it was too late.

He paused. 'By too late,' he said, 'I mean . . .' Some fastidiousness over language seemed to prevent him from finishing the sentence.

Hitler spoke impatiently into the silence.

'Too late for our bodies to be consumed.'

I glanced around me. Everyone appeared perfectly composed.

The man with the notebook leaned over and whispered something in Hitler's ear.

'Bormann reminds me that we shall need a lot more petrol than appears to be in the bunker,' Hitler said. 'How much do you think we need, Bormann?'

Bormann consulted his notebook. 'With the arrival of Field Marshal von Greim and the Flight Captain the day before yesterday, I think about twelve hundred litres.'

'Well, I suppose it can be obtained. Make a note, will you, Bormann, to ask the SS men to bring some in. We don't want it left until the last moment and then bungled.'

My frozen stare rested on the general. His eyes flicked towards me, but did not meet mine.

As Bormann wrote in his book, the Propaganda minister continued: 'The suicide of our leader and Früulein Braun will of course take precedence. Their bodies will be burnt by an SS squad in the Chancellery garden, Bormann and myself officiating. Some of you might also like to be present. This act will be the signal for our own, lesser scarifices.'

Hitler laid his hand on the box. 'I have sufficient cyanide to provide everyone who requires it with a lethal dose.'

The dog yawned and snapped at something in its sleep.

'Ideally,' said the Propaganda minister, 'our remains would be disposed of by the SS troop guarding the bunker, but in the circumstances we can't be sure that there will be enough of them left to make a thorough job of it.'

'They must be *ordered* to,' said Hitler.

'It's a question of getting enough petrol here in time,' said Bormann.

'In that case we ought to start getting it in now,' said the minister.

'Quite,' said Bormann, and then for a while nothing happened. I realized that Bormann was waiting for the minister of Propaganda to leave the room to give the order, and the minister of Propaganda was waiting for Bormann to leave the room to give the order.

Hitler passed his hand over his eyes and said, with great weariness, 'See to it, Schaub,' and one of the adjutants present got up and went out.

'Speaking as a medical man,' said Stumpfegger, breaking a heavy silence on my left, 'I should point out that it is actually quite difficult to burn a human body completely. Burning more than twenty bodies, unless the heat is intense, is a major task, and I think we have to resign ourselves . . .'

'Means will be devised,' Hitler's voice cut in, dismissing argument. 'I can't be expected to think of everything. You will devise means.'

He took a small brass key from his pocket and fitted it to the brass lock on the box.

Sound outside the room seemed to recede as he lifted back the lid, so that in spite of the constant rumble of the shelling it was possible to hear the hinges creak. Hitler's eyes dilated over the contents, and the eternal restlessness of his hands stilled as he brought the box on to his lap and held it there. I caught a glimpse of worn blue satin, like that which had lined a box in which my father kept surgical instruments.

He raised his head and I saw how aged he had become. But the eyes were like an eagle's.

One by one we began to go up and accept the poison from him. He gave me a clear glass phial the size of a fingernail, that touched my skin like ice. I looked into the box where the phials lay ranked, and felt my head swim.

In the morning I went to talk to the general. I had slept little.

He was propped up on his pillows. He turned his head as I came in and gave me an odd smile, sad and courteous, which I hadn't seen on his face before and didn't like.

I said, 'Did you know what everyone here was planning?'

'Planning?'

'Mass suicide. SS cremation squads. The necessity of getting in enough petrol.'

'Does it matter if I did?'

'If you did, you could have told me.'

'Anyone else could have told you, come to that.'

There was a pause. I found that I was very cold. I clutched my arms, to keep from shivering.

I said, 'Are you in agreement with it?'

'Of course.'

'You will take the poison?'

'Gladly, for Germany.'

His blue eyes gazed at me. They were fierce and dreamy.

'For Germany,' I repeated. Then, with an effort, for I was having to fight against the weight that was pulling me down to the place where they all were: 'What possible good can it do Germany?'

'It will be a beacon for the future,' he said. 'An act of sacrifice. Buried like a diamond . . .'

'You don't bury diamonds, you dig them up.'

I listened to the thudding of the shells.

I said, 'Do you really believe that all the people who went up and collected a bottle of poison last night are going to take it?'

'You should be ashamed to say that.'

'Are *you* going to take it? Really? Unscrew the little stopper and tip it into your mouth?'

'Yes, really!' He shouted it. It took too much of his strength, and he lay back on the pillows looking drained.

I realized that in his state of wretchedness death was probably not unattractive.

'Well, I'm certainly not going to!'

'Then why did you accept it?'

'He does something to my mind.'

'A pity you are unable to rise to the greatness of the occasion.'

'I fail to see the greatness of the occasion. I think it's morbid and hysterical.'

He stared past me at the wall. 'You have always been allowed a lot of licence, haven't you?'

I perched on the operating table. My head had cleared.

'Everyone in this bunker,' I said, 'is mad. And everyone who comes here goes mad in a few days. It has not yet happened to me, but it has happened to you because you are in a weakened state. I think the sooner we get out of here the better.'

'No one's keeping you here,' he said. 'Hitler will be glad to give you permission to go. He wants companions in his last hour on earth, not captives.'

'You know quite well I can't leave without you.' I was exasperated. My chances of getting through the Russian lines on foot were negligible. Everyone was very clear what the Russians did to women. There was only one way out of Berlin: by air.

He appeared to acknowledge this. He said, 'You didn't have to come here. I tried to dissuade you.'

'I don't blame you for that,' I said.

'You could have been killed twenty times over on that flight.'

'That's a different matter.'

I sat swinging my legs. There didn't seem much else to say.

'You look so angry,' he said. 'I didn't mean to trap you here. Perhaps Rechlin will send another aircraft.'

'If they do, will you get on it?'

'No, but there is no reason why you shouldn't.'

I didn't know whether to believe him or not. But it was a secondary point. I said, 'Do you think they will try to send another aeroplane?'

He did not reply.

About an hour later, as I was taking what passed for exercise through the corridors, a man I hadn't seen before hurried past me in the direction of Hitler's quarters. He was clutching several sheets of paper and his face was screwed tight with apprehension.

I was in the upper complex when I felt the shock wave. Not a shell, but worse. I retraced my steps at once.

As I entered the lower corridor, I flinched back.

Hitler's frame blocked the light in the passageway outside his room. His right hand was clenched tight, and with it, from time to time, he struck the wall beside him. The fingers of his left hand were thrust clawlike into a lacerated ball of paper. His entire body was in the grip of a fierce trembling, but his eyes shone steadily, like baleful moons.

From his lips poured a torrent of hatred so obscene, murderous and annihilating that I held on to the bulkhead for support.

The bunker's other occupants stood like stone in doorways.

The voice screamed of treachery. It raved of plots, death and extermination. In the depths of its lust to kill was an uncomprehending woundedness. It demanded vengeance, vengeance, vengeance.

When at last it fell silent I saw the same sickness on every face. One by one, people turned and went into their rooms. Hitler sagged like a puppet, and EB came up behind him and put her painted hands on his head and led him away.

The general had been standing at the door of the sickroom. He was lying on the bed when I got there.

'What's happened?' I asked.

'Himmler has been trying to negotiate with the enemy. It was picked up on Swedish radio.'

'*Himmler?*'

'Yes, faithful Heini.'

Faithful unto death. That was what the badge meant, the skull badge the SS wore.

I said, 'Doesn't he know what happened to Goering?'

'Presumably. It was his men who arrested Goering.' The general closed his eyes. 'I need to rest now.'

I went and sat in one of the armchairs. The Western was back. I leafed through it. Someone had underlined, in its entirety, the last chapter, in which the imprisoned hero was dramatically rescued from an underground cell.

Major Reinhardt came and sat beside me.

He said, 'You're still here, then.'

'Yes.'

'Hmm.' He smoothed a cigarette pensively between his fingers. Then he said, 'Well, that's cooked Fegelein's goose.'

'Sorry?'

'Himmler's man, isn't he?' He drew his finger across his throat.

Later I went up the four flights of concrete steps that led to the Chancellery garden. I thought I might find Major Reinhardt there, enjoying his cigarette, but I didn't. The air was searing and full of sulphur, it made my lungs labour and my eyes smart, but it was real air, not the air of the bunker. Behind me the Chancellery loomed like the ruins of Rome.

Berlin was in flames. I looked to the south-west, where Wenck's army should be triumphantly demolishing the coloured buttons set out on Hitler's map, but there saw no sign of Wenck.

I saw something, though. I saw them take out Fegelein from the neighbouring shelter a hundred yards away, stand him against a tree and shoot him.

The shelling that night was the worst we had experienced. The bunker seemed to rock with it, and the air was full of a fine dust. It covered the chairs and tables, it covered our hair, clothes and faces. In the dim light we looked like phantoms.

No one spoke much. Hitler's outburst of rage had exhausted us all. Axmann had reported that the Russians were in Potsdamer Platz, establishing positions from which they would presumably attempt to over-run the Chancellery the next morning.

I lay on my blanket watching the ceiling flake and crack, and listening to the limping step of the Propaganda minister as he walked up and down, up and down the corridors.

At about half past midnight a guard came in and roused the general with an order. I did not have to hear it to know what it was. Nor did he: I had sensed his restlessness for hours, and that it had little to do with the pain of his foot. He got off the bed, and I heard him peg his difficult way down the passage with the crutches Stumpfegger had found for him.

He was back twenty minutes later. I had dozed in his absence. Perhaps I knew it was the last chance I would get for a long time. I felt him looking down at me.

He said, 'We're leaving. There's a plane waiting near the Brandenburg Gate.'

I was already thrusting my arm into the sleeve of my jacket.

The next sentence I did not expect. 'He wants to see you.'

I walked along the damp, already decomposing corridor, through the ante-room and to the door of Hitler's study. There I stopped, as though I had walked into a barrier, although the door was slightly ajar. Through the gap came a sound of shuffling paper, and then another sound which I recognized: the click of buttons against each other as they are laid out on a map. There I stood, unable to move and unable to knock, until the grating voice called out, shocking me, 'Who's there?'

Quickly I identified myself.

'Then come in.'

The eyes, in parched grey flesh, moved up from their continual preoccupation as I entered.

'Flight Captain, I have just seen the field marshal.' As he continued speaking, his speech accelerated. 'The Russian positions around the Chancellery must be destroyed before dawn, this is essential, or there is no hope for us. The task can only be carried out by the air force, and you will fly the field marshal to Rechlin so that he can issue the order.'

I said that I would fly the field marshal to Rechlin gladly.

'I have laid a second duty on him, and I lay it on both of you. The traitor Himmler is in the north, he is plotting there, he hopes to succeed me.' The words were slipping into incoherence. The will held them in check, as it held in check what the facial muscles were trying to do, and the dancing left leg, and the shuddering arm.

'You must tell Doenitz – '

He stopped. I thought his mind had gone. He stared in front of him for what seemed an endless time. I swallowed, and the sound filled the room.

He made a great effort.

'Doenitz has command in the north. He must arrest Himmler. It is my dying wish.'

He braced his hands on the table top and began to push himself to a standing position, and I thought I was dismissed. But not yet.

'Faithful unto death,' rasped the tortured voice. 'So much for promises. I can trust one other human being in the world, and my dog.'

Something happened to me when I heard this. I cannot explain it. I have never been able to explain it, what he did to me and countless others.

'Will you be faithful?' the voice insisted, pursuing me where I tried to hide from it. There was no hiding from it, or from the eyes. In the abyss of those eyes I saw something I knew and I recoiled in horror, as if I had seen a living creature twisting in a pit of torment. And then I felt myself, too, falling into the pit, abandoning reason for unreason and, in the moment before the eyes released me, willingly.

The general and I went up to the outside, to the hellish night, where the Bücker waited for us, shrouded like a bat in the shadows.

With the help of two S S men I wheeled the little aircraft on to a bit of uncratered pavement. The Russians had almost reached this section of the East-West Axis, and in a freak lull in the gunfire I heard Russian speech.

We helped the general into the small passenger seat, stowing the crutches hastily. The constant artillery flashes had illuminated the plane, and as I started the engine a shell landed twenty yards ahead of us. The Bücker would present a perfect target as it climbed.

I wrenched the plane round on full right rudder. She protested, and tried to lurch into a shell-crater, but I held her steady and a moment later was racing down the pavement in the other direction, whipping the engine and praying for lift, with the general shouting 'You're crazy! You are out of your mind!' in my ear. Not quite. I'd done this before.

The wheels were up. Air gusted unreliably beneath the wings. I fought for height, willed every inch of it, knowing I must not raise the nose a fraction further or the aeroplane would stall. We were climbing, but erratically, and of course not fast enough for safety, and here came the obstacle which made this trick so desperate. Out of the smoke loomed the stone mass of the Brandenburg Gate. And now I had to raise the nose, and as I did so my eyes flicked back and forth from the horses on top of the Gate to the speed indicator, which naturally was falling, and surely if it fell any further the aeroplane would stall, it must stall . . .

The pompous statuary glided beneath us. I dropped the nose a fraction to recover speed, and almost at once went into a steep turn. Tracer streamed into the sky over the starboard wing. The trick had worked. By the time the gunners had realized we were not taking off into the wind, but with it, and had started to track us, we were out of the greatest danger and circling higher.

I circled, climbed, and hid in the smoke until the guns were far below me and the fighter swarms intent on bigger prey. From thirteen thousand feet, under stars, we looked down on the cauldron of Berlin.

I set course for Rechlin and flew on over blackened fields and burning villages, caught from time to time in the white blaze of a searchlight, out of which I would flick, spiralling.

CHAPTER TWENTY-FIVE

'Did you know what the SS were doing in Russia?' I say to the general as the lorry bumps into the outskirts of Lübeck.

'Yes,' he says. 'Of course I did.'

I have the sense that this was all I wanted, and that now I could let it go. Because what else is there to say, what is it possible to say?

But he wants to say more.

'It was ghastly, the whole thing. I loathed it.'

The words don't fit. Yet it is better than nothing.

'But you allowed . . .' I say.

'What could one do?'

'Refuse.'

'Refuse!' He laughs. 'And be shot. Or perhaps not, just sacked. The point is, what would it have achieved? If I hadn't commanded that air corps . . .'

'Somebody else would have?'

'Exactly.'

'You remember General Ploch?'

'Of course.'

'He . . .'

He what?

'He carried out his duty,' says the general, 'as far as I'm aware.'

The lorry begins to lurch over mounds of broken paving stones.

'Duty,' I repeat.

'Soldier's duty,' says the general. 'Start questioning orders, and where do you go from there? Anything can be questioned, at that rate.'

'Perhaps it should be,' I suggest.

He settles his head back, in an exhausted fashion, against the side of the truck, but brings it forward again because the jolting is intolerable.

370

'It isn't just soldiering which is impossible without obedience,' he says. 'Government's impossible without it. It's the foundation of everything.'

I am silent. Not because I have no reply.

'You don't understand obedience,' he says. 'It's because you're a woman.'

'I understand it. And I am not a good example of a woman.'

'I don't know what you mean.'

'Naturally.'

'A soldier's obedience is his honour,' he says, after a moment or so.

'Is that what you mean by honour? To obey, however hard it is?'

'Yes, that's what I mean by it.' His eyes move over the moonscape the RAF have made of Lübeck. 'It's the only thing that's left now.'

Of course it is. For the first time I see it as he must. Everything of his world has gone. The saluting, the certainties, the faith in caste and country. The hallowed words are empty, the ideas have been turned obscenely on their heads. For an old soldier, there is no longer sky above or earth beneath. There is only the simplest thing of all, the first and hardest thing. Self-abnegation, obedience.

I say, and it comes out harsh, 'Didn't you once tell me you were a Christian, General?'

There's a lot of it in the upper ranks of the armed forces. Old Catholic families. Hitler never stamped it out.

'Yes,' he says.

'How do you square that concept of honour with your conscience? Surely the whole point of having a conscience is to use it.'

He looks out of the open back of the truck for a long time. I have no idea what he is seeing, but it is not the bombed streets.

In the end he says, so quietly I almost do not catch it, 'Oh, for pity's sake leave me alone. Haven't you ever done anything you're ashamed of?'

The medieval centre of Lübeck, through which I wandered with Peter eating gingerbread, is occupied by hills of rubble. On these hills, greyish shadows flit and linger. They are children, picking through the ruins. As the truck passes, they turn and watch it with professional interest. In a glance they estimate the total value of the vehicle if reduced to its components. The value is reckoned in cigarettes. Cigarettes buy anything.

We pull up outside a tall building which has a rakish appearance. Mattresses have been stuffed into the empty window frames of the top storey, and a sign hanging by one corner above a wrought-iron balcony proclaims that this was once the Hotel Montenegro. It looks a dubious home for the air force, Lübeck sector, but an airman stands with his rifle in the doorway, and as I help the general over the broken pavement, and the lorry loaded with the Gauleiter's carpets rumbles off to SS barracks, he presents arms.

We go down a carpeted hallway which smells unmilitary and has watercolours on the walls.

Something is strange here, which has nothing to do with the incongruous atmosphere of the building. The general and I stand, testing this strangeness, outside a door which has a piece of ruled exercise paper pinned to it. On the paper is written 'Commanding Officer'. There should be a guard on duty here, but there is none. It is the middle of the evening, and someone is listening to music on the radio. In the whole building there is no other sound. The music is the funeral march from *Götterdämmerung*.

The music finishes. There is what seems a very long pause. Then a voice begins speaking. It is a voice I don't know: it is dry, as dry as sand, and it sounds old. It tells us that it is the voice of Grand Admiral Doenitz.

The general lifts the end of a crutch to bang on the door, but doesn't do it.

I open the door.

Five senior officers sit around a table, intently leaning forward their heads almost meeting over the wireless set. They are wholly absorbed in the words coming over the air waves, being broadcast to every corner of Germany.

I listen, and shudders begin to run from the top of my head to the soles of my feet.

He is dead. His hand drops from us.

'In deepest grief,' says Doenitz, 'the German people bow.'

The weight of that hand.

'I take over the leadership of the German people at this fateful hour . . .'

At my side the general trembles.
'God will not abandon us,' says the voice on the radio.
We step forward into the room.